$\mathcal{S}$ophia inched closer to the dock's edge and reached one gloved hand toward his, considering how best to board the bobbing craft without losing her dignity overboard.

The moment her fingers grazed his palm, his grip tightened over her hand. He pulled swiftly, wrenching her feet from the dock and a gasp from her throat. A moment of weightlessness—and then she was aboard. Somehow his arm had whipped around her waist, binding her to his solid chest. He released her just as quickly, but a lilt of the rowboat pitched Sophia back into his arms.

"Steady there," he murmured through a small smile. "I have you."

A sudden gust of wind absconded with his hat. He took no notice, but Sophia did. She noticed everything. Never in her life had she felt so acutely *aware*. Her nerves were drawn taut as harp strings, and her senses hummed.

The man radiated heat. From exertion, most likely. Or perhaps from a sheer surplus of simmering male vigor. The air around them was cold, but he was hot. And as he held her tight against his chest, Sophia felt that delicious, enticing heat burn through every layer of her clothing—cloak, gown, stays, chemise, petticoat, stockings, drawers—igniting desire in her belly.

And sparking a flare of alarm. This was a precarious position indeed. The further her torso melted into his, the more certainly he would detect her secret: the cold, hard bundle of notes and coin lashed beneath her stays.

Also by Tessa Dare

Goddess of the Hunt

SURRENDER
OF A SIREN

A Novel

Tessa Dare

BALLANTINE BOOKS • NEW YORK

Surrender of a Siren is a work of fiction. Names, characters, places, and incidents are the products of the author's imagination or are used fictitiously. Any resemblance to actual events, locales, or persons, living or dead, is entirely coincidental.

A Ballantine Books Mass Market Original

Published in the United States by Ballantine Books, an imprint of The Random House Publishing Group, a division of Random House, Inc., New York.

BALLANTINE and colophon are registered trademarks of Random House, Inc.

This book contains an excerpt from the forthcoming book *A Lady of Persuasion* by Tessa Dare. This excerpt has been set for this edition only and may not reflect the final content of the forthcoming edition.

ISBN 978-0-345-50687-0

Cover illustration: Doreen Minuto

Printed in the United States of America

www.ballantinebooks.com

OPM 9 8 7 6 5 4 3 2 1

CHAPTER
ONE

GRAVESEND, DECEMBER 1817

In fleeing the society wedding of the year, Sophia Hathaway knew she would be embracing infamy.

She'd neglected to consider how infamy *smelled*.

She paused in the doorway of the fetid dockside tavern. Even from here, the stench of soured ale accosted her, forcing bile into her throat.

A burly man elbowed her aside as he went out the door. "Watch yerself, luv."

She pasted herself against the doorjamb, wondering at the singular form of address implied in "luv." The man's comment had clearly been directed toward *both* of her breasts.

With a shiver, she wrapped her cloak tight across her chest.

Taking one last deep breath, she sidled her way into the dank, drunken confusion, forbidding her gray serge skirts to brush against anything. Much less any*one*. From every murky corner—and for a squared-off tea caddy of a building, this tavern abounded in murky corners—eyes followed her. Suspicious, leering eyes, set in hard, unshaven faces. It was enough to make any young woman anxious. For a fugitive young lady of quality, traveling alone, under the flimsy shield of a borrowed cloak and a fabricated identity . . .

Well, it was almost enough to make Sophia reconsider the whole affair.

An unseen someone jostled her from behind. Her gloved fingers instinctively clutched the envelope secreted in her cloak. She thought of its brethren, the letters she'd posted just that morning, breaking her engagement and ensuring a scandal of Byronic proportions. Seeds of irrevocable ruin, scattered with the wind.

A cold sense of destiny anchored her rising stomach. There was no going back now. She could walk through far worse than this shabby pub, if it meant leaving her restrictive life behind. She could even endure these coarse men ogling her breasts, so long as they did not glimpse the secret strapped between them.

Her resolve firmed, Sophia caught the eye of a bald-headed man wiping a table with a greasy rag. He looked harmless enough—or at least, too old to strike quickly. She smiled at him. He returned the gesture with a completely toothless grin.

Her own smile faltering, she ventured, "I'm looking for Captain Grayson."

" 'Course you is. All the comely ones are." The gleaming pate jerked. "Gray's in the back."

She followed the direction indicated, moving through the crowd on tiptoe in an effort to keep her hem off the floor. The sticky floorboards sucked at her half boots. Toward the back of the room, she spied a boisterous knot of men and women near the bar. One man stood taller than the others, his auburn hair looking cleaner than that of his company. A brushed felt beaver rested on the bar nearby, an oddly refined ornament for this seedy den.

As Sophia angled for a better view, a chair slid out from a nearby table, clipping her in the knee. She bobbled on tiptoe for a moment before tripping forward. The hem of her cloak caught on her boot, and the cloak wrenched open, exposing her chest and throat to the sour, wintry air. In her desperate attempt to right herself, she clutched wildly for the wall—

And grasped a handful of rough linen shirt instead.

The shirt's owner turned to her. "Hullo there, chicken," he slurred, his breath rancid with decay. His liquor-glazed eyes slid over her body and settled on the swell of her breasts. "Fancy bit of goods you are. By looks, I would have priced you beyond my pocket, but if you's offerin' . . ."

Had he mistaken her for some dockside trollop? Sophia's tongue curled with disgust. Perhaps she was disguised in simple garments, but certainly she did not look *cheap*.

"I am not offering," she said firmly. She tried to wriggle away, but with a quick move, he had her pinned against the bar.

"Hold there, lovely. Jes' a little tickle, then."

His grimy fingers dove into the valley of her bosom, and Sophia yelped. "Unhand me, you . . . you revolting brute!"

The brute released one of her arms to further his lascivious exploration, and Sophia used her newly freed hand to beat him about the head. No use. His fingers squirmed between her breasts like fat, greedy worms burrowing in the dark.

"Stop this," she cried, making her hand a fist and clouting his ear, to no avail. Her efforts at defense only amused her drunken attacker.

"S'all right," he said, chuckling. "I likes my girls with plenty o' pluck."

Desperation clawed at her insides. It wasn't simply the insult of this lout's hands on her breasts that had her panicking. She'd forfeited her genteel reputation the moment she left home. But his fingers groped closer and closer to the one thing she dared not surrender. If he found it, Sophia doubted she would escape this tavern with her life intact, much less her virtue.

Her attacker turned his head, angling for a better look down her dress. His grimy ear was just inches from her mouth. Within snapping distance. If she bit it hard enough, she might startle him into letting her go. She had all but made up her mind to do it, when she inhaled another mouthful of his rank sweat and paused. If her choices were putting her mouth on this repulsive beast or dying, she just might rather die.

In the end, she didn't do either.

The repulsive beast gave a yawp of surprise as a pair of massive hands bodily hauled him away. Lifted him, actually, as though the brute weighed nothing, until he writhed in the air above her like a fish on a hook.

"Come now, Bains," said a smooth, confident baritone, "you know better than that."

With an easy motion, her rescuer tossed Bains aside. The brute landed some feet away, with the crunch of splintering wood.

Sagging against the bar with relief, Sophia peered up at her savior. It was the tall, auburn-haired gentleman she'd spied earlier. At least, she assumed him to be a gentleman. His accent bespoke education, and with his dark-green topcoat, fawn-colored trousers, and tasseled Hessians, he cut a fashionable silhouette. But as his arms flexed, the finely tailored clothing delineated raw, muscled power beneath.

And there was nothing refined about his face. His features were rough-hewn, his skin bronzed by the sun. It was impossible not to stare at the golden, weathered hue and wonder—did it fade at his cravat? At his waist? Not at all?

The more she peered up at the man, the less she knew what to make of him. He had a gentleman's attire, a laborer's body . . . and the wide, sensuous mouth of a scoundrel.

"How many times do I have to tell you, Bains? That's no way to touch a woman." His words were addressed to the lout on the floor, but his roguish gaze was fixed on her. Then he smiled, and the lazy quirk of his lips tugged a thin scar slanting from his jaw to his mouth.

Oh yes, that mouth was dangerous indeed.

At that moment, Sophia could have kissed it.

"The proper way to touch a woman," he continued, sauntering to her side and propping an elbow on the bar, "is to come at her from the side, like so." In an attitude of perfect nonchalance, he leaned his weight on his arm and slid it along the bar until his knuckles came within a hair's width of her breast.

Mouth of a scoundrel, indeed! Sophia's gratitude quickly turned to indignation. Had this man truly yanked one lout off her just so he could grope her himself? Apparently so. His hand rested so close to her breast, her flesh heated in the shadow of his fingers. So close, her skin prickled, anticipating the rough texture of his touch. She wished he *would* touch her, end the excruciating uncertainty, and give her an excuse to slap the roguish smirk from his face.

"See?" he said, waggling his fingers in the vicinity of her bosom. "This way you don't startle her off."

Coarse laughter rumbled through the assembled crowd.

Retracting his hand, the scoundrel lifted his voice. "Don't I have the right of it, Megs?"

All eyes turned to a curvy redhead gathering tankards. Megs barely looked up from her work as she sang out, "Ain't no one like Gray knows how to touch a lady."

Laughter swept the tavern again, louder this time. Even Bains chuckled.

Gray. Sophia's heart plummeted. What was it the bald man had said, when she asked for Captain Grayson? *Gray's in the back.*

"One last thing to remember, Bains," Gray continued. "The least you can do is buy the lady a drink." As the tavern-goers returned to their carousing, he turned his arrogant grin on Sophia. "What are you having, then?"

She blinked at him.

What was she having? Sophia knew exactly what she was having. She was having colossally bad luck.

This well-dressed mountain of insolence looming over her was Captain Grayson, of the brig *Aphrodite*. And the brig *Aphrodite* was the sole ship bound for Tortola until next week. For Sophia, next week might as well have been next year. She needed to leave for Tortola. She needed to leave now. Therefore, she needed this man—or rather, this man's *ship*—to take her.

"What, no outpouring of gratitude?" He cast a glance toward Bains, who was lumbering up from the floor. "I suppose you think I should have beat him to a pulp. I could have. But then, I don't like violence. It always ends up costing me money. And pretty thing that you are"—his eyes skipped over her as he motioned to the barkeep—"before I went to that much effort, I think I'd at least need to know your name, Miss . . . ?"

Sophia gritted her teeth, marshalling all her available forbearance. She needed to leave, she reminded herself. She needed this man. "Turner. Miss Jane Turner."

"Miss . . . Jane . . . Turner." He teased the syllables out, as if tasting them on his tongue. Sophia had always thought her middle name to be the dullest, plainest syllable imaginable. But from his lips, even "Jane" sounded indecent.

"Well, Miss *Jane* Turner. What are you drinking?"

"I'm not drinking anything. I'm looking for you, *Captain* Grayson. I've come seeking passage on your ship."

"On the *Aphrodite*? To Tortola? Why the devil would you want to go there?"

"I'm a governess. I'm to be employed, near Road Town." The lies rolled effortlessly off her tongue. As always.

His eyes swept her from bonnet to half boots, stroking an unwelcome shiver down to her toes. "You don't look like any governess I've ever seen." His gaze settled on her hands, and Sophia quickly balled them into fists.

The gloves. Curse her vanity. Her maid's old dress and cloak served well for disguise—their dark, shapeless folds could hide a multitude of sins. But as she'd dressed herself for the first time in her life that morning, her fingers shook with nerves and cold, and Sophia had assuaged their trembling with this one indulgence, her best pair of black kid gloves, fastened with tiny black pearl buttons and lined with sable.

They were not the gloves of a governess.

For a moment, Sophia feared he would see the truth.

Balderdash, she chided herself. No one ever looked at her and saw the truth. People saw what they wanted to see . . . the obedient daughter, the innocent maiden, the society belle, the blushing bride. This merchant captain was no different. He would see a passenger, and the promise of coin.

Long ago, she'd learned this key to deceit. It was easy to lie, once you understood that no one really wanted the truth.

"Lovely, aren't they? They were a gift." With a gloved flourish, she held out her letter. The envelope bore the wear and marks of a transatlantic voyage. "My offer of employment, if you'd care to examine it." She sent up a quick prayer that he would not. "From a Mr. Waltham of Eleanora plantation."

"Waltham?" He laughed, waving away the letter.

Sophia pocketed it quickly.

"Miss Turner, you've no idea what trials you're facing. Never mind the dangers of an ocean crossing, the tropical poverty and disease . . . George Waltham's brats are a plague upon the earth. One your delicate nature and fine gloves are unlikely to survive."

"You know the family, then?" Sophia kept her tone light, but inwardly she loosed a flurry of curses. She'd never considered the possibility that this merchant captain could claim an acquaintance with the Walthams.

"Oh, I know Waltham," he continued. "We grew up together. Our fathers' plantations shared a boundary. He was older by several years, but I paced him for mischief well enough."

Sophia swallowed a groan. Captain Grayson not only *knew* Mr. Waltham—they were friends and neighbors! All her plans, all her carefully tiered lies . . . this bit of information shuffled them like a deck of cards.

He continued, "And you're traveling alone, with no chaperone?"

"I can look after myself."

"Ah, yes. And I tossed Bains across the room just now for my own amusement. It's a little game we seamen like to play."

"I can look after myself," she insisted. "If you'd waited another moment, that revolting beast would be missing an ear."

He gave her a deep, scrutinizing look that made her feel like a turned-out glove, all seams and raw edges. She breathed steadily, fighting the blush creeping up her cheeks.

"Miss Turner," he said dryly, "I'm certain in that fertile female imagination of yours, you think sailing off to the West Indies will be some grand, romantic adventure." He drawled the phrase in a patronizing tone, but Sophia wasn't certain he meant to deride *her*. Rather, she surmised, his tone communicated a general weariness with adventure.

How sad.

"Fortunately," he continued, "I've never known a girl I couldn't disillusion, so listen close to me now. You're wrong. You will not find adventure, nor romance. At best, you'll meet with unspeakable boredom. At worst, you'll meet with an early death."

Sophia blinked. His description of Tortola gave her some pause, but she dismissed any concern quickly. After all, it wasn't as though she meant to *stay* there.

The captain reached to retrieve his felt beaver from the bar.

"Please." She clutched his arm. Heavens. It was like clutching a wool-sheathed cannon. Ignoring the warm tingle in her belly, she made her eyes wide and her voice beseeching. The role of innocent, helpless miss was one she'd been playing for years. "Please, you must take me. I've nowhere else to go."

"Oh, I'm certain you'd figure something out. Pretty thing like you? After all," he said, quirking an eyebrow, "you can look after yourself."

"Captain Grayson—"

"Miss. Jane. Turner." His voice grew thin with impatience. "You waste your breath, appealing to my sense of honor and decency. Any gentleman in my place would send you off at once."

"Yes, but you're no gentleman." She gripped his arm again and looked him square in the eye. "Are you?"

He froze. All that muscle rippling with energy, the

rugged profile animated by insolence—for an instant, it all turned to stone. Sophia held her breath, knowing she'd just wagered her future on this, the last remaining card in her hand.

But this was so much more thrilling than whist.

"No," he said finally. "No, I'm not. I'm a tradesman, and I need to turn a profit. So long as you've silver to pay your passage, the brig *Aphrodite* has a waiting berth."

Relief sighed through her body. "Thank you."

"Have you trunks?"

"Two. Outside with a porter."

"Very well." His mouth curved in a slow, devilish smile. A conspiratorial smile. The sort of smile a young lady of fine breeding didn't acknowledge, let alone return.

So naturally, wicked thing that she was, Sophia smiled back.

"Well," he murmured, "this is going to be a challenge."

"What is?" she asked, feeling suddenly disinclined to put up much of a fight.

"Retrieving your trunks, with you clinging to my arm."

"Oh." Yes, she was still clinging to his arm, wasn't she? Drat. And yet—she wasn't quite ready to let it go.

Maybe it was the lingering desperation from her episode with Bains, or the flood of profound relief that accompanied her rescue. Perhaps it was a perverse fascination with this enigma of a man, who possessed the brute strength to toss grown men around, and just enough charm to be truly dangerous. Or maybe it was simply the feel of his rock-hard muscles beneath her hand, and the knowledge that she'd made them flex.

Sophia couldn't say. But touching him made her feel exhilarated. Powerful and alive. Everything she'd been waiting her whole life to feel. Everything she'd been prepared to travel halfway across the globe to find.

In running away, she had made the decision to embrace infamy.

And lo, here he was.

The girl really needed to let him go.

This was the voyage Gray went respectable. And it was off to a very bad start.

It was all her fault—this delicate wisp of a governess, with that porcelain complexion and her big, round eyes tilting up at him like Wedgwood teacups. She looked as if she might break if he breathed on her wrong, and those eyes kept beseeching him, imploring him, making demands. *Please, rescue me from this pawing brute. Please, take me on your ship and away to Tortola. Please, strip me out of this revolting gown and initiate me in the pleasures of the flesh right here on the barstool.*

Well, innocent miss that she was, she might have lacked words to voice the third quite that way. But, worldly man that he was, Gray could interpret the silent petition quite clearly. He only wished he could discourage his body's instinctive, affirmative response.

He didn't know what to do with the girl. He ought to do the respectable thing, seeing as how this voyage marked the beginning of his respectable career. But Miss Turner had him pegged. He was no kind of gentleman, and damned if he knew the respectable thing. Allowing a young, unmarried, winsome lady to travel unaccompanied probably wasn't it. But then, if he refused her, who was to say she wouldn't end up in an even worse situation? The chit couldn't handle herself for five minutes in a tavern. Was he truly going to turn her loose on the Gravesend quay? What would he tell George Waltham then?

Damn it. After years of aimless carousing, Gray had reached the point in his life where, for one reason and another, he actually wanted to behave in an honorable fashion. The trouble was, somewhere in all those years of aimless carousing, he'd mislaid his sense of honor. He could sail through a cyclone and not lose his course. He could navigate a woman's body in the dark. But his moral compass had grown rusted with disuse.

However . . . he never lost sight of the bottom line. And so, with this governess putting him to the test, Gray reverted to his usual method of making decisions—he opted for profit. Miss Jane Turner was a passenger. He had a ship with empty berths. The decision was simple. He was a tradesman, and this was business. Strictly business.

He had no business studying the exquisite alabaster sweep of her cheekbone.

And she had no business clutching his arm.

"Miss Turner," he said sternly, in the same voice he gave orders to his crew.

"Yes?"

"Let me go now."

She released his arm, blushing fetchingly as she did so and looking up at him through trembling lashes. Gray sighed. If it wasn't one thing, it was another.

"I've one last piece of business, then. Stay here."

With that imperious command, he crossed the tavern. Bains sat at a table, hunkered over a fresh tankard of ale. Gray clapped a hand on his shoulder and leaned over to speak in his unwashed ear. A few more stern words, a few coins, and there was one more quandary resolved to his profit.

"Now then, Miss Turner. We can be on our way." Grasping her firmly by the elbow, he whisked her out the tavern door.

"You gave him money?" Struggling under his grip, she twisted to look back toward Bains. "After what he did to me, what you did to him . . . You *paid* him?"

Ignoring her question, he caught the porter's eye. "The lady's belongings," he commanded briskly.

The porter wrapped beefy forearms around the larger of her two trunks. Gray reached for the smaller one, hefting it onto his shoulder and holding it balanced there with one hand. He took three paces before he realized she wasn't following.

He paused long enough to toss a comment over his shoulder. "Come along, then. I'll take you out to the *Aphrodite*. You'll be wanting to meet the captain."

CHAPTER
TWO

The captain?

Sophia stood staring numbly after him. Had he just said he'd introduce her to the captain? If someone else was the captain, then who on earth was this man?

One thing was clear. Whoever he was, he had her trunks.

And he was walking away.

Cursing under her breath, Sophia picked up her skirts and trotted after him, dodging boatmen and barrels and coils of tarred rope as she pursued him down the quay. A forest of tall masts loomed overhead, striping the dock with shadow.

Breathless, she regained his side just as he neared the dock's edge. "But . . . aren't you Captain Grayson?"

"I," he said, pitching her smaller trunk into a waiting rowboat, "am *Mr.* Grayson, owner of the *Aphrodite* and principal investor in her cargo."

The owner. Well, that was some relief. The tavern-keeper must have been confused.

The porter deposited her larger trunk alongside the first, and Mr. Grayson dismissed him with a word and a coin. He plunked one polished Hessian on the row-boat's seat and shifted his weight to it, straddling the gap between boat and dock. Hand outstretched, he beckoned her with an impatient twitch of his fingers. "Miss Turner?"

Sophia inched closer to the dock's edge and reached one gloved hand toward his, considering how best to board the bobbing craft without losing her dignity overboard.

The moment her fingers grazed his palm, his grip tightened over her hand. He pulled swiftly, wrenching her feet from the dock and a gasp from her throat. A moment of weightlessness—and then she was aboard. Somehow his arm had whipped around her waist, binding her to his solid chest. He released her just as quickly, but a lilt of the rowboat pitched Sophia back into his arms.

"Steady there," he murmured through a small smile. "I have you."

A sudden gust of wind absconded with his hat. He took no notice, but Sophia did. She noticed everything. Never in her life had she felt so acutely *aware*. Her nerves were drawn taut as harp strings, and her senses hummed.

The man radiated heat. From exertion, most likely. Or perhaps from a sheer surplus of simmering male vigor. The air around them was cold, but he was hot. And as he held her tight against his chest, Sophia felt that delicious, enticing heat burn through every layer of her clothing—cloak, gown, stays, chemise, petticoat, stockings, drawers—igniting desire in her belly.

And sparking a flare of alarm. This was a precarious position indeed. The further her torso melted into his, the more certainly he would detect her secret: the cold, hard bundle of notes and coin lashed beneath her stays.

She pushed away from him, dropping onto the seat and crossing her arms over her chest. Behind him, the breeze dropped his hat into a foamy eddy. He still hadn't noticed its loss.

What he noticed was her gesture of modesty, and he gave her a patronizing smile. "Don't concern yourself,

Miss Turner. You've nothing in there I haven't seen before."

Just for that, she would not tell him. Farewell, hat.

To a point, he was correct. She likely had nothing in there he had not seen before. He'd certainly seen a sovereign in his life, and a banknote or two. He may have even seen almost six hundred pounds' worth of them, all lined up in a tidy row. But he likely hadn't seen them in the possession of a governess, because no woman with that sort of money would ever seek employment.

That scuffle with Bains in the tavern had only underscored her peril. She needed to focus on the tasks at hand. Escaping England and marriage. Guarding her secrets and her purse. Surviving until her twenty-first birthday, when she could return to claim the remainder of her trust. And in aid of it all, keeping men out of her stays.

After untying the boat, Mr. Grayson wedged himself onto the narrow plank across from her and gathered the oars.

"You don't have a boatman?" she asked. Their knees were practically touching, they sat so close together. She sat up a bit, widening the gap.

"Not at the moment." Levering one oar, he pushed off from the dock.

She frowned. Surely it wasn't usual, for the ship's owner and principal investor to row himself to and from the quay. Then again, surely it wasn't usual for the ship's owner and principal investor to have the shoulders of an ox. As he began to row in earnest, the bold, rhythmic power of his strokes entranced her. The soft splash of the oars cutting through the water, the confident motions of his hands, the way strength rippled under his coat again, and again, and again . . .

Sophia shook herself. This was precisely the sort of observation she ought to avoid.

With reluctance, she dragged her gaze from his muscled shoulders and settled it on a more benign prospect. *Burnt sienna.* To capture the color of his hair, she would start with a base of burnt sienna, mixed with a touch of raw umber and—she mentally added, as the boat drifted through a shaft of sunlight—the faintest trace of vermillion. More umber at the temples, where sideburns glossed with pomade slicked back toward his slightly square-tipped ears. A controlled touch would be needed there, but the breeze-tossed waves atop his head invited loose, sinuous brushstrokes, layered with whispers of amber. Indian yellow, she decided, lightened with lead white.

The mental exercise calmed her nerves. These wild, mutinous passions that ruled her—Sophia might never master them, but at least she could channel them into her art.

"Was it a convent you escaped, Miss Turner?" He turned the boat with a deft pull on one oar.

"Escaped?" Her heart knocked against her hidden purse. "I'm a governess, I told you. I'm not running away, from a convent or anywhere else. Why would you ask that?"

He chuckled. "Because you're staring at me as though you've never seen a man before."

Sophia's cheeks burned. She *was* staring. Worse, now she found herself powerless to turn away. What with the murky shadows of the tavern and the confusion of the quay, not to mention her own discomposure, she hadn't taken a good, clear look at his eyes until this moment.

They defied her mental palette utterly.

The pupils were ringed with a thin line of blue. Darker than Prussian, yet lighter than indigo. Perhaps matching that dearest of pigments—the one even her father's generous allowance did not permit—ultramarine. Yet within that blue circumference shifted a changing sea of color—green one moment, gray the next . . . in the shadow of a half-blink, hinting at blue.

He laughed again, and flinty sparks of amusement lit them.

Yes, she was *still* staring.

Forcing her gaze to the side, she saw their rowboat nearing the scraped hull of a ship. She cleared her throat and tasted brine. "Forgive me, Mr. Grayson. I'm only trying to make you out. I understood you to be the ship's captain."

"Well," he said, grasping a rope thrown down to him and securing it to the boat, "now you know I'm not."

"Might I have the pleasure, then, of knowing the captain's name?"

"Certainly," he said, securing a second rope. "It's Captain Grayson."

She heard the smirk in his voice, even before she swiveled her head to confirm it. Was he teasing her? "But, you said . . ."

Before Sophia could phrase her question—or even decide exactly which question she meant to ask—Mr. Grayson shouted to the men aboard the ship, and the rowboat lurched skyward. A splinter gouged her palm as she gripped the seat. The boat made a swift, swaying ascent.

As they reached deck level, Mr. Grayson stood. With the same sure strength he'd exhibited on the dock, he grasped her by the waist and swung her over the ship's rail, setting her on deck and releasing her an instant too soon. Her knees wobbled. She put out a hand to grab the rail as a pair of crewmen hoisted her trunks aboard. She, and everything she owned in the world, now resided on this creaking bowl of timber and tar. The ship jogged with a passing wave, and dizziness forced her eyes closed.

"Miss Turner?"

She turned back to face Mr. Gr . . . or Captain . . . *Him,* whoever he was.

Instead, she found herself staring into the starched cravat of a different man. A *very* different man.

It wasn't as though she'd never seen a man like him before. Many of England's best families kept Negro servants in their employ. In fact, black footmen were quite the fashion in the *ton*—their presence hinted at lucrative foreign holdings, and ebony skin made an aesthetically pleasing contrast with a powdered wig.

But this man's skin was not ebony. Rather, the tone of his complexion more accurately matched the warm gloss of a ripe hazelnut, or strong tea lightened with a drop of milk. He wore no wig at all, but a tall gray hat. And beneath the hat, his brown, tightly curled hair was cropped close to his scalp. His dark-blue greatcoat was as well-tailored and elegant as any dandy's. Golden-brown eyes regarded her from a fine-featured face.

He was handsome, and—to Sophia's further confusion—handsome in a vaguely familiar way.

"Miss Turner." Mr. Grayson stepped forward, shrinking the triangle. "Allow me to present Captain Josiah Grayson."

She slid her gaze from the black man just long enough to shoot *him* a sharp glare. "You said *you* were Mr. Grayson."

Both men smiled. Sophia set her jaw.

"I *am* Mr. Grayson. And this"—he clapped a hand on the black man's shoulder—"is Captain Grayson."

She looked from one man to the other, then back again. "You share the same name?"

Their smiles broadened.

"But of course," Mr. Grayson said smoothly, that thin

scar on his chin curving up to mock her. "Brothers usually do."

Gray watched with satisfaction as a blush bloomed across those smooth, delicate cheeks. Perhaps he was enjoying Miss Turner's confusion a bit too much. But damn, ever since he'd lifted Bains off her in the tavern, he'd been enjoying everything a bit too much. The way the circumference of her waist so perfectly filled his crooked arm. The feel of her soft, fragile body pressed up against his in the rowboat. The clean, feminine scent of her—hints of powder and rose water and another scent he couldn't quite place. Something sweet.

And the way she kept staring at him. Bloody hell. It heated his blood, made him want things that even he recognized as less than respectable.

So it was a relief now, to let her blink up at his brother for a bit.

"Brothers." She looked from Gray to Joss and back again. Her gaze sharpened, seemed to refocus somewhere behind him. Gray fought the urge to turn and look over his shoulder.

"Yes of course," she said slowly, tilting her head to one side. "I ought to have seen it at once. The squared-off tip, the little notch above the lobe . . ."

He exchanged an amused glance with Joss. What the devil was this about notches and tips?

"You have the same ears," she finished, a smile tipping the corner of her mouth as she made a smooth curtsy.

Gray paused a beat, then gave a soft laugh. There was a self-assured grace to her movements that he found oddly entrancing, and now he understood why. This was a gesture of satisfaction, not deference. She curtsied not to please, but because she was pleased with herself.

In short, the girl was taking a bow.

And damned if he wasn't tempted to applaud. She hadn't been destined for employment, he would stake the ship on that. Gentle-bred, certainly, despite those deplorable garments. From a wealthy family, he surmised, fallen on hard times. Those fine gloves were only a subtle clue; it was her bearing that made the confession. Gray knew how to discern the true value of goods beneath layers of spit and varnish, and Miss Turner . . . Miss Turner was a quality piece.

She straightened. "I am honored to make your acquaintance, Captain Grayson."

"The honor is mine," Joss replied with a smooth bow. "You travel alone, Miss Turner?"

"Yes. I am to be employed, near Road Town."

"She's to be governess to George Waltham's whelps," Gray interjected. "Needless to say, I attempted to caution her against taking such a thankless post."

"Miss Turner." Joss's voice took on a serious tone. "As captain of this vessel, I must also question the prudence of this journey."

Miss Turner foraged in her cloak. "I . . . I have a letter, from Mr. Waltham."

"Please, don't misunderstand me," Joss said. "It's not your employment I'm concerned for, it's your reputation. We have no other passengers aboard this ship."

No other passengers? Gray cleared his throat.

Joss shot him a look. "Save my brother, of course. A young, unmarried woman, traversing the Atlantic without a chaperone . . ."

Gray shuffled his feet impatiently. What was Joss on about? Surely he didn't intend to refuse her passage?

"Perhaps you would do better to wait. The *Peregrine* sails for Tortola next week."

Hell. He did intend to refuse her passage.

"No," she objected. "No, please. Captain, I appreciate

your concern for my reputation. Had I any prospects other than this post, had I any family or friends who would take exception . . . I might share your concern. As matters stand, I tell you with complete honesty"—she swallowed—"there is no one who will care."

Gray tried, very hard, to pretend he hadn't just heard that.

She continued, "If you can ensure my safety, Captain Grayson, I can promise to behave in strict accordance with propriety."

Sighing hard, Joss shifted his weight. "Miss Turner, I'm sorry, but—"

"Please," she begged, laying a delicate hand on his brother's arm. "You must take me. I've nowhere else to go."

Joss's expression softened. Gray was relieved to learn he wasn't the only man that wide-eyed plea worked on. For no definable reason, he was also annoyed, to watch it plied on another man.

"Take pity, Captain Grayson. Surely Miss Turner must be fatigued." Gray spied the old steward limping down the deck. "Stubb, kindly show Miss Turner to the ladies' cabin. Berth seven is vacant, I believe."

Stubb gave an amused cackle. "They're all vacant, I believe."

Well, yes. But they'd all be full on the voyage home, thanks to the dwindling profits of sugar plantations. Scarcely anyone was traveling to the West Indies anymore, save Methodist missionaries. And, apparently, the occasional winsome governess.

Seeming to recognize defeat, Joss bowed. "Welcome aboard the *Aphrodite,* Miss Turner. I hope your voyage is pleasant."

The young lady curtsied once again before Stubb escorted her to the narrow stairs that led belowdecks.

Gray watched Miss Turner descend into the belly of the ship, knowing that for good or ill, this voyage had just become a great deal more interesting.

"Where's Bains?" Joss asked suddenly. "What are you doing, rowing yourself back to the ship? Is he following with more cargo?"

"No. I let him go."

"You let him go? What the devil for?"

"Something's wrong with his eyesight." Any man who mistook Miss Turner for a dockside whore had to be losing his vision. Not to mention, Gray didn't want a sailor who had a habit of taking what wasn't offered him. In voyages past, that attitude might have been a desirable trait, but not anymore. The *Aphrodite* was a respectable merchant ship now.

Joss's jaw clenched. "You can't let him go. He's my crewman."

"It's already done."

"I can't believe this. You go ashore for two hours of trade, and somehow you've exchanged an experienced sailor for a governess."

"Well, and goats. I did buy a few goats—the boatman will have them out presently."

"Damn it, don't try to change the subject. Crew and passengers are supposed to be my responsibility. Am I captain of this ship or not?"

"Yes, Joss, you're the captain. But I'm the investor. I don't want Bains near my cargo, and I'd like at least one paying passenger on this voyage, if I can get one. I didn't have that steerage compartment converted to cabins for a lark, you realize."

"If you think I'll believe your interest in that girl lies solely in her six pounds sterling . . ."

Gray shrugged. "Since you mention it, I quite admired her brass as well."

"You know damn well what I mean. A young lady, unescorted . . ." He looked askance at Gray. "It's asking for trouble."

"Asking for trouble?" Gray echoed, hoping to lighten the conversation. "Since when does the *Aphrodite* need to go *asking* for trouble? We've stowed more trouble than cargo on this ship." He leaned back, propping both elbows on the ship's rail. "And as trouble goes, Miss Turner's variety looks a damn sight better than most alternatives. Perhaps you could do with a bit of trouble yourself. It's been a year, you know."

Joss's face drew tight. "It's been a year, two months, and seventeen days. I have troubles enough of my own, Gray. I'm not looking for more." He turned and stared out over the harbor.

Damn. Gray knew he shouldn't have said that. It was just—well, he missed the old, piss-at-the-devil Joss. He missed his brother.

He kept hoping the old Joss would surface someday, once he released all that pain dragging him down. But the chances of that seemed even less likely, now that Gray had made him captain. Navigating the sea would be the least of Joss's worries on this, his first voyage in command. Navigating the balance of power between a green captain and fifteen men more accustomed to plundering cargo than protecting it—now *that* was treacherous going. *Here there be monsters.*

And Joss was worried—perhaps rightly—that having an attractive, unmarried young lady aboard would cock it all up.

"I'll keep the girl out of trouble," Gray said, in what seemed to him a rather magnanimous gesture. "I'll watch out for her."

"Oh, I've no doubt you will. But who's going to watch out for you?"

Gray's nerves prickled. So, it wasn't the girl Joss was concerned about. No, he expected Gray to cock it all up.

"Right, Joss. I'm an unprincipled, lecherous bastard." He paused, waiting for his brother to argue otherwise. He didn't.

Gray protested, "She's a governess, for the love of gold. Prim, proper, starched, dull." *Soft,* he thought in counterpoint. *Delicate, sweet. Intriguing.*

"Ah. So you'll dally with any chambermaid or serving wench who'll lift her skirts, but you'd draw the line at seducing a governess?"

"*Yes.* Have a look at me, man." Gray smoothed his brushed velvet lapel, then gestured upward at the banners trimming the freshly tarred rigging. "Look at this ship. I'm telling you, my libertine days are over. I've gone respectable."

"It's easy to change your coat. It's a great deal harder to change your ways."

Gray sighed heavily. He'd never been a model brother, and God knew he'd never be a saint. But whether Joss believed it or not, he'd worked damn hard to launch this business. He'd worked damn hard for *them*—to give this patched-together family of theirs some security, the place in society their father had forfeited decades ago. He'd talked investors into entrusting him with thousands of pounds; he'd promised the insurers he could be trusted to safely deliver the cargo.

Yet his own brother didn't trust him to keep out of a girl's skirts.

The irony would have struck him as humorous, had it wounded him any less. Had it been any less deserved. Gray rubbed his face with one hand and tried again, all trace of joking gone from his voice. "Listen, Joss. I won't pursue her."

"She's beautiful."

"I won't pursue her," Gray repeated slowly. "And I thought that you weren't looking."

Joss stared back out at the water. "I was widowed, Gray. I didn't go blind."

No, not blind, Gray thought. *Just . . . numb.*

When Joss turned and caught him staring, Gray just smiled and shook his head. "The girl's right, you know. We both have his ears." He pushed off the rail and straightened, pulling a hand through his hair.

His uncovered, wind-mussed hair.

"Witch's tit," he muttered. "When did that happen?"

Joss raised an eyebrow. "What's that?"

Gray wheeled about, searching the deck and glancing over the rail. "I've lost my damn hat."

Joss broke into low laughter.

"It's not funny. I just bought that hat. I *liked* that hat. Cost me a bloody fortune, that hat."

Joss laughed again, and this time Gray laughed with him. Yes, that hat had cost him a bloody fortune. And now that hat had purchased him a moment of carefree laughter with his brother, on the deck of the *Aphrodite*. An echo, somehow, from a happier time past.

Gray smiled to himself. Damn, but he loved a good bargain.

CHAPTER
THREE

Surely there was a man in there somewhere, Sophia thought. Somewhere under all that hair.

The hunched, ancient steward shuffled down the narrow staircase, whistling a jaunty tune as he went. She followed, treading gingerly on the bowed boards. As her eyes adjusted to the dim lighting, she took in the greasy, gray tangle of hair that hung midway down the man's back, the grizzled froth of beard that extended nearly as far down in front, the lightly furred forearms exposed by his loose checked tunic.

" 'Ere we are, miss," he announced. "Ladies' cabins." He pushed aside a thin curtain of dark fabric, and they entered a small, low-ceilinged chamber with a round table and chairs occupying the center. Sunlight streamed into the space from a skylight above. Four doors opened off the small room, two on either side. The steward crossed to the door marked "Seven" and opened it with a flourish. "Your berth, miss."

"Thank you, Mr. . . ."

"Just Stubb, miss."

"Thank you, Stubb."

"The privy's just there." He nodded toward a small door. "Go through the cabin this way, and you'll hit top steerage—that's where all the provisions are kept—and then the forecastle. Go the other direction, and you have the gentlemen's cabin, the galley, then the captain and mates' cabins at the stern. But if you need anything, you just call on me, miss."

"Thank you, Stubb."

"I'll 'ave your trunks down in a wink, then." He bowed extravagantly, sweeping the floor with the fringe of his beard.

Sophia entered her berth and shut the door, then turned a slow circle in place. There wasn't room to do much else. The little closet, for lack of a better term— her family's Mayfair town home boasted cupboards larger than this—consisted of a narrow bed protruding from the wall at shoulder height, storage space beneath the bunk, and a small writing desk that folded down from the wall.

No chair.

Sophia removed her bonnet and knotted the ribbons together, then hung it from a peg driven into the wall. She might have sat down, but there was nowhere to sit. She could have lain down, but she wasn't certain how to vault herself into the high bed. Instead, she returned to the common area and sat at the table, dropping her head into her hands.

Had she succumbed to seasickness already? The gentle rolling of the anchored ship seemed insufficient to occasion this amount of dizziness. The whole vessel was a study in contradictions. The captain who wasn't a captain. The governess who wasn't a governess. Two men— one white, one black—claiming the close kinship of brotherhood.

Strangely enough, she believed the last. Something about their square-tipped ears, and the way their angular jaws balanced those arrogant grins . . . They were like two garments cut from the same pattern, but fashioned from different cloth.

Ah, yes. They were half brothers, of course. This overdue realization of the obvious gave Sophia a bit of peace. Apparently, her flow of comprehension had not been dammed entirely. Merely slowed, to the trickling rate of syrup.

She knew what—or rather, *whom*—to blame for that.

Him, and his insufferable teasing. Coming to her rescue in the tavern, only to humiliate her further. Deliberately misleading her about the captain's identity simply to gather amusement from her befuddlement. And possessing the unmitigated gall to do it all looking so handsome, with that roguish smirk and the mocking scar beneath it.

How did he get it, that scar? So thin and straight, slanting from the cleft of his chin to the corner of his mouth. From a blade of some sort, most definitely. Perhaps a stray swipe of a knife in a bawdy-house brawl. Or maybe a more honorable man had called him out in a duel, to avenge his callous acts of insolence toward unsuspecting ladies. A flick of the rapier could make such a scar. But if *he* had walked away from the duel with a scratch, what had become of his opponent?

Her imagination ran wild with the notion, painting a vivid scene in her mind. She could visualize the knot of muscle in his arm, sketch the straining sinew in his wrist as he loomed over his trembling rival, lifting the sword for a lethal blow—

" 'Ere we are, then."

Sophia's head jerked up.

Stubb reappeared in an aura of grizzled hair, followed by two sailors each balancing one end of her stacked trunks. The steward directed, "It's berth seven, what's marked for the lovely miss."

Her trunks deposited, Sophia stood to offer her thanks. At that moment, however, the ship gave a sudden lurch, and she found herself tossed right back in the chair.

"Anchors aweigh!" The call came echoing through the grated skylight. "All hands! All hands!"

The three men hurried back the way they'd entered, and Sophia followed them up the narrow staircase and onto the deck.

What a glorious commotion awaited her there—the sailors shouting and hauling and climbing into the rigging like spiders scaling webs. She craned her neck to watch their progress, shading her eyes with one hand. One by one, the square sails unfurled, four apiece on each of the two soaring masts. The wind quickly found and filled the sails, puffing them out like frogs' throats.

She went to the rail and stayed there for hours, watching the river widen beneath them and the dense clamor of Gravesend diffuse into pastoral calm. Before she expected it, the Thames spat them out into a wide basin of churning water. They had yet to reach the open sea, but the arms of land on either side grew increasingly distant, as the tide tugged the *Aphrodite* free of England's embrace. Daylight was fading, and tendrils of fog wound over her neck and before her eyes, obscuring her view of the low, chalky banks.

Sophia fought the childish impulse to wave farewell. She clung to the lip of wood instead—for strength, and for stability, as the vessel's pitching grew increasingly violent. The ship crested a large swell, then dipped into a gray-green valley. Cold, salty spray rushed up to sting her eyes and cheeks.

It must be the fog, she thought, squeezing her eyes shut and wiping her cheeks. Or the steady rocking of the ship, like a cradle. Perhaps it was the encroaching darkness and the muted roaring of the sea that made her feel, for the first time in many years, so very small.

And so very, very alone.

But then, suddenly, she wasn't.

"Homesick already? Or merely seasick?" Mr. Grayson joined her at the rail.

Sophia tried not to look at him. It was a struggle.

When a few moments passed without her reply, he said, "I'd offer a few soothing words, but they'd only be lies. It'll get worse before it gets better."

She didn't ask which type of sickness he referred to. Both, she suspected. "Are the waves always this large?"

But when she turned to him, he'd disappeared. A shout drew her gaze heavenward. Above her, sailors called to one another as they ascended the rigging again. Her stomach churned, just watching them sway back and forth against the backdrop of greenish sky. Sophia clutched the rail and shut her eyes.

"Be reasonable. It's just a few clouds," came a low murmur, behind her.

"Aye, a few big, black clouds to the West. You know as well as I do, a storm's coming."

"A bit of a blow, perhaps. The *Aphrodite*'s weathered far worse. Reef the topsails, keep all hands at the ready."

There was a pause, thick with enmity.

"Not in the Downs," came the terse reply. "I'll not risk springing a mast our first night at sea. We'll drop anchor and furl the sails, and we'll wait it out."

"Joss, you're behaving—"

"I'm behaving as the captain of this ship, Gray. If you don't start affording me the respect that deserves, I'll order you below." The voice sank deeper still. "And if you dare contradict me in front of my crew, I'll throw your arse in the brig."

A burst of spray hit Sophia's face again, startling her eyes open. With droplets of seawater clinging to her eyelashes, she slowly rotated her neck until the two brothers came into focus.

The men glared at each other, and the fog swirling

around them took on the charged heat of steam. Apparently, the Grayson brothers shared no more affection than Sophia and her sister did.

The captain turned toward the ship's bow, calling, "Mr. Brackett!"

A third man joined them. The fog and spray obscured the features of his face, but Sophia could see he was tall and lean, standing ramrod straight despite the waves.

"Mr. Brackett," said the captain, "see that *all* passengers"—he shot another glance at his fuming brother—"are returned to their cabins. Furl the topsails and prepare to drop anchor."

"Aye, aye, Captain." Mr. Brackett strode forward, sharp cheekbones and blade-thin nose slicing through the fog. He began barking orders, and the crew exploded into activity.

"Come along then, Miss Turner." Stubb took her elbow and urged her toward the companionway hatch. They crossed the deck in a lurching gait as the waves rolled beneath.

Once they were safely below, Stubb left her alone, only to return a few moments later with a bucket threaded over his arm. Behind him followed another of the sailors—an impossibly tall and broad-shouldered black man whose size required him to nearly double over and turn sideways just to thread his body through the compartment entry.

"Levi 'ere will be putting up the deadlights." Stubb tilted his hoary crown toward the black man as he bent to lash the chair legs to the table's bolted base.

"Deadlights?" Just the sound of the word left Sophia cold, and she braced herself against the table to receive its meaning.

"Shutters for the cabin windows," the steward explained. "To keep out the storm and sea."

Levi nudged past her, squeezing into her berth. He carried a circular plate, drilled 'round with screw holes.

Stubb passed the bucket to Sophia. "You're like to have need of this."

She looked down at the leather pail. "Am I to bail out the seawater, then?"

Stubb cackled with laughter. "Levi! The lovely miss thinks she'll be put to work, bailing out the bilge!" Levi made no reply as he emerged from her berth, but Stubb laughed twice as loudly to compensate. "Nay, miss. If we take on some sea, there's a pump in the hold."

"Then why the bucket?" Sophia asked. The ship dropped suddenly, and her stomach rolled with it. "Oh. That."

"Now don't be worried about the waves, miss. Save your concerns for the lightning."

"Lightning?" She didn't like the sound of that.

"Aye. Strange things occur when lightning strikes a ship. That electric fluid bounces all through the hull, and woe to the sailor caught holding a bit of metal." Stubb fluffed his whiskers. "What do you think turned this beard of mine to white?" He flashed a toothless grin. "Had me a whole set of gold teeth. All melted to slag."

"You're teasing me."

"I am not," the steward said, though he threw Sophia a sly wink. "Just ask Levi here. He won't speak a word to contradict me."

Neither would he speak a word to support you, she surmised. The black man hadn't broken his silence since entering. But arms crossed and face stony, he looked capable of supporting the London Bridge.

"Don't you know?" the old man continued. "That's why they call me Stubb. Before the lightning struck, I used to have a wooden leg."

"A wooden . . ." Sophia stared at the steward's bare,

furred feet for a moment before Stubb broke into loud, toothless laughter.

"No, don't worry yerself about a little blow like this one, miss," Stubb said, backing his way out of the cabin. "We'll come through it fine."

Once the men had left, taking the lamp along with them, Sophia fumbled her way into her berth. It was dark as a pocket, and even if she had some light by which to undress or unpack her trunks, the boat's turbulent motions made it difficult just to remain upright.

She settled for removing her gloves, and then her cloak, reaching into the folds to retrieve her "letter of employment." This she tucked beneath her bodice, where it curled around her purse. She groped with her feet until she located her trunks. Then, climbing atop them and clinging to the edge of the bunk for balance, she spread her cloak across the high, flat plank and—between groaning tilts of the ship—managed to scramble into bed.

That letter—it was a stroke of good fortune that neither Captain nor Mr. Grayson had been inclined to examine it. Her handiwork could easily deceive someone unacquainted with either party, but Mr. Grayson possessed intimate knowledge of the Waltham family. He would be certain to notice something amiss.

It all had begun as a lark, a joke. While tucked away at a country house party, Sophia had amused her friend Lucy Waltham by drafting a nonsense letter to Lucy's cousins in Tortola, whom she had never met. At the time, Sophia's sole motive had been to needle Lucy about her suitor, Jeremy Trescott, the Earl of Kendall. But the romance of it all, the idea of her scribblings floating across the sea to a tropical clime, had gripped Sophia and refused to let go. She posted the letter on a whim, signing Lucy's name but giving her own London address. Then

Lucy had married Jeremy, and Sophia had become engaged, and Tortola had been forgotten.

Until a week ago, when Sophia received a reply.

My dear cousin Lucy, the letter read.

Although your kind letter arrived addressed to Papa, he has bade me reply, since he assumes we are nearly of an age. I am Emily, his eldest, recently turned sixteen, and I am happy to oblige his request. Compared to the hardships I am typically made to endure, such as minding my four incorrigible siblings, penning a letter is a true delight.

At any rate, I extend to you our entire family's felicitations on your marriage and our fondest hopes for your happiness. Would that I could invite you and your new husband to visit us here in the West Indies, but Papa threatens daily that we shall soon depart for America, as soon as he finds a buyer for our land. How desolate I shall be, to bid farewell to our beloved home, Eleanora, where I have been born and bred and lived so many happy years.

Forgive me, I must end. I hear the telltale clanging that informs me young George and Harry have taken to fencing on the veranda again.

Fondest regards from your cousin,
Miss Emily Waltham

On first reading, the letter was merely a welcome source of amusement, during a week that held levity in short supply. But that was before Sophia learned that her dowry was actually a trust, and only her twenty-first birthday stood between her and complete financial independence. Before she wandered into that gallery in Queen Anne Street and saw that magnificent painting of a ship braving a stormy sea, and dared to imagine that she, too, could brave the world. Before everything changed—or, more accurately, before Sophia realized she never would.

Then the letter became a plan. A new sheet affixed to the original envelope, some doctoring of the address, and Sophia Hathaway—or rather, Miss Jane Turner—had an offer of employment. An escape.

And she had to escape. She'd been escaping for years now, through clever lies and wicked fantasies. Surely Sophia was the only girl at school who kept a secret folio of naughty sketches buried beneath the obligatory watercolor landscapes. The only debutante at Almack's who mentally undressed unsuspecting gentlemen between dainty sips of ratafia. Surely none of the other young ladies in the Champions of Charity Junior Auxiliary lay abed at night with their shifts hiked to their waists, dreaming of pirates and highwaymen with coarse manners and rough, skillful hands.

She was a perfect fraud. And no one saw the truth. Least of all the dear, deluded man who had wished to marry her.

Now she'd done it. She'd run away, in the most scandalous fashion imaginable, ensuring she could never return. Thanks to her farewell notes, by now half of London would be under the impression she'd eloped with a French painting master named Gervais. Fabricated or no, her ruin was complete. No longer was Sophia the pretty ribbon adorning a twenty-thousand-pound dowry, a trinket to be bartered for connections and a title. At last, she'd be her own person, free to pursue her true passion, experience real life.

Well. If she'd wished to experience real life, she'd gotten her wish indeed. A very real storm howled around her, the thunder rumbling in rebuke, as if the world had conspired to put her bravery to the test. She huddled into her cloak and took deep, slow breaths, as if by calming her inner tempest of emotions, she might tame the storm without.

It didn't work, in either respect.

Gray seethed with anger.

Having been ordered belowdecks in such insulting fashion, he thundered his way down to the gentlemen's cabin. Once inside his tiny berth, he wrestled out of his coat. Between the cramped size of the room and the rolling of the ship, the experience was like tumbling a chambermaid in a closet, only far less pleasurable. One particularly impatient yank on his sleeve earned him bloodied knuckles when his fist banged the low ceiling.

When he'd ordered the *Aphrodite* converted to accommodate passengers, the builder had given him an option. Did he want four gentlemen's cabins, similar to the ladies'? Or would he prefer to squeeze six smaller berths into the same space?

Gray's answer? Six, of course. No question about it. Two extra beds meant two extra fares. He hadn't dreamed he'd one day occupy one of these cramped berths.

Six feet of angry man, lashed into a five-foot bunk, in the midst of a howling gale—it wasn't a recipe for a good night's sleep. Gray craved the space and comfort of his former quarters aboard the *Aphrodite*—the captain's cabin. But as his brother had so officiously pointed out, Gray wasn't the captain of this ship anymore.

Throw his arse in the brig, had Joss threatened? Gray tossed indignantly, his chest straining against the ropes that held him in the child-sized bed. The ship's brig didn't sound so bad right now. He'd put up with a few iron bars, the rancid bilgewater and rats, if it meant he could stretch his legs properly. Hell, this room was so damned small, he couldn't even get his blasted boots off.

He kicked the wall of his berth, no doubt scuffing the shine on his new Hessians. He hated the cursed things anyway. They pinched his feet. Why the devil he'd thought it a brilliant notion to get all dandified for this voyage, Gray couldn't remember. Just who was he trying to impress? Stubb?

No, not Stubb.

Bel. It was all for Bel.

Gray couldn't forget the way she'd looked at him when he'd left last year. The disappointment welling in those big eyes, as dark and doleful as any medieval icon's. Hadn't she learned by then to stop expecting so damned much of him? He'd never lived up to his little sister's ideal. He wasn't sure any man could.

But now Gray could show her he'd changed. As much as it was within his power to change, at any rate. He'd given up the reckless, albeit far more entertaining, life of a privateer and become a successful tradesman. The owner of a shipping concern, with two new vessels in construction besides the *Aphrodite,* and investors lining up to back more. Able to offer her a home in London, a comfortable life, whatever else she might desire.

Bel might have preferred he grow a conscience, rather than build a fortune. But Gray knew better than to waste his time. If a scoundrel like him had any hope of Heaven, it rested solely on the strength of Isabel Grayson's prayers.

Prayer wouldn't help him tonight. From Gray's experience, the best ward against seasickness was to turn one's mind to sin.

Surprising, then, that his thoughts drifted to Miss Turner.

He thought he'd outgrown admiring her sort, those delicate English roses. Give him an exotic orchid. A voluptuous woman with unbound hair and bold, dark eyes, who knew what she was about. Girlish blushes, demure smiles—they'd lost their allure for Gray years ago.

But still he thought of her. He could no more rid his mind of her than command the storm to cease. Tossing fitfully in his bunk, he recalled her near-breakable beauty, her delicate scent. And the feel of her body pressed against his for those few seconds in the rowboat. Not just the enticing sensation of her soft, pillowy breasts flattening against his chest, but beneath them, a pulse racing like a bird's, pounding against his torso through all those layers of womanly flesh and wool. As if something caged inside her was clamoring for escape. Begging him to set it free.

It was then he discovered an unhappy consequence to all his tossing and turning. One of the ropes binding him to his bed had drifted south—and now cinched his body at a most unfortunate latitude.

Damn it to hell.

He undid the ropes and wrestled out of the bed. What the devil was happening to him? His little brother had him confined to his cabin. A prim governess had him tied in knots. And worst—he'd been off the sea so long, he was losing his instincts. Joss had been right; the storm was growing violent.

Arms braced against either side of the corridor, Gray made his way from the gentlemen's cabin to the companionway. He needed to see the storm for himself, judge how the ship's new rigging and spars were weathering the gale.

But when he reached the stairs, his plans changed. There was a girl in his way.

Miss Turner stood perched on the third rung of the ladder, straining on tiptoe to peek through the half-open hatch. Had Gray been the superstitious sort, he might have thought her a ghost. Her fingers were white, delicate webs where she clutched the handle of the hatch with one hand and the ladder with the other. Flashes of luminous beauty alternated with darkness. Each fork of lightning illuminated her finely wrought features and the droplets of spray clinging to her hair and eyelashes.

No, she wasn't a ghost. But she was a vision just the same.

"Miss Turner," he said, bracing one shoulder against the wall.

She didn't turn around.

Gray cleared his throat and tried again. "Miss Turner."

Now she startled, nearly losing her grip on the ladder. "Mr. Grayson. I . . ." Her voice caught, and she dabbed her face with her sleeve. "I wanted to see the storm."

"And how do you find it?"

"Wet."

Gray chuckled, surprised.

"And beautiful," she continued, as another bolt of lightning threw her features into relief. "Out here on the water, with no solid land beneath—it's so different. As though there's no boundary between sky and sea, and we're simply at Nature's mercy. It's so wild and gothic."

"It's dangerous, is what it is."

"Yes, precisely." Another bright flash revealed the curve of a smile.

Gray frowned. What was she doing, smiling at him in a storm? Sending electric pulses through his blood with each glimpse of her pale, haunting beauty? She ought to be huddled in her bunk, fearing for her life.

He crossed the small space in one stride, gripping the ladder with one hand and offering her the other, to assist her descent. "Wise passengers wait out a storm in their berths."

"Do they?" she whispered, taking his hand. "What does that make us, then?"

Now this, this was danger. He didn't miss the coy lilt in her voice, nor the tremor of her rain-dampened shoulders, an unconscious shiver that all but begged for his embrace. No, she didn't even realize the invitation she'd made, but the signs were unmistakable to Gray. He'd seen this reaction, many times before, and he knew better than to be flattered by it. It was nothing more than instinct.

Any port in a storm.

"It doesn't make *us* anything," he said, helping her down. The feel of her chilled, slender fingers in his triggered all manner of instincts. "It makes me a concerned investor. And it makes you a girl with an overactive imagination. Go back to your berth."

The lightning had ceased, but her eyes sparked with a fire all their own. "But I—"

"You're not safe here." He wrenched open the door to the ladies' cabin and waved her through it. "Go to bed, Miss Turner."

Yes, go to bed, he thought, as she wordlessly swept through the door and he drew it shut behind her. *Go to your bed, before I sweep you off to mine.*

CHAPTER
FOUR

Sophia woke with a start, alone and disoriented in the dark. Her pulse responded first, pumping panic through her veins at a furious rate. She pressed her hand to her heart, and her fingers curled around her purse. Awareness returned in a dizzy rush.

A faint silvery glow leaked under the door of her berth. It was morning. And if it was morning, that must mean she'd survived the night.

She turned onto her side. Every muscle screamed with pain. Her skirt and cloak were still heavy with damp, resisting her feeble attempts to rise. Perhaps she didn't need to move, after all.

Oh, but she did. She drew a deep breath, then wished she could spit it out. The air was thick with humidity and rank with the odors of sickness and bilge. She slid from her bunk, ignoring the protestations of her aching limbs, and flung open the door of her berth.

She lunged for the staircase, scrambling up on her hands and knees. A salty breeze nipped at her ears as she emerged headfirst into the gray dawn. She inhaled a deep, bracing breath of fresh air. The thought of returning below held no appeal whatsoever. Yet neither could she remain like this, head and neck protruding from a hole in the deck, like some species of seafaring marmot.

She climbed abovedecks and struggled into an upright position, planting her feet in a wide stance to buffer the ship's rolling. Sophia closed her eyes. Either the ship was caught in a whirlpool, or her head was spinning like a top. She looked toward the nearest rail—only five paces away, perhaps six. Beyond it, the English coastline appeared to teeter on a fulcrum. She bowed her head, focused her gaze on the deck beneath her, and took one step. Two.

Then the deck pitched suddenly, and her locked knees buckled. She was falling, spinning, out of control.

She was caught.

"Steady there." Two large hands gripped her elbows. Her fingers instinctively closed over two strong arms. Sophia barely had time to register the feel of superfine wool and hard muscle beneath her fingertips, a brief instant to catch a glimpse of two gray-green eyes.

And then she vomited all over two slightly scuffed, tassel-topped Hessians.

"I . . ." She coughed and sputtered. Mr. Grayson's iron grip on her elbows refused to relax, preventing her from turning away. "Sir . . . Release me, I beg you."

"Absolutely not. You're not steady on your feet. This way, then." He guided her sideways, nudging her to take small steps and twirl slightly right—the most mortifying waltz Sophia had ever endured. He backed her against a small crate. "Sit down."

She obeyed, sinking onto the rough wooden slats gratefully. Still holding her fast by the elbows, he crouched before her. She could not bear to meet his eyes.

"Stay here," he ordered. "I'll come back presently."

Oh, please don't. Sophia cringed as his soiled boots carried him away. The instant his footsteps faded, she pulled a handkerchief from her cloak and wiped her brow. She willed her head to stop spinning, so she could rise to her feet unaided and make her escape. But he was too fast for her. Within the space of two minutes, he was back, boots rinsed—with seawater, she supposed—and steaming tankard in hand.

"Drink this." He wrapped her trembling hands around the tankard. Delicious warmth prickled through her chilled fingers.

"What is it?"

"Tea, with treacle and lemon. And a touch of rum." When she merely stared at the drink, he added, "Drink it. You'll feel better."

Sophia raised the mug to her lips and sipped carefully. Fragrant steam warmed her from the inside out. The syrupy sweetness coated her throat, masking the bitter taste of bile. She sipped again. "Thank you," she finally managed, keeping her eyes trained on the liquid sloshing in the tankard. "I'm . . . I'm sorry about your boots."

He laughed. "You *should* be sorry." He crouched beside her. Sophia stubbornly stared into her tankard. "I despise these boots," he continued. "I'd just been contemplating yanking them off my feet and tossing them overboard. But now it seems I'll have to keep them." Surprise tugged her gaze up to his. He grinned. "For sentimental reasons."

Don't do it, she told herself. *Don't smile back.*

Too late.

"Mr. Grayson . . ."

"Please." His elbow nudged her thigh. An accident? He did not apologize. "After that, I believe you can call me Gray."

His gaze sparked—a hint of silver flashing in murky green—and Sophia became suddenly, painfully aware of the picture she must present. Soiled, wrinkled dress still damp at the hem, flax-colored hair teased loose from its pins. The pale, wan complexion of illness.

And yet . . .

His eyes did not merely skim her surface. Instead, they focused some distance beneath her stained garments, plumbing the depths of her appearance in a most disconcerting way.

Despite the chill, a light sheen of perspiration bloomed over her thighs.

"Mr. Grayson. I thank you for the tea." Sophia shifted the tankard to one hand and shook out the handkerchief she'd kept in her palm. A sudden puff of wind wrenched it from her grasp.

His hand darted out, and he caught the fluttering scrap of white effortlessly, as though it were a dove trained to fly to his hand.

Sophia reached for it. "Once again, I thank you."

He whisked it out of her grasp. "Save your thanks. I haven't given it back." He fingered the eyelet trim. "Perhaps I'll decide to keep it. For sentimental reasons."

It came to her so easily, the flirtatious response. He had only to look at her, and her caution collapsed in the flick of a fan. "You shouldn't tease, Mr. Grayson. It isn't at all charitable."

"Ah, but I'm a tradesman. I'm interested in profit, not charity. And I asked you to call me Gray." He leaned closer, and now—at this diminished distance—Sophia would have sworn his eyes were not green at all, but a pale blue.

Piercing blue.

"You have money, don't you?"

Her mouth went dry. *He knew.* From the handkerchief? It must be too fine, too embellished. Obviously it belonged to a lady of wealth. Curse it. If only Sophia had had more time to plan her escape, she would have managed a better disguise. It had been difficult enough to leave her painstakingly selected trousseau behind and take only her everyday linens. She hadn't had time to assemble a coarser wardrobe, nor even any notion of where the poorer classes shopped.

"I beg your pardon?" Her fingers tightened around the rapidly cooling tankard.

"Money. You do have money, don't you? You never paid your fare yesterday. It's six pounds, eight. If you haven't the coin, I'll have no choice but to hold you for ransom once we reach Tortola."

Her fare. Sophia sipped her tea with relief. If Mr. Grayson was this concerned over six pounds, he surely had no idea he was harboring a runaway heiress with nearly one hundred times that amount strapped beneath her stays. She suppressed a nervous laugh. "Yes, of course I can pay my passage. You'll have your money today, Mr. Grayson."

"Gray."

"Mr. Grayson," she said, her voice and nerves growing thin, "I scarcely think that my moment of . . . of indisposition gives you leave to make such an intimate request, that I address you by your Christian name. I certainly shall not."

He clucked softly, wrapping the handkerchief around his fingers. With hypnotic tenderness, he reached out, drawing the fabric across her temple.

"Now, sweetheart—surely my parents can be credited with greater imagination than you imply. Christening me 'Gray Grayson'?" He chuckled low in his throat. "Everyone aboard this ship calls me Gray. Sorry to disappoint you, but it's no particular privilege. There's but one woman on earth permitted to address me by my Christian name."

"Your mother?"

He grinned again. "No."

She blinked.

"Oh, now don't look so disappointed," he said. "It's my sister."

Sophia slanted her gaze to her lap, cursing herself for playing into his charm. If the sight of him drove the wits from her skull, the solution was plain. She mustn't look.

But then he pressed the handkerchief into her hand, covering her fingers with his own, and Sophia could not retrieve the small, defeated sigh that fell from her lips. His touch devastated her resolve completely. His hand was like the rest of him. Brute strength, neatly groomed. She heartily wished she'd thought to put on gloves.

He leaned closer, his scent intruding through the pervasive smell of seawater—wholly masculine and faintly spicy, like pomade and rum.

"And sweetheart, if I did make an *intimate request* of you"—his thumb swept boldly over the delicate skin of her wrist—"you'd know it."

Sophia sucked in her breath.

"So call me Gray." He released her hand abruptly.

Disappointment—unbidden, imprudent, *unthinkable* emotion—cinched in Sophia's chest. Distance from this man was precisely what she wished. Well, if not precisely what she wished, it was exactly what she needed. He looked at her as though he'd laid all her secrets bare, and her body as well.

She pushed the tankard back at him, leaving him no choice but to take it from her hands. "I shall continue to address you as propriety demands, Mr. Grayson." She cast him a sharp look. "And you certainly are *not* at liberty to call me 'sweetheart.'"

He donned an expression of wide-eyed innocence. "That isn't what it stands for, then?" Teasing the handkerchief from her clenched fist, he ran his thumb over the embroidered monogram.

S.H.

"You see?" He traced each letter with the pad of his finger. "Sweet. Heart. I thought surely that must be it. Because I know *your* name is Jane Turner."

His lips curved in that insolent grin. "Unless . . . don't tell me. It was a gift?"

At least this time she made it to the rail.

And there Sophia clung, until she was certain she must be casting up remnants of Michaelmas dinner. Until the heavy footfalls of those soiled boots told her that he'd left.

Back in her berth, she dipped a clean, *unembroidered* handkerchief into a basin of fresh water. Stripped down to her drawers and stockings, she sponged the icy water over her neck and face, then between her breasts and under her arms. After toweling dry, she dusted her body with scented rice powder.

She still felt filthy.

With trembling fingers, she restrapped the heavy bundle around her ribs. She tugged a clean chemise over her head and cinched up her stays.

She still felt exposed.

She brushed out her hair with sharp yanks, as if to punish the feeble mind beneath the tingling scalp. Of all the times and places to go distracted over a man! During her Season, she'd been courted by no fewer than nine of the *ton*'s most eligible bachelors. No dukes or earls among them, to her parents' dismay, but she had become engaged to the most coveted catch of the *ton*—the supremely charming Sir Toby Aldridge. And never, not once, in all those waltzes and garden strolls and coy conversations, had Sophia's perfect composure been shaken. She knew how to manage attractive men; or rather, she knew how to manage herself around them.

She knew nothing. She was an idiot, an imbecile, a

simpleton, and a ninny. Boarding a ship under an assumed name, then whipping a monogrammed handkerchief from her cloak?

Sophia yanked and twisted her hair into a severe style, then stabbed the coiled knot with several hairpins.

Foolish, foolish girl. If Mr. Grayson learned about that money, he would know her instantly for a fraud. He could take her purse away, or hold her captive in hopes of extorting more. Worse, he could turn out to be a gentleman after all, and simply return her to her family.

Be calm, she bade herself, taking a deep breath.

Considering his friendship with the Walthams, Mr. Grayson was bound to discover her deceit eventually. But by the time the ship reached Tortola, she would be just weeks from her twenty-first birthday. Just weeks away from freedom. If Mr. Grayson possessed some shred of gentlemanly honor that might compel him to return a ruined debutante to England—and Sophia doubted he did—it would already be too late. By then, her trust and her future would belong to her alone.

Her anxiety somewhat allayed, Sophia reached for her dress. It pained her to put on the same wrinkled gown, but she had no choice. Her trunk accommodated only four dresses in addition to the one she wore. Two were last summer's muslin frocks, to wear once they reached the tropics. The third was not a dress at all, but rather a smock for painting, and the fourth . . . the fourth was pure folly.

Once dressed, she turned her attention to the smaller trunk, which held her dearest treasures. Paints, charcoal, pastels, palette, brushes—and one hundred sheets of heavy paper, divided into two parcels, each wrapped tightly in oilcloth. One hundred sheets to ration over a month, perhaps longer.

Although she might have allowed herself three, Sophia

withdrew only two sheets of paper. She gathered up a small drawing board and a stub of charcoal before neatly repacking her artist's cache. As she replaced the oilcloth packet, her hand brushed against the worn leather cover of a small book. Smiling, she lifted the volume to the top of the trunk.

The Book.

Given to her by her friend Lucy Waltham, now the Countess of Kendall, this tiny volume had proved an invaluable source of both information and inspiration. *The Memoirs of a Wanton Dairymaid*, the title read. Its contents were, as one might expect, ribald accounts of a dairymaid's trysts with her gentleman employer. As a whole, Sophia had found The Book shocking, titillating, and woefully lacking in illustrations. This last, she had set out to remedy.

She flipped through the first half of the book, now painstakingly embellished with pen-and-ink sketches of the wanton dairymaid and her gent in various states of undress. She had planned to return it to Lucy when she finished, but now . . . A pang of loneliness pinched in her chest. Even if she did see Lucy again, her friend would be forced to cut her. A countess didn't consort with fallen women.

A sudden image sprang to her mind. A frenzy of colors, textures, tastes . . . Snow-white petticoats bunched at her waist. Straw strewn on a stable floor. The warm gush of an overturned pail of milk. Miles of smooth, bronzed skin. The taste of salt on her tongue and the scrape of rough whiskers against her neck.

She threw the book back in her trunk and shut it quickly. Irrepressible dreamer she might be, but Sophia was *not* a wanton dairymaid. And Mr. Grayson, as he was so fond of reminding her, was no gentleman.

The air inside the cabin had grown uncomfortably

close. She needed to clear her mind. She needed to draw. To gather all this diffuse, unruly sensation within her and force it through the tip of her pencil, onto paper where it could be caged by four margins. Safe. She tucked charcoal and paper under her arm and mounted the ladder, intending to sketch on deck.

The instant her head emerged through the hatch, however, Sophia's plans changed.

She found herself face-to-face with a goat.

With a rude bleat, the goat snatched a sheet of paper from her grasp and crumpled it between its jaws. Sophia watched in confounded outrage as the goat casually masticated and swallowed her precious parchment. When the animal extended its long, narrow tongue in every indication of lunching on her second sheet, Sophia startled into action. She grabbed her drawing board with both hands and smacked the impertinent animal on the nose.

"Easy there, sweetheart." Mr. Grayson's deep voice carried from somewhere above. "That's my investment you're bludgeoning."

Sophia stared at the goat. She paused a half-second to imagine Mr. Grayson's handsome features superimposed on that furry, blunt-nosed visage. Then she whacked it over the head again.

My, but that felt good.

Evidently, the goat did not agree. It grasped the corner of Sophia's board with its teeth and pulled. Sophia tugged back with all her strength. She lost her footing on the stair and tumbled backward into the cabin. The goat fell with her. Or rather, the goat fell on top of her.

Drat.

Bleating indignantly, the goat scrambled to its feet, its forelegs and hindlegs on either side of Sophia's midsection. Sophia struggled to raise herself up on her elbows. Her serge skirt had flipped up, exposing her stockings.

The powerful stench of farm animal smothered her like a goat-hide blanket. Two pendulous teats dangled before her eyes, swaying gently with every motion of the ship.

"Well, well." Mr. Grayson's teasing tone carried down the staircase. The remaining sheet of paper fluttered to a rest near Sophia's elbow. The goat ingested it with alacrity. "This is a very pretty picture. What a fetching dairymaid you make, Miss Turner."

CHAPTER
FIVE

"Goats." Joss swore. "Why did it have to be goats?"

"Can't have empty space on a merchant vessel." Gray tore his gaze from the rustic tableau belowdecks. Now *there* was an image that would haunt his dreams. The girl already owed him one night's rest. "Space wasted is money lost. And we'll have fresh milk all the way to Tortola. You'll be thanking me soon enough."

"And when you purchased them, did you pause to consider just where we'd house the bloody beasts?"

"No need to be disparaging, Joss." Gray tugged the ear of the brown-and-white nanny. "These bloody beasts are from Hampshire's finest stock. They'll fetch a good price. And I thought they'd stay put in the hold."

"Evidently, you thought wrong."

"Must have chewed through their ropes last night." Gray paused, considering. "We'll put them in the gentlemen's cabin. Damned berths are too small for human habitation anyway."

"I see." Joss tapped the toe of his boot against the deck. "And I suppose you're going to look after them there? Clean up after them? Milk them?"

"Don't be absurd. Stubb and Gabriel can share the milking. As for the tending . . . That green hand of yours is fresh off the farm, isn't he? Ah, there he is." He whistled through his teeth. "Boy!"

A pale-faced youth trotted across the deck, a thick coil of rope threaded over his arm.

"What's your name, again?"

"Davy Linnet, sir."

"How old are you, Davy?"

"Fifteen, sir."

"Come from the farm, have you?"

The lad shifted his feet. He regarded the goats warily. "Yes, sir."

"Then I suppose you know how to tend a goat."

The boy hesitated, looking toward Joss.

"Well?" Gray asked. "Do you know a goat's teat from her tail, or don't you?" When the boy still paused, he added, "Speak up now, or I'll ask you the same about girls."

"I've tended goats, sir. It's just . . . I wasn't expecting to tend them at sea. I rather thought I was finished with that."

Gray laughed. "A man can't shake his past, Davy. And don't I know it. Take them down to the gentlemen's cabin, then. One to a berth." He raised his voice and spoke in the direction of the hatch. "And rescue Miss Turner from that animal under her skirts."

Davy stowed his coil of rope and grabbed a cannon rammer from the rack at the ship's rail. He prodded one goat's flank with the blunt end. "Get along, then."

"So, if the goats are in the gentlemen's cabin," Joss asked, turning toward the helm, "where do you intend to sleep? Not curled up with your flock, I imagine."

"No. There's always the la—"

"The ladies' cabin?" Joss stopped. His eyes narrowed. "Think again."

"I suppose the for—"

"And don't think about bunking in the forecastle. I'll

not have you in there carousing with the crew, undermining my authority."

Gray shrugged. "Then that leaves steerage, it would seem. I'm certain Davy can spare some room for me amongst the barrels." He shook his head. "I own the damn ship, and I'll be bedding down in steerage with the green hand."

"Don't look to me for sympathy," Joss said. "I didn't want your bloody goats. Or their milk."

"Oh, you'll drink their milk. You'll drink it, and you'll thank me for it." Gray teetered on the brink of anger, and his brother's smirk pushed him over the edge. "Damn it, I've taken on risks for this business, Joss. I've made sacrifices. All so the family . . . so *you* can reap the benefits. I wish you'd cease throwing them back in my face."

Gray knew instantly he'd gone too far. Lately, conversing with Joss was like swimming through shark-infested waters. And the steely glint in his brother's eye signaled an imminent attack.

"*You*. Want to tell *me*. About sacrifices." Joss took a step toward him, his voice rough. "I reap the benefits, do I? My family reaped the sugarcane that paid for this ship. They lived and died for it. And you may own the damn ship, but you don't own me."

Damn it to hell. Whenever Gray thought they'd finally moved past the inequity of their births, he found himself quite rudely corrected. It wasn't as though Gray could change the fact that he'd been the firstborn, legitimate son. As the younger brother, Joss would never have had the same opportunities as Gray, whether he'd been born of a mistress, a wife, or in this case, a slave.

"Joss, that's unfair. You know the fact we're of different mothers didn't matter to our father. It's never mattered to me."

"It matters to some. I've the scars to prove it."

"As do I."

Shaking his head, Joss studied the mainmast towering above them. "Go bugger one of your goats, Gray."

"*Joss.*"

Ignoring Gray entirely, Joss turned to his second mate. "Mr. Wiggins! Summon all hands. Prepare to weigh anchor."

Gray walked away. There wasn't anything more he could say. At least, there wasn't anything more he knew how to say. He'd just have to keep quiet, he supposed. Keep quiet, and look after the money. There wasn't any way he could change the past and little enough he knew to do in the present. He'd never had any talent for morality—that, he gladly left to Bel. But if he looked after the money, everything else would fall into place.

Even the goats.

"Sir, you owe me a debt."

Sophia dodged Mr. Grayson's elbow as he wheeled to face her. She had him right where she wanted him. With the mast directly behind him, and rigging to either side, he had nowhere to escape.

"Mr. Grayson." She took a deep breath and clenched one hand into a fist at her side. The other hand she raised into the space between them, brandishing a sheet of clean parchment. "You—and your goat—owe me two leaves of high-quality paper. Heavy stock, free of markings. I expect restitution."

He rubbed one palm along his jaw, then slid it back to cup his neck. "*Paper?*" One eyebrow arched as he took in her disheveled appearance. "You're all worked up over a few sheets of paper?"

Suddenly self-conscious under his gaze, Sophia smoothed a lock of hair behind her ear. After the theft of her paper and the humiliation of landing in a farmyard tangle, she had relied upon her indignation to shield her from Mr. Grayson's charms. Perhaps she had overestimated the protective quality of pique.

Although she still wore the same bedraggled garment she'd been wearing since the moment of their introduction, he'd changed his attire. His tailored navy-blue topcoat and buff trousers were the height of fashion. His unruly waves of hair had been tamed with a touch of pomade, and the light growth of beard only increased his roguish good looks. The sole defect in his appearance remained the scuffed boots, which had now suffered all manner of abuse, from saltwater to sickness.

He looked unforgivably handsome. The sheet of paper crumpled in Sophia's grip. Drat him, now he owed her three.

"Paper," he repeated.

"Yes, paper. It may be just 'a few sheets of paper' to you, but to me, it's . . . well, it's *paper*." Sophia was painfully aware of how idiotic she sounded. "I have a very limited supply, you see, and it's simply too dear to be wasted on livestock."

"I see." His brows knit together as he stared at the sheet in her hand.

"No, you don't." Sophia felt tears pricking the corners of her eyes. Of all the absurd occasions to cry. She'd told herself she could leave everything else behind—her family, her friends, her belongings—so long as she had her art. Only now she found herself missing everything else a bit more than she'd planned, and to have her creative outlet threatened by this, this *beast*—not to mention his goat . . . She sniffed fiercely. "Of course, you don't see. How could you? You're thinking it's just a bit of paper, but it isn't at all. It's . . ."

"It's *paper*."

Blinking back her tears, Sophia turned to stare resolutely at the horizon. "Yes, precisely."

"Now, sweetheart, where's that lacy little handkerchief when you need it?"

After a furtive swipe at her eyes, Sophia crossed her arms.

"Ho there, boy!" A sharp voice cut through their conversation. "Go aloft and set the fore royal."

"Aye, aye, Mr. Brackett."

A youth about Sophia's height hurried between them and paused at the base of the rigging. She recognized him as the boy who'd removed the unwelcome goat from her cabin.

"First time then, Davy?" Mr. Grayson asked.

The youth swallowed audibly. "First time at sea, sir."

Mr. Grayson clapped him on the shoulder. "Just take your time. The royal's not nearly so tricky as the topgallant—it's higher, but there's no need to go out on the yardarm. Stick to the rigging. Keep your feet on the ropes and your eyes on your hands, and you'll be fine."

The lad nodded. He mounted a part of the rigging that formed a tarred, narrow ladder and began to climb, his face grim. Sophia watched, breathless, as he quickly gained the first of the perpendicular beams that held each of the *Aphrodite*'s square-rigged sails. There, some twenty feet above the deck, he reached a sort of railing that surrounded the mast, where he paused before resuming his climb.

"That's it, Davy," Mr. Grayson called. "Look lively, then."

The boy moved on to a new set of tiered ropes and resumed climbing. "How far up does he have to go?" Sophia cupped a hand over her eyes.

"To the royal yard." Mr. Grayson met her puzzled expression. "All the way."

She tilted her head back and let her gaze follow the mast skyward. She couldn't discern whether she actually glimpsed the top, or whether the towering column simply faded into the distance. The prospect was dizzying.

"But that's so high!" She blinked up at the mast again. "And on his second day at sea?"

"Exactly. If he's to be a sailor, he must become accustomed to the feel of the rigging and the motion of the ship. The officers do him no favors if they coddle him at the outset."

Sophia looked up again. Davy had reached the next yard. He paused there for some moments, clinging to the rigging. He was only halfway to the top of the mast, yet so high she could no longer distinguish the features of his face. The mast swayed back and forth with each pitch of the ship.

"What if he falls?" she asked, swallowing hard.

Mr. Grayson shrugged. "From where he's at now? He'd be a mite banged up, but he'd live."

"From the royal yard?"

"Well, then he'd likely die. Whether he hit the deck or the sea, it wouldn't much matter. But don't worry, sweetheart. He won't fall."

Just then, Davy's boot slipped in its foothold. The boy caught himself quickly, but not before Sophia gasped and clapped a hand to her mouth. The sheet of crumpled paper fell from her grasp. It never hit the deck. Mr. Grayson snagged it easily between his first finger and thumb. He smoothed the sheet against his embroidered waistcoat before handing it back.

"Wouldn't want to waste another sheet of paper," he said with a slight smile. "But you see, sweetheart—we sailors catch on quickly. A sailor with slow reflexes is a dead sailor."

Sophia looked back up to the rigging. She and Mr.

Grayson weren't the only ones watching Davy's progress. From the mainmast, bow, helm—all eyes were fixed on the boy. The crewmen watched his ascent with great interest and whispered speculation, as though it were a horse race or a prizefight.

When Davy reached the next yard, a clamor of approval rose up from the deck. "That's the topgallant now, boy," a burly sailor called out. "Almost home!"

When the boy hesitated, clinging to the mast, Mr. Grayson cupped his hands around his mouth. "Get on with it then, Davy! The goats are getting lonesome!"

The youth began the last, most perilous section of his climb. Sophia could not bear to watch any longer. She focused on the planks beneath her feet instead, and then—when the suspense became too great to tolerate— she let her gaze slide to Mr. Grayson's hand where it hung at his side.

Sophia kept her eyes trained on that hand—the strong, sculpted fingers, the palm ridged with callus. With that hand, he'd caught her handkerchief, the paper, and Sophia herself on more than one occasion. If Davy stumbled, surely that hand would reflexively move to catch *him*. She stared at his hand because she knew—so long as it dangled loose at Mr. Grayson's side, the boy was safe.

She was safe.

Oh, no. Where had that thought come from? An absurdity, that. He was dangerous, Sophia reminded herself. He could expose her deceits and force her back to a miserable existence, and she, who could recite falsehoods effortlessly to dukes and doormen alike, lost all power to dissemble whenever he drew near. And yet, despite all this—or perhaps because of it?—standing in his broad shadow, Sophia began to feel strangely safe. Protected.

She shook herself. It would seem seasickness or Mr. Grayson's teasing, or most likely both, had rendered her completely nonsensical. Logic demanded she flee to the cabin that instant and remove herself from the influence of that potent, self-assured charm.

But she didn't.

Instead, she inched closer.

He felt it, her sudden nearness. A warm, feminine propinquity that drew his every nerve to attention. He didn't need to look.

He didn't need to, but he did.

God, she truly was exquisite.

Even his grief-blinded brother had called her beautiful, but that word wasn't quite enough. There was a rightness to her face somehow, a quality that resonated in his bones. Like the clear ring of fine crystal clinked in celebration, or the echo of a whisper in a cathedral.

Exquisite.

A raucous cheer announced young Davy's success, and Gray looked up to the royal yard to see the square sail unfurling high above, like a handkerchief.

The loud clanging of the bell cut through the crew's whoops and whistles. Mr. Brackett stood on the raised deck toward the ship's stern, his expression forbidding. "This isn't a circus, you louts! All hands back to work!"

The sailors returned to their duties, grumbling among themselves. If Gray couldn't fault the officer for chasing the sailors back to work, at least he could make up for their absence by congratulating young Davy heartily on his descent.

"Well done, boy." He clapped a hand on the youth's trembling shoulder. "You'll be in the forecastle with the sailors soon enough. Perhaps by the time we cross the Tropic."

"Thank you, sir." The boy wiped his brow with his sleeve.

"How do you feel?"

"Like I'm going to be sick, sir."

Gray laughed and stepped back quickly. "Just do me a favor, boy. Spare my boots a second baptism."

Stifling a nervous giggle, Miss Turner gave the boy a warm smile. "You're very brave, Mr. Linnet."

Gray observed the blanched, tight skin over her knuckles where she gripped the edges of her cloak. He knew she'd been sick with worry for the boy. Even now, she was struggling to mask her true emotions behind that gracious smile—because she understood, as Gray did, how important it was for Davy's confidence, that he never see her fear.

But Gray saw it. He'd felt it, as she'd inched closer to him. Even now, she stood so close that their shadows bled together on the deck.

Her vulnerability disarmed him, somehow; and that smile had him envying a fifteen-year-old green hand like he'd never envied a prince. Gray was seized by the absurd notion to climb the mast himself, just to bask in that warm approbation.

Davy lurched off toward the rail, and Gray laid a hand at the base of Miss Turner's spine, turning her in the opposite direction. That lovely smile aside, she didn't look too well herself. With a light yet firm touch, he ushered her up the steps onto the elevated deck at the helm. She made no protest.

Damn, but she fit so perfectly under his palm. Gray imagined his hand could nearly span the width of her waist. He tested the idea, fanning his fingers over the small of her back. She shivered under his touch, but did not pull away.

In fact, she seemed to shrink closer.

"It's all right, sweetheart," he murmured in her ear. "The lad came through it admirably. So did you."

She wheeled to face him, those heavy woolen skirts swirling about his legs. A strange swell of protectiveness rose in his chest. Driven by some impulse he could no better understand than he could deny, Gray lifted her hand to his lips, pressing a warm kiss to her fingers.

"Now," he murmured, "what were we discussing?" For the life of him, he couldn't hold a thought in his head.

"Paper. You . . . you still owe me two sheets of paper."

"You still owe me six pounds, eight shillings," he said softly. "Not to mention a new pair of boots. So I think you're rather ahead."

Indeed, Gray was losing ground fast. Those lovely eyes, her whisper-soft skin, the sweet scent that only grew more potent as the warmth between them built . . . If they stood like this much longer, he wouldn't give tuppence for anything but gathering her in his arms, covering her lips with his, and ravaging that pert blossom of a mouth.

No, no. What was he thinking? One didn't ravage an English rose of a governess. This was a girl who'd expect to be kissed sweetly. Chastely. Tenderly.

Hell. The word "chaste" wasn't even in his vocabulary. And Gray didn't do anything tenderly.

"Sweet, I hate to break it to you. But no matter how many sheets of paper you fill with letters home—there's no mail coach stopping by."

"No, it's not for letters. You don't understand."

"So explain it to me."

"I . . ." She looked up at him again, those big eyes searching his. There was a story behind that desperate gaze. One that wouldn't fit on two sheets of paper, nor even two hundred, he supposed.

He squeezed her hand. *Go on,* some fool part of him urged. *Tell me everything.*

She never had a chance.

"I beg your pardon, Miss Turner." Joss stood at Gray's shoulder, looking as though someone had mixed bilge-water into his tea. "I need a word with my brother, if I may."

"Yes, of course, Captain. Mr. Grayson was just . . . explaining the workings of the ship." She attempted to tug her hand from Gray's grasp, shooting him a pained look when he refused to relinquish his prize.

Gray said smoothly, "Actually, we were discussing debts. Miss Turner still owes me her fare, and I—"

"And I told you, you'll have it today." Beneath that abomination of a skirt wrapped about his leg, she planted her heel atop his booted toe and transferred all her weight onto it. Firmly. Once again, Gray regretted trading his old, sturdy boots for these foppish monstrosities. Her little pointed heel bit straight through the thin leather.

With a tight grimace, Gray released her hand. He'd been about to say, *and I have her handkerchief to return.* But just for that, he wouldn't.

"Good afternoon, then." A sweet smile graced her face as she stomped down on his foot again, harder. Then she turned and flounced away.

He made an amused face at Joss. "I think she likes me."

"In my cabin, Gray."

Gray gritted his teeth and followed Joss down the hatch. Whether he liked being Gray's half brother or not, Joss was damn lucky right now that he was. Gray wouldn't have suffered that supercilious command for any bond weaker than blood.

"You gave me your word, Gray."

"Did I? And what word was that?"

Joss tossed his hat on the wood-framed bed and stripped off his greatcoat with agitated movements. "You know damn well what I mean. You said you wouldn't pursue Miss Turner. Now you're kissing her hand and making a spectacle in front of the whole ship. Bailey's already taking bets from the sailors as to how many days it'll take you to bed her."

"Really?" Gray rubbed the back of his neck. "I hope he's giving even odds on three. Two, if you'll send young Davy up the mast again. That got her quite excited."

Joss glared at him. "Need I remind you that this was *your* idea? You wanted a respectable merchant vessel. I'm trying to command it as such, but that'll be a bit difficult if you intend to stage a bawdy-house revue on deck every forenoon."

Gray smiled as Joss slung himself into the captain's chair. "Be careful, Joss. I do believe you nearly made a joke. People might get the idea you have a sense of humor."

"I don't see anything humorous about this. This isn't a pleasure cruise around the Mediterranean."

"You think I don't know that?" Gray paced toward the windows spanning the ship's stern. "Believe me, I know perfectly well what's at stake here. They're my stakes, damn it."

Joss made a dismissive snort. "You don't need to remind me whose money it is."

"Yes, it's my money and my ship, but I've entrusted them both to you."

"No you haven't. You're ordering my crew around, questioning my decisions . . ."

"So that's what this is about. The storm yesterday?"

"The storm, the goats, Bains, the girl. You've countermanded me at every turn, and we're only a day out from land. I'm telling you, if you want a captain who thinks only of profit, with no regard for the comfort and safety of people aboard—"

No regard for people? Oh, now Gray was getting angry. This was all about his regard for people—two rather important people, one of whom stood glaring at him with murder in his eyes. The other being the principal reason for his presence on this ship. Fetching his baby sister for her London debut was something he'd been waiting to do for years. That task, Gray wouldn't delegate.

"I want a captain who doesn't furl the sails and drop anchor at the sight of a few clouds," he said. "And yes, damn it, I need a captain with the fortitude to put up with a few goats and governesses, if that's what it takes to turn a profit." He rounded the table to stand toe-to-toe with his brother. "What's happened to you? We used to churn up these seas like a pair of sharks. We took everything, feared nothing."

"We were young. And stupid."

"Maybe so, but we were great. We sailed the fastest ship on the Atlantic. The *Aphrodite* captured more prize than any other privateer in service of the Crown, and we didn't do it by playing safe." Gray put a hand on Joss's shoulder and lowered his voice. "The war's over. And I don't need to tell you how much of that money's sunk into this venture. We have to conquer honest trade now. We have to chase success with everything we've got."

"*We?* What's all this talk of 'we'? When did that word enter your vocabulary?" Joss shrugged off his hand.

"When did you become such an insufferable ass? It's always been 'we.' *We* were supposed to be full partners, until *you* changed your mind."

"Oh, are we going to tally broken promises now? Be my guest, but I'm warning you . . . I don't think that's an argument you want to start."

Gray took a slow breath, forcing himself to remain calm. "What's past is past. I've done what I can on my own, but now *we* have to make this work. We owe it to Bel. And to Jacob."

"I see. It's your money, but it's our obligation." Joss shrugged off Gray's hand. "Don't presume to tell me what I owe my own son. I'll be damned if I'll take lessons on family duty from you."

Gray stared at his brother. Their father's ears aside, he scarcely recognized Joss anymore. When he wasn't cutting the pitiful figure of a mourning widower, he was being a downright prick. Why couldn't he see this was all for the good of the family? That Gray had worked all these years, assumed all these risks—for him and Bel, and now Jacob?

"Miss Turner may be a sweet-looking lass," Joss said, "but you've got to look the other direction. Aside from my responsibility as captain to guard her personal safety, I can't afford the melodrama that accompanies your *affaires*, Gray. You know full well what it'll do to the crew if they know you're bedding her under their noses. And what happens when you tire of her? Need I remind you of the French captain's widow? That incessant wailing did wonders for shipboard morale."

"Perhaps I won't tire of her," Gray protested, just to be contrary. Because, apparently, that was how brothers behaved.

"Perhaps a dolphin will fly out of your arse. And here's an argument even you can't refute. Grayson Shipping doesn't need a reputation for delivering damaged goods. You want me to hand George Waltham an impregnated governess?"

"I wouldn't get her with child. Give me that much credit, at least."

"I give you credit for nothing. Let's try this one last time, shall we? You made me this ship's captain. If I'm the captain, what I say goes. And I say you don't touch her. If you can't abide by my orders, take command of the ship yourself and let me go home."

"Go home and do what? Squander your fortune and talent on dirt farming?"

"Go home and take care of my own family. Go home and do what I damn well please, for once."

Cursing, Gray leaned against the wall. He knew Joss would make good on that threat, too. It hadn't been easy, coaxing his brother out of mourning. Gray had resorted to outright bullying just to convince him to take command of the *Aphrodite,* threatening to cut off his income unless he reported to London as agreed. But he needed Joss, if this shipping concern was to stay afloat. He'd worked too hard, sacrificed too much to see it fail.

And if Joss didn't become a willing partner, it all would have been in vain.

"Stay away from the girl, Gray."

Gray sighed. "We're on the same ship. I can't help but be near her. I'll not promise to refrain from touching her either, because the girl seems to lose her footing whenever I'm around. But I give you my word I'll not kiss her again. Satisfied?"

Joss shook his head. "Give me your word you won't bed her."

"What a legend you're making me! Insinuating I could bed her without even kissing her first." Gray worried the edge of his thumbnail as he considered. "That might prove an amusing challenge, now that you suggest it."

Joss shot him an incredulous look.

"With some other lady, on some other ship." Gray raised his hands in a defensive gesture. "I'll not bed her. You have my word. And don't think that's not a great sacrifice, because it is. I'd have her in two, three days at the most, I tell you."

"Once again—not amusing."

"For God's sake, Joss, it's a joke. What do you want, an apology? I'm sorry for kissing Miss Turner's hand, all right?"

Joss shook his head and flipped open the logbook. "No, you're not."

"Yes, I am." The odd thing of it was, Gray was telling the truth. He knew he was being an ass, but the joking was easier than honesty. For all his teasing, he hadn't kissed her hand with the intent to seduce, or to judge if she tasted as sweet as he'd dreamed. He'd kissed her fingers for one reason only. Because they were trembling, and he'd wanted them to stop. It was wholly unlike him, that kiss. It was not a gesture he thought it wise to repeat. The girl did something strange to him.

Gray tried again. "I'm sorry for kissing Miss Turner's hand." He crossed to stand opposite his brother's chair. "I'm sorry for arguing about the storm. I'm sorry for sacking Bains. Hell, I'll even say I'm sorry for the goats. I'm sorry you had the great misfortune to be sired by my degenerate father, and I'm sorry you're stuck with an equally degenerate half brother."

Joss looked up sharply.

Gray said, "I'm sorry Mara died."

Joss looked back down.

Gray sat down across from him. "But I'm not sorry I made you the captain of this ship, Joss. *Joss.*" He waited until his brother met his gaze. "You're the only one I can trust. I need you to command this ship, and I'll not jeopardize that in any way. I won't countermand you again. I'll stay out of any disputes." He fanned his fingers out over the blotter and recalled the slender width of Miss Turner's waist. Then he closed his hand into a fist. "I said I wouldn't pursue Miss Turner. I won't."

Joss snorted.

"Damn it, I wish one of these days you'd learn to trust me."

His brother looked him in the eye. "Not half as much as I wish you'd give me a reason to."

CHAPTER
SIX

Sophia was hungry. Suddenly, ravenously hungry.

A near brush with disaster could do that to a woman.

She followed the stairs down into the belly of the ship. Hadn't Stubb mentioned the galley was down here somewhere? She couldn't remember where.

Pausing at the bottom of the stairs, she propped one hand on the ladder to steady herself. Her heart throbbed in her chest. The air was too thick. Her breaths were shallow, and she was faint with hunger.

She'd come so close to confessing everything.

If only he weren't so infuriating and so solicitous, all at once. One or the other, she knew how to resist, but insolence and charm made a potent brew indeed. The way he'd soothed her concern with rough fingers, even as his words teased. The way he'd guided her with a light touch at the small of her back, kissed her fingers so tenderly . . . they could have been in an elegant ballroom, preparing to dance a quadrille.

By all evidence—his fine attire, cultured accent, proud bearing, the rare flash of politesse—Mr. Grayson was a man who could move in the highest echelons of English society, but delighted in doing just the reverse. For a moment, she'd thought: If she told him everything, perhaps he would understand.

Perhaps he was a runaway, too.

Foolish, foolish girl. He understood profit. He understood six pounds, eight shillings. Mr. Grayson was no different from any fortune-hungry suitor of the *ton*. Or for that matter, from even her own family. He looked at her and saw gold, tied up with a pretty bow. And she would give him his blasted gold and have done with him—just as soon as she had something to eat.

Instead of turning left into the ladies' cabin, Sophia went right. She emerged into a cabin quite similar to her own in appearance, but distinguished by the strong smell of goat. Holding her sleeve to her nose, she passed through the common area quickly and stepped through a door on the opposite side.

"Shut the bloody door, then!" The voice thundered at her through a cloud of steam.

Sophia complied hastily.

A tall, lean black man stood over a pot of boiling water, carving chunks from a peeled potato with a large knife. "Not time for mess now, is it?" he said without looking up. "That's six bells just sounded, and I ain't so old as I can't hear, nor so stupid as I can't count. So off with you then, you greedy bastard, and come back in an hour."

Sophia would have obeyed this request, but she was momentarily shocked immobile. No one, in all her twenty years of genteel privilege, had ever addressed her in such a coarse manner. Much less a Negro cook. She couldn't quite name the sensation that overtook her. It wasn't anger, or shame. It was more a sense of complete disorientation. As if God, in a fit of boredom, had thought it might be amusing to flip the globe on its ear.

The cook flung the knife down and wiped his hands on an apron. "I told you, you can bugger off. You're not getting nothing until—" He turned, saw Sophia, and froze.

They stood there, staring at each other, not speaking, until the pot boiled over.

"Bloody hell." The cook grabbed an iron and wrenched

open the stove, poking vigorously at the fire. Sparks shot out to mingle with the steam.

"I beg your pardon," Sophia said. "I only hoped to ask for a bit of bread. Perhaps . . ." The cook swore again as he banged the stove shut, and she jumped. "Perhaps a drop of tea."

"No, it's I who must beg your pardon, miss." He wiped his hands on his apron again, leaving dark smudges of soot. "Have a seat, Miss . . . ?"

"Miss Turner."

"Have a seat then, Miss Turner." He pulled a three-legged stool up to a square, butcher-block table and patted it with his hand. "I'm Gabriel."

Sophia sat down quickly. It was a comfortable stool, and a comfortable space. A square little room, lined with cabinets and the stove to one side. Overhead, the ceiling hovered a foot or so above deck level, letting fresh air and sunlight in from all four sides. The aromas of cooking food had her stomach grumbling.

"I'll fetch your bread and tea," the man said. Now that he'd ceased swearing, the exotic cadence of his voice intrigued her. Unlike the sharp commands the seamen volleyed from rigging to deck, Gabriel's speech was smooth and resonant. "I'm not accustomed to having passengers aboard." He looked her over, and a white, toothy smile split his face. "For a moment there, I thought you were an angel, come to take me up to Heaven."

She winced. "No, I'm not an angel." She knew he meant to be conciliatory, but he may as well have called her a beetle, for all the pleasure that appellation conveyed. "I'm a governess."

His angel, Toby had always called her. *His innocent dove.* He would wax nearly poetic about how perfect she was, how beautiful and pure.

He had no idea.

"Forgive me," he'd whisper after each kiss, swallowing hard between ragged breaths. "You're so lovely, I can't help myself. But don't be frightened, my angel. I shan't press you further. I'm so sorry."

But Sophia hadn't been sorry, or frightened in the least. She recited the demure deferrals that come as naturally as embroidery to any young lady of accomplishment, but she left these encounters feeling frustrated and curious. She longed to be pressed further. Pressed further, harder, and in unspeakably intimate places.

A lifetime of playing Toby's perfect angel had loomed before her like a living hell. She had no use for purity; Sophia wanted passion. So she'd run away. She'd fled the dream wedding—and dream groom—of every young lady in England, on the slim hope of finding it.

But at the moment, she would settle for some tea, and a morsel of bread.

"I apologize for cursin' at you like that." He put a kettle on the stove. "I thought you were one of the sailors, come looking for extra food. Can't let 'em have a morsel more than their allotment, the greedy beggars. You give them one biscuit extra, and they'll expect the same every day until we make port." He set a hunk of bread before her. "That's the last of the bread, miss. Enjoy it."

Sophia bit into it gratefully. Stale bread had never tasted so delicious. "I'd gladly forgive you anything for a cup of tea. But what if," she asked, swallowing, "what if I had been Captain Grayson? Or Mr. Grayson?"

Gabriel made a dismissive wave of his hand. "I been chasing Gray and Joss out of one kitchen or another since they was boys. They know better than to run afoul of old Gabriel." He reached for a canister of tea and paused. "But it might have been that Mr. Brackett. And something tells me he'd not take kindly to being told to bugger off." He shrugged, scooping tea into a tin pot.

"Lots of changes for an old man like me. Not used to men of Brackett's type aboard this vessel. Nor beautiful young misses like yourself."

"But you can't be old," Sophia insisted. Gabriel laughed, and she peered through the steam at his face. Smooth, unwrinkled skin with the sheen of polished mahogany stretched over high cheekbones and a flat nose. His laughter revealed a full set of straight, white teeth. Only the faintest dusting of white in his close-cropped hair hinted at advancing age.

The kettle whistled.

"And what do you mean, you're not accustomed to passengers?" Sophia propped her elbow on the table and rested her chin in her hand, entranced by the steaming trickle of water from kettle to teapot. "Are all the berths typically occupied by goats, then?"

Gabriel chuckled. "Now don't disparage the goats, Miss Turner. They'll give you milk for your tea, and a taste of chowder on Sundays." He set a tin mug on the table before her and ladled a generous amount of treacle into it. "But these cabins are all new, miss. Used to be just steerage all through, from galley to forecastle. The *Aphrodite* is a whole new ship inside. It's like her maiden voyage.

"We needed all that space during the war," he continued, pouring tea into her cup. "For extra crewmen and guns. Powder and cannonballs, too. And the ship had to leave port half-empty at least, so we'd have room for prize cargo and prisoners."

Sophia blinked at him, ignoring the delicious-smelling tea before her. "Cannonballs? Prisoners? Was the *Aphrodite* a warship, then?"

"No, miss." He smiled and went back to his pot of potatoes on the stove. "*This* crew, falling in with the British Navy? No, the *Aphrodite* was a privateer vessel. Brought in three-and-sixty prizes—French ships, American ships. And she brought Gray more money in five years at sea than the old Mr. Grayson lost in thirty years of farming sugarcane."

Sophia's hand plunked down on the table. "But privateers . . . aren't they nearly the same as pirates?"

"No, miss. There's a world of difference between the life of a privateer and a pirate."

"Less violent?"

Gabriel shook his head. "About the same, there."

"More honorable."

"Not necessarily. That would depend on the particular privateer and the particular pirate."

"Then how is it different?"

"Why, privateering's legal, of course. Sanctioned by the Crown. Can't be hanged for a privateer."

"I see."

" 'Course, the war's over now." Gabriel sprinkled the dish with pepper before removing the pot from the stove. "No more privateering to be had. So we've got to turn respectable, Gray says. It was either that, or turn pirate." Gabriel winked at her. "And I'm rather attached to my neck."

Sophia sipped her tea, amazed. She was the lone female passenger—the lone passenger, really—aboard a ship crewed entirely by men who might as well be pirates, except that they couldn't be hanged. And Mr. Grayson, with his arrogant swagger and mercantile lust, was their erstwhile, unhangable pirate king.

Mercy.

She drained the rest of her tea in one long draught, capped with an audible swallow. "Thank you for the refreshment," she said, rising to her feet. Blood rushed from her head, leaving her dizzy. The steam was suddenly too thick to breathe. "I . . . I believe I'll go take some fresh air."

As she hurried on deck, her mind was awhirl. All that time that Mr. Grayson had been touching her, teasing her . . . she'd been consorting with a *pirate*. If he had the slightest inkling that she carried hundreds of pounds beneath her stays, he'd surely stop at nothing to get it. And yet, she could not bid caution to overtake the gothic thrill. For Heaven's sake, a *pirate*.

She could be in danger, she admonished herself.

She could be plundered.

The possibility really ought to have frightened her more than it did.

Perhaps she could not escape the man, but she had to tamp down this response he incited in her. There was only one thing for it. She would go to her cabin and sketch. Something simple, innocent. Rosebuds, apples, blocks of wood. Anything but him.

Then something fell to the deck with a loud thud, startling Sophia to a halt. It was a knotted length of rope, only a few feet long, and it had landed almost at her feet. A rather small object to have made such a noise. It must have fallen from high above.

Shading her eyes with her hand, Sophia craned her neck and looked upward. Davy Linnet descended the rigging hand over hand, like a monkey. For all his nervousness earlier, he looked born to the ropes now. He landed at her feet in a graceful swoop. "Beg yer pardon, miss." He picked up the offending coil and, flashing a shy smile, made an ungainly bow.

Sophia graced him with her best debutante's smile, gratified by the manner in which his pale cheeks colored when she did. At least someone on this ship knew how to treat a lady. "Mr. Linnet, I wonder if I might trouble you for a favor."

The youth swallowed, his expression suddenly earnest. "Anything, miss. Anything."

CHAPTER
SEVEN

Over the next few days, Gray found himself partnered in an absurd sort of quadrille. Miss Turner was always in his sights, but rarely within reach. And when their paths collided occasionally, as much by accident as by design, she quickly twirled away from him, to be lost in the dance once again.

Just as well.

He learned the pattern of her activities. She came abovedecks shortly after breakfast, presumably to take some fresh air. Then she would disappear again, usually until the dogwatches in late afternoon. A sailor's favorite time of day, the dogwatch—when work slowed and the sun hung low in the sky and dinner loomed hopefully on the horizon. It was the time of day when those who had pipes would play them, and those who had cards would gather 'round, and men with no talent for music or gambling might light a pipe instead. Only natural, then, that Miss Turner would be drawn to the deck at that hour, lured by the air of camaraderie and the sounds of laughter or song.

He couldn't imagine how she passed her time between forenoon and dusk. What did ladies do with themselves on a transoceanic voyage? Sewing? Reading? Gray himself grew itchy with idleness. He found little to do, save charting the latitude religiously and circling the deck, pausing to chat with the sailors now and then. Every once in a while, a sail might appear on the horizon. And, according to his right of whimsy as captain, Joss might or might not decide to hail the ship and let the carved goddess adorning the *Aphrodite*'s prow curtsy to a kindred figurehead.

Odd, to watch the ships approach willingly now, rather than flee.

"Say!"

The shout drew Gray's attention. A knot of sailors surrounded young Davy, who appeared as riled up as a fifteen-year-old green hand could get.

Davy stood nose-to-chest with O'Shea, jabbing a finger into the Irishman's chest. "Give it back then, you big, ugly—"

"Watch yer mouth there, boy! Mind who you're talking to." O'Shea gave him a half-strength push that sent Davy sprawling into Quinn, one of the new men. Quinn shouted in protest and threw a swift elbow, knocking Davy to the deck.

Gray strode over to join the group. A bit of good-natured hazing never hurt a new boy. He had to learn his place among the crew. But Gray had never countenanced cruelty on his ship. And this was, he reminded himself, still *his* ship. Wordlessly, he extended a hand to Davy and hauled him to his feet. The crewmen nudged one another, silencing the laughter.

"What's the problem, O'Shea?" Gray knew better than to solicit Davy's version of the conflict first. Shipboard hierarchy was sacred.

The Irishman shrugged. "Boy's got himself all worked up over a bit of paper."

"Paper?" Gray laid a hand on Davy's sleeve.

Davy struggled in Gray's grip. "It's *my* paper, you great lout."

"And I said I'll give it back to ye, now didn't I, ye wee

bugger?" O'Shea clenched his fists and turned to Gray. "Can I hit 'im, Gray? Let me hit 'im. He insulted me mum, the little piece of sh—"

The bell clanged at the helm. All wheeled to view Mr. Brackett, wearing his usual black overcoat and equally dark expression. "Back to your stations, all of you!" He stomped to the skylight above the galley and called down, "Cook! No grog tonight for larboard watch!"

"Aye, aye, Mr. Brackett." Gabriel's voice wafted up on a cloud of steam.

The men grumbled in chorus, and Davy took a few dull knocks to the kidneys. "Ow!"

"Better let me have the paper, O'Shea," Gray said. "I'll have a talk with the boy here about minding his place."

O'Shea handed him a crumpled sheet of parchment before heading back toward the ship's bow.

Gray turned to the boy. He cleared his throat, summoning the serious tone he reserved for reprimands and funerals and other rare occasions. "Now, Davy. It's bad form, and generally a bad idea, to run afoul of O'Shea. Or any of the crewmen, for that matter. You're together on this ship for the next month, you realize. Life at sea isn't all grog and sunshine. Your mates hold your life in their hands, and you don't want to give them any reason to lose their grip."

"Yes, sir," came the boy's sullen reply. "It's just . . ." He gestured toward the crumpled paper in Gray's hand. "Have a look at it, sir."

Gray smiled. "What is it, then? A love letter from your girl back on the farm?" He released Davy's sleeve and smoothed the paper against his chest before glancing down at it.

He nearly dropped the page.

It was a charcoal sketch of young Davy Linnet. And it was a revelation.

"Miss Turner done it," Davy said simply.

She had, indeed. The boy's likeness was rendered in deft, light strokes, and in stunningly faithful detail. It wasn't anything like the schoolgirl sketches most young ladies produced—generic, blocky human figures distinguishable only by the shade of the subject's hair, or the line of his nose. Every inch of this sketch was inimitably *Davy*. The restless energy in his stance and rumpled tufts of dark hair. The awkward ears and too-large hands he'd eventually grow into. The spark of youthful optimism in his eye, hedged by the self-conscious, lopsided quirk of his lips, a shadow of future irony. In a single sketch, the artist—for this was most certainly the work of an artist—had captured the boy Davy was and the man he would one day become. It wasn't merely a likeness; it was a *portrait*.

It made Gray feel wistful for his boyhood. It made him feel strangely humbled and alone. It made him want to garrote the bloody goat that had eaten Miss Turner's two sheets of paper and turn the ship around just to buy her more.

And most of all, it made Gray greatly curious—and a little bit afraid—to know what Miss Turner saw when she looked at *him*.

"Thought I'd save it for my mum," Davy said, "so she'll not forget what I look like. Miss Turner only worked on it while I was off-watch, Mr. Grayson. Said I was doing her a favor, giving her a subject to practice on." The boy scrubbed at his face with his sleeve and craned his neck to look over Gray's shoulder. "Never had a portrait of myself before. Is it like me enough?"

"Very like," Gray said quietly. Then he cleared his throat and forced a grin. "You're a handsome devil, Mr. Linnet. Give it a few years, and you'll be breaking the ladies' hearts on two continents."

"Oh, no," Quinn called from the crow's nest. "Lad's up to his ears in love with Miss Turner. Aren't ye, boy? She's all he can talk about, Gray. Don't go tempting him with talk of other girls. There'll be no other lady for him—not this voyage, anyway."

Davy colored and stammered. "I . . . It's not . . ."

Gray laughed and clapped a hand on his shoulder. "I can't fault your choice, Davy. She's a beautiful woman, and talented at that."

Davy shifted his weight awkwardly. "Well, and of course she won't look at me. I do know that, sir. I just . . ."

"You're just a normal lad of fifteen. I was one once myself, you realize. And I never caught the eye of a lady half so fine as Miss Turner." He gave the sketch one more lingering gaze before returning it to Davy.

"And she must think a great deal of you, Davy," he said, chuckling. "She's given you a whole sheet of paper."

As Sophia emerged from the hatch, she immediately recognized Mr. Grayson's roguish laughter, coming from somewhere to her right.

She turned left.

An overnight rain had scrubbed the inverted basin of sky to a bright, cloudless blue. The sun shone down with unmitigated audacity, and the crest of each wave gleamed. Their collective brilliance was almost painful to behold; like a sea of diamonds.

This should have been her wedding day.

Sophia wondered if the sun was shining on a small, picturesque chapel in Kent. What had happened, she wondered, to the hundreds of hothouse flowers especially cultivated for the occasion? She thought of the wedding breakfast, so carefully planned to the last gilt demitasse spoon. Was the pastel pyramid of almond- and rose-flavored ices waiting stoically for her return, a fashionably Egyptian monument to her betrayal?

Even if they'd managed to keep her disappearance concealed until now . . . when she failed to appear for her own wedding, the secret would be out. Rumors of her elopement with the mysterious Gervais would leap from lady to lady like fleas in a church pew. She'd be the talk of the *ton*—although not quite the way her social-climbing parents would have hoped.

What an elaborate joke she'd played on them all. What a laugh.

So why did she feel like crying?

Standing on tiptoe and clutching the wooden pins, she leaned over the ship's side, staring hard into endless waves and swirling trails of foam. A single tear fell from the corner of her eye, dropping into the seawater with all the significance of a grain of sand strewn in a desert.

A flash beneath the waves caught her gaze. A smooth dart rose up from the blue-green depths, then sank beneath the surface again. Sophia waited, holding her breath. It surfaced once more, a bolt of quicksilver slicing through the waves, pacing the *Aphrodite*'s brisk progress.

A sailor nearby called to another, and the two men joined her at the rail, marking the elegant creature's course.

"What is it?" Sophia wondered aloud, her eyes never leaving the water.

"It's just a dolphin-fish, miss," one of the crewmen answered.

The creature leapt from the water, its sleek, shimmering form sailing through the air before disappearing once more beneath the waves. It leapt again, and then again, carving playful, exuberant arcs through the spray, trailing silver-dipped rainbows in its wake.

The fish's course veered, bringing it even closer to the

ship's hull. Sophia admired the creature's flat snout and the sharp blade of its fin, running the full length of its spine. But most marvelous of all were the bold, iridescent shades decorating its scales.

"It's beautiful," she said.

A harpoon shot out from the sailor's hand, skewering the fish with a sick squelch.

"It's dinner," the crewman said cheerfully. The two men dropped a net over the side and hauled their thrashing catch aboard.

Gagging, Sophia pressed a hand to her mouth and turned away.

"Now don't be squeamish, miss," the crewman said. "You'll miss the colors."

The colors? Sophia peeked over her shoulder. The men had the fish completely aboard now, and its flat body thumped uselessly on the planked deck.

"See, miss? The colors are starting."

As the sailor spoke, the bold hues of the fish's scales began to shimmer and change. Sophia stepped toward it, fascinated. Its light-blue belly deepened to the truest cobalt. A stripe of fresh green turned electric with gold. Sophia had never seen colors so vivid—not in nature, not in paintings. Not even in her dreams. The fish was a living rainbow.

A dying rainbow, rather. Its arcing body eventually went pale and limp, turning as colorless as the decking. Having withdrawn their harpoon, the crewmen returned to the rail to look for more. And there the fish lay, gutted and lifeless.

Sophia had never felt so disillusioned. The stark reality of life and death had been splashed in her face like so much seawater. She realized, with sudden clarity, that all her life she'd been raised to view the world as a collection of objects assembled for her amusement, her admiration, her consumption. But now she understood—nothing existed for beauty alone. Even a beautiful fish still died, was still food.

She'd left home seeking to experience real life, true passion, grand adventure. Well, this was real life, and it wasn't pretty. And every moment she stood here, staring blankly at the deck and crying pointless tears, was a moment of real life wasted.

"Here's another," one of the sailors called, flinging his harpoon back into the sea. A second later, he crowed with triumph. "Got 'im in one."

Sophia rushed back to the rail and peered over the edge at the thrashing fish churning the waves to froth. A giddy thrill warmed her toes.

The crewman began to pull in the rope, hand over hand.

"May I help bring it in?" she asked.

"What?" the sailor grunted, not losing his pace.

"May I?" She jerked her chin at the struggling fish and laid one hand on the rope, above his. She had reeled in a fish before—granted, it was a smallish trout, plucked from a stream in the English midlands. But still, the principle appeared the same.

He stared at her a moment, then shrugged. "Don't see why not."

Sophia grasped the rope with both hands, and he showed her how to brace one foot on the bulwark and pull hand over hand, letting the rope fall in a neat coil at their feet.

"Ready to try it yerself?" he asked.

She nodded, and he released the rope.

"Ah!" Sophia gave a sharp cry as several yards of cable slid straight through her grip. The dolphin-fish was swifter than she'd expected, and stronger, too. Now she'd made matters worse by giving it more slack, more room to struggle.

"Shall I help you, miss?" the sailor asked.

"No, thank you. I'll do." Bracing her foot and tightening her grip, Sophia clenched her teeth and began to pull, arm over arm. For every arm-length of rope she pulled in, it seemed the dolphin-fish took three. What with all this thrashing, the fish would probably resemble mincemeat by the time she hauled it aboard.

But she *would* haul it aboard, if it was the last thing she did. And she would rejoice to see even minced fish on her plate tonight, instead of salt pork.

After a minute, the task seemed to grow easier, presumably because the fish grew weaker. But just when she thought she had it netted, the dolphin-fish made one last desperate surge for freedom, dragging her a few steps toward the bow. Her boot caught in the coiled rope, and she very nearly tripped. She managed to pull up, however, and regain control. Her efforts were rewarded with a rousing chorus of whistles and cheers.

"That's the way, miss!"

"You've got 'im now!"

Slowly pivoting her head from one side to the other, Sophia realized she'd amassed quite an audience. Evidently her battle with the fish made for high entertainment. Ah, well. Let the men laugh. She was having fun, too.

She smiled as she resumed pulling in the catch.

In fact, she was having the time of her life.

Jesus Christ. The chit was going to get herself killed.

From the stern, Gray looked on in disbelief as Miss Turner played tug-o-war with a fish and the crew watched with glee. What the hell were they thinking?

"What the hell are they thinking?" Joss came to Gray's side. "Mr. Wiggins," he ordered, "tell the men—"

"Don't bother," Gray called out, vaulting over the rail that separated helm and quarterdeck. "I'll put a stop to it myself."

Long strides carried him across the decking, while Gray tried to hold panic at bay. Devil take it, when had the *Aphrodite* become so damned long? Up at the bow, Miss Turner lost her footing, tripping over the coiled rope, and Gray very nearly lost his breakfast.

"Bloody idiots," he muttered, as a prelude to the worse invectives running through his mind. Only a fool let a fish thrash at the end of a rope like that, churning up the froth, leaving a wake of blood and innards on the waves. It was a cretinous way to catch a fish, and a surefire method of attracting a—

"Shark!"

And from there on, it all went so fast. But so slowly, at the same time.

Had the girl any common sense, she would have dropped the line at once. But she had no sense. She made no sense. She was a pale English rose of a governess, adrift in a watery wilderness, on her way to a grueling post on a godforsaken island, when any fool could have told her—a woman so lovely need never work for her keep.

Had the men around her any sense, they would have cut the rope immediately. But they were idiots, bloody shite-for-brains idiots, too entranced by the pretty girl in peril to reach for their knives.

Had Gray his own knife, he would have drawn it. But he wasn't wearing his knife, because he wasn't the captain on this ship, was he? Nor an officer, nor even part of the crew. He was just a stupid, overdressed passenger who hadn't strapped on a goddamned knife that morning because it might ruin the lines of his goddamned brand-new coat.

No, he didn't have his knife. But he had his legs, powering him the remaining yards to the bow. He had his arms, lashing around Miss Turner just as the shark's jaws snatched the dolphin-fish carcass and dragged it under the waves. And he had his voice, that authoritative tone of command. The voice that carried over storms, and gunfire, and howls of pain.

"Let go of the line." He grabbed her forearms and shook them. Jesus, she'd been holding on to the thing for so long, her instinct was to tighten her fingers further. Precisely the wrong thing to do. As the shark lunged away, the cable streamed through her two-fisted grip, no doubt taking the skin of her palms along with it.

"Let it go!" he ordered. "Now!"

She did. Her shaking fingers were white; her palms were abraded and raw.

And damn it to hell, he stared at those ruined hands an instant too long.

By the time Gray attempted to pull her back from the rail, the shark had spooled out several more yards of rope. The rope that lay coiled and tangled about her foot, that was.

"Cut the bloody line!" he commanded, tightening his arms around her slender frame and jamming his boot down on top of hers.

The rope cinched like a noose about their ankles, yanking their feet out from under them. She screamed as together they fell to the deck, then skidded toward the rail, tugged by their intertwined legs. In a matter of seconds, they would either be pulled overboard entirely, or have their legs torn off. Neither alternative sounded particularly pleasant. Gray shoved his free boot against the bulwark, bracing himself for what he knew would be a futile, and brief, wrestling match with a shark. He gritted his teeth. "Someone. Cut. The. Damn. Line."

Thwack.

Someone did.

Gray lifted his head to spy Levi's hand on an ax handle, and the blade several inches deep in the rail. "Thank you," he huffed, letting his head fall back against the deck.

And now here he lay on the forecastle, holding Miss Turner as if they were two spoons in a drawer. The crown of her head tucked neatly under his chin, and her round little bottom nestled between his thighs. She was damp with sweat, and panting for breath. Gray was struck by the ridiculous notion that he'd had a dream the other night, very much like this. Except they'd been wearing fewer clothes. And there hadn't been a half-dozen gawking seamen standing about.

And what did she say, his dream girl? This exquisite, rose-scented siren who would smile as she pulled him to his death?

"Well," she said. "That was exciting."

CHAPTER
EIGHT

"That"—Mr. Grayson slammed the door of the captain's cabin—"was the most breathtaking display of stupidity I have ever witnessed in my life."

Sophia cringed in her chair as he plunked a basin of water on the table. Liquid sloshed over the side, trickling toward the floor. With jerky motions, he removed a flask from his breast pocket, unscrewed the top, and added a splash of brandy. Then he threw back a healthy swallow, himself.

She'd never seen him so agitated. He took everything as a joke, laughed off confrontation, deflected insult with a roguish smile.

"You're angry," she said.

"Damn right, I'm angry. I'd like to string every one of those bloody idiots up to the yardarm and shout them deaf."

"So why are you here, shouting at me?"

He yanked open a drawer and removed a box. When he flung it on the table and flipped the latch, the box proved to be a medicine kit, crowded with brown glass vials and plasters and rolls of gauze.

"Because . . ." With a sullen sigh, he dropped into the other chair. "Shouting the crew deaf is the captain's privilege. And I'm not the captain. So I'm here instead, playing nursemaid. Give me your hands."

She lifted her clenched hands to the table and slowly

uncurled her fingers. Across each palm was painted a wide, angry swath of red.

Swearing under his breath, he gingerly lifted one of her hands and laid it across his own. His tanned, weathered fingers dwarfed hers.

With his free hand, he dipped a piece of gauze into the basin. "This will hurt."

"It already hurts."

"It will hurt more."

Sophia winced as he sponged the wound. Yes, it did hurt more. It hurt worse when she looked at it, so instead she looked at him. She hadn't come this near to him in days, not since they watched Davy Linnet climb the mast. Now she drank in every detail of his rugged, handsome face: the strong jaw sporting several days' growth of beard, that thin scar tracing a path to his sensuous lips, the faint creases at the corners of his eyes, the result of weather or laughter or both. His was a face sculpted by real life, and it wasn't pretty.

It was captivating.

"Do you realize you could have died?" he asked gruffly.

Sophia bit her lip. She did understand, in some way, that together they had just cheated death. Perhaps she ought to be rattled now, shaking with terror—but instead, she felt nothing but alive. Gloriously alive, and connected to this man, as though that rope were still binding her ankle to his.

He dipped the gauze again. "Why didn't you let go of the line when I told you to?"

"I don't know. I wasn't thinking."

"That's obvious. For a governess, you don't have much sense." He blew lightly across her palm, raising the hairs on the back of her neck. His gray-green eyes locked with hers. "For a governess, you don't make much sense."

And now a shiver swept down to her toes.

He released the one hand and took up the other, dunking a fresh piece of gauze. Swabbing at her wound, he said, "You're a puzzle, Miss Turner, but none of the pieces fit. That abhorrent gown cannot have been made for you. Your gloves were a gift. The loss of two sheets of paper has you in tears, and even your handkerchiefs bear someone else's monogram."

Panic coursed through her body, drawing every nerve to attention. He blew over her palm again, and this time the sensation nearly undid her.

"You've been avoiding me," he said.

"You've been avoiding me, too."

"Don't change the subject."

I didn't think I had. Her heartbeat pounded as he dressed her wounds, winding the bandage tightly around her palm. "I told you, I—"

"You told me you'd pay your fare that day, and you've been avoiding me ever since. I know why, Miss Turner."

"You do?"

"I do." He bandaged her other hand.

Oh, God. How much did he truly know? Should she stick with her old story? Invent a new one? Normally, Sophia could weave an entire web of lies with the same effortless talent of a spider spinning silk. But he'd always thrown her off balance, from their very first meeting, and now . . . now she was wounded and in pain, and he was caring for her so tenderly. And when she closed her eyes, she saw the angry, gaping maw of a shark—but she felt his arms around her, holding her fast. Protecting her. All she could think of was how right it felt, and how much she wanted to feel it again.

"You've been lying to me all along, haven't you?"

She couldn't answer. Her voice simply wouldn't work.

"Look at you," he said, his gaze running over her face. "Gone white as sailcloth. I knew it. You never intended to pay your fare. You don't have a shilling to your name, do you?"

Sophia blinked at him. What to say? She needed to keep her money—which meant she needed to keep it secret. He was offering her a gift, with his ridiculous, wrongheaded, oh-so-male assumption. She would be a fool not to take it.

"Do you?" he repeated, his thumb tightening over her wrist.

Casting her eyes to her lap, Sophia released a breathy, dramatic sigh. "What will you do with me?"

"I don't know what to do with you," he said, his voice growing curt with anger again. "Deceitful little minx. I'm of half a mind to put you to work, milking the goats. But that's out of the question with these hands, now isn't it?" He curled and uncurled her fingers a few times, testing the bandage. "I'll tell Stubb to change this twice a day. Can't risk the wound going septic. And don't use your hands for a few days, at least."

"Don't use my hands? I suppose you're going to spoon-feed me, then? Dress me? Bathe me?"

He inhaled slowly and closed his eyes. "Don't use your hands *much*." His eyes snapped open. "None of that sketching, for instance."

She jerked her hands out of his grip. "You could slice off my hands and toss them to the sharks, and I wouldn't stop sketching. I'd hold the pencil with my teeth if I had to. I'm an artist."

"Really. I thought you were a governess."

"Well, yes. I'm that, too."

He packed up the medical kit, jamming items back in the box with barely controlled fury. "Then start behaving like one. A governess knows her place. Speaks when spoken to. Stays out of the damn way."

Rising to his feet, he opened the drawer and threw the

box back in. "From this point forward, you're not to touch a sail, a pin, a rope, or so much as a damned splinter on this vessel. You're not to speak to crewmen when they're on watch. You're forbidden to wander past the foremast, and you need to steer clear of the helm, as well."

"So that leaves me doing what? Circling the quarterdeck?"

"Yes." He slammed the drawer shut. "But only at designated times. Noon hour and the dogwatch. The rest of the day, you'll remain in your cabin."

Sophia leapt to her feet, incensed. She hadn't fled one restrictive program of behavior, just to submit to another. "Who are you, to dictate where I can go, when I can go there, what I'm permitted to do? You're not the captain of this ship."

"Who am I?" He stalked toward her, until they stood toe-to-toe. Until his radiant male heat brought her blood to a boil, and she had to grab the table edge to keep from swaying toward him. "I'll tell you who I am," he growled. "I'm a man who cares if you live or die, that's who."

Her knees melted. "Truly?"

"Truly. Because I may not be the captain, but I'm the investor. I'm the man you owe six pounds, eight. And now that I know you can't pay your debts, I'm the man who knows he won't see a bloody penny unless he delivers George Waltham a governess in one piece."

Sophia glared at him. How did he keep doing this to her? Since the moment they'd met in that Gravesend tavern, there'd been an attraction between them unlike anything she'd ever known. She knew he had to feel it, too. But one minute, he was so tender and sensual; the next, so crass and calculating. Now he would reduce her life's value to this cold, impersonal amount? At least back home, her worth had been measured in thousands of pounds, not in *shillings*.

"I see," she said. "This is about six pounds, eight shillings. That's the reason you've been watching me—"

He made a dismissive snort. "I haven't been watching you."

"*Staring* at me, every moment of the day, so intently it makes my . . . my skin crawl and all you're seeing is a handful of coins. You'd wrestle a shark for a purse of six pounds, eight. It all comes down to money for you."

"*Yes.*" He slammed a fist, knuckles-down, on the table. Everything in the cabin rattled, from the glass-paned cabinet to Sophia's teeth. The brute strength in the gesture was a tiny bit frightening and wildly arousing, and he glared at her mouth so hard, she was almost certain he would kiss her.

She was very certain she wanted him to.

But then he stepped back, doubling the distance between them, and gave her a lazy shrug. That smile—that damnable arrogant grin—tipped his mouth and sent that ghost of a kiss sliding right off his lips. The insolent scoundrel was back.

"It all comes down to money, sweet. Anyone who tells you different is lying. If it didn't all come down to money, you wouldn't be headed for a governess post in Tortola, would you?"

He had her there. "No. I suppose I wouldn't."

"This is business. Strictly business. Mind you don't give me more trouble than you're worth, or I'll strand you in some Azorean fishing village and never look back."

"You wouldn't dare."

"You don't think?" He paused in the door and lifted a brow. "Well, sweetheart, somewhere there's a French captain's widow who'd correct that assumption."

* * *

Gray spent an endless afternoon in steerage, turning pages of a book he lacked the concentration to read. No matter how hard he stared at the blocks of dark print swimming on the pages, he couldn't see words.

He could only see her.

As the afternoon light faded, he let the book fall against his chest. He shut his eyes and tried to sleep.

He could only see her.

When the bells rang for the second dogwatch, he gave up. Tossing the book aside with a curse, he rose from his hammock and prepared to go abovedecks. If the image of her lovely face was going to haunt him no matter what he did, he might as well suffer the torment in person.

Ah, but it wasn't just her lovely face that haunted him. Nor the soft, lush body he was increasingly desperate to see liberated from that woolen cocoon. It was the way she'd so willingly owned up to the truth. The way her spirit had sparked when he'd told her to put aside her art. The way she'd practically made sweet, innocent love to him with her eyes when he'd said he cared if she lived or died.

Good Lord. The laughable irony of it. He'd wasted weeks of his adolescence memorizing sonnets, spent years perfecting little murmured innuendos. Only to learn the most seductive phrase in the English language was something akin to: All things being equal, I'd rather not see you mauled by a shark.

Business, he admonished himself as he shrugged back into his topcoat. This was strictly business. He promised Joss he'd watch out for the girl. After today, there was no doubt she needed watching over. And watching over her was a great deal easier when she was in his sights.

When he gained the quarterdeck, however, he found it deserted. All the sailors were knotted at the ship's bow. The volume of their laughter told Gray the rum was flowing freely. The officers stood sober at the helm. In the middle, there was no one. She'd stayed below.

Gray joined his brother at the stern, propping one elbow on the rail. "It's a fair wind tonight."

"Aye. Is Miss Turner well?"

"She was well enough when I left her."

In silence, they watched the sun slide over the curve of the earth. A loud whoop rose up from the crew at the other end of the ship.

Gray shook his head. "I can't believe you're allowing the men to drink, after what they did today."

"It's Saturday. Wives and sweethearts, you know."

"I don't care if it's the devil's own birthday. If this ship were under my command, they'd not taste a drop until the Tropic."

Joss made a derisive sound. "Fortunate thing she's not under your command, then. You know as well as I, what a fool decision that would be. In fact, after what *you* did today, you ought to go join them."

Gray sighed. He knew his brother was right. Brushes with death were commonplace at sea, and a true sailor learned to shrug them off with a laugh or a smile. One moment, a man could be scaling the rigging—a false move, a soft splash, and the next moment, he'd be gone. Lives were gambled and lost on the whims of fate. When fortune did work in a man's favor and he survived a narrow scrape, it was bad form to brood. Made the crew tense, and even more prone to accidents.

No, the only thing for it was to go on with life. To smile, to joke, to drink and make merry. To toast wives and sweethearts, just as they did every Saturday.

Funny, for Joss to remind him of this. Of all the men who needed to smile, laugh, and just get on with life.

"Come have a drink with me then," Gray said, nudging his brother with his elbow.

Joss shook his head. "No sweetheart to toast. No wife, either."

"So raise a glass to her memory."

"Not tonight." Joss pushed off the rail and headed for the hatch, only pausing long enough for one last remark—a remark that summed up just about every word Joss had spoken to Gray since the day Mara died: "Go on without me."

And Gray still hadn't figured out how to argue back.

Once his brother had disappeared belowdecks, Gray ambled toward the bow of the ship, to join the weekly celebration. In fact, he began the celebration a bit early by pausing to take out his flask and toss back a large swallow.

He froze, flask tilted to his lips, when the music stopped and he heard a light, flirtatious, most distinctly *feminine* laugh coming from the assembled crew.

It had to be her. He knew this simply because she was the only female aboard—not because he recognized her laugh. And that had him tossing back another draught of brandy, to think that he'd been several days in a beautiful woman's proximity and not yet made her laugh. How utterly unlike him.

How depressing.

A few paces more, and one glance confirmed his suspicion. There Miss Jane Turner sat, balancing a tankard between her fingertips, the skirts of her ill-fitting gown draped across an overturned crate. Damn it, hadn't he just told the chit she was to stay aft of the foremast?

Bailey struck a few notes on the pipes, and the crew launched into another rousing song. Gray waited a full verse before approaching her, prowling around her periphery and coming to rest behind her right shoulder. A few of the men gave him friendly nods, but most were too absorbed in their spirits and song to pay him any mind.

"What are you doing?" she asked, flicking him a glance through the swaying lamplight.

"Who, me?" he murmured. "I'm simply leaning against the foremast. You know, this tall bit of timber you weren't to go past."

She sipped her drink.

Gray pushed off the mast and crouched at her side. If she'd turn and look at him, they would be eye-to-eye. But she didn't. "The better question is, what the hell are *you* doing?"

"I'm enjoying myself," she said lightly, taking another drink. "I suggest you do the same." She passed the tankard to him and applauded with wild enthusiasm as the song came to its tuneless end.

Gray peered at the half-empty tankard, then lifted it to his nose and sniffed. Straight, unadulterated rum, the girl was drinking. That would explain the enthusiasm. Her applause concluded, she snatched the tankard back and downed a swallow to do a sailor proud.

Bloody hell. Gray suspected the only thing worse than watching over a prim governess would be watching over a soused one.

"Gray!" O'Shea pushed through the crowd and thrust a brimming mug into his hand. "Just in time for another round of toasts." O'Shea lifted his own cup high. "To the fair Maureen, and her lovely bits. She's firm in the arse, and soft in the—"

"Head," Gray interrupted, prodding the Irishman's bulk with his shoulder. "Got porridge for brains, if she dallies with the likes of you."

While the men laughed and drank "To fair Maureen," Gray reached for Miss Turner's elbow. "Come along, then. You don't belong here."

"I was invited here," she ground out. "And I'm not going anywhere."

"It's no place for ladies." He squeezed her elbow firmly and lifted her to her feet.

"Your turn, Gray," O'Shea said.

He shook his head. "I'm not here to drink. I'm here to see our little Miss Turner back to her cabin. It's past her bedtime."

She glared at him. He glared right back.

"Come on, Gray," another sailor called. "Just one toast."

Miss Turner raised her eyebrows and leaned into him. "Come on, Mr. Grayson. Just one little toast," she taunted, in the breathy, seductive voice of a harlot. It was a voice his body knew well, and vital parts of him were quickly forming a response.

Siren.

"Very well." He lifted his mug and his voice, all the while staring into her wide, glassy eyes. "To the most beautiful lady in the world, and the only woman in my life."

The little minx caught her breath. Gray relished the tense silence, allowing a broad grin to spread across his face. "To my sister, Isabel."

Her eyes narrowed to slits. The men groaned.

"You're no fun anymore, Gray," O'Shea grumbled.

"No, I'm not. I've gone respectable." He tugged on Miss Turner's elbow. "And good little governesses need to be in bed."

"Not so fast, if you please." She jerked away from him and turned to face the assembled crew. "I haven't made my toast yet. We ladies have our sweethearts too, you know."

Bawdy murmurs chased one another until a ripple of laughter caught them up. Gray stepped back, lifting his own mug to his lips. If the girl was determined to humiliate herself, who was he to stop her? Who was he, indeed?

Swaying a little in her boots, she raised her tankard. "To Gervais. My only sweetheart, *mon cher petit lapin*."

My dear little rabbit? Gray sputtered into his rum. What a fanciful imagination the chit had.

"My French painting master," she continued, slurring her words, "and my tutor in the art of passion."

The men whooped and whistled. Gray plunked his mug on the crate and strode to her side. "All right, Miss Turner. Very amusing. That's enough joking for one evening."

"Who's joking?" she asked, lowering her mug to her lips and eyeing him saucily over the rim. "He loved me. Desperately."

"The French do everything desperately," he muttered, beginning to feel a bit desperate himself. He knew she was spinning naïve schoolgirl tales, but the others didn't. The mood of the whole group had altered, from one of good-natured merriment to one of lust-tinged anticipation. These were sailors, after all. Lonely, rummed-up, woman-starved, desperate men. And to an innocent girl, they could prove more dangerous than sharks.

"He couldn't have loved you too much, could he?" Gray grabbed her arm again. "He seems to have let you go."

"I suppose he did." She sniffed, then flashed a coquettish smile at the men. "I suppose that means I need a new sweetheart."

That was it. This little scene was at its end.

Gray crouched, grasped his wayward governess around the thighs, and then straightened his legs, tossing her over one shoulder. She let out a shriek, and he felt the dregs of her rum spill down the back of his coat.

"Put me down, you brute!" She squirmed and pounded his back with her fists.

Gray bound her legs to his chest with one arm and gave her a pat on that well-padded rump with the other.

"Well, then," he announced to the group, forcing a roguish grin, "we'll be off to bed."

Cheers and coarse laughter followed them as Gray toted his wriggling quarry down the companionway stairs and into the ladies' cabin.

With another light smack to her bum that she probably couldn't even feel through all those skirts and petticoats, Gray slid her from his shoulder and dropped her on her feet. She wobbled backward, and he caught her arm, reversing her momentum. Now she tripped toward him, flinging her arms around his neck and sagging against his chest. Gray just stood there, arms dangling at his sides.

Oh, bloody hell.

She stared up at him, with those wide, searching eyes. Fair glossed over with rum, those eyes, but beautiful nonetheless. And those lips—soft, swollen, pouting, just begging to be kissed. God, he wanted to kiss her. Kiss her long and slow and deep, until he was drunk on her sweet, rum-scented breath.

She pursed those lovely lips together—

And then she laughed. She bent her head and buried her face in his coat and laughed, long and loud, until her shoulders shook with it.

"This isn't funny," he said weakly. Weakly, because he didn't truly want her to stop. So stupid, this small thrill of triumph. At last, he'd made the pretty girl laugh.

"Oh, but it is. Those men up there . . . What do you think they think we're doing down here?"

It took Gray a moment to follow her through that labyrinth of a question.

"They'll think we're lovers," she cooed, bursting into laughter again.

"Sweetheart, you'd better pray they do." He put both hands on her waist and pushed her away. But she wouldn't release his neck. They did a strange imitation of a Russian dance as he walked her backward, until she collided with a wall. He pinned her to the paneling with his hands on her hips and his most intimidating glare drilling into her eyes. "You'd better pray that they think I'm down here rogering you within an inch of your precious life. Because that's the only way you'll sleep undisturbed tonight. They won't try a thing, if they think you're mine."

Her fingers curled into the locks of hair at his nape. She toyed with them idly, letting her fingernails rake over his skin. Her bandaged palm brushed his neck.

"Stop that," he said hoarsely.

She didn't. A muscle in his thigh began to quiver.

"Stop that," he repeated. "You're not supposed to be using your hands."

"I'm not using them much." She rested her chin on his chest and peered up at him. "How many teeth does a shark have, I wonder? It seemed like hundreds."

"I have no . . . no idea." He groaned as her finger traced the sensitive groove behind his ear. His eyelids fluttered.

"No, don't close your eyes," she said. "I like the way you look at me. So hungry. So dangerous. As if you're a pirate . . . and I'm a prize worth far more than six pounds, eight shillings."

"You're drunk is what you are."

"Mmm. And you're a man. A big, strong man with the softest, most lovely hair." Her fingers slid up, caressing his scalp until he was fully, excruciatingly aroused.

She started giggling again. Gray had never been much for giggling women, but damned if her soft, rolling laughter wasn't driving him insane with desire. He could stop that giggling. He could kiss her quiet, fondle her breathless.

"Do you want to know why I'm laughing?"

"No."

"Come on, Gray," she mimicked saucily, her hips wriggling under his hands. "You're no fun anymore."

"No," he growled. "I'm not." *I've gone respectable,* he reminded himself, *as of this voyage.* Damned if he could remember why, or what was the bloody rush. Why hadn't he waited another month to reform? The start of the new year would have been a logical choice. What kind of a fool made resolutions in December?

"I'll tell you anyway," she whispered. "It's your hair. It's such a beautiful color, this dark, delicious brown, with the red undertones all through. And up here"—her fingers danced up his temples—"little strands of gold." She frowned with concentration, as though it cost her a great deal of effort to focus her eyes. "It reminds me how, from the very first time I saw you, I've been wanting . . ."

She broke off giggling again.

And damn it, now he did want to know why. He wanted very, very much to know why. Because Gray didn't find this situation amusing in the slightest. His body was aching with quite serious need. Whatever scraps of resolve he possessed were quickly disintegrating, and his trembling fingers couldn't—or just plain wouldn't—hold her off anymore. Releasing her hips, he braced both hands on the wall, caging her between his arms.

There, now he wasn't even touching her.

But she was touching him. Still stroking her soft fingers through his hair, now pressing her warm body to his. His straining erection finally met with the welcome friction of her belly, and it was all he could do not to grind against it. He ought to walk away. Walk straight out of the room without looking back.

But he couldn't. God, he just couldn't. She felt too good. She wanted him, and *that* felt too good. The wanting, he could resist. But this feeling of being *wanted*—it was always his undoing. His little siren would pull him straight to his death, all the way to damnation, and he was literally inches away from giving in and enjoying the ride.

"I've been wanting," she breathed, "so very much . . . to paint you."

To paint him?

He laughed. Oh, what fun he could have with her. "Sweetheart, I . . ."

Gray's voice trailed off as a vivid image appeared in his mind. Not Miss Turner naked and writhing beneath him—though that image would certainly haunt his dreams.

No, he saw her charcoal sketch of young Davy Linnet. The perception in it, the attention to detail. And suddenly, Gray formed a vision of himself through those all-seeing, artist's eyes.

He saw an unshaven brigand, inches away from plundering an innocent governess who was far from home and full in her cups. A man poised to break his word to his only brother, *again*—as though it were an easy habit. A fraud in foppish boots, trying to buy his way into the graces of his sister and society because he lacked the merit to earn their respect.

In that fraction of a second, Gray glimpsed his own portrait, and he did not like what he saw. He might never be the picture of respectability, but he'd be damned if the world would remember him like this.

With a harsh growl, he pushed off against the wall. She fell back against the paneling, her bandaged hands dangling at her sides.

"This is not going to happen," he said, as much to himself as to her. He paced away in agitation and ran his hands through his hair, as if he could brush off the memory of her delicate, teasing touch.

"Why not? Don't you want me to—"

"No. I don't want anything from you. I don't want you to paint me. I don't want you to touch me. I don't want to see you distracting the crew. I don't want to see you baiting sharks. I don't want to see you. At all."

She blinked at him. No more giggles now.

But Gray wasn't done. "You—" He shook a finger at her. "You are so bloody stupid. You have no idea how damned lucky you are. Do you know what could happen to you, crossing the ocean alone with no money and no chaperone? Do you have any notion what a dangerous game you play, going addled with rum and then prancing before the crew like a common harlot?"

She swallowed hard.

"*If* I wanted you," he said, bracing one hand on the wall above her shoulder and looming over her in an attitude of threat, "I could have had you days ago, your very first night on this ship. I'd probably have tired of you by now. Your innocence would be gone, and you'd have thrown it away. For nothing. Maybe if you were especially good, I'd have knocked a few shillings off your fare."

Her eyes went wide. The drunken gloss in them was gone.

Good. Maybe now she'd behave with some sense. Hadn't he warned her from the first? He'd never met a girl he couldn't disillusion.

Gray took a step backward, then another. Easing his way toward the door.

"So be a good little governess, Miss Turner. Go to your berth, blockade the door, crawl into your bunk, and say your prayers. And thank Almighty God in Heaven that I don't want you."

CHAPTER
NINE

Curse the sun.

Sophia's eyelids fluttered open. A narrow crease of daylight greeted her, winking from underneath the door. She squeezed her eyes shut, recoiling in pain. Her head pounded. Her hands throbbed. Her body ached all over, no doubt from yesterday's wrestling matches with fish and men.

Oh, God. Men.

Fragmented memories of last night floated to the surface of her consciousness, began piecing themselves into a picture. A picture that made her sick.

She groped wildly for the water basin and retched into it.

What on earth had she done? She'd announced to a dozen disorderly sailors that she'd just finished a torrid affair with a Frenchman and was currently searching for his replacement. Then she'd plastered herself to Mr. Grayson, murmuring all manner of rubbish and winding her fingers through that dark, thick hair.

And oh, it had been so soft.

She didn't know which was more humiliating: the fact that she'd offered herself to him with all the finesse and enthusiasm of a back-alley whore? Or the fact that he'd refused?

I don't want you, he'd said.

No, this was the most humiliating fact: For all her bodily aches and pains, the severest wound was to her pride. A proper, well-bred young lady would have praised God that, despite all her imprudent, scandalous behavior, she'd awakened this morning with her virtue intact. But Sophia had long ago decided to leave her proper, well-bred life behind and embrace infamy.

And now, infamy himself wouldn't have her.

I don't want you.

His words had cut her like a knife. Each time they echoed in her mind, the knife twisted.

Who *would* want her, after the way she'd behaved? Heavens, if she hadn't been born into wealth and guarded so closely all these years, what kind of sordid end would she have come to? One that would make even a wanton dairymaid blush. If Toby could see her now, he'd be congratulating himself on his lucky escape.

A light knock sounded at her door. Sophia winced.

"Who is it?" Her voice was scratchy and feeble.

"It's breakfast," came Stubb's voice. He cackled. "Compliments of your sweetheart, Germaine."

"Gervais," she moaned, diving back under her blanket. Good Lord, how could she face him again? How could she face anyone on this ship?

She couldn't, it turned out, for quite some time.

She spent three whole days cloistered in her cabin, taking her meals in solitude, spending the daylight hours hunched over a sketch, venturing only to the privy and back. Stubb broke her seclusion a few times a day, to deliver meals and change the dressings on her wounds.

Eventually, her boredom eclipsed her embarrassment. By her estimate, there were three weeks or more remaining in this journey. She couldn't remain holed away in the cabin that long. She needed fresh air and light, and inspiration for her artist's eye.

On the fourth morning, Sophia removed the bandages

from her hands and gingerly stretched the new pink skin covering her wounds. Then she gathered her drawing board and charcoal—and any scrap of courage she could find—and climbed abovedecks.

The ship was unnaturally quiet. Although she stared at the boards beneath her feet, she could feel all heads swiveling in her direction. Mr. Grayson's head wasn't among them. She would have sensed it, had he been there. She was all too familiar with the prickling heat of his gaze.

Taking a deep breath, she hiked her chin, squared her shoulders, walked all of five paces to a low stool, and sat down. There, that hadn't been so difficult.

She was vaguely conscious of the sailors talking and laughing among themselves. No doubt her antics four nights ago were the source of their amusement. Sophia didn't know what she'd do if any of them approached her, hoping to be the next "Gervais." Despite the humiliation of being hauled from the deck in such barbaric fashion, she hoped Mr. Grayson had been correct in saying they'd not make advances if they thought she was his.

Of course, if they thought she was his, they were dead wrong.

I don't want you.

Enough. She'd been reliving those events for days now, ruminating over the implications and castigating herself—and, when regrets became tiresome, savoring the memory of his wavy hair caught in the webs of her fingers, or the sensation of his strong hands encircling her waist . . .

Enough. It was time to go back to work. Once she put charcoal to paper, a bubble of concentration formed around her, blocking out all distractions.

She drew a kitten, of all things. A kitten, with wide eyes and sharp little claws, wiggling back on its hindlegs as if preparing to pounce. Pounce on what, she had not yet decided.

A shadow fell over her paper, and a low whistle sounded from some feet above. Sophia froze, afraid to look up.

"Would ye look at that. Got his sights on a wee mousie, has he?"

It was O'Shea. Sophia sighed with relief. She didn't know all the crew by name yet, but O'Shea's thick brogue—and mammoth size—distinguished him from the crowd. "I hadn't yet decided," she answered him, tilting her head to the side. "I was thinking, perhaps a cricket. Or maybe a snake."

"Brave puss."

Sophia shielded her eyes with her hand and peered up at the Irishman's face. His hard eyes wandered from her hand, to her face, to the sketch in her lap. He made a gruff noise in his throat—the sort of noise men make when they're working up to saying something and don't quite know how to get it out, but want to keep up the aura of brute masculinity in the midst of their indecision.

He was making Sophia nervous. He meant to ask her something, and she was afraid to learn just what.

"Yes?" she prompted.

"The crew . . . We had it out between ourselves, Miss Turner. There were a bit o' scuffling, but I came out on top." He suddenly crouched before her, transforming his silhouette from tree-trunk to boulder in an instant. His craggy face split in a devilish grin. "I get to be first."

"We drew lots, Miss Turner. It's my turn next."

Sophia looked up from her drawing board. Quinn stood before her, wringing his tarred sailor's cap in massive, knob-knuckled hands, wearing an expression more fit for a funeral than a portrait-sitting. "Do take a seat, Mr. Quinn."

The man lowered his weight onto the crate opposite, bracing his arms on his knees. "What am I to do?"

With her fingernail, Sophia sharpened the stub of charcoal. "You needn't do anything but sit there." She gave him a small smile, then quickly looked down again, as it clearly made him uncomfortable. "Why don't you tell me about yourself?" She directed her question to the paper as she began to rough in the oval of his face.

He scratched his chin. "Not much to tell. Born in Yorkshire, I was. My father moved us to London when I was a lad. Got pressed into the Navy when I was sixteen, and I've not called dry land home since."

"You don't have a wife then? No family of your own?" Sophia kept her tone light, stealing furtive glances at Quinn's hawk's-beak nose and heavy brow between questions.

"Not as yet, miss."

"But surely you've a sweetheart for Saturdays?"

Quinn gave a rough laugh. "Oh, I've one for every day of the week, Miss Turner."

Sophia stilled her charcoal and lifted an eyebrow. "What a relief to learn that your calendar is full, Mr. Quinn. For I warn you, I shan't be tempted to stray from Gervais."

He laughed then, and his posture relaxed. Sophia was relieved, too. In the week since that night, her drunken toast had become just another shipboard joke. Mr. Grayson had returned abovedecks quickly enough to prevent the crew from suspecting an affair. Neither had the men taken Gervais seriously, thank Heaven, and she was coming to understand why. Most of their toasts weren't based in reality, either. Life at sea was a dangerous business. The men flirted with death on a daily basis, and they laughed off their close calls. But even if they could escape death, they could not escape loneliness. It was an ever-present shadow that they worked to shrug off—through song, drink, embroidered tales.

Sophia could wholeheartedly relate to that sentiment. She knew loneliness, all too well. And having a fantasy lover—well, for the first time in her life, it didn't make her feel isolated. Here, she was just like everyone else.

She set to work on her sketch, keeping Quinn occupied with questions about his childhood, his home, his service in the war. Asking a man to recall his past invariably caused him to look away, as though his memories marched along the horizon. And while Quinn focused on that far-off time, Sophia could study his features openly without making him ill at ease. She noted the small divot between his eyebrows that appeared likely to become a furrow with time. She observed the tar embedded under his fingernails and in the creases of his palms; stains that would likely never wash off. And when he spoke of his nephew, she caught the faintest hint of a smile at the corner of his eyes.

How different it was, to draw people—*real* people with lives of sweat and labor, each a unique challenge. A far cry from sketching the same old vases of flowers and copies of copies of great masterworks. It gave Sophia a surprising amount of pleasure to simply talk with the men and gain their confidence. When they sat down before her, they trusted her to collect all their weathered features and tiny imperfections and commit them to paper, to assemble them into likenesses for their wives, their sweethearts, themselves. It felt somehow important. When she handed them the completed sketch, she gave them something of value that came from her talent, not from her fortune or her pretty face.

Of course, it also helped pass the time. And it kept Sophia, for those few hours a day, from thinking of *him*.

He was everywhere on the ship; there was no escaping him. Even if she remained in her cabin most of the day, the skylight was always open, and through it flowed steady streams of sunshine and fresh air and his voice.

Mr. Grayson, as she'd learned from the first, was not a quiet man. He spoke often. He spoke loudly. And when he spoke, people listened. Including her.

The coarse shouts of the sailors, their muttered curses . . . the periodic clanging of the ship's bell, the scrape of chains across the deck, the creaking of the ship's wooden joints . . . All these sounds had blended into a flotsam of sound that now floated beneath Sophia's consciousness. But never his voice. Mr. Grayson's baritone rang out over all, assailing her at the most awkward moments.

She would be dressing in her chamber, bared to the waist, lacing her stays with a newly gained efficiency, and Mr. Grayson would choose that particular moment to linger above the cabin and scandalize young Davy Linnet with a ribald joke. It irritated Sophia beyond reason, that he could bring her nipples to tight peaks without even occupying the same room. Without even knowing he did so.

At least, she prayed he did not know he did so. Sometimes she wondered.

She might have been the sole person Mr. Grayson aroused with a simple laugh or phrase, but she certainly wasn't the only one he affected. When the crew fell idle on a calm afternoon and the sluggish silence grew thick, those were the times Mr. Grayson chose to sing. As though he'd been waiting for Nature herself to grow still in anticipation of his performance.

He'd burst out with a song—some bawdy, coarse sailor's shanty, sung with all the reverence of a hymn—and by the time he'd reached the end of the first verse, the entire crew would have joined him. The chorus would ring from every mast, and down in the cabin, Sophia would smile despite her best efforts not to.

At other times, he'd smooth over a brewing argument with a jest, delivered in a smooth, disarming tone. Or his casual comment about the wind would be followed by swift adjustments in the rigging. With that clear, pleasing baritone, Mr. Grayson directed the crew just as surely as the rudder steered the ship.

"I know what you're thinking, Gray." O'Shea's brogue lilted down through the skylight one warm morning, while Sophia was hard at work.

Mr. Grayson responded, a raw longing in his voice. "Aye. It would be so easy to take her."

Sophia nearly dropped her quill.

"We've the advantage of the wind," O'Shea said.

"And a faster ship," Gray replied. "We'd be on her stern in no time."

Ships. Sophia breathed again. *They were speaking of ships.*

"Those were the days." O'Shea gave a low whistle. "One cannonball to the rudder . . ."

"Wouldn't even need that. She'd accept our terms with little more than a signal shot and a smile."

She could hear that smile in his voice.

He continued, "Cannons are for amateurs. Seizing a ship intact . . . it's all in the approach. From the moment that sail appears on the horizon, you act as though it's already yours. All that remains is to inform the other captain."

Now Sophia smiled with him. She knew exactly what he meant. It was the same attitude she'd carried with her into the bank that day. A half-hour later, she'd walked out with six hundred pounds. She wished she could tell

Mr. Grayson that story. He would find it amusing, no doubt. She could almost hear the ringing laugh he'd give when she described the red-faced clerk and the way she'd . . .

How curious.

She'd barely spoken with Mr. Grayson in over a week. How could she have done, after that horrid night? But somehow, through these overheard conversations and stray remarks, she'd come to know him quite well. She'd come to *like* him.

She'd come to think of him as a friend. He'd saved more than her life that day.

There was no denying it now, after the conversation she'd just overheard. She had to face up to the truth she'd been avoiding.

He could have had her that night, so easily. Conquest was his specialty, as he'd just said. Ships, women . . . whatever Mr. Grayson wanted, he took. And he *had* wanted her, at least in the carnal sense, despite all his protests to the contrary. When she'd pressed up against him so shamelessly, she'd felt his unmistakable arousal. She'd made herself his for the taking, and he had walked away.

Of course, he wasn't the first person to guard her virtue. Her family, her schoolmistresses, her companions—even her own betrothed—all her life, she'd been surrounded by a fortress of people, all devoted to keeping her untouched. Because her virtue was currency, a token to be bartered for social connections. Would any of those same people give two straws about her virginity, had Sophia been a lowborn, penniless orphan? She doubted it.

But Mr. Grayson did. He thought her a poor, friendless governess, with no connections worth mentioning and no one to care. And still, he'd guarded her virtue when, in a moment of drunken foolishness, she would have thrown it away.

In running away from home, Sophia had seized control of her fortune. But she'd also seized control of her body. Her nouveau-riche parents had been desperate for one of their daughters to marry a title. When her older sister, Kitty, had failed to do so, their hopes had transferred to Sophia. But to marry without passion or love, simply for money and connections—it would have made her the worst sort of whore. Sophia didn't want to lose her virginity as a means of completing a transaction. She dreamed of a different experience, one of passion and emotion and breathtaking romance.

And she'd have lost that dream, if not for him.

Maybe he'd been right. Maybe she ought to thank Almighty God in Heaven that he didn't want her.

What did it mean then, that she couldn't?

Rising to her feet, she packed away her quill and ink. Maybe she couldn't tell Mr. Grayson the story of her own conquest. Maybe he wouldn't speak to her at all. But the day was fine, and there was a sail on the horizon, and she simply couldn't stay put in the cabin a moment longer. She wanted to be in the center of the activity, enjoying the warm rays of the sun.

Oh, who was she fooling?

She wanted to be near *him*.

Gray froze as Miss Turner emerged from the hold. For weeks, she'd plagued him—by day, he suffered glimpses of her beauty; by night, he was haunted by memories of her touch. And just when he thought he'd finally wrangled his desire into submission, today she'd ruined everything.

She'd gone and changed her dress.

Gone was that serge shroud, that forbidding thundercloud of a garment that had loomed in his peripheral vision for weeks. Today, she wore a cap-sleeved frock of sprigged muslin.

She stepped onto the deck, smiling face tilted to the wind. A flower opening to greet the sun. She bobbed on her toes, as though resisting the urge to make a girlish twirl. The pale, sheer fabric of her dress billowed and swelled in the breeze, pulling the undulating contour of calf, thigh, hip into relief.

Gray thought she just might be the loveliest creature he'd ever seen.

Therefore, he knew he ought to look away.

He did, for a moment. He made an honest attempt to scan the horizon for clouds. He checked the hour on his pocket watch, wound the small knob one, two, three, four times. He wiped a bit of salt spray from its glass face. He thought of England. And France, and Cuba, and Spain. He remembered his brother, his sister, and his singularly ugly Aunt Rosamond, on whom he hadn't clapped eyes in decades. And all this Herculean effort resulted in nothing but a fine sheen of sweat on his brow and precisely thirty seconds' delay in the inevitable.

He looked at her again.

Desire swept through his body with startling intensity. And beneath that hot surge of lust, a deeper emotion swelled. It wasn't something Gray wished to examine. He preferred to let it sink back into the murky depths of his being. An unnamed creature of the deep, left for a more intrepid adventurer to catalog.

Instead, he examined Miss Turner's new frock. The fabric was of fine quality, the sprig pattern evenly stamped, without variations in shape or hue. The dressmaker had taken great pains to match the pattern at the seams. The sleeves of the frock fit perfectly square with her shoulders;

in a moment of calm, the skirt's single flounce lapped the laces of her boots. Unlike that gray serge abomination, this dress was expensive, and it had been fashioned for her alone.

But it no longer fit. As she turned, Gray noted how the neckline gaped slightly, and the column of skirt that ought to have skimmed the swell of her hip instead caught on nothing but air.

He frowned. And in that instant, she turned to face him. Their gazes caught and held. Her own smile faded to a quizzical expression. And because Gray didn't know how to answer the unspoken question in her eyes, and because he hated the fact that he'd banished the giddy delight from her face, he gave her a curt nod and a churlish "Good morning."

And then he walked away.

Gray burst into the galley. "Miss Turner is not eating."

The cramped, boxed-in nature of the space, the oppressive heat—it seemed an appropriate place to take this irrational surge of resentment. If only his emotion could dissipate through the ventilation slats as quickly as steam.

"And good morning to you, too." Gabriel wiped his hands on his apron without glancing up.

"She's not eating," Gray repeated evenly. "She's wasting away." He didn't even realize his hand had balled into a fist until his knuckles cracked. He flexed his fingers impatiently.

"Wasting away?" Gabriel's face split in a grin as he picked up a mallet and attacked a hunk of salted pork. "Now what makes you say that?"

"Her dress no longer fits properly. The neckline of her bodice is too loose."

Gabriel stopped pounding and looked up, meeting Gray's eyes for the first time since he'd entered the galley. The mocking arch of the old man's eyebrows had Gray clenching his teeth. They stared at each other for a second. Then Gray blew out his breath and looked away, and Gabriel broke into peals of laughter.

"Never thought I'd live to see the day," the old cook finally said, "when you would complain that a beautiful lady's bodice was too loose."

"It's not that she's a beautiful lady—"

Gabriel looked up sharply.

"It's not *merely* that she's a beautiful lady," Gray amended. "She's a passenger, and I have a duty to look out for her welfare."

"Wouldn't that be the captain's duty?"

Gray narrowed his eyes.

"And I know my duty well enough," Gabriel continued. "It's not as though I'm denying her food, now is it? I'm thinking Miss Turner just isn't accustomed to the rough living aboard a ship. Used to finer fare, that one."

Gray scowled at the hunk of cured pork under Gabriel's mallet and the shriveled, sprouted potatoes rolling back and forth with each tilt of the ship. "Is this the noon meal?"

"This, and biscuit."

"I'll order the men to trawl for a fish."

"Wouldn't that be the captain's duty?" Gabriel's tone was sly.

Gray wasn't sure whether the plume of steam swirling through the galley originated from the stove or his ears. He didn't care for Gabriel's flippant tone. Neither did he care for the possibility of Miss Turner's lush curves disappearing when he'd never had any chance to appreciate them.

Frustrated beyond all reason, Gray turned to leave,

wrenching open the galley door with such force, the hinges creaked in protest. He took a deep breath to compose himself, resolving not to slam the door shut behind him.

Gabriel stopped pounding. "Sit down, Gray. Rest your bones."

With another rough sigh, Gray complied. He backed up two paces, slung himself onto a stool, and watched as the cook grabbed a tin cup from a hook on the wall and filled it, drawing a dipper of liquid from a small leather bucket. Then Gabriel set the cup on the table before him.

Milk.

Gray stared at it. "For God's sake, Gabriel. I'm not six years old anymore."

The old man raised his eyebrows. "Well, seeing as how you haven't outgrown a visit to the kitchen when you're in a sulk, I thought maybe you'd have a taste for milk yet, too. You did buy the goats."

Gray shook his head. He lifted the cup to his lips and sipped cautiously at first, paused, then drained the cup quickly, as if it held rum rather than goat's milk. It coated his tongue, tasting bland and creamy and smooth. Innocent. Gray looked down at the empty cup ruefully. He wished he'd made it last a bit longer.

Gabriel took up his mallet and started pounding again, and Gray looked up sharply, about to ask the old man to leave off and find some quieter occupation. A task more conducive to . . . to Gray's pondering, or yearning, or regretting, or whatever damn fool thing he'd sat down to do. But a glimpse of something fluttering behind the cook's shoulder stole the complaint from his lips.

Another sketch—this one of Gabriel—hung on the wall above the water cask. It swiveled gently on a single tack; or rather, the paper hung plumb with gravity while the whole ship swiveled around it. She'd captured

Gabriel's toothy, inoffensive grin and the devilish gleam in his eye, and the effect of the paper's constant, subtle rocking was to make the image come alive. Softly, strangely—the portrait of Gabriel was *laughing*.

Gray shook himself. Laughing at *him*, most likely.

"She comes here?" he asked.

"Aye. That she does. Every morning." Gabriel straightened his hunched spine and adopted a cultured tone. "We take tea."

Gray frowned. One more place he'd have to avoid—the galley at morning teatime. "See to it that she eats something. Slip more milk in her tea. Make her treacle duff every day, if she cares for it. Are you giving her a daily ration of lime juice?"

Gabriel smiled down at the salt pork. "Yes, sir."

"Double it."

"Yes, sir." Gabriel's grin widened.

"And stop grinning, damn it."

"Yes, sir." The old man practically sang the words as he pounded away at the meat. "Never thought I'd live to see the day."

CHAPTER
TEN

It was Christmas Eve morning, and Sophia's mood could only be described as morose. She sat in the cabin, which felt incongruously warm considering the holiday. Paper, inkwell, and quill sat before her on the table. By now, she'd adapted her artistic technique to the ocean's ceaseless rolling. Her inkwell she affixed to the tabletop with a large dab of melted wax, so it could not easily be dislodged into her lap. The paper she braced under straps of leather she'd removed from her trunk and stretched over the tabletop. And as she laid quill to paper, she kept the joints of her arm and wrist loose to buffer any sudden lurch of the ship.

She'd illustrated three-quarters now of The Book, meticulously documenting the wanton dairymaid and her lover in each of their amorous attitudes. This morning, however, lewdness did not excite her. She flipped to the epilogue, wherein the gentleman proposed marriage to his lover and together they embarked on a long and fruitful union. Without any excess of concentration, Sophia began sketching a scene of the couple picnicking together beneath the shade of a willow tree. The dairymaid, now dressed in a lady's finery, sat on a blanket, legs extended before her, ankles crossed, her gaze searching the horizon. The gentleman lay with his head in her lap, looking up at the sky. They did not regard each other, but the easy intimacy of their postures gave them the air of a couple very much in love.

"Ahoy! Ship ahoy! Larboard bow! All hands!"

The ship bustled into activity, and Sophia recognized the familiar sounds of the off-watch sailors thundering up from the forecastle, the mainsail being backed against the mast. The boat slowed and swung around.

She recapped her inkwell and wiped her hands on her apron hurriedly. "Speaking" with another ship could take minutes or hours, depending on the circumstance. Sometimes the captains merely exchanged names and destinations in a friendly "how-do" fashion, like two ladies crossing paths in the park. In other instances, long conversations and trade might take place. The other day, Mr. Grayson had boarded a Portuguese trader and returned with a crate of bartered goods.

But whether the encounter lasted minutes or hours, Sophia—like everyone else aboard—did not want to miss it. Nothing rivaled the sight of a sail approaching. It served as a comforting reminder that the *Aphrodite* was not simply drifting the globe alone. A promise that civilization and society awaited them at the end of this journey, somewhere.

She hastened abovedecks, shielded her eyes with her hand, and performed a slow circle. There was no ship to be seen, not even a single puffed sail hugging the horizon. Yet the men were all assembled on deck, buzzing with anticipation. All the sailors, at least. Mr. Grayson was notably absent, as were the captain, his officers, and Stubb.

Confused, Sophia approached Quinn. "I thought we were to speak with another ship."

A wide grin split Quinn's weathered face. "That we are, miss."

"But . . ." Sophia scanned the distance again, and her voice trailed out to sea.

"Oh, 'tisn't a ship coming across the sea," Quinn said. "Nay, we're expecting a visitor come *up* from the sea. We've crossed the Tropic of Cancer. And that means we've got to appease old Triton before we go any further."

Sophia looked around at the milling crewmen. "Triton? *Up* from the sea? I don't understand."

"It's a sailors' tradition, miss." O'Shea approached, his thick brogue cutting through Sophia's confusion. "The Sea King himself comes aboard to have a bit of sport with those crossing the Tropic for the first time, like the new boy there." He nodded toward Davy, who stood to the side, looking every bit as confused as Sophia but unwilling to own to it.

Quinn crossed his massive forearms over his chest, stacking them like logs. "And Triton always collects his tax, of course."

"His tax?" Sophia asked.

O'Shea gave her a sly look. "Best be ready with a coin or two, Miss Turner. If you can't pay his tax, old Triton just might sweep ye down to the depths with him and keep ye there forever."

Quinn chuckled, shooting the Irishman a knowing look. "Knowing old Triton, it wouldn't be surprising if he did just that."

O'Shea winked at the crewman. "Could hardly blame him."

Sophia's heart pounded, and with every wild thump it slammed against the purse secured beneath her stays. Was this "Triton" the seafaring equivalent of a highwayman, then? Some sort of pirate?

"Where are the officers?" she asked Quinn. "Doesn't the captain greet any approaching vessel?"

"The captain and his mates tend to steer clear of Triton. Sailors' business, this is."

Well, if Sophia had been looking for an excuse to flee

belowdecks, she'd just been handed one. But before she could move, a voice called out, "All hands at attention! Prepare to greet yer king! The ruler of the ocean depths himself, and with him today comes his fair mistress, the Queen!"

Coarse laughter rippled through the crowd. None of the sailors seemed the least bit distressed at receiving this visitor, Sophia noted. Of course, none of them had much to lose.

Two sailors hauled on ropes, hoisting the jolly boat up to the ship's side, revealing two apocryphal figures standing in the center of the small craft. At first glance, Sophia only saw clearly the shorter of the two, a gruesome creature with long tangled hair and a painted face, wearing a tight-fitting burlap skirt and a makeshift corset fashioned from fishnet and mollusk shells. The Sea Queen, Sophia reckoned, a smile warming her cheeks as the crew erupted into raucous cheers. A bearded Sea Queen, no less, who bore a striking resemblance to the *Aphrodite*'s own grizzled steward.

Stubb.

Sophia craned her neck to spy Stubb's consort, as the foremast blocked her view of Triton's visage. She caught only a glimpse of a white toga draped over a bronzed, bare shoulder. She took a jostling step to the side, nearly tripping on a coil of rope.

"Foolish mortals! Kneel before your king!"

The assembled sailors knelt on cue, giving Sophia a direct view of the Sea King. And even if the blue paint smeared across his forehead or the strands of seaweed dangling from his belt might have disguised him, there was no mistaking that persuasive baritone.

Mr. Grayson.

There he stood, tall and proud, some twenty feet away from her. Bare-chested, save for a swath of white linen draped from hip to shoulder. Wet locks of hair slicked back from his tanned face, sunlight embossing every contour of his sculpted arms and chest. A pagan god come swaggering down to earth.

He caught her eye, and his smile widened to a wolfish grin. Sophia could not for the life of her look away. He hadn't looked at her like this since . . . since that night. He'd scarcely looked in her direction at all, and certainly never wearing a smile. The boldness of his gaze made her feel thoroughly unnerved, and virtually undressed. Until the very act of maintaining eye contact became an intimate, verging on indecent, experience.

If she kept looking at him, she felt certain her knees would give out. If she looked away, she gave him the victory. There was only one suitable alternative, given the circumstances. With a cheeky wink to acknowledge the joke, Sophia dropped her eyes and curtsied to the King.

Mr. Grayson laughed his approval. Her curtsy, the crew's gesture of fealty—he accepted their obeisance as his due. And why should he not? There was a rightness about it somehow, an unspoken understanding. Here at last was their true leader: the man they would obey without question, the man to whom they'd pledge loyalty, even kneel.

This was *his* ship.

"Where's the owner of this craft?" he called. "Oh, right. Someone told me he's no fun anymore."

As the men laughed, the Sea King swung over the rail, hoisting what looked to be a mop handle with vague aspirations to become a trident. "Bring forth the virgin voyager!"

Sophia's stomach gave a panicked flutter. What in God's name did Mr. Grayson intend to do to her? She half-feared, half-yearned to find out. Then the flutter spread pleasantly downward, and the balance tipped in favor of yearning.

But the sailors took no notice of her. Instead they pushed Davy Linnet to the fore.

"Here he is, yer majesty!" Quinn called out. "New boy, first time crossing the Tropic."

Mr. Grayson leveled his "trident" at the lad. "If you wish to cross my sea, young man, you must submit yourself to questioning. And you must tell the truth, do you understand? No one lies to the Sea King. If you attempt to deceive me, I shall know it. And then I'll suck you down into the depths of the ocean to live with the eels, never to be heard from again."

Davy glanced around him, looking uncertain whether to laugh or tremble. "Aye, sir."

"Aye, your *majesty*," Triton corrected.

Davy shuffled his feet. "Aye, yer majesty."

A pair of crewmen pushed a barrel against the mast, and Davy was made to stand upon it. Somewhere in the crowd, a sailor made a crude remark. The men erupted into laughter.

Mr. Grayson banged his mop-handle trident on the deck for silence—once, twice. The men hushed, and he turned to Davy. "Now then, boy, tell me your name."

"Davy Linnet, sir."

Bang went the mop handle. "Your majesty."

"Davy Linnet, yer majesty."

"What is your age, Davy Linnet?"

"Fifteen, sir."

Bang.

Davy jumped. "Fifteen, yer majesty."

Mr. Grayson began to circle the lad at a leisurely pace. "From whence do you hail, Davy Linnet?"

"From Sussex. Town of Dunswold. Yer majesty."

"How many siblings have you?"

"Five, yer majesty. Four sisters and one brother."

"Are your parents living?"

"Both, sir. Er, yer majesty."

Mr. Grayson turned slowly on his heel, his arm muscles flexing as he propped the makeshift trident on one shoulder. The drape of his toga slipped, and he casually repositioned the fabric with his free hand. But not before Sophia glimpsed a shocking scar near his collarbone—an irregular circle of pink, puckered flesh nearly the size of her palm. She pressed her own hand to her throat.

"And tell me, Davy Linnet," Mr. Grayson continued, "given a choice, do you prefer brown bread or white?"

"White, yer majesty."

"Ale or grog?"

"Grog, yer majesty." Davy began to relax, a shy smile playing on his face. Clearly, he'd anticipated a harsher interrogation than this.

He'd anticipated correctly.

"Ever stolen anything, Davy Linnet?"

The boy's smile vanished, and his brow creased. "Wh-what?"

"Have you"—Mr. Grayson leveled the mop handle at the boy—"ever stolen anything? Are you a thief?"

Davy hedged. "Well, I've nicked a scrap here and there in my time. Food, mostly."

"Mostly?"

Davy's eyes hardened. "Mostly." Mr. Grayson held his silence, but the youth did not elaborate. Finally, he added, "Weren't much to go around in the Linnet house."

Mr. Grayson gave him a stern look. "So hunger excuses theft, does it?"

"N-no, sir. No, yer majesty."

"Would you steal from your crewmates?"

"No," Davy shot back, resolute. He looked around at the sailors. *"No."*

Bang.

"No, yer majesty."

Mr. Grayson turned a slow circle. "What if you were hungry?"

"No, yer majesty. Not from my crewmates. Can't steal from those as share everything. If I'm going hungry, it means everyone's going hungry."

Mr. Grayson gave a stiff nod, obviously satisfied with Davy's response. He paused a long beat. Then his posture changed abruptly as he leaned back against the ship's rail. "Have you a wife, Davy Linnet?"

The boy chuckled, obviously relieved at the change of subject. "No, yer majesty."

"No? I do hope it's not for lack of trying. How many sweethearts have you had?"

Davy's cheeks colored. "None, yer majesty."

"Tumbled any girls, Davy Linnet?"

Davy's face went scarlet. He mumbled, "N-no."

Bang.

"No, yer majesty," the boy amended quickly. "Not yet."

This last drew a roar of laughter from the crew and a smirk from the Sea King. Davy's posture relaxed.

"How about love? Ever been in love, Davy Linnet?"

The boy went rigid again. His eyes flitted to Sophia for an instant, and her heart squeezed. She knew the boy harbored an infatuation for her—everyone aboard the ship knew it—and she knew just as certainly it wasn't anything to approach the love he'd one day feel for a wife. But then, one couldn't tell a fifteen-year-old his emotions were less than real.

The silence stretched as the entire assembly awaited the boy's response. Quinn grinned and winked at Sophia. Davy swallowed hard.

Mr. Grayson rapped his staff against the barrel, causing Davy to sway. "The truth, boy. Or the eels."

The boy studied his feet for a moment. Then his head shot up and he met Mr. Grayson's eyes directly. "Aye, sir. I'm in love."

Raucous laughter burst like a thunderclap, quickly organizing itself into a bawdy chant. Davy's face flushed red as a cake of vermillion. Sophia bit her lip, inwardly aching for him. Not even when he'd climbed the mast that first day at sea, white-knuckled and shaking with fear, had she ever witnessed such courage. The irony pricked at the corners of her eyes. She couldn't remember ever hearing those words and truly believing them—not from her family, not from her friends. She'd been courted by a legion of suitors and even been betrothed, but her first sincerely-uttered declaration of love came from this brave, earnest boy.

Davy's admission must have affected the Sea King, too. For though he kept his face carefully composed, Mr. Grayson neglected to bang his trident and elicit the required "yer majesty."

Sophia longed to gauge Mr. Grayson's reaction further, but she kept her gaze trained on the youth. Davy stood tall, despite the jeering of his crewmates. She prepared to reward him with a gracious smile, should he look in her direction, though she suspected he'd be too proud to do so.

And he was. The boy stared stubbornly at Mr. Grayson. "Any more questions, yer majesty?"

Another storm of laughter swept through the crew.

Bang.

Silence.

"Only one, Davy Linnet. Have you coin to pay your tax?"

The lad blinked. "Tax?"

"Aye, your tax. There's a price for crossing these waters unharmed. And if you cannot pay it with coin, you must suffer the consequences." Mr. Grayson nodded toward Stubb, who pushed forward another barrel, this one open at the top and sloshing with liquid. A stench wafted from the barrel—odors of tar and rotting fish mingling with the pervasive aroma of stirred-up bilge.

Davy's nose wrinkled as he regarded the noxious brew from his high vantage point. "I . . . I haven't a coin to my name, yer majesty."

"Well, Davy Linnet," Mr. Grayson continued smoothly, "if you can't pay the tax, you must be dunked."

Stubb pulled out a rusted strap of metal and waved it above his head. "Dunked and shaved!"

The men erupted into cheers. Levi and O'Shea took Davy by either leg, lifting him toward the bilge-filled barrel.

Sophia knew she shouldn't intervene. The boy would come to no harm, she told herself. It was just a bit of bilgewater. Clearly all of the sailors had suffered some similar hazing their first voyage, or they wouldn't be taking such glee in Davy's plight. But the lad had already endured too much humiliation, and endured too much of it on her account.

"Stop!" she called out.

To a one, the crewmen froze. A dozen heads swiveled to face her.

Sophia swallowed and turned to Mr. Grayson. "What about me? I'm also a virgin voyager."

His lips quirked as his gaze swept her from head to toe and then back up partway. "Are you truly?"

"Yes. And I haven't a coin to my name. Do you plan to dunk and shave me, too?"

"Now there's an idea." His grin widened. "Perhaps. But first, you must submit to an interrogation."

A lump formed in Sophia's throat, impossible to speak around.

Mr. Grayson raised that sonorous baritone to a carrying pitch. "What's your name then, miss?" When Sophia merely firmed her chin and glared at him, he warned dramatically, "Truth or eels."

Bang.

Excited whispers crackled through the assembly of sailors. Davy was completely forgotten, dropped to the deck with a dull thud. Even the wind held its breath in anticipation, and Sophia gave a slight jump when a sail smacked limp against the mast.

Though her heart pounded an erratic rhythm of distress, she willed her voice to remain even. "I've no intention of submitting myself to any interrogation, by god or man." She lifted her chin and arched an eyebrow. "And I'm not impressed by your staff."

She paused several seconds, waiting for the crew's boisterous laughter to ebb.

Mr. Grayson pinned her with his bold, unyielding gaze. "You dare speak to me that way? I'm Triton." With each word, he stepped closer. "King of the Sea. A god among men." Now they stood just paces apart. Hunger gleamed in his eyes. "And I demand a sacrifice."

Her hand remained pressed against her throat, and Sophia nervously picked at the neckline of her frock. This close, he was all bronzed skin stretched tight over muscle and sinew. Iridescent drops of seawater paved glistening trails down his chest, snagging on the margins of that horrific scar, just barely visible beneath his toga.

"A sacrifice?" Her voice was weak. Her knees were weaker.

"A sacrifice." He flipped the trident around, his biceps

flexing as he extended the blunt end toward her, hooking it under her arm. He lifted the mop handle, pulling her hand from her throat and raising her wrist for his inspection.

Sophia might have yanked her arm away at any moment, but she was as breathless with anticipation as every other soul on deck. She'd become an observer of her own scene, helpless to alter the drama unfolding, on the edge of her seat to see how it would play out.

He studied her arm. "An unusually fine specimen of female," he said casually. "Young. Fair. Unblemished." Then he withdrew the stick, and Sophia's hand dropped to her side. "But unsatisfactory."

She felt a sharp twinge of pride. Unsatisfactory? Those words echoed in her mind again. *I don't want you.*

"Unsatisfactory. Too scrawny by far." He looked around at the crew, sweeping his makeshift trident in a wide arc. "I demand a sacrifice with meat on her bones. I demand . . ."

Sophia gasped as the mop handle clattered to a rest at her feet. Mr. Grayson gave her a sly wink, bracing his hands on his hips in a posture of divine arrogance. "I demand a goat."

CHAPTER
ELEVEN

The stench of live goats had permeated the *Aphrodite* for weeks. Now, the more pleasing aroma of cooked goat battled for precedence. Gray found it a refreshing change, but the remaining livestock didn't seem to agree. They bleated loudly in their berths, protesting the sudden decrease in their number.

Gray picked his way through the barn that had formerly been the gentlemen's cabin, careful not to brush up against anything. He'd just bathed and dressed, and it wouldn't do to show up at Christmas Eve dinner with goat dung on his boots.

He passed into the galley and was greeted by a cloud of fragrant steam. The exotic scent of spices mingled with the tang of roasting meat. Startled, Gabriel choked on a sip from a tankard. In the corner, Stubb quickly shoved something behind his back. The old men's eyes shone with more than holiday merriment.

"Happy Christmas, Gray." Gabriel extended the tankard to him. "Here. We poured you some wine."

Gray waved it off with a chuckle. "That my new Madeira you're sampling?"

Gabriel nodded as he downed another sip. "Thought I should taste it before you serve it to company. You know, to be certain it ain't poisoned." He drained the mug and set it down with a smile. "No, sir. Not poisoned."

"And the figs? The olives? The spices? I assume you checked them all, too? For caution's sake, of course."

"Of course," Stubb said, pulling his own mug from behind his back and taking a healthy swallow. "Everyone knows you can't trust a Portuguese trader."

Gray laughed. He plucked an olive from a dish on the table and popped it into his mouth. Rich oil coated his tongue. "Did you find the crate easily enough?" he asked Stubb, reaching for another olive.

The old steward nodded. "It's all laid out, just so. Candles, too."

"Feels like Christmas proper." Gabriel tilted his head. "Miss Turner even gave me a gift."

Gray followed the motion, squinting through the steam.

I'll be damned.

A small canvas sat propped on the cabinet. Painted on it was a deceptively simple seascape. Masterful brushstrokes captured the swirling motion of the water and the dance of the breeze. Fading sunlight kissed the waves with brilliance.

And as was the case with all Miss Turner's work, Gray found himself genuinely moved by it—not only by the painting's beauty, but by the care that occasioned its creation. She'd given Gabriel a window for the galley, just as surely as if she'd cut a hole in the ship's side and installed a pane of glass. She'd given him a gift, indeed.

Stubb said, "She made a sketch of Bailey for his wife. Now he's fashioning her these little canvases from spare bits of wood and sailcloth."

"Doesn't Bailey have sails to mend?" he grumbled. "I'm not paying the man to make canvases."

Gabriel shrugged, throwing him an offended look. "I just give the man his biscuit three times a day. I don't keep track of how he spends his time."

Gray knew he was being an ass, but he found it damned maddening, this constant assault of her artistry. These little scraps of beauty strewn about his ship. Dazzling his eyes, yanking him about with little tugs on his gut. Their collective effect left Gray feeling more than a bit resentful. But not so resentful that he'd ceased looking for them—hell, *hoping* to find them—in a manner that verged uncomfortably on habit.

Not that any of her sketches or paintings were for *him*.

He turned to Stubb. "Did she give you a present, too?"

The man smiled through his grizzled beard. "Aye. It's in steerage. Lovely little painting of a mermaid."

"Good Lord." Gray sanded his palm on his bearded jaw.

The steward picked up a wooden spoon and prodded Gray in the side. "They're waiting for you, you know. Get in there, so we can serve."

Gray hurried through the passage before Stubb could prod him again. He traversed the small corridor of the officers' berths and entered the captain's cabin. The men rose as he entered, Joss at the head of the narrow table, flanked by the other officers.

"Merry Christmas," he mumbled, suddenly self-conscious. He nodded to the men, then turned and made a bow to Miss Turner before sliding into the chair opposite.

Stripes.

Out of habit, Gray immediately noted the answer to his question. The persistent, ever-present question that plagued his days, popped into his mind whenever he saw her or anticipated seeing her. Which was nearly all of the time.

Which frock would she be wearing? Sprigs or stripes?

Gray harbored a slight preference for the stripes. Not only did the darker color suit her complexion, but the neckline plunged in an enticing manner, displaying a wedge of sheer chemise. The sprigged gown had a higher, square neckline, and only one flounce to this frock's two.

But then . . . The sprigged gown had tiny buttons down the side—fourteen buttons, to be exact, and though just mentally undoing them was enough to drive Gray mad with frustration, that mile-long stretch of minuscule pearl dots was some comfort. The fastenings of this striped gown, by contrast, were completely invisible. Were there little hooks, he wondered, under the sleeves? Hidden in the seams somewhere?

Miss Turner coughed and shifted in her seat.

Dear God. Gray shook himself, realizing he'd just spent the better part of a minute openly staring in the direction of her breasts. At a distance of no more than two feet. Worse—he'd wasted that blasted minute obsessing about hooks and buttons, when he could have been scanning for the shadow of an areola, or the crest of a nipple.

Damn.

And now he had no choice but to drop his gaze and study the china.

It did look well, the porcelain. The acanthus pattern complemented the scrollwork on the silver quite nicely. Odd, to be drinking Madeira from teacups, but at least they were better than tin. The white drape beneath it all was nothing of quality, but the lighting was dim, and it would do.

Gray put out a hand to straighten his fork.

"The table looks lovely," she said, to no one in particular.

Dear God. Once again, she jolted him back into reality, and Gray realized he'd spent the better part of two minutes now fussing over china and table linens. First dressmaking, now table-setting . . . If it wasn't for the fact that her voice called straight to his swelling groin, Gray might have begun to question his masculinity.

What the hell was happening to him?

He wanted her. He wanted her body, quite obviously. More disturbing by far, he could no longer deny that he wanted her approval. And he wanted both with a near-paralyzing intensity, though he knew he could never have one without sacrificing the other.

Then she extended her slender wrist to reach for the teacup, and Gray remembered the reason for this entire display.

He wanted to see her *eat.*

"Where's Stubb?" he growled, tetchy with hunger. All sorts of hunger.

"Right behind you, sirs and madam." Stubb shuffled in, bearing a steaming tureen. "First course, soup." He moved around the table, beginning with Miss Turner, ladling generous helpings of creamy chowder into their bowls.

Silence reigned, save for the light clink of silver on china. Gray ate his soup quickly, scarcely tasting it, scalding the roof of his mouth in the process. Then he sat back and sipped Madeira from his teacup, trying not to stare at her as she daintily spooned chowder to her lips.

Perhaps he was going mad.

Next to him, Wiggins cleared his throat. "You must forgive us, Miss Turner. We seamen are poor dinner companions, I fear. We are accustomed to eating quickly, efficiently, with little conversation. And we are certainly unused to the company of a beautiful lady."

Gray coughed, setting his teacup down on its saucer with a crack.

Miss Turner swallowed slowly and laid down her

spoon. "I am most grateful for company this evening, even of the quiet variety. I am no great conversationalist, myself."

Gray snorted. Not a conversationalist. The girl had coaxed the life story out of every sailor on this ship.

She had just picked up her spoon again when Joss spoke.

"You do not find the voyage too tedious, Miss Turner?" Joss asked. "I regret that you are left to entertain yourself, being the sole passenger."

She laid down her spoon. "Thank you, Captain, but I find sufficient activity to occupy my hands and my mind. Reading, sketching, walking the deck for fresh air and healthful exertion. I'm surprisingly content, living at sea."

Gray's heart gave an odd kick.

"But it's Christmas, Miss Turner. You are away from your home." Brackett's voice was cool. "Surely you must miss your family?"

"Yes, of course. I do." She folded her hands behind her half-full bowl of chowder. "I miss . . . Oddly enough, I miss oranges. We always had oranges at Christmas, when I was a child."

"Yes," said Joss, his lips curving in the rare hint of a smile. "Yes, so did we. Didn't we, Gray?"

Oranges. They wanted oranges. As if it could be so simple, to go back to the time when happiness came in a knobby round package and fit in the palm of one's hand. And yet, were there oranges to be had at that moment, Gray would have traded the ship for a crate of them. He watched as Miss Turner lifted a spoonful of soup to her lips with agonizing slowness. He stared, fascinated, as her lips parted, revealing the tip of her tongue . . .

"I say, Miss Turner—" Wiggins again.

Her spoon paused in mid-air.

Gray crashed his fist on the table. "Christ, man! Can't you see the lady is trying to eat?" Crossing his arms, he slumped back in his chair. Its wooden joints creaked in protest.

And now everyone put down their spoons.

Gray felt their eyes on him. He kicked the table leg, frustrated with himself, with her, with his goddamned boots. They still pinched his feet.

Stubb shuffled in, accompanied by Gabriel this time. "Main course," the old steward called.

"There's meat-and-kidney pie," Gabriel announced proudly, setting the dish in the center of the table. "Made the crust from biscuit meal. Thought my arm would fall off from pounding."

"And here's the roast!" Stubb lowered his offering to the table, a well-browned haunch that smelled of grease and savory. Olives and small, white rounds of goat's-milk cheese ringed the meat.

"Thank you, gentlemen." Joss wrenched the carving knife from the roast, and a trickle of rich juices flowed forth.

Conversation was adjourned, by unanimous decree.

Generous helpings of meat and pie, along with second and third cups of Madeira, did much to improve the general mood. Seemingly gripped by holiday nostalgia, Wiggins prattled on and on about his children. During a particularly inane monologue on little Master Wiggins's affinity for his schoolmaster, Brackett pushed back from the table and excused himself to resume his watch on deck. Gray helped himself to more roast, taking the opportunity to slide an extra slice onto Miss Turner's plate.

She glanced up at him, her expression a mixture of shock and reproach.

And this was his reward for generosity.

He gave a tense shrug by way of excuse, then replaced

the knife and fork and busied himself with his own food. He felt her staring at him.

That was it. If she was entitled to stare at him, he was damned well going to stare back. And if this governess was going to reprimand him like an incorrigible charge . . . well, then Gray was going to misbehave.

Letting his silver clatter to the china, he balled his hands into fists and plunked them down on either side of his plate. "You say you miss your family, Miss Turner? I wonder at it."

Her glare was cold. "You do?"

"You told me in Gravesend you'd nowhere to turn."

"I spoke the truth." Her chin lifted. "I've been missing my family since long before I left England."

"So they're dead?"

She fidgeted with her fork. "Some."

"But not all?"

He leaned toward her and spoke in a low voice, though anyone who cared to listen might hear. "What sort of relations allow a young woman to cross an ocean unaccompanied, to labor as a plantation governess? I should think you'd be glad to be free of them."

She blinked.

He picked up his fork and jabbed at a hunk of meat. His voice a low murmur, he directed the next question at his plate. "Or perhaps they're glad to be free of you?"

Something crushed his foot under the table. A pointy-heeled boot. Then, just as quickly, the pressure eased. But her foot remained atop his. The gesture was infuriating, and somehow wildly erotic.

He met her gaze, and this time found no coldness, no reproach. Instead, her eyes were wide, beseeching. They called to something deep inside him he hadn't known was there.

Please, she mouthed. *Don't.*

She bit her lip, and he felt it as a visceral tug. That unused part of him stretched and ached. And at that instant, Gray would have sworn they were the only two souls in the room. In the world.

Until Wiggins spoke again, confound the man.

"How strange you must find it, Miss Turner," the second mate said, "celebrating the holiday in this tropical climate. Not a typical English Christmas, is it?"

Sophia cleared her throat. "No indeed." God bless Mr. Wiggins. She extricated herself from Mr. Grayson's enigmatic gaze and reached for her Madeira. Loath to field further questions of any variety, she passed the burden of conversation like a hot serving dish. "Would you agree, Captain Grayson?"

Beneath the table, she allowed her foot to slide back down to the floor. That was a mistake. In the next heartbeat, his boot clamped over hers like a trap.

Sophia kept her gaze trained on the captain. His thin black eyebrows rose. "I'm afraid I couldn't say, Miss Turner. All of my Christmases have been spent at sea, or on Tortola."

Sophia wriggled her foot madly, but it was no use. Mr. Grayson's Hessian pinned her nankeen half boot to the cabin floor. She shot him an angry glare, but he had taken a sudden interest in searching the depths of his Madeira.

"Yes, of course," Sophia replied to the captain. "Mr. Grayson," she said pointedly, hoping to draw the scoundrel's attention, "mentioned to me that your father owns a plantation there. What crop did you tell me your father raises, Mr. Grayson?"

He refused to look up. Shrugging, he set down his cup and began worrying his thumbnail. "I didn't tell you."

"Sugar," the captain answered. "It was a sugar plantation, Miss Turner, but our father died several years ago."

"Oh." Sophia forced herself to turn to the captain, though her gaze wanted to linger on Mr. Grayson's face, study the shadows that flickered there. "I'm sorry to hear it."

"Are you?" The words were a low, casual murmur. So faint, Sophia wondered if she'd imagined them. She looked around the table. If anyone else had heard the remark, they gave no sign.

Her foot stopped struggling beneath the weight of his boot, and the pressure eased. The contact remained.

"Who manages the property now?" She pushed an olive around her plate. "Have you an older brother, or a land agent?"

The two brothers exchanged a strange look.

"The land is no longer in the family," Captain Grayson said tersely. "It was sold."

"Oh. That must have been a difficult decision, to sell your boyhood home."

Captain Grayson rested one elbow on the table. "Once again, Miss Turner, I couldn't say. Was it, Gray?"

"Was it what?" Mr. Grayson clearly wished to evade the question. Sophia knew he'd been heeding the conversation, and she winced with discomfort as his leg tensed, crushing her toes once more.

"Pudding!" With his usual flourish, Stubb swept through the cabin door and added the dish to the table. As he uncovered the dome-shaped pudding, the aromas of figs and spices and brandy mingled with the familiar comfort of treacle-scented steam. A Christmas miracle, indeed. Sophia's mouth watered.

"The lady asked a question, Gray." The captain leaned forward, ignoring both Stubb and pudding. His voice took on a steely edge. "Was it a difficult decision, to sell our boyhood home? I've told her I couldn't say, seeing as how I wasn't involved in that decision. So the question falls to you. Was it difficult?"

Mr. Grayson clenched his jaw. His eyes narrowed as he regarded his brother. "No. It wasn't difficult in the least. It was the only profitable course."

The captain's mouth quirked in a humorless smile, and he sat back. "There's your answer, Miss Turner. Decisions never give my brother pause, so long as the profitable course is clear. He keeps his conscience in his bank account."

Sophia's gaze darted back and forth from brother to brother. The men warred silently, a battle of stony glares and firmed jaws and tight grips on silver. Then Mr. Grayson's posture suddenly relaxed, and, as Sophia had seen him do on so many occasions, he took the advantage with a roguish smile. Charm was always his weapon of choice.

"So that's why Gray's never married." Mr. Wiggins gave an easy chuckle. He leaned over the table to slice into the pudding, dispelling the tension between the brothers. "A rich man may keep his conscience in a vault, but we poor men have to marry ours."

Mr. Grayson made a show of smiling at the jest. But his grin faded, and for a moment Sophia saw what she had never before noticed, in those dozen occasions. It cost him something, that roguish smile. Behind it, he looked . . . weary. Empathy gripped her before she could push it away. She'd spent many evenings in many ballrooms, struggling under the weight of feigned levity. Fooling everyone but herself.

He looked up suddenly and caught her staring. Sophia blushed, feeling as though she'd walked in on him in his bath.

And that thought made her blush deeper still.

Mr. Wiggins rescued her again. "Without my wife, I wouldn't know what to do with myself. I can't even decide what color waistcoat to order at the tailor's." He gave Sophia a playful glance, his eyes merry with wine. "Do tell, Miss Turner, how is it such decisions come naturally to the fairer sex?"

Sophia smiled. "For you, Mr. Wiggins, the choice is clear. With your dark coloring, an ivory waistcoat would definitely suit you best."

The man beamed, tucking into his pudding. A trickle of brandy sauce dribbled down his lapel. Cursing, he dabbed it with his sleeve.

"But then, ivory does show stains most dreadfully." She looked down at her plate, testing the pudding's texture with her fork. "You see, sir, there are some of us for whom decisions are no trial. Living with those choices . . . now *that* is our burden." She gave Mr. Grayson a cautious glance.

His boot released hers, and Sophia felt oddly bereft. She wiggled her toes inside her stocking. After all that time, she worried they might never regain sensation.

She need not have been concerned. For Mr. Grayson did not retract his foot. He merely moved it to the floor, to rest alongside hers. And then he stretched his leg and slid that foot forward, so that the edge of his boot caressed her from toe to heel.

Oh, yes. Her sensation was intact. And not only in her toes. A hot tingling spread like flames throughout her body, and her heart began to bounce in her chest. Sophia froze, her fork poised in mid-air. She stared down at her plate, afraid he'd see the crimson staining her cheeks.

Then his ankle brushed hers. Her heart leapt into her throat. And before she knew what was happening, the warm weight of his calf was crooked around her own, his leg twining with hers in an intimate embrace. The posture instantly recalled their tussle with the shark—boots lashed together, bodies entangled, chests heaving with the exhilaration of escape.

Oh, and now Sophia blushed *everywhere*. Her lips, her nipples, the cleft between her legs—she felt every pink part of her body swelling and turning deep red.

"Is there something wrong with your pudding, Miss Turner?"

Curse the arrogant charm in his voice. Curse her body's response to it. She closed her eyes, then opened them. "No."

Teasing, teasing man. He'd rejected her once before; she'd be a fool to throw herself at him again. She ought to pull her leg away, Sophia told herself. Kick him in the shin; stab his thigh with her fork as though it were a slab of roast goat. But she didn't want to do any of those things. She wanted to sit like this for hours, letting his strong leg support her own. Feeling alive and exhilarated and desired . . . and not the slightest bit alone.

And beyond this dinner, this night, this secret embrace—Sophia wanted more. She wanted to be as close to him as she possibly, humanly could. She wanted *him*. This night was her chance, and this time she wasn't scared or uncertain or drunk on rum. This time, she wouldn't let him get away.

The decision was easy to make. Living with it would be another matter.

"No," she repeated boldly, looking up. No longer caring if he saw her wanton blush or noted her shallow breath or heard her wildly thumping pulse. His eyes issued a challenge, and she met it without blinking, trading him smile for smile. "Everything is quite to my liking."

CHAPTER
TWELVE

"What the hell was that?" Joss turned on him the moment Gabriel cleared the last of the china.

"What the hell was what?" Gray pulled a flask from his breast pocket and offered it to his brother.

Joss waved it away. "You know damn well what I mean. Something's going on between you and Miss Turner, I know it."

Gray uncapped the flask and took a sip. "What makes you say that?" He circled the table, discreetly examining the angle of the tablecloth and the perspective from the captain's chair. Surely Joss couldn't have seen what had taken place under the table. Even if his brother had noticed, he could demand all the answers he wished. Gray had no desire—or words—to explain it.

For the first time since he'd left England, Gray gave thanks for the thin, impractical leather of those dandified Hessians. The feel of her lithe, shapely leg against his . . . She'd accepted the contact so readily, blushed so attractively. Beneath that table, they'd formed some sort of alliance.

And then she had extended a clear verbal invitation.

If he went to her berth right now, she would be expecting him. At last, he could solve the mystery of what held together that damned striped frock. Or . . . he could simply rip it from her body.

Gray shoved the image aside before his groin could react further.

Joss did his bit to provide distraction. "How did she know about the plantation?"

"I told her in Gravesend, before we even set sail. The minute she mentioned Waltham."

They stared at each other.

"And on that topic," Gray continued, "what the hell was *that* about? Interrogating me about selling the land?"

"Miss Turner brought it up."

"You continued it. Why this resentment now, Joss? It's been almost eight years, and until M—" Gray bit off the end of that sentence. Joss didn't need another reminder of his wife's death. "Until recently, you never once complained. At the time, you told me you understood."

"At the time, I was nineteen years old."

"And I was three-and-twenty. Not precisely a man of the world. I did my best. I've done my best ever since. And if my best doesn't meet your high expectations, I don't know what to say. Except that it's no surprise."

"Don't play the martyr with me. You're the one who didn't keep his word. And speaking of your word and its dubious worth, don't change the subject. I saw the looks you and Miss Turner were exchanging. The lady goes bright pink every time you speak to her. For God's sake, you put food on her plate without even *asking*."

"And where's the crime in that?" Gray was genuinely curious to hear the answer. He hadn't forgotten that shocked look she'd given him.

"Come on, Gray. You know very well one doesn't take such a liberty with a mere acquaintance. It's . . . it's *intimate*. The two of you are intimate. Don't deny it."

"I do deny it. It isn't true." Gray took another swig from his flask and wiped his mouth with the back of his hand. "Damn it, Joss. Sooner or later, you're going to have to trust me. I gave you my word. I've kept it."

And it was the truth, Gray told himself. Yes, he'd touched her tonight, but he'd never pledged not to touch her. He had kept his word. He hadn't bedded her. He hadn't kissed her.

God, what he wouldn't give just to kiss her . . .

He rubbed the heel of his hand against his chest. That same ache lingered there—the same sharp tug he'd felt when she'd brought her foot down on his and pursed her lips into a silent plea. *Please,* she'd said. *Don't.* As if she appealed to his conscience.

His conscience. Where would the girl have gathered such a notion, that he possessed a conscience? Certainly not from his treatment of her.

A bitter laugh rumbled through his chest, and Joss shot him a skeptical look.

"Believe me, I've scarcely spoken to the girl in weeks. You can't know the lengths I've gone to, avoiding her. And it isn't easy, because she won't stay put in her cabin, now will she? No, she has to go all over the ship, flirting with the crew, tacking her little pictures in every corner of the boat, taking tea in the galley with Gabriel. I can't help but see her. And I can see she's too damn thin. She needs to eat; I put food on her plate. There's nothing more to it than that."

Joss said nothing, just stared at him as though he'd grown a second head.

"Damn it, what now? Don't you believe me?"

"I believe what you're saying," his brother said slowly. "I just can't believe what I'm hearing."

Gray folded his arms and leaned against the wall. "And what are you hearing?"

"I wondered why you'd done all this . . . the dinner. Now I know."

"You know what?" Gray was growing exasperated. Most of all, because *he* didn't know.

"You care for this girl." Joss cocked his head. "You care for her. Don't you?"

"*Care* for her."

Joss's expression was smug. "Don't you?"

The idea was too preposterous to entertain, but Gray perked with inspiration. "Say I did care for her. Would you release me from that promise? If my answer is yes, can I pursue her?"

Joss shook his head. "If the answer is yes, you can—and should—wait one more week. It's not as though she'll vanish the moment we make harbor. If the answer is yes, you'll agree she deserves that much."

Wrong, Gray thought, sinking back into a chair. Regardless of the answer, he knew she deserved far better. Damn it, he couldn't even enjoy the fantasy of destroying that striped frock. Because he knew she'd only one other to wear, and he'd be too concerned over whether she possessed the needle and thread to mend it. Because the pattern might never match up right again; the stripes would be off, and the effect would be a bit less lovely than before. Because he would have taken something from her, destroyed something beautiful and perfect . . . and never again would she look at him with those clear, trusting eyes and tug on his heart.

Please. Don't.

Gray punched his thigh. This was why when he took a fancy to a woman, he pursued her, sampled her, and moved on. Becoming acquainted first ruined everything.

Agitated, he hooked a finger under his neck cloth and pulled it loose. "Care for her," he muttered. "How could that be possible? I've scarcely gone near the woman in weeks."

"I don't know how it's possible, but it seems to be

true. In fact, I think you're half in love with her. More than half, perhaps."

Rising from his chair, Gray straightened to his full height. "Now wait. I'm half out of my mind with lust, I'll grant you that. More than half, perhaps. But I'm certainly not in love with that girl. Don't forget who you're talking to, Joss. I keep my conscience in my bank account, remember? I don't even know what love looks like."

Joss paused over his desk. "I know what love looks like. Using up all those Portuguese goods on one meal, killing a valuable goat, bringing out porcelain from the cargo hold . . . Crack one plate, and you'd lose half the set's price. Serving meat onto a lady's plate." He shrugged. "Love looks something like that."

Gray ran his hands through his hair, shaking off the lunatic notion before it could take root in his brain. "I'm telling you, I'm not in love. I'm just too damned bored. I've nothing to do on this voyage but plan dinner parties. And it's about to get worse. No chance of cracking a plate tonight." He jerked his chin at the lamp dangling from a hook, which on any normal night would have been swaying in time with the waves. "If you hadn't noticed, we're becalmed."

"I'd noticed." Joss grimaced and motioned for the flask. Gray tossed it to him. "Good thing we've given the men a fine meal and grog tonight. Becalming's never good for the crew's morale."

"Not good for the investor's morale, either." Gray rubbed his temples. "Let's hope it doesn't last."

The calm lasted for days. For all of Christmas Day, and all of Boxing Day, too. The idleness that began as a welcome holiday quickly became a hardship to all aboard the *Aphrodite*. By the third morning, the same men who'd spent Christmas singing and joking were sniping at one another and grumbling under their breath at every order. Without wind, there was little for them to do but mend the rigging and scrape the chains. Men's equivalent of needlework, Sophia mused, eyeing the foot-long marlinespikes the sailors used to reeve and splice the lines. The crew had her sympathy. She'd always detested needlework.

The sky was cloudless, the air was listless, the men were restless. And above all, it was hot. Hotter than Sophia could ever have dreamed. The tropical air smothered her like a thick, woolen blanket.

With no breeze, the cabin became an oven. Sophia had no intention of staying inside. The men rigged an unused sail into a canopy, and she sat on a crate beneath it, fanning herself with her drawing board and sketching from time to time. Watching the mast's shadow crawl across the dock. Sitting absolutely, perfectly still.

Mr. Grayson, by contrast, was in constant motion. He roamed between hold and deck, fore and aft, seemingly the most restless man aboard. Sophia hadn't known what to expect, after their furtive exchange beneath the dinner table. She'd lain awake half that night, counting the bells that marked each half-hour. At first, sensual excitement clanged through her with each sharp ring. As hours passed, the buzzing pulses turned to pangs of trepidation. Then, as night gave way to morning, hollow disappointment reigned. Capricious, teasing man. Why hadn't he come? Surely he couldn't have desired any clearer invitation.

But he hadn't appeared that night. Not the next morning, either. By the time she finally crossed paths with him the following afternoon, his mumbled "Merry Christmas" was the extent of their exchange.

It seemed they were back to silence.

I don't want you.

She tried to ignore the words echoing in her memory. They weren't true, she told herself. She was an expert at deceit; she knew a lie when she heard one.

Still. What else to believe, when he avoided her thus?

Although he rarely spoke *to* her over the next two days, Sophia frequently overheard him speaking *of* her. Even these remarks were the tersest of commands: "Fetch Miss Turner more water," or "See that her canopy doesn't go slack." She felt herself being tended, not unlike a goat. Fed, watered, sheltered. Perhaps she shouldn't complain. Food, water, and shelter were all welcome things.

But Sophia was not livestock, and she had other, more profound needs. Needs he seemed intent on neglecting, the infuriating man.

On their third morning of calm, Captain Grayson ordered the crew to put in the longboat. This order was met by loud grumbles and curses among the sailors.

"What is it?" Sophia asked as O'Shea stomped past.

"The captain's ordering us to go out in the longboat and tow the ship. He's hoping if we move around, we'll find some wind. But rowing in this heat . . ." The big Irishman squinted and wiped his brow with his forearm. "It'll be a bitch."

O'Shea walked off without even apologizing for his language. Sophia couldn't blame him. She would be cursing, too, if she had to perform hard physical labor under this blistering sun.

The men took three shifts, each with one officer and four men out in the longboat, rowing with all their might for an hour to make little discernible progress. Sophia watched with sympathy, but also with fascination. While out on the longboat, the men removed their shirts, and she took the opportunity to make discreet sketches. Even from a distance, she could plainly see their cord-like muscles, their vivid scars and exotic tattoos. These men were a far cry from the languid Greek marbles she'd been taught to copy. They were imperfect, perspiring, striving, and most of all, *real*.

But soon the heat swamped even this diversion, as the pencil slipped from Sophia's sweaty grasp and rolled away.

Drat.

She couldn't be bothered to chase it.

One hour blurred into another after that. The men continued through their rotations, one crew rowing, the other overhauling rigging, the third at rest. Mr. Grayson had disappeared belowdecks.

Davy Linnet walked past, and Sophia perked. "Good afternoon, Davy," she said, smiling. Ever since the Tropic crossing, she'd made an extra effort to favor Davy in front of his crewmates. Even in this sweltering heat, courage deserved its reward.

"Good afternoon, Miss Turner." He ducked his head to hide a shy grin.

"You're looking very well, Davy. I'd wager you've gained a stone since we left England. They won't be able to call you 'boy' much longer." She tilted her head in coquettish fashion. "Do they have you in the forecastle yet?"

He shook his head and scratched the back of his neck. "Still have a lot to learn, miss. I'll make it there soon."

"I'm certain you will." She smiled again, and the lad blushed. Sophia knew how much he craved admittance to the forecastle, where all the sailors bedded down. He'd been sleeping in steerage since the voyage began, and there he would remain until he'd proven himself, in both ability and character.

"Man aloft to splice the fore topgallant lift!"

From around the foremast, Quinn grumbled and began moving toward the ratlines.

"I'll do it." Davy dodged in front of the sailor, throwing him off balance.

Quinn gritted his teeth, but profanity flowed freely through the gaps. "Out of my way, boy, or I'll throw you to the sharks."

"I said, I'll do it." Davy held out a hand. "Lend me your marlinespike."

Quinn gave him a skeptical look. "This is sailor's work, boy. Have you spliced a cable before?"

"I've practiced on deck."

The older man harrumphed and elbowed the boy aside.

With a glance in Sophia's direction, Davy stepped in front of him again. He stood undeterred even when Quinn puffed his chest and drew up to full height, a full head taller than the youth.

"Let me do it," Davy insisted. "How can I learn if you don't give me a chance to try?"

Quinn paused, staring up at the mast. Then he wiped his brow and looked back at the boy. "If you want to climb up there in this heat, I won't stop you." He unknotted the marlinespike from his belt and slapped the needle into Davy's outstretched palm. "Don't cock it up, or I'll gut you myself."

With those words of encouragement, Davy sprang into the rigging. She watched his ascent for a while, and then he climbed out of her sight, behind the canopy. Sophia decided her loyalty to Davy did not extend that far, as to wilt and freckle in the tropical sun while he repaired a bit of rope. She would conserve her energy for congratulating him once he finished.

She waited, chin propped in her hands. Her eyelids grew heavy. She was drifting . . . drifting . . .

Thwack.

The sharp noise jolted her awake.

"Ho, there! Get down here, boy!" She recognized Mr. Brackett's harsh bark.

Sophia scrambled out from under the canopy. The crew gathered around the foremast, watching in ominous silence as Davy slowly descended the ratlines. At the center of the scattered group stood Mr. Brackett, hands planted on either hip, and legs braced wide in an attitude of imminent threat.

"Ahoy! All hands!"

She shook herself, trying to dispel the drowsy haze from her brain. What could Davy have done that would warrant this assembly, resembling nothing so much as a shipboard trial, with Mr. Brackett looking like judge and executioner in one?

Then she saw it, sticking out of the deck like a giant's dart—the marlinespike driven straight into the planks. That must have been the loud thwack she'd heard. Davy had dropped it from the topgallant yard. If it had struck a man . . . Despite the heat, Sophia shivered. It was a miracle no one on deck had been killed.

She might have counted their blessings too soon.

As Davy finally reached the deck, Mr. Brackett's expression spelled quiet murder. He walked over to the offending sliver of iron, planted a boot on the board it had pierced, grasped the spike with both hands, and pulled it free with one swift yank. He brandished it before Davy, jabbing the point into the center of the boy's chest. "Careless, Linnet. Very careless."

The boy stood a bit taller, but Sophia noticed his left knee begin to shake.

"I'm sorry, sir. My hand was sweaty. It just slipped. It won't happen again, sir." Davy's voice cracked as he spoke.

"I'd like to believe that, Linnet. But I think I'd better teach you a lesson. Just to be certain."

Teach him a lesson? What could the man mean? Sophia scanned the deck. The captain was out in the longboat. Mr. Wiggins was presumably belowdecks, resting. For the moment, the ship was Mr. Brackett's to command.

And Sophia could tell, he wasn't about to let the men forget it.

The air and the water were so calm, so still, that every word echoed off the decking, as though it were a stage. And Brackett definitely had an air for the theatrical. He circled the men, turning his hawkish glare from one sailor to the next, letting his boots clunk ominously with each slow step. He held his audience rapt.

"This crew is the most indolent band of curs I've ever seen. I've been itching to give you men a taste of real discipline." Brackett turned to Davy. "Do you really mean to be a sailor, boy? Do you think you have what it takes?"

Davy nodded, once.

"Well, you can't handle a marlinespike, can you? But perhaps you can handle a taste of the lash."

Sophia leapt forward. "No!"

Mr. Brackett turned to her. "Miss Turner, this isn't a fit spectacle for ladies. You ought to return to your cabin."

"No. You can't do this. I won't allow it."

The moment the words escaped her throat, Sophia knew she'd made a grave mistake. If Davy had any hope of leniency, she'd just erased it. Brackett's black eyes pinned her, as dark and unyielding as obsidian. He would never back down now. To spare Davy at her behest would be tantamount to surrendering authority in front of his crew. Unthinkable.

"I apologize for offending your genteel sensibilities,

Miss Turner. Justice can be an ugly business. Now, I advise you to go belowdecks."

"Go on, Miss Turner," Davy said. "I've had my share of beatings. It's nothing I haven't felt before."

And of course he didn't want her to see, the brave boy. Sophia cast him an apologetic look. Then she firmed her chin and spoke to Brackett. "Thank you, I will stay. If you can perform this atrocity, you can perform it in front of me." Perhaps the man would go lightly on Davy with her here. Or maybe she could swoon at a fortuitous moment and put a stop to it altogether.

"If you wish." Brackett turned on his heel, swinging the marlinespike around like a compass needle, ultimately selecting Quinn as its true north. "You there. String Linnet up to the yardarm."

Muffled curses rose up from the assembled crew. Quinn shifted his weight uneasily. Brackett swung 'round again, making another swiping threat with the marlinespike, and losing his hat in the process. The men dropped back in silence.

The sweat on Sophia's neck went cold.

"Remove your shirt, Linnet." When the boy simply stood in place, Brackett hooked the tip of the marlinespike into Davy's collar and yanked, ripping the coarse tunic from neck to waist. Then he reached out with his free hand to tear the shirt away from the youth's torso, exposing a smooth, pale chest.

Brackett rested the marlinespike on his shoulder like a dueling pistol and turned to Quinn. "String. Him. Up."

Quinn did not move. Braced in a wide stance, arms crossed over his chest, he was a towering mountain of muscle. And he received Brackett's command with all the stony indifference of a mountain that had just been ordered to jump. *Make me*, his gaze said. *I'd like to see you try.*

Sophia wanted to believe the man felt some allegiance to Davy, but she suspected the heat factored strongly in his defiance. If Quinn hadn't wanted to climb the mast ten minutes ago, he could hardly relish the idea of hauling a boy up with him now.

Mr. Brackett did not seem angered by Quinn's mute refusal. Instead, Sophia thought he looked oddly gratified. His face lit with a smug, expectant grin. "Do you disobey a direct order then, Quinn?"

Quinn did not move.

"Insubordination," said Brackett, circling Quinn slowly, "is a serious infraction. I advise you to reconsider. I'll say it but one more time, Quinn." Brackett punctuated each word with a jab to the sailor's chest. "String. Him. Up."

Quinn shrugged off the spike, as a horse twitches its flank to dislodge a fly.

Brackett sneered, sweat trickling off his brow. His black hair was soaked with perspiration, matted to his scalp like raven feathers. Whether it was the heat, the power of command, or both—this scene had unleashed something dark in the man. Something terrifying. His eyes were wild, and he wielded the marlinespike like one of the devil's own tormentors.

"I was going to make an example of the boy there, but now I think you"—he jabbed Quinn again—"will make a better example by far."

With sudden, agile fury, Brackett swung the heavy iron spike and hit Quinn square in the back of his knee. The man's leg crumpled beneath him, and he dropped to the deck with a heavy thud.

Sophia clapped a hand over her scream.

Quinn groaned and rolled to his knees. Brackett twirled the marlinespike in his hand and hammered him between the shoulder blades with the blunt end, sprawling him face-first onto the deck. Before the sailor could recover from the blow, Brackett had his boot planted on the man's neck, holding him down.

The assembled crew stood frozen, the men glancing frantically from one to another. Sophia understood their hesitation. Even if their captain would not countenance such violence—and Sophia felt certain he wouldn't—to overpower Brackett would be mutiny.

Quinn struggled to rise. Brackett crushed his heel down on the man's neck, stifling all protest.

Sophia glanced toward the ship's prow. It was impossible to see the longboat from here. If only she could make some sort of signal . . . or call out to the captain.

"Fetch me the lash," Brackett ordered, pointing the marlinespike at Davy. "And be quick about it, or I'll double your strokes."

Sophia didn't wait for Davy's response. She turned on her heel and bolted down the stairs belowdecks, racing through the ladies' cabin and passing into steerage.

"Mr. Grayson!" She wove through the jumbled crates. He would make everything all right, she knew it. He had to. "Mr. Grayson! Gray!"

A hand snagged her elbow.

"Come to me at last, have you?"

It was stifling hot in the compartment, and Sophia was overwrought. At the sound of his sleepy baritone and the reassuring feel of his hand on her skin, she nearly melted. He leaned against the stacked crates, rubbing sleep from his eyes with his sleeve. "What is it, sweet?"

"Come quickly," she said, removing his hand from her elbow and tugging him back toward the stairs.

At the frantic tremor in her voice, he snapped into seriousness. She yanked on his arm, but he did not move. "What is it?" he repeated, his eyes searching hers.

"It's Davy. And Quinn . . . he's going to flog them."

"Who?"

"Mr. Brackett."

With a muttered curse, he shook off her grip and charged past her, making his way through the ladies' cabin and taking the ladder three rungs at a time. Sophia hurried behind him.

"What the devil is going on here?" Mr. Grayson demanded.

The scene looked much as Sophia had left it. Was it possible only a minute had passed? Brackett still held Quinn under his boot, at the point of the marlinespike. Around him, the crewmen stood in a half-circle, sweat streaming from their brows under the midday sun. At the sight of Mr. Grayson, they visibly relaxed. The only one missing was Davy.

"Ah, Mr. Grayson. Good afternoon." Mr. Brackett greeted him calmly, his eyes hard as stone.

"Where's the boy?"

"I've sent him to fetch the lash. This one"—he shifted his weight to Quinn's neck—"needs to learn who his superiors are."

"There's no lash on this ship, Brackett. I don't permit flogging. Never have."

Brackett smirked. "Small wonder, then, that your crew is so worthless. They're well overdue for their dose of discipline. And if you've no lash . . . well, I'm certain something can be improvised."

"Ahoy!" The call came from the front of the ship. The longboat had returned. A few of the sailors began backing away from the scene, toward the prow. They looked toward Mr. Grayson for permission, and he dismissed them with a nod.

"That'll be your captain, Brackett. You may stand down."

Mr. Grayson's voice remained so calm, so authoritative; his posture was relaxed. His coat and trousers hung haphazardly from his frame, in contrast to Mr. Brackett's orderly rows of buttons, glaring in the sun. He was unarmed, unkempt, unruffled. Yet there was no doubt in anyone's mind who had the upper hand. Once again, Mr. Grayson had assumed command of a scene without even breaking a sweat.

Meanwhile, Sophia trembled so violently, her ribs rattled against her stays. She felt an arm take her elbow, steadying it. Swiveling her head, she found Stubb standing beside her.

"The boy's below," he whispered. "When he come looking for the lash, I told him to stay out of sight."

Sophia swallowed and nodded.

Mr. Grayson crossed his arms over his chest. "Stand down, Brackett. If there's discipline to be meted out, the captain will handle it."

Brackett removed his boot from Quinn's neck, only to give him a swift kick in the ribs. The sailor groaned at his feet, and the officer's mouth twisted in a sick smile. "I'm first mate. I don't work for the captain. I work for you."

Mr. Grayson's eyes hardened. "Not any longer, you don't."

The captain strode across the deck, wiping his brow before replacing his hat. Four sailors followed him, still shirtless from their stint in the longboat.

"What's going on? We heard a commotion." The captain spied Quinn groaning in pain on the deck and knelt beside him. "Good God. He didn't fall from the rigging?"

"No." Mr. Grayson nodded toward Brackett. "Captain Grayson, you should know that Mr. Brackett has been relieved of his duties as first mate of the *Aphrodite,* effective immediately. How you accommodate his presence on this ship for the remainder of the voyage is yours to decide. I recommend the brig."

"I see." Joss looked around at the assembled sailors, his demeanor suddenly grave. He rose to his feet, pulling his cuffs straight. "Stubb, tend to Quinn." He turned to the shirtless sailors. "Levi, O'Shea. Show Mr. Brackett his new quarters in the brig. Gray—" He tilted his head toward Sophia. "Get her belowdecks. And keep her there."

Mr. Grayson nodded.

Levi and O'Shea took the snarling Brackett between them, one on either arm, and together they herded him down into the hold. As they passed, Sophia gasped. Levi's back was a gnarled mass of healed scars, braided one over the other in the middle, branching out toward both shoulders. She wondered, were they the result of his permanent silence, or the cause?

"Come, sweetheart. You need to rest." Mr. Grayson's hand pressed against the small of her back.

Sophia shook her head. She couldn't tear her eyes away from the horror that was Levi's back. Not until he disappeared belowdecks. "I thought you said you don't permit flogging."

"I don't. That's why."

CHAPTER
THIRTEEN

Miss Turner went limp in his arms. Gray thought for a moment she'd swooned. But when he looked down at her, he found only thick-fringed eyes gazing back up at him, swimming with confusion and unshed tears. She hadn't fainted at all. She'd simply fallen against him and trusted him to catch her.

Behind him, Joss barked orders to the crew, and to Mr. Wiggins, now first mate. The men scurried back to their stations. Still, the two of them stood there, her back pressing flat and warm against his chest. Gray wrapped his arms about her and steered her toward the companionway. Shoring up her slender frame with an arm about her waist, he guided Miss Turner down the stairs and into the ladies' cabin.

And then came the moment to ease her into a chair. But he found he didn't want to release her. She fit so perfectly against him, and he suddenly allowed himself to feel how very much he'd been yearning to do exactly this. Hold her close. Hold her tight. Not let go.

Together they leaned against the doorframe. One of them was shaking, and Gray worried it might be him.

She leaned her head against his arm. "I knew you'd put a stop to it. I tried, but I only made matters worse. But I knew they'd listen to you. They all listen to you. And I knew you'd never allow such a thing to continue."

Good Lord, Gray thought. Here he held this woman

in his arms while she made him out to be some sort of . . . not a saint, exactly, but a man possessing a shred of honor. And all the while she trembled against his body, soft and damp and warm, never suspecting the dozens of ways in which he longed to dishonor them both.

Would she still allow him to hold her like this, encircled in his arms, her backside pressed against his swelling groin, if she could read his thoughts? If she knew that when she tilted her head to bury her face in his sleeve, she gave him a direct view of the alabaster curve of her neck, the carved ivory of her collarbone, and the exquisite image that would haunt his dreams—the soft, rose-scented valley between her breasts?

God, what a lecherous bastard he was.

He'd been ashamed of many things in his life, but never before had he felt so ashamed simply to be a *man*, a part of this violent, brutish race of creatures who flogged one another, beat helpless boys with marline-spikes, and lusted after unsuspecting governesses while they were overset with emotion. This woman was bred for better things, deserved better things. Better than this ship, this life. Better than a base, craving creature like him.

"You should sit down." He brought his hands to her shoulders and guided her to a chair.

She sank into it slowly, folding her hands on the table in front of her. Well, and now what? He certainly couldn't leave her alone in this state. Her eyes were dark hollows in an ashen face; her lips quivered.

Gray paced the cabin. He couldn't comfort her without mauling her. He couldn't go abovedecks and put his crew to rights, because they weren't his crew to command.

Impotent. He'd been rendered impotent, in more ways

than one. Gray nearly laughed with the realization. It was not a sensation he'd ever thought to experience, in any sense of the word. Coupled with this heat . . . he would go mad with frustration. He rubbed his hand under his collar, then made a fist and punched the wall.

"What will happen to Mr. Brackett?" Her voice was flat, remote.

"He'll stay in the ship's brig until we dock."

She gave him a blank look.

"It's a jail," he explained. "More of a cage, really. Down in the hold."

"A *cage*? How horrible."

"It's for his own safety, as much as anything. What he did . . . it wasn't any worse than what officers on other ships do every day. But now that he's no longer an officer, the sailors might be tempted to exact revenge."

"Why did you dismiss him from duty, then? Why not let him remain an officer until we reach Tortola?"

"Even if Brackett's actions *had* been justified, I couldn't have kept him in the post. He's lost all authority with the crew now. My interference assured that."

"It's all my fault." Her voice shrank. "I'm so sorry."

"*No.*" She jumped, and Gray bit the inside of his cheek. *Bloody hell.* Hadn't she seen enough coarseness today, without him losing all sense of civility? He forced his emotions back down to a simmer. "Don't be sorry. You were right to help. You were right to fetch me."

She relaxed, and Gray resumed prowling the cabin. "What the devil was Davy doing up there with a marlinespike? That's what I'd like to know. It's a sailor's duty."

She put her head in her hands. "I'm afraid that's my fault, too. I'd been talking to him about moving up to the forecastle, and I . . . I think he wanted to impress me."

Gray choked on a laugh. "Well, of course he did. You ought to take care how you bat those eyelashes, sweetheart. One of these days, you're likely to knock a man overboard."

The legs of her chair scraped the floor as she stood. The color returned to her cheeks. "If Davy was trying to impress me, it's as much your fault as mine."

"How is that *my* fault?" Gray's frustration came right back to a boil. He hated himself for growling at her, but he couldn't seem to help it.

"You're the one who humiliated him in front of the crew, with all those questions. You goaded him into saying he . . . well, you know what he said."

"Yes, I know what he said." Gray stepped toward her until only the table separated them. "I know what he said. And don't pretend you didn't enjoy it. Don't pretend you don't use those men to feed your vanity."

"My vanity? What would you know about feeding my vanity? You don't so much as breathe in my direction. At least the sailors speak to me. And if that entire 'King of the Sea' display wasn't one long exercise in feeding your own vanity, I'm sure I don't know what is." She jabbed one finger on the tabletop and lowered her voice. "Those men may flirt with me, but they worship you. You know it. You wanted to feel it. Bask in it. And you did so at Davy's expense."

"At least I only teased the boy. I'm not the one poised to break his heart."

She blinked. "It's only infatuation. He's not really in love with me."

He pounded the table. "Of course the boy's in love with you! They all are. You talk to them, you *listen* to their stories—even Wiggins's prattling, God only knows why. You draw them little sketches, you make them paintings for Christmas. You remind them of everything they've left behind, everything they pray they'll one day hold again. And you do it all looking like some sort of Botticelli goddess, surely the most beautiful thing they've ever laid eyes on. Damn it, how's a man to *keep* from falling in love with you?"

Silence.

She stared at him.

She blinked.

Her lips parted, and she drew a quick breath.

Say something, Gray silently pleaded. *Anything.* But she only stared at him. What the hell had he just said? Was it truly that bad? He frowned, reliving the past minute in his mind.

Oh, God. Gray rubbed his face with one hand, then gave a sharp tug on his hair. It was that bad. *Damn it to hell.* If Joss were here, he'd have a good laugh at his expense.

"Have you . . ."

"Have I what?" Gray prompted, promptly kicking himself for doing so. God only knew what she'd ask now. Or what damn fool thing he'd say in response.

"Have you ever seen a Botticelli? Painting, I mean. A real one, in person?"

The breath he'd been holding whooshed out of him. "Yes."

"Oh." She bit her lip. "What was it like?"

"I . . ." His hand gestured uselessly. "I haven't words to describe it."

"Try."

Her eyes were too clear, too piercing. He swallowed and shifted his gaze to a damp lock of hair curling at her temple. "Perfect. Luminous. So beautiful, your chest aches. And so smooth, like glass. Your fingers itch to touch it."

"But you can't."

"No," he said quietly, his gaze sliding back to meet hers. "It isn't allowed."

"And you care what others will allow?" She took a step toward him, her fingers trailing along the grooved tabletop. "What if you were alone, and there was no one to see? Would you touch it then?"

Gray shook his head and dropped his gaze to his hands. "It's not . . ." He paused, picking over his words like fruits in an island market. Testing and discarding twice as many as he chose. "There's a varnish, you see. Some sort of gloss. If I touched it with these rough hands, I'd mar it somehow. Make it a bit less beautiful. Couldn't live with myself then."

"So—" She leaned one hip against the table's edge, making her whole body one sinuous, sweeping curve. Gray sucked in a lungful of heat. "It isn't the rules that prevent you."

"Not really. No."

Silence again. Vast and echoing, like the long, marble-tiled galleries of the Uffizi.

And then, at last: "It's still your fault."

"What is?"

"Everything. Davy. Of course he wants to prove himself now. How did you expect him to react, asking him all of those questions? Grilling him in front of all the crew, in front of me?" She wilted into the chair. "You should have known better. You should have *done* better."

There she went again, appealing to his hypothetical sense of honor. Pulling at her neckline as she did it, sending jolts of desire straight to his groin. Confirming he'd no true honor at all.

"I mean, how would you feel, your whole life exposed like that in front of all those men?"

"The men respect me because they know I've been

through it, too. Just like all of them received the same treatment once. No secrets between sailors, Miss Turner. Unlike some"—he threw her a glance—"I've nothing to hide."

"Is that so?" Her gaze sharpened.

Gray nodded.

"Well, then. What is your name?"

He crossed his arms over his chest. So this was her game, was it? Very well. If she wished to question him, he would answer. She was free to learn every vile, brutish thing about him. That would teach her to appeal to some imaginary sense of decency. "Benedict Adolphus Percival Grayson. The same as my father's."

"I thought you said there was only one woman permitted to address you by your Christian name."

"And it's still the truth. Don't get excited, sweetheart. I've not given you leave to use it. You may, however, call me Gray." *Please,* he added silently.

She shook her head. "What is your age, Mr. Grayson?"

"I am two-and-thirty this coming year. Miss Turner."

"From whence do you hail?"

Gray eased back in his chair. "I was born and raised on Tortola, as you know. The Grayson family tree is rooted in Wiltshire. My grandfather was a gentleman of some standing, and my father was his typically wayward second son. For his sins, which were legion, my father was exiled to Clarendon—that was the name of our plantation—to mend his dissolute ways."

"And did he?"

"What do you think?" He reclined in his seat, propping one boot on the table between them.

A smile tugged at her lips. "How many siblings have you, Mr. Grayson?"

"In truth, I could not say. My father's acknowledged children number three. I have one brother, whom you have met, and one sister, whom you have not. We are all of different mothers. So to answer your earlier question, it would seem the West Indies proved an ineffective remedy for dissolution." He watched her for signs of shock or displeasure. Her brow, however, remained as placid as this godforsaken sea.

"I know your father is . . ."

"Dead."

She cleared her throat. "Yes, dead. Is your mother still living?"

"No. She died when I was an infant. I've no memory of her at all."

A single crease scored her forehead. "I'm sorry."

"Are you?"

The words simply rolled off his tongue, uttered with no particular inflection or intent. But Miss Turner snapped to attention. Gray fought the urge to fidget under her scrutiny.

"Yes," she said, a note of defiance in her voice. "I am sorry. It's a tragic thing, to have no memory of your mother."

Gray shrugged. "Better than having some memory of her, and feeling the pain of the loss."

"Do you truly believe it's better?"

He frowned and tugged at his ear.

"I didn't think so."

Gray put a hand on the armrest and shifted his weight. Perhaps allowing this interrogation hadn't been such a brilliant idea after all. Miss Turner was supposed to be the one growing uncomfortable, not him.

"Brown or white?" She propped her chin in one hand and stared at him.

"Excuse me?"

"Bread, Mr. Grayson. Given a choice, do you take brown bread or white?"

He chuckled. "Brown, if there's butter. If not, white."

"Ale or grog?"

"Ale. Chased with brandy." *Not a bad idea,* he thought, reaching into his coat for his flask. He unscrewed the cap and lifted it to his lips.

"Have you ever stolen anything, Mr. Grayson?"

He froze, looking at her over the flask. With deliberate slowness, he tipped it back until the fiery liquor spread down his throat. Then he wiped his mouth, recapped the flask, and replaced it carefully in his breast pocket. "Of course."

She tilted her head and raised one eyebrow, inviting him to elaborate.

"Where shall I begin? With the typical childhood petty thievery? Pineapples, chickens, my father's stickpin . . . I could go on for several minutes there. Shall I detail for you all the dozens of ships I've boarded, the boatloads of precious cargo I've seized? Privateering is sanctioned thievery, perhaps, but theft nonetheless." He drummed one finger lightly on the tabletop. "I've made stealing a way of life, Miss Turner. I could go on about it for hours. How much elaboration do you care to hear?"

She paused a moment, considering. "You're not ashamed to own to it, then. Your thievery."

"In most cases, no. I'm not."

"Then in some cases, you are? What is it you're ashamed of stealing, Mr. Grayson?"

Gray wrestled with her clear, unwavering gaze. Dare he make the confession? It would serve his purpose well, expose him for the blackguard he was. The girl ought to know just what sort of man she regarded. Then maybe she'd cease looking at him with those trusting eyes, expecting things of him she had no right to expect. Expecting things he had no way or means of giving.

Dropping his gaze to the floor, he rubbed a thumb

across his lower lip. "I stole my brother's inheritance." His own voice sounded strange, oddly hollow. His whole body felt oddly hollow. "Twice."

"Well," she said. He glanced up to find that her expression held not disdain or shock, as he might have expected. As such an admission deserved. Rather, she looked intrigued.

"The pineapples and chickens, the dozens of ships . . ." She traced a groove in the tabletop with her finger. "All these I can easily imagine. But stealing an inheritance . . . twice? However did you manage that?"

"It's a long story."

"I've no pressing engagements."

"I was in England, on break from Oxford, summering in Wiltshire at my grandfather's estate. We received word that my father had died. My grandfather took the news hard. I think the old man always held out hope that his prodigal son would one day make good, return to the fold. When that hope was extinguished . . ." Gray cleared his throat. "He suffered an apoplexy within the week and never recovered."

She made a small, crooning noise in the back of her throat. "You lost your father and your grandfather in the space of one week?"

"No. My father had already been dead for two months."

"Yes, but still. You'd only just learned of it." She hugged herself.

Gray frowned as she stroked her shoulder, inflaming his own long-buried hurt even as she soothed herself. Damn it, she was supposed to be reviling him, not pitying him. And certainly not sympathizing with him. "Do you want me to finish the story or not?"

"I'm sorry. Go on."

He spoke briskly now, as if conducting a business

transaction. "My grandfather left Clarendon to my father. In the event my father was no longer living, the lands were to be divided between my father's male children."

"You and Captain Grayson."

"Yes." He leaned forward over the table. "But you see, sweetheart, they didn't know about Joss. I gather my father neglected to mention his half-African by-blow in his annual estate report. The solicitors had no idea."

"But if he's illegitimate . . . Would he have stood to inherit at all?"

He turned his hand palm side up and studied the blunt, clipped edges of his fingernails. "Perhaps not. No way to tell without explaining matters to the executors."

"And you didn't." Her eyes turned from curious to piercing. "You accepted the lands, and then you sold them. Without asking your brother."

Gray nodded.

"Did you divide the proceeds with him, after the fact?"

"No. I bought this ship and had it fitted for privateering. It was all in my name, but I promised him we would split the proceeds after the war."

"And did you?"

Gray shook his head. "No. I gave him what share he earned as first mate, and not a penny more. I took the rest, bought a house in London, and started Grayson Shipping."

"Grayson Shipping," she repeated. "Not Grayson Brothers Shipping."

"Grayson Shipping. The ships, the investment, the risks, the profit—it's all mine. I am my brother's employer, not his partner."

"My goodness." She sat back in her chair, still regarding him intently. "Yes, I think you are rightly ashamed."

And there it was. The prim face of censure he'd been seeking. A strange sense of satisfaction descended on him. Divine justice, perhaps. Other men, better men, confessed their sins to priests and saints, but Gray had chosen for his confessor this governess. The most beautiful woman he'd ever set eyes on, in all his years of chasing pleasure from one horizon to the next. The only woman to stir this desperate yearning in his breast. And this was his penance—to watch her shrink back into her chair, to see those clear eyes glaze with mistrust as she at last recognized him for the devil he was.

Yes, this was his due. And she wasn't finished yet, his petite, austere inquisitor. No, there was so much sin yet to be revealed.

"Go on, then," he prompted.

She gave him a quizzical look.

"Conclude the interrogation, sweetheart. You've more questions to ask."

She stared hard into a corner of the cabin. "Are you married, Mr. Grayson?"

"No. I'm not the marrying sort."

"Have you had many sw—" She paused. "Many sweethearts, then?"

"Yes. Many."

She winced, almost imperceptibly, but he felt it like a flick of the lash. Still, she turned to meet his eyes again. Brave girl.

Ask it, he urged silently. *Make the confession complete.*

"And how many lovers, Mr. Grayson?"

CHAPTER
FOURTEEN

"I couldn't say."

"I'm afraid that answer's not an option." Sophia smiled and rapped the table with her fist, grateful for the chance to tease. "Truth or eels, Mr. Grayson."

He did not smile back. "I tell you most truthfully, Miss Turner—I couldn't say. I lost count years ago. It's been fifteen years since I tumbled my first tavern wench. And in those fifteen years, I've traveled three seas and four continents, sampling the ladies in every port. If it's a number you require, then you count them. I can't."

Sophia blinked, waiting for that devilish, teasing grin to appear. But it didn't. He wasn't teasing at all.

She hadn't been under any illusions that he led a life of chastity. But for a shrewd tradesman, who lived his life by numbers and amounts, to lose count . . . the actual number must be great indeed. The man sitting across the table from her had bedded countless women, from every corner of the globe. The thought repulsed her and, in some shameful way, thrilled her. But most of all, it disappointed her. Regret stung her somewhere between the shoulder blades, and her spine stiffened.

"Well," she said finally, unable to mask the bitterness in her voice. "It's a miracle you're not dead of the pox."

"It's not a miracle. It's a combination of caution and sheepgut."

"More to your credit, then. And here you've remained

seemingly hale and stout, despite fifteen years of such strenuous exertion. A remarkable feat. No wonder you seem so proud of your exploits."

"Do I?" His jaw tightened.

"With good health, you may have every expectation of decades of further debauchery."

"Sweetheart, that's my greatest fear."

"Which part? The good health, or the debauchery?"

"The decades."

Sophia studied his face. Fidgeting under her scrutiny, he lowered his gaze and scratched the thick growth of beard along his jaw. She'd been wrong, she realized. He did not take pride in his exploits at all. "What about love?"

He did not look up. "What about it?"

"The many sweethearts, the countless lovers . . . How many of them did you love, Mr. Grayson?"

He linked his hands behind his head and stared up at the ceiling. "Every last one of them, sweet. Every last one."

Sophia rolled her eyes. "Well, that's the same as saying none."

He shrugged and continued to stare up at the ceiling. "Is it?"

Another question perched on the tip of her tongue. Sophia hesitated, then asked it anyway. "And did any of them love you?"

He leveled a cool gaze at her. "Only the fools." There was such pride there in his eyes, mingled with such pain.

Then, suddenly, his fist crashed to the tabletop. Sophia jumped in her seat.

"I think it's time I asked the questions, don't you?" He rose to his feet and began pacing the cabin. "I know your name already, Miss *Jane* Turner."

Sophia had the impulse to interrupt, to correct him.

But she couldn't. Guilt pinched in her chest. He'd just bared his life to her. Why hadn't she the courage to do the same?

"What is your age, then?"

"I am twenty." At least *that* was the truth.

"Twenty," he repeated, in a tone of dismissal. "Only twenty. So young. What can you know of the world?"

"More than you would credit. What can you know of me, to draw such a conclusion?"

He swung around and leaned a hand on the table. "What can I know of you, indeed. How much of the world have you seen, then, Miss Turner? From whence do you hail?"

He loomed over her, his bulk and strength intimidating. But the intensity in his eyes was more disquieting by far. "Kent."

He laughed and stood erect again. "Oh, Miss Turner hails from the wilds of Kent, does she? Known for its savage garden parties, Kent. Are your parents living?"

"Yes, both."

"Have you siblings?"

"One sister."

"What a charming little family." Sophia began to interject, but he spoke over her. "Brown bread or white?"

"White."

"White bread. But of course. Nothing but the best for Miss Turner. I suppose I can skip the next question, as well. I'm well aware of your taste for rum."

Sophia bristled at the malice in his voice, and the brutal way in which his hand sliced the air. "Actually, I prefer claret."

"Claret." He smirked. "Well, I'm sorry I cannot accommodate your tastes, Miss Turner, to offer you white bread and claret at every meal."

"You know I've no such expectation." Pressing her

hands to the tabletop, she rose to her feet. "Why are you behaving in this fashion?"

He leaned over the table, placing his hands flat to mirror hers. "In what fashion would you like me to behave? I can't be other than I am, sweetheart. You've known from the start, I'm no gentleman. I'm a liar, a thief, a libertine . . . and worse." He leaned closer, and she swayed forward, as if pulled by a thread. His face was but a handsbreadth from hers. Close enough to kiss.

His gaze fell to her lips, his voice distilling to a rough whisper. "You say you have no expectation of white bread and claret? Sweet . . ." The word swirled over her lips, and Sophia's eyes fluttered shut. "You would do well to form no expectations at all."

Her eyes flew open. He pushed back and straightened until his dark hair swept the cabin ceiling. Sophia retreated slowly, her heart drumming in her breast. A sad, yet satisfied look came over his face as he folded his arms across his chest.

He meant to push her away. She understood it now. Telling her of the history with his brother, boasting about the countless women. And now, with this ruthless interrogation. This was the same man who had held her so tenderly not a half-hour ago, practically declared love for her in a moment of honest anger. The man who wanted her so fiercely, she could taste it on his breath. The man she desired so much, she ached for him, body and heart. And now he was pushing her away. Using his sordid past to drive a wedge between them.

Well, Sophia had a sordid past of her own. Her sins might not have been as numerous or as salacious, but they were every bit as black as his. And she was not going to allow yet another man to paint her as some sort of perfect angel, above desire, too pure to touch.

She skirted the table, closing the distance between them. "We're not finished."

"Sweet, I think we were finished before we began."

She shook her head, laying a hand on his arm. "You've more questions to ask me."

His mouth quirked in a half-smile. Unfolding his arms, he caught her hand in his. Sophia wished that the glassy sea would roll beneath them, pitching her into his arms. But the calm held.

"Don't try to tell me," he said, tracing her fingers with his, "that these soft, delicate hands have committed theft."

"But they have."

"Of what? Ribbons? A bit of lace, perhaps?" He folded her fingers over her palm and returned her hand to her side. "Perhaps a few leaves of paper?"

"Paper of a sort." Banknotes were paper, weren't they?

"Whatever your petty sins, sweet, I'm certain I could buy and sell them with the coin in my waistcoat pocket."

He had no idea. Lowering her eyes, Sophia pressed her hand to the purse beneath her stays. True, the money was hers in name. But hadn't it been nearly Toby's, by rights? Even now, he could be bringing suit against her parents, demanding the dowry she'd denied him when she ran away. What she'd done . . . It wasn't so very different from Mr. Grayson's deceit. She'd stolen her own inheritance. "You'd be surprised at the cost of my sins."

But before she could elaborate, he jabbed a finger under her chin, tilting her face to his. Just as quickly, his hand fell away. "Don't tell me you're married?"

Laughter bubbled up in her throat. "Of course not. No." A surge of guilt chased the laughter away. She should have been married, by now.

Still, she willed the smile to remain. Her laughter seemed to please him, as did her response. He began to look himself again, and Sophia inwardly rejoiced.

"How many sweethearts, then?"

"Many."

His eyebrow quirked. "Don't count the men aboard this ship."

"Even without them . . ." She gave him a coquettish smile. "Still several."

"And have there been lovers?"

The disdain in his voice, the smug curve of his lips . . . Sophia knew he expected her answer to be a prim denial. He would be wrong. She would not confirm his impression of her as untouched, innocent. He needed to understand that he was not beneath her. Nothing was beneath her, not theft, not deceit. Certainly not passion.

There was only one way to show him her true nature.

And that was to lie.

"Yes. One."

He drew a sharp breath through his teeth. Sophia turned, taking two steps away. She clenched her fists until her fingernails bit into her palms, willing herself to be calm. After all, this was a lie she'd told many times before.

"But you look so surprised," she began, glancing at Mr. Grayson over her shoulder. "I told you weeks ago about Gervais. My painting master, and my tutor in the art—"

"The art of passion," he finished for her. He gave her a look of utter skepticism. "Yes, I remember. I didn't believe you then, either."

"It doesn't matter whether or not you believe me," she lied, sweeping across the cabin. "He was tall and lean and divinely handsome, with jet-black hair and silver eyes and long, sculpted fingers. And he loved me desperately."

"Oh, they always do."

"He loved me," she insisted. "Desperately." Brushing a lock of hair from her forehead, she continued, "Oh, but it wasn't affection that drew us together. It was raw, animal passion."

Chuckling, he crossed his arms over his chest. "Animal passion? What could you know of animal passion?"

She flushed under his bold gaze. This bit would not be difficult to fudge. Between the lessons of one wanton dairymaid and her proximity to this intensely attractive man, she'd gathered a thing or two about animal passion.

"It began with smoldering glances, exchanged across crowded rooms." Her fingers trailed along the tabletop as she sauntered toward him. "And then, little excuses to touch each other. Every brush of his skin on mine . . ." She grazed a single fingertip against the back of his hand. ". . . made me shiver with longing."

He caught her wrist in his grip. Her breath caught in her throat.

"Well," she said, "I'd imagine you know how the rest progressed."

"I'd imagine I do." He released her wrist, and something flickered in his eyes. The beginnings of belief. "So you're telling me this is the reason you're bound for Tortola, to become a governess. You were ruined."

Sophia gave a tiny nod. How considerate of him, to do half the lying for her. Her words gained momentum, tumbled forth into the stagnant air. "We became too reckless. Once Gervais gave me a taste of paradise, nothing could keep us apart. I escaped my chaperone whenever I could, stole out to meet him in the middle of the night. The closets, the carriage house, even a hackney cab—our trysting knew no boundaries. Gervais even came to see me in Kent, during one of our house parties."

"A house party?" He wagged a finger at her. "I knew you came from quality. I knew you were not bred to be a governess."

She threw him a saucy look. "I was not bred to be a wanton, either. But so I became."

"A wanton. *You.*"

Sophia searched her memory, mentally flipping through the chapters of The Book. *Details,* she told herself. Details would convince him.

"We agreed to meet in the stables. It was too risky for Gervais to be seen near the house. I stole a dairymaid's costume and tucked all my hair under a straw cap with a wide brim. So long as I kept my head down, no one could recognize me. When I arrived in the stables, he startled me from behind the door. Without a word, he grabbed me up in his arms and carried me into the loft. There he had lit a dozen candles, and strewn rose petals and blankets over a bed of sweet-smelling hay."

"A dozen lit candles in a stable full of dry hay? You're lucky you survived the experience, sweetheart. You could have been tinder."

Sophia raised her eyebrows and stiffened her posture. "Our love was an inferno. I thought I *would* go up in flames, so glorious was our pleasure that night."

He covered his eyes with a hand and laughed, loud and long. "What a vivid romantic imagination you have."

"It's not imagination. I'm telling you the truth!" Panic gnawed at her stomach. If she couldn't convince him now, she would certainly lose him. His opinion of her would be confirmed, and he'd only think her more naïve than ever. Desperate, she approached him steadily until they stood toe-to-toe. Perhaps physicality could persuade where words could not.

"Don't you believe me?" Crossing her arms, she framed

her bosom for his appraisal. His eyes took the bait. Then, in a choreographed fit of pique, she whirled away. Men preferred to give chase, Sophia knew. She might be a virgin, but she understood how to draw a man to her side.

Her pounding heartbeat filled the humid silence. The room had grown dark. So curious here in the tropics, how night fell like a thunderclap. No lingering dusk, no mystic hour of twilight. Just light, and then dark.

"Rose petals." His voice dropped, and she counted his slow footfalls as he moved to stand behind her. She felt his breath whispering against her nape, his gaze burning a trail along her neckline. Then he leaned in, hovering inches from her shoulder as he drew a slow, deep breath through his nose. A low, seductive growl rumbled from his throat and reverberated down her spine. "I believe the rose petals."

Slowly, he brushed a wisp of hair from her shoulder. His finger never grazed her skin, but the sensation of the silken lock gliding over her neck had Sophia quivering. She shut her eyes, feeling the feather-light caress *everywhere*.

"Did you love him?" he asked. "This Gervais?"

The last question. She should have been expecting it, but it took her completely by surprise. "Yes, of course," she blurted out, unthinking.

She slowly turned to face him in the dark. Mr. Grayson battened his reaction before she could gauge it, but Sophia knew she'd made a misstep. If he'd been thinking of sharing her bed tonight, he was now thinking twice. How ironic, that there was nothing to cool a man's ardor like the mention of love.

And what would he ask her now? Their little script was at an end. Sophia waited breathless in the dark, hoping some question, request—or kiss—would fall from his lips.

The cabin door scraped open, and a lamp threw flickering light between them. He took a step back.

Stubb shuffled in, struggling under a heavy tray. "Here's dinner," he announced, hanging a lamp on a hook above them. "Sorry it's late, but it's been a busy day."

Mr. Grayson nodded. "I'll leave you to your meal then, Miss Turner."

"I brought service for two." Stubb plunked tin plates and serving dishes on the table. "All passengers are to take their meals in the ladies' cabin until further notice. Captain's orders." The old man glanced at Gray. "The captain wants you both to stay belowdecks until we get our wind back. He'd said you'd understand, Gray."

"Aye," Mr. Grayson replied. "I understand." He gave Sophia a guarded look. "But I'll leave you to your dinner just the same."

"You're not hungry?" Stubb lifted the cover from a serving dish. At the smell of the salted-beef stew called lobscouse, Sophia's empty stomach complained loudly.

"Miss Turner will better enjoy her meal without my presence," Mr. Grayson said, backing toward the steerage passage. "As for me, I'll hold till breakfast. I find I've little appetite this evening."

Then he left. But not before flashing her one last searching, hungry glance.

Sophia smiled. He was a very poor liar.

CHAPTER FIFTEEN

Gray's body complained at him all night long. His empty stomach groused, when he might have filled it at dinner. His joints protested the cramped hammock swaddling him, when he might have been sharing a soft mattress with an even softer companion. And of course there was the ever-present ache of unfulfilled lust in his groin.

But beyond all this, his mind was in turmoil, and his heart—his heart was unmoored completely. Wrenched free of its anchor and set adrift. He'd no idea how to secure it again.

She wasn't a virgin.

So she claimed.

Don't question it.

At last, with that one bit of information, everything about the girl made sense. The fine clothes, the cultured air, the governess post. The spark in her eyes, and the way she responded to his touch. The way she touched him. She understood passion; she knew what pleasure they could share.

Still he passed the night alone.

Because she offered more than pleasure. She offered her heart. She offered trust. God, she'd practically thrust it upon him, and Gray didn't want it. He had enough people to look after, and he'd already disappointed them all. It was only a matter of time before he'd fail her, too.

Even so, by daybreak Gray had already washed and

dressed. He sat on a crate, tapping his boot and fidgeting with his pocket watch until eight bells sounded for the forenoon watch. Breakfast time. He could ignore the needs of his stomach no longer. Neither could he ignore this other gnawing ache inside him—the need to see her.

He hadn't the faintest idea what he'd say to the girl; as little as possible would be best. Gray fetched up a book, tucked it under his arm, and headed for the ladies' cabin door.

The aroma of freshly brewed tea greeted him. Miss Turner stood over the table, arranging a half-dozen small pots next to the breakfast tray. After yesterday's dramatic events and a restless night, it surprised Gray to see her standing there looking so . . . normal. Almost domestic. The knot of anxiety in his chest unraveled.

"Good morning." Without looking up, she unscrewed the lid off one of the pots and dabbed at its contents with a fingertip.

"Are you planning to poison my tea?" Gray drew out a chair and sat down, plunking his book down on the table and helping himself to a biscuit.

"Nothing quite so dreadful." She looked up at him, and the coquettish gleam in her eyes had him coughing around his mouthful of food. Yes, everything was as usual. The mere sight of her, so beautiful, so close—stole his very breath. Which left him completely unprepared for the words she spoke next. "I'm going to paint you."

"Paint me?" Vivid, sensual memories flooded his mind. Her fingers threaded in his hair, her body pressed against his. Gray doubted she even remembered that night, drunk as she'd been. Of course, he couldn't forget it.

"You don't mind, do you? I need to practice, and it is something to pass the time." Pushing aside a mug of tea, she began unfolding a small easel. "Unless you had some other activity in mind?"

Gray cleared his throat and lowered his gaze to his book. He had many other activities in mind. "I had planned to read."

"And so you still may." She threaded her arms through the sleeves of a smock and tied it behind her back. "Just allow me enough time to rough in the outline of your features, and then you can read your book while I complete the rest."

"I'm not certain . . ."

She set down a trio of brushes, lining them up from smallest to largest. "I'm running out of subjects, you see. I've sketched or painted nearly everyone else on the ship."

"I'd noticed."

She paused, staring hard at the brushes. "Had you?"

"Yes."

Her gaze lifted to his. "And . . . ?"

And what? What could he possibly say? That her sketches filled him with envy and yearning? That they revealed to him hidden qualities in men he'd worked alongside for years, and showed him more than he'd ever wanted to know of her heart? That he'd spurned this same request—and *her*—weeks ago, precisely because he dreaded the moment she turned that artist's eye on him and perceived the true quality of his soul? Irony tugged the corner of his mouth into a half-smile. Let her see it, then. Her supply of black pigment would be exhausted completely. She'd never burden him with that trusting look again.

He drained his mug of tea and threw it down like a gauntlet. "Very well."

Smiling, she propped a canvas on the easel. "Very well."

"What am I to do?"

"Just be at ease." She threw him an amused glance. "Much as I'd rejoice to feel the sea rolling beneath us, I don't believe you're in any imminent danger of being thrown to the floor."

Gray followed her gaze to his hand where it clenched the arm of his chair. Annoyed with his own transparency, he folded his hands across his chest, sliding one boot along the floorboards as he reclined in the chair. "I am perfectly at ease."

"How is it," she asked, scratching with a pencil as her narrowed gaze alternated between him and the canvas, "that the son of a dissolute gentleman, raised on a West Indian sugar plantation and educated at Oxford, after inheriting land and an income, decides to make his life at sea?"

Gray stared at her.

She ceased sketching and cast him an expectant look, tucking a stray wisp of hair behind her ear.

"What? You want me to talk? I thought I was supposed to remain still."

"You are supposed to be at ease. And reminiscing, I find, usually puts a subject at ease."

Not this subject.

She turned back to her sketch. "Did you dream of becoming a sailor as a boy?"

Gray laughed. "No. I'd never been aboard a ship until I was sent off to Oxford. I was sick and miserable for the whole first week at sea. Couldn't eat a thing. A stroke of luck, as it turned out, for the sailors caught and ate a tainted fish. Nearly all of the crew fell ill; four of them died."

"Good Heavens."

"I offered my assistance to the captain. He put me to work, and I just took to it, somehow. By the time we crossed the Tropic, I was setting and furling sails like an able seaman. Between shifts in the rigging, I learned everything the captain had to teach me about windpower and navigation. When we reached England, I asked him if I could stay on, and he made me second mate. Didn't make it to Oxford for another year and a half."

"I wonder that you bothered to go at all."

"I nearly didn't." He scratched his chin. "But the war was brewing. And a letter finally caught up with me, saying my father had taken ill—that sobered me. Both Joss and Bel were still underage, and I knew there'd be no one to look after them if he died. Figured I'd best stay put for a while, so they'd know where to find me if they needed me. Oxford seemed as good a place as any. Only finished three terms, as it happened."

"Because your father did die." Catching the pencil between her teeth, she wiped her hands on the apron of her smock.

"Yes."

She removed the pencil from her mouth and turned her head to stare at him. Her eyes did not meet his, however. Rather, Gray fancied that she studied his ear, or perhaps the line of his jaw. He scratched his neck self-consciously, feeling his whole body heat under her unabashed appraisal.

"And that's when you sold the land," she said, returning her attention to the canvas. "And became a privateer?"

He nodded.

"But if you were concerned for your brother and sister, why did you not simply go home? Keep running the plantation?"

Gray exhaled roughly. "For a host of reasons. But all of them had to do with money. Sugar prices were plummeting; tariffs kept increasing. West Indian plantations were no longer the profitable enterprises they'd once been. We would have been mired in debt within the year." He shook his head. "It never would have worked. If I'd told the executors about Joss, it would have meant months of delay, and I couldn't be certain he'd even agree to sell. I found a buyer for the land, and I had the opportunity to buy this ship and obtain a letter of marque, so I seized it. And then I seized over sixty ships in the name of the Crown." Gray couldn't keep a hint of pride out of his voice. "I've never regretted my decision. It was the only profitable course."

She cast another scrutinizing glance at him, this time in the direction of his hairline. Gray's own eyes rolled heavenward, as if he could follow the line of her gaze.

"Does this occur often, that the ship is becalmed?"

Gray shrugged. "Not every voyage. But often enough."

"How long does it usually last?"

"There's no way of telling. Hours. Days. A week."

She brushed a stray wisp of hair behind her ear. "A week's delay? That must affect your profit most adversely."

"Aye, it does."

He looked up at the skylight beseechingly. This must be hell. He was losing money by the hour, he was made to suffer the unattainable temptation of the most beautiful woman he'd ever seen, and it was bloody *hot*. Without any fresh breezes to stir it, the air inside the cabin grew increasingly stale as the sun inched higher in the sky. It was barely mid-morning, and sweat was already beading under Gray's cravat. He looked back at Miss Turner, admiring the graceful, dewy curve of her bare neck as she bent her head. The temperature inside the cabin increased another degree.

She sat back and tilted her head to one side, studying the canvas. "Surely it wasn't the *only* profitable course, privateering. There are so many risks involved, such unpredictability. I mean, you might have married."

"Married?"

"Yes, of course. That's what most eligible gentlemen in financial straits do, isn't it? You came from a good family and had some land to your name ... surely you could have found a young heiress or wealthy widow to marry you, and then you might have done as you pleased. After all," she said, her eyes meeting his, "it's not as though you lack sufficient charm to woo ladies. And you're certainly handsome enough, in your own way."

"Handsome *enough*. In my own way."

She bent her head again. "Oh, stop looking so smug. I'm not flattering you, I'm merely stating facts. Privateering was not your only profitable course of action. You might have married, if you'd wished to."

"Ah, but there's the snag, you see. I didn't wish to."

She picked up a brush and tapped it against her palette. "No, you didn't. You wished to be at sea. You wished to go adventuring, to seize sixty ships in the name of the Crown and pursue countless women on four continents. That's why you sold your land, Mr. Grayson. Because it's what you wanted to do. The profit was incidental."

Gray tugged at the cuff of his coat sleeve. It unnerved him, how easily she stared down these truths he'd avoided looking in the eye for years. So now he was worse than a thief. He was a selfish, lying thief. And still she sat with him, flirted with him, called him "charming" and "handsome enough." How much darkness did the girl need to uncover before she finally turned away?

"And what about you, Miss Turner?" He leaned forward in his chair. "Why are you here, bound for the West Indies to work as a governess? You, too, might have married. You come from quality; so much is clear. And even if you'd no dowry, sweetheart ..." He waited for her to look up. "Yours is the kind of beauty that brings men to their knees."

She gave a dismissive wave of her paintbrush. Still, her cheeks darkened, and she dabbed her brow with the back of her wrist.

"Now, don't act missish. I'm not flattering you, I'm merely stating facts." He leaned back in his chair. "So why haven't you married?"

"I explained to you yesterday why marriage was no longer an option for me. I was compromised."

Gray folded his hands on his chest. "Ah, yes. The French painting master. What was his name? Germaine?"

"Gervais." She sighed dramatically. "Ah, but the pleasure he showed me was worth any cost. I'd never felt so alive as I did in his arms. Every moment we shared was a minute stolen from paradise."

Gray huffed and kicked the table leg. The girl was trying to make him jealous. And damn, if it wasn't working. Why should some oily schoolgirl's tutor enjoy the pleasures Gray was denied? He hadn't aided the war effort just so England's most beautiful miss could lift her skirts for a bloody Frenchman.

She began mixing pigment with oil on her palette. "Once, he pulled me into the larder, and we had a feverish tryst among the bins of potatoes and turnips. He held me up against the shelves while we—"

"May I read my book now?" Lord, he couldn't take much more of this.

She smiled and reached for another brush. "If you wish."

Gray opened his book and stared at it, unable to muster the concentration to read. Every so often, he turned a page. Vivid, erotic images filled his mind, but all the blood drained to his groin.

As the sun inched higher in the sky, the crosshatched shadow of the grated skylight crept down the wall of the cabin and began its slow crawl across the floor. Soon the sun was directly overhead, painting the table with a checkerboard of shadows.

Feeling drowsy and sluggish, Gray hooked a finger under his sweat-dampened cravat and tugged. He stole a glance at Miss Turner over his book. Her pale muslin gown had wilted with the heat, clinging to her form in a most appealing manner. She rotated her neck slowly, stretching with a lithe, sensual grace.

"Is there any more tea?" Gray asked.

"No." She took up a handkerchief and pressed it to her brow, then her glistening, flushed décolletage.

He shifted uncomfortably, feeling a new source of heat pool in his groin. "I'll get after Stubb to bring water. In a minute." He bent his head and closed his eyes and tried to think of anything cool. Those pretty flavored ices all the fashion in Mayfair, the ones he'd be certain to take Bel to sample. The trout stream in Wiltshire where he'd spent that summer between years at Oxford. Ale, fresh from the cellar in winter. Snow.

Gray had a sudden image of Miss Turner standing in an English winterscape, dressed in rich velvet and dusted with powdery white snowflakes. Tiny crystals of ice clinging to her fur-trimmed gloves, her mantle, her hair, her thick fringe of eyelashes. Her pale skin contrasting with plump, flushed lips. An angelic apparition.

Except that he couldn't do to an angel what Gray saw himself doing with this snow-covered siren. He imagined himself licking a snowflake from her cheek, and his tongue curled around the sharp burst of cold. In his mind's eye he tasted another, and another—and they were sweet. She was a rose-flavored ice, a delicacy beyond anything he'd ever tasted, and he was devouring her, taste by impossibly tiny taste. Snowflake by snowflake. Until he tumbled her back into the snow and bared the creamy mounds of her breasts, the plump berries of her nipples, the juicy curves of her delicious body—and feasted.

CHAPTER
SIXTEEN

Sophia counted six clangs of the bell before Mr. Grayson jolted fully awake. He looked up at her, startled and flushed. As though he'd been caught doing something he shouldn't.

She smiled.

Rubbing his eyes, he rose to his feet. "Will I shock you, Miss Turner, if I remove my coat?"

Sophia felt a twinge of disappointment. When would he stop treating her with this forced politesse, maintaining this distance between them? How many tales of passionate encounters must she spin before he finally understood that she was no less wicked than he, only less experienced? Perhaps it was time to take more aggressive measures.

"By all means, remove your coat." She tilted her eyes to cast him a saucy look. "Mr. Grayson, I'm not an innocent schoolgirl. You will have to try harder than that to shock me."

His lips curved in a subtle smile. "I'll take that under advisement." She watched as he shook the heavy topcoat from his shoulders and peeled it down his arms. He draped the coat over the back of a chair before sitting back down. The damp lawn of his shirt clung to his shoulders and arms. A pleasant shiver rippled down to Sophia's toes.

"It doesn't suit you anyway," she said, loading her brush with paint.

He gave her a bemused look as he unknotted his cravat and pulled it loose. She inwardly rejoiced. Now, if only she could convince him to do away with his waistcoat . . .

"The coat," she explained, when his eyebrows remained raised. "It doesn't suit you."

"Why not? Is the color wrong?" The sudden seriousness in his tone surprised her.

"No, the color is perfectly fine. It's the cut that's unflattering. That style is tailored to gentlemen of leisure, lean and slender. But as you are so fond of telling me, Mr. Grayson, you are no gentleman. Your shoulders are too broad for fashion."

"Is that so?" He chuckled as he undid his cuffs. Sophia stared as he turned up his sleeves, baring one tanned, muscled forearm, then the other. "What style of garments would best suit me, then?"

"Other than a toga?" He rewarded her jest with an easy smile. Sophia dabbed at her canvas, pleased to be making progress at last. "I think you need something less restrictive. Something like a sailor's garb. Or perhaps a captain's."

"Truly?" His gaze became thoughtful, then searching. "And even dressed in plain seaman's clothes, would you still find me handsome *enough*? In my own way?"

"No." She allowed his brow to crease a moment before continuing. "I should find you surpassingly handsome. In every way." She mixed paint slowly on her palette and gave him a coy look. "And what of my attire? If you had your way, how would you dress me?"

"If I had my way . . . I wouldn't."

A thrill raced through Sophia's body. Her cheeks burned, and her eyes dropped to her lap. She forced her gaze back up to meet his. Now was not the moment to lose courage. Nothing held sway over a man's intentions like jealousy. "Gervais once kept me naked for an entire day so he could paint me."

He blinked. "He painted a nude study of you?"

"No. He painted *me*. I took off my clothes and stretched out on the bed while he dressed me in pigment. Gervais called me his perfect, blank canvas. He painted lavender orchids here"—she traced a small circle just above her breast—"and little vines twining down . . ." She slid her hand down and noted with delight how his eyes followed its path. "I feigned the grippe and refused to bathe for a week."

Desire and jealous rage warred in his countenance, yet he remained as immobile as one of Lord Elgin's marble sculptures. What would it take to spur the man into action? Frustrated, she blew a wisp of hair off her face and nodded in the direction of his arm. "Would you pass me the little pot of red?"

He frowned down at the scattered cakes of pigment. "Which one is the red?"

"The vermillion. Just there at your elbow. You see it."

"This one?" He handed her a pot of Vandyke brown.

Sophia flung her palette on the table and stretched for the red pigment herself. "If you don't wish to help me, just say so. There's no need to tease."

"Calm down, sweetheart. I'm not teasing you at all. I don't see colors the way most people do, it seems."

"What do you mean, you don't see colors?"

He shrugged. "I see some colors. Just not as many as other people seem to see. You say, 'red, green, brown' . . . they all look the same to me. If a sapphire lies next to an amethyst, I can't tell them apart. Apparently, I had an uncle who was the same way. Once my tutor stopped beating me for mislabeling my Latin exercises, it's never troubled me." He turned his attention back to his book.

"But . . . but that's tragic! To go through life without color? Unable to appreciate art, or beauty?"

He laughed. "Now, sweet—hold your brush before you paint me a martyr's halo. It's not as though I'm blind. I have a great appreciation for art, as I believe we've discussed. And as for beauty . . . I don't need to know whether your eyes are blue or green or lavender to know that they're uncommonly lovely."

"No one has lavender eyes."

"Don't they?" His gaze caught hers and refused to let go. Leaning forward, he continued, "Did that tutor of yours ever tell you this? That your eyes are ringed with a perfect circle a few shades darker than the rest of the . . . don't they call it the iris?"

Sophia nodded.

"The iris." He propped his elbow on the table and leaned forward, his gaze searching hers intently. "An apt term it is, too. There are these lighter rays that fan out from the center, like petals. And when your pupils widen—like that, right there—your eyes are like two flowers just coming into bloom. Fresh. Innocent."

She bowed her head, mixing a touch of lead white into the sea-green paint on her palette. He leaned closer still, his voice a hypnotic whisper. "But when you take delight in teasing me, looking up through those thick lashes, so saucy and self-satisfied . . ." She gave him a sharp look.

He snapped his fingers. "There! Just like that. Oh, sweet—then those eyes are like two opera dancers smiling from behind big, feathered fans. Coy. Beckoning."

Sophia felt a hot blush spreading from her bosom to her throat.

He smiled and reclined in his chair. "I don't need to

know the color of your hair to see that it's smooth and shiny as silk. I don't need to know whether it's yellow or orange or red to spend an inordinate amount of time wondering how it would feel brushing against my bare skin."

Opening his book to the marked page, he continued, "And don't get me started on your lips, sweet. If I endeavored to discover the precise shade of red or pink or violet they are, I might never muster the concentration for anything else."

He turned a leaf of his book, then fell silent.

Sophia stared at her canvas. Her pulse pounded in her ears. A bead of sweat trickled down the back of her neck, channeling down between her shoulder blades, and a hot, itchy longing pooled at the cleft of her legs.

Drat him. He'd known she was taunting him with her stories. And now he sat there in an attitude of near-boredom, making love to her with his teasing, *colorless* words in a blatant attempt to fluster her. It was as though they were playing a game of cards, and he'd just raised the stakes.

Sophia smiled. She always won at cards.

"Balderdash," she said calmly.

He looked up at her, eyebrow raised.

"No one has violet lips."

"Don't they?"

She laid aside her palette and crossed her arms on the table. "The slope of your nose is quite distinctive."

His lips quirked in a lopsided grin. "Really."

"Yes." She leaned forward, allowing her bosom to spill against her stacked arms. His gaze dipped, but quickly returned to hers. "The way you have that little bump at the bridge . . . It's proving quite a challenge."

"Is that so?" He bent his head and studied his book. Sophia stared at him, waiting one . . . two . . . three beats before he raised his hand to rub the bridge of his nose. Quite satisfactory progress, that. Definite beginnings of fluster.

"Once, during one of my lessons with Gervais, I was sketching Michelangelo's *David,* from a plate in a book. Only, I could not capture the muscles of the forearm at all."

"Him again?" He heaved a bored sigh as he turned another page.

"Gervais stood up"—Sophia pushed back from the table and rose to her feet—"wrenched off his coat, and rolled his shirtsleeve up to the elbow." She placed her hand flat on the table, directly in front of Gray.

"He took my hand and dragged my fingers over every slope and sinew of his arm." As she spoke, Sophia traced the tendons of her planted wrist with her free hand. When she skimmed her fingers up to the hollow of her elbow, she heard his breath catch. *Good.* More progress.

"And after touching them," she said, "I had no trouble sketching those muscles at all."

Gray snapped his book shut, tossed it aside, and stared up at her in challenge. The dark intensity in his eyes gave Sophia a heartbeat's pause. Slowly, she stretched one hand toward his face. "Now . . . hold perfectly still."

His eyes closed as she touched one finger to the bridge of his nose. With deliberate slowness, she traced the uneven, bronzed slope with her fingertip. His breathing grew husky. At last she broke the contact. He kept his eyes closed.

She ran a thumb across his left eyebrow, then drew a bold line from his temple to his cheekbone. His skin was softer than she'd expected, and oddly cool beneath her fingertips. She dragged her fingers down into the rough growth of beard along his jaw, flattening her hand to let the bristles rasp against the sensitive skin of her palm.

He drew a ragged breath that verged on a groan, but his eyes remained shut. He held perfectly still.

Something hot and hungry surged through Sophia's veins. Desire, mingled with the heady thrill of power. She traced the contours of his brow, skimmed over the soft, vulnerable curves of his eyelids. His lashes, long and curved as a child's, trembled under her touch, and a sweet pang of tenderness swelled in her heart. She followed the circumference of his face, running one fingertip down to the cleft of his chin, then climbing the thin scar slanting to the corner of his mouth. He exhaled roughly, and Sophia felt the heat of his breath swirling through her blood. Emboldened, she slid her thumb along the ridge of his lower lip.

His hand shot up to capture hers, holding it pressed against his cheek. He looked up at her mournfully, his hair mussed and his breathing labored.

Oh, yes. Fluster accomplished.

"Gray." She leaned closer, the damp fabric of her shift tangling around her thighs.

He tensed. "Don't do this. I'll only hurt you."

"I'm not an innocent, Gray. I know what you want. Can't you tell I want it, too?" She leaned over to whisper in his ear. "I could show you colors. Colors like you've never dreamed. The cool blue of my eyes . . ." She blew gently over his neck and watched the tendon there go rigid. "The golden silk of this hair . . ." She wound a stray lock around her finger and brushed it over his cheek.

"Sweetheart . . ."

Sophia hovered above him, bringing her lips within an inch of his. "I could teach you the taste of perfect, luscious, rose-petal pink."

He shook his head, almost imperceptibly. "I said I wouldn't pursue you."

"Is that so? Well, as it happens, I'm tired of being pursued. I'm rather enjoying taking the other role."

"Sweet, believe me, I'm not worth pursuing. And if I . . ." He squeezed his eyes shut, then opened them again. "If I let this happen, I never will be. I gave my word, and for once I want to keep it. I'm a scoundrel, by trade and vocation, and I'm all wrong for a girl like you."

"A girl like me? But I'm already ruined."

"Ruined? Because you've known pleasure? There's nothing about you that's ruined. You're young and beautiful and full of dreams. You're exquisite." He touched her face. "Perfect."

Tears pricked at her eyes. Such sweet words. How she wished she deserved them.

His fingers caught a stray lock of her hair. "This tutor who attempted to ruin you, he was clearly an amateur. But sweet . . . to my shame, I've had a great deal of practice. I'm trying to go respectable. I'm trying to be a better man."

"You're trying to be someone you're not. And it's making you miserable." She pressed her free hand to his other cheek, framing his face between her palms. "You do have the face of a scoundrel . . ."

"You see me clearly, then."

"But what of the man beneath? There's so much more to you, I know it. I *feel* it. A passion for life. Such strength . . ." Hooking her fingers under his collar, she slid her palm toward his muscled shoulder. "And this heart." Her fingers strayed lower over his chest, grazing the border of his scar.

He winced. With a low growl, he pulled her hands away. "Sweetheart, I . . ." He released a gruff sigh, and his face shuttered. "I can't."

"I see." Sophia sat up, feeling the sting of defeat.

"I'm sorry." He dragged a hand through his hair. "You can't imagine how sorry."

"You *should* be sorry." She put a hand on either arm of his chair and balanced above him. If he bent his head, it would rest on the waiting pillows of her breasts. He looked quite aware of that fact. "Very . . . very . . . sorry."

Sophia returned to her chair with a playful flounce, hoping to conceal the manner in which her thighs still quivered and her heart ached. "All right, then," she said lightly, taking up her palette and coating her brush with paint. "I will finish my painting. You may go back to your book."

She kept her attention focused on the canvas before her. In her peripheral vision, however, she could see that Gray's book remained closed on the table. She could hear his breathing, slow and thick. Even in this hothouse of a cabin, she could feel his radiant male heat burning through her thin muslin gown and chemise.

The task of appearing unaffected by this open lust grew increasingly difficult. After a few minutes, her arm ached from clutching the palette so tightly. Sophia laid both palette and paintbrush on the table and began to knead the spot where her neck met her shoulder, massaging the sore knot of muscle there. The tendrils of hair against her neck were damp with perspiration.

"Touch yourself for me."

Sophia froze. Her heart stopped beating. Surely she hadn't heard what she thought she'd—

"You heard me." His chair slid around the table to rest beside hers. "I promised I wouldn't touch you. So touch yourself for me."

Her pulse roared back to life, and the pounding rhythm of her heart echoed in dull, forceful beats at the apex of her thighs. Sophia shut her eyes. The suggestion was shocking and thrilling and altogether unspeakable. Impossible. She had to think of a response. A scathing set-down to dash cold water over his ardor. Over hers. She had to douse this wild passion coursing through her veins.

But there was no cold water. Only hot, liquid desire beading on her forehead, trickling down between her breasts. She'd begun this game of bluffing. She could hardly back down now, when losing the game meant losing *him*.

As if they moved of their own accord, her fingers left the crest of her shoulder and slowly wandered down the lace-edged slope of her neckline.

"*Yes.*" The soft hiss of the word slid over her skin like a caress. "Yes. Touch them for me."

Her nipples puckered instantly, drawing to hard peaks against her chemise. She hesitated, eyes still tightly shut. Her breath heaved in her chest, lifting the top of her breast against her fingers with each inhalation.

"Yes, sweet. Touch them for me. Five-and-twenty days we've been on this ship. Four-and-twenty nights I've dreamt of cupping those breasts in my hands. I'm aching to hold them, to feel them firm and round and soft under my fingers. God, they're so soft, aren't they, sweetheart? Just like your hands, your wrists, your lips. You're so soft, soft as petals all over."

The deep baritone of his voice rumbled through her, each word setting off a tremor in her core. Sophia bit her bottom lip to keep it from quivering. Curling her fingers around the fabric of her dress and chemise, she dragged them over her shoulder and slowly down, until the neck-line would stretch no further. She dipped her fingers under the fabric and lifted her breast, liberating the damp, heavy globe from her bodice. Hot air swirled over her nipple. She shivered, imagining it to be his breath.

He was silent for a moment that stretched into an age. Sophia kept her eyes clamped shut, dying a slow, quiet death of exposure and shame. What on earth was she doing, exposing her breast to this man? So wanton, so loose. He'd known she would do it. He'd encouraged her just to tease. To regain the upper hand. If she opened her eyes, he'd be smirking at her. Mocking her.

"Dear God," he finally breathed. "You are so beautiful. So perfect. Smooth and fair and creamy and round. And sweet, oh sweet. It's as though I can taste you. Touch your nipple for me."

Hardly believing what she was doing, Sophia dragged her thumb over the straining peak. White light burst through the darkness behind her eyelids.

"Yes," he groaned. "Do it again."

She obeyed.

"Again. God, I want to lick you there. I want to run my tongue around and around and then pull you into my mouth and suckle you hard. Tug on it, sweet. Yes, just like that. I want to lose myself in that softness and feel your arms around me while I suckle you until you moan."

Sophia rolled her nipple between her thumb and forefinger, imagining his strong, rough hands on her. His lips and tongue caressing her, sucking her. Her breath rushed out in a long, low sigh.

"Yes, louder. Moan for me. Let me hear you."

Moaning, Sophia cupped her other breast through the fabric of her dress, teasing the taut, hidden bud.

"I want to touch you. All of you. I want to see and stroke every perfect, beautiful inch of you. Your breasts. Your navel. The backs of your knees. Every last toe. I want to taste you all over. Lick that powder you use right off of your skin. I want to know every secret, hidden part of you. I want to know how it is that you smell like a damned rosebush in the middle of the ocean."

Her tongue darted out to wet her lips. He groaned. "Oh, sweet. If you knew what you do to me. I'm aching for you."

It occurred to Sophia that he might be touching himself, too. Perhaps it ought to have shocked her, that thought. Instead, it drove her to a new peak of excitement. She slid down in her chair, her legs falling apart slightly. Between her thighs, she felt achy and hot. Drenched with sweat and desire.

"Lift your skirts," came the hoarse command. "Let me see you. I have to see you."

Lost in a dark haze of passion, Sophia was past thinking, past shame. Her hands slid from her breasts to the tops of her thighs. She fisted her hands in the thin muslin and slowly hitched the fabric up, baring her ankles. Then her calves.

"More. Higher."

She obeyed, rucking the muslin up over her knees, smoothing one palm against her sensitive inner thigh.

"Oh, sweet Heaven. Look at you. No stockings, no garters. No drawers, either? Tell me there are no drawers."

She arched her spine slightly, her head lolling against the back of the chair. She skimmed her hand higher to bare the smooth expanse of her thigh.

He released a ragged sigh. "No drawers, either. I'll never take you back to England now. This is how I want you, always. Here, in the tropical heat—no petticoats, no stockings, no drawers. Ready for me at any time. And you are ready for me, aren't you, sweet? You're so hot and wet. God, how I want to taste you. You're delicious, even from here."

Sophia's heart was pounding so hard, she feared it would explode. Her head spun, dizzy with heat. Her mouth fell open. She was panting. She felt shameless and sensual and more boldly feminine than she'd ever felt in her life.

"Touch yourself for me." His voice took on a new urgency, grew rough and demanding. "You know the place, I know you do. Touch yourself for me."

His voice held her in such thrall, she was powerless to disobey, even if she'd wanted to. But she didn't want to. She wanted to do everything he told her. She wanted to be here, always, in this sultry tropical fog of desire, and let him do whatever he would with her. Her fingers brushed over the damp nest of curls at the juncture of her thighs, parting the slick folds of her sex to find that swollen, sensitive bit of flesh.

"Oh yes, sweet. Do it for me. I want to taste you there. I want to be in you, feel you tight and clasping around me. I want you moaning for me. Under me. On top of me. I want to have you in every way known to man, and then invent a dozen more. Touch it for me. Imagine it's me there, touching you. In you."

The climax broke through her in a crashing wave. She arched up off the chair, her breath caught in a strangled cry. Pleasure jolted through her again and again, until she went limp in its aftermath, shuddering.

A blissful peace washed over her first.

Followed by awareness.

Then shame.

Oh, God. What had she just done? With shaking hands, she pushed her skirt back down over her knees. She brought one hand to her still-naked breast and the other to her eyes, squeezing them shut tight. But not tight enough. Hot tears leaked through her trembling lashes.

"Oh no, sweet. No."

He whispered so tenderly, but the sound of his voice

only served as a cruel reminder that he was *there*. He had *seen*. The tears came harder, spilling down her cheeks.

"No, sweet, don't cry." His voice was low and close to her ear. "Are you—" He paused. "Are you thinking of him?"

She shook her head no.

"Then why do you cry? Surely you're not embarrassed?"

Sophia sobbed against her hand.

"Oh, sweet. Please don't. Don't cry, or I'll cry with you. You're the most lovely, most perfect thing I've ever seen in all my life, and I could weep for the sheer beauty of you." Rough fingers smoothed the hair from her brow. "Don't ever be ashamed, not with me."

He tugged her hand away from her face. She kept her eyes shut tight as he kissed her fingertips, one by one, then turned her hand over to plant a heartrendingly tender kiss upon her palm.

Sophia opened her eyes. The ceiling flashed bright above her at first, through a blurry haze of tears. She blinked and sniffed. Never in her life had she felt so vulnerable. The burdensome disguise she'd been wearing the entire voyage—wearing her entire life, it seemed— had been stripped away. No more deceptions, no more fantasies. This was all that remained: a weary, wanton, lonely girl with one hand clasped to her naked breast and the other pressed against his lips.

She'd bared herself before him, in every way. As she'd never dared reveal herself to anyone. More truth had passed between them in the last ten minutes than any conversation could relay, and still he held her, soothed her. Would his lips still form such tender words and soft kisses, if he knew the complete truth?

He kissed her palm again. "Don't cry. I'd die before

I'd let anything or anyone hurt you. I couldn't bear to think I'd caused you such distress." He pressed her hand against his bearded cheek. She felt his lips graze her temple. "Sweet," he whispered against her ear. "You're safe with me. Always."

Sophia turned her head slowly, until her gaze locked with his. His eyes—they were the purest cerulean blue, and fathoms deep. She caressed his cheek with her thumb. "Oh, Gray."

CHAPTER
SEVENTEEN

She said his name, and it pierced him. Like a needle-thin dagger that threaded right between his ribs to embed itself in his heart.

And like any sudden wound, it caught him completely off-guard. It hurt. It sent him into shock.

What had just happened? He'd been reading; she'd been painting. They'd argued over paint, discussed colors. He'd teased her until she blushed, and she'd teased him back. She'd touched his face. Oh, how she'd touched him. Then suddenly he was viewing the most erotic display he'd ever witnessed in his life. And that included several erotic displays he'd paid good money to watch.

He'd said things to her. Wild, depraved fantasies he'd never voiced to any woman without paying her handsomely first. Perhaps a few things he'd never said to any woman at all. And she'd listened, and complied. Willingly. With sensual abandon and such sweet trust, it made his heart ache. He'd said anything and everything that came into his mind, to keep her going. To bring her to that peak of pleasure and watch her while she came.

That much was good. Very good.

But then she'd cried, and he'd said more. He would have said anything, promised her everything to soothe her. Now he stared into her red, weepy eyes, suddenly realizing how very close he'd come to doing just that—promising her everything—and it scared him into a cold sweat. She dragged that soft, soft thumb across his cheek, and his knees actually trembled. Trembled, damn it!

Gray had no idea what the hell was happening to him, but he knew that it had to be bad. Very bad.

Her lips were pouty and swollen with passion and just begging to be kissed, long and slow and deep. His groin was still throbbing with the memory of her erotic little gasps, her back arched in ecstasy.

Oh, Gray, she said. Oh, Gray, indeed. As in, oh Gray what the holy hell has come over you and what the devil do you intend to do about it?

He took the coward's way out. He looked away.

"I thought you were painting a portrait. Of me."

She turned her head, following his gaze to her easel. A vast seascape overflowed the small canvas. Towering thunderclouds and a violent, frothy sea. And slightly off center, a tiny ship cresting a massive wave.

"I *am* painting you."

"What, am I on the little boat, then?" It was a relief to joke.

The relief was short-lived.

"No," she said softly, turning back to look at him. "I'm on the little boat. You're the storm. And the ocean. You're . . . Gray, you're everything."

And that was when things went from "very bad" to "worse."

"I can't take credit for the composition. It's inspired by a painting I once saw, in a gallery on Queen Anne Street. By a Mr. Turner."

"Turner. Yes, I know his work. No relation, I suppose?"

"No." She looked back at the canvas. "When I saw it that day, so brash and wild . . . I could feel the tempest churning in my blood. I just knew then and there, that I had something inside me—a passion too bold, too grand to keep squeezed inside a drawing room. First I tried to deny it, and then I tried to run from it . . . and then I met you, and I saw you have it, too. Don't deny it, Gray. Don't run from it and leave me alone."

She sat up, still rubbing his cheek with her thumb. Grasping his other hand, she drew it to her naked breast. Oh, God. She was every bit as soft as he'd dreamed. Softer. And there went his hand now. Trembling.

"Touch me, Gray." She leaned forward, until her lips paused a mere inch away from his. "Kiss me."

Perhaps that dagger had missed his heart after all, because the damned thing was hammering away inside his chest. And oh, he could taste her sweet breath mingling with his. Her lips were so close, so inviting.

So dangerous.

Panic—that's what had his knees trembling and his heart hammering and his lips spouting foolishness. It had to be panic. Because something told Gray that he could see her mostly naked, and watch her toes curl as she reached her climax, and even cup her dream-soft breast in his palm—but somehow, if he touched his lips to hers, he would be lost.

"Please," she whispered. "Kiss me."

"I can't." For the second time that day, he pulled her hand away from his face. For the first—and, he suspected with distressing certainty, the last—time ever, he slid his hand from her breast. "I just can't."

The pain in her eyes devastated him. "Then I suppose you'd better leave."

The bell clanged through the silence, insistent and ceaseless. An alarm to match the frantic pounding of Gray's heart. Did the whole ship know the danger he was in?

But as his consciousness filtered back, he became aware that the dull thunder in his ears wasn't his pulse. It was real thunder. And the roar of breath rushing in and out of his lungs was drowned out by the howl of distant wind. The ship gave a lazy tilt, and a small cake of pigment rolled the length of the table before crashing to the floor. Then a wild lurch cleared the rest of her paints and had them both grasping the bolted table for balance.

"All hands! All hands!"

Gray pushed back in his chair, glancing up through the ventilation grate. As he rose to his feet, another sudden dip swept the chair out from under him. "Sweetheart, I—"

"I understand, Mr. Grayson." Her voice was weak. "Go. Please, just go."

And with one last look in her welling eyes . . . God help him, he left.

Gray emerged from the companionway to a scene eerily similar to the one on Miss Turner's canvas. The *Aphrodite* hurdled over white-capped swells, and a bank of forbidding black clouds clung to the horizon.

As he made his way to the helm, seawater dashed over his linen-clad shoulders, reminding him he'd left his coat belowdecks. Regret hollowed out his chest. His coat was the least of what he'd left there. Any shred of courage or decency he possessed. His heart, the shriveled, black thing it was.

And her.

Above him, a pair of sailors were deftly reefing the main topsail. Gray envied them. That was what he needed: He needed to work. He needed to perform hard, physical labor until he was numb to the fingertips and blind with exhaustion. He needed to sweat her out of his system.

He met Joss at the ship's wheel. "Seems we've got our wind back."

"Aye," Joss said. "And then some. I don't like the look of those clouds."

Thunder rumbled in the distance.

"Nor the sound of them," Gray added.

Joss lifted a spyglass to his right eye, squeezing the left shut. "There's a sail approaching to windward. I've given orders to lie-to and hail her, see what they can tell us about the squall. Perhaps they've just come through it."

"Or around it."

Joss lowered the spyglass to give him an enigmatic look. "What are you doing abovedecks, anyhow?"

"The cry went up for all hands."

"You're not a hand. You're a passenger."

"I may not *be* a hand, but I've got two perfectly good hands, and if I sit on them a second longer, I'll go mad."

Joss stared at Gray's open collar, where his cravat should have been knotted. "She's really getting to you, isn't she?"

"You have no idea," Gray muttered.

"Oh, I think I do."

Gray ignored his brother's smug tone. "Damn it, Joss, just put me to work. Send me up to furl a sail, put me down in the hold to pump the bilge . . . I don't care, just give me something to do."

Joss raised his eyebrows. "If you insist." He lifted the spyglass to his eye and began scanning the horizon again. "Batten the hatches, then."

Gray tossed a word of thanks over his shoulder as he descended to the quarterdeck and went to work, dragging the tarpaulins over the skylights and securing them with battens. As he labored, the ship's motions grew more violent, hampering his efforts. He saved the vent above the ladies' cabin for last, resisting the urge to peer down through the grate. Instead, he first secured one end, then blanketed the entire skylight with one strong snap on the canvas.

"Ahoy! Ahoy!" Wiggins leaned forward over the prow, hailing the approaching ship, its puffed scudding sails a stark contrast against the darkening sky.

Gray moved to cover the companion stairs, reaching inside the gaping black hole and groping for the handle to draw the hatch closed.

Something—or someone—groped him back.

When the skylight was battened, the cabin went instantly black. Sophia felt the sudden, suffocating darkness, even though her eyes were clamped shut, the heels of her hands pressed flat against them to stem the tide of tears.

What was happening?

She stood up on shaky legs, smoothing her frock over her hips and adjusting her bodice in the dark. Fumbling in the darkness, she felt her way toward the cabin door and opened it. A square of light pierced the darkness overhead—the companionway hatch.

She moved toward the stairs and placed a foot on the bottom riser. When she reached forward to grab hold of the ladder's edge, however, her hand met instead with something warm, solid, and strong.

An arm.

"Sweet," a voice said. A large hand closed over her wrist.

His voice. *His* hand.

She nearly wept anew. He was still there. In some absurd, maudlin spike of self-pity, she'd prepared herself to never see him again.

"What are you doing?" he demanded, his shadowy face protruding through the hatch. "Get back in your cabin."

Oh, but of course he was still there. His mere presence signified nothing, she told herself sternly. It wasn't as though he'd any means of escaping the ship. If he had, he surely would have taken it.

Even so, she hadn't the courage to let him go.

She used his arm as leverage, hauling herself up the stairs even as the ladder pitched and rolled beneath her. "What's happening?" The salty breeze whipped loose strands of hair across her face, and she used her free hand to tuck them behind her ear. She gripped his arm with the other.

"There's a storm coming." Deep lines etched his face. His own hair clung to his brow in thick, wet locks. "You need to remain below."

"This isn't so bad," she protested, pulling the hair from her face once again. "It isn't even raining."

He caught her chin in his hand and stared down at her face. For a breathless moment, Sophia thought he intended to kiss her.

She thought wrong.

"Look." He swiveled her head toward the ship's bow.

"Oh." The wind whipped the sound from her lips as quickly as she uttered it. Before them, the sky boiled with towering, greenish-black clouds. If Sophia hadn't suffered through enough geography lessons to know better, she would have thought they'd sailed to the very end of the earth and were about to tumble off the map into a churning void.

He turned her face back to his. The threat in his eyes was no less murderous than that of the sky. She'd never seen him look so forbidding. "Now go below. And stay there."

"Are you coming with me?"

His lips thinned. "No."

"Ahoy!"

Shouts drew their attention to starboard, where a tall ship backed its mainsail in preparation to speak with the

Aphrodite. Peering through the spray, she could barely make out the ship's name painted on its side: the *Kestrel.*

The wind accelerated, screaming through the rigging overhead. The ocean's surface erupted in a thousand white-edged crests, like a sea monster bearing row upon row of menacing teeth.

"Get below!" Gray steered her back toward the hatch.

Then the sky cracked open in a flash of white, just as thunder quaked the deck beneath their feet. For a terrifying, endless moment, the world blanked. There was no sight, no sound, only the pungent scent of sulfur and weightless shock.

With a swift yank on her wrist, Gray twirled her into his chest, wrapping his arm across her torso and forcing her down to the deck. Sophia cowered between the wooden planks beneath her and the human fortress of warmth and strength surrounding her. Protecting her. She took a mental inventory of her limbs, making sure they were all still there. Yes, there were her legs, curled awkwardly into her belly. One arm was pinned beneath her; with her other hand she still clutched his sleeve. She slid her trembling hand down toward his wrist, rejoicing to feel his pulse pound against the crook of her thumb. Her own heart thudded against her ribs. Muffled noises reached her ears—men shouting, wood splintering. But the only sounds that Sophia cared about were these twin rhythms: his heart, and hers.

After a few moments, the weight pressing her to the deck eased, and she felt herself lifted to her feet.

"Can you stand?"

She nodded, locking her knees as she rested her back against his chest. "Was . . ." Her throat worked. "Was that lightning? Did it strike the ship?"

"Yes. And no." His grip tightened over her wrist. "It struck theirs."

She craned her neck to look up at his face. His features pale and drawn, he stared hard out over the ship's rail. Sophia followed his gaze.

At first she scarcely noticed it, the faint red glow at the tip of the *Kestrel*'s mainmast. The ship was still some distance away, and Sophia had to squint to make it out. But it was there. Gray's arm went slack about her, and she took a step forward. The light seemed to disappear for a moment, then sparked feebly and glowed anew, like an ember in a dying fire.

But this fire was not dying.

The captain appeared at Gray's side. Together, the two men stared up at the red glow. "Gray, can you see—"

"Yes."

A tongue of flame spurted from the tip of the mast. Sophia felt Gray's whole body stiffen. Fire slithered down a length of rope, igniting one tip of the topmost yardarm.

"Damn it, why don't they raise the alarm?" the captain asked. "Where is her crew?"

"After a blast like that . . ." Gray's voice took on a steely edge. "Dead, some of them. Stunned or maimed, at least."

A swell tipped the deck, and Sophia stumbled back against his chest. His chin scraped the crown of her head. They fit together so perfectly. Since the day he'd helped her board this ship, she'd fallen time and again into his embrace. To her, the truth was plain. His arms belonged around her. If only he would let her into his heart.

She turned her head and rested her brow against his shoulder. "Gray," she whispered.

He tensed and pulled back. But he didn't let her go.

The captain cupped his hands around his mouth. "Put in the boats!" he shouted toward the men at the bow. "Brace the mainsail aback!"

"You're falling back?" Gray asked.

"What choice do we have?" The captain scrubbed his face with one hand. "There's no telling which direction that mast will fall. We can't risk the *Aphrodite* catching fire. I'll put in the boats. If there are any survivors, they'll make their way overboard."

"Not if they're injured or trapped in the hold, they won't."

"What do you propose to do, Gray?"

His reply was quiet, but firm. "Board it."

"What?" Sophia pulled out of his grip and turned to face him.

"What?" The captain's expression mirrored her sense of alarm. "Board a burning ship? Gray, are you mad?"

"You act as though we've never done it before. This used to be our livelihood, boarding burning ships. That mast is a fuse. It'll send the whole ship up in smoke if it's not cut down before those flames reach the deck." He clapped a hand on his brother's shoulder, his lips thinning in a tight smile. "Come on, Joss. It'll be like old times."

"In old times, any blaze we faced was the result of our own cannonfire. You know a lightning strike can spark fires all through a ship. Even now, there could be a blaze in the hold. If there's a keg of powder, a cask of rum nearby . . . The whole thing could go any moment."

"Then we'd best look lively, hadn't we?" Gray strode toward the rail, shouting up at the sailors, "Mainsail haul! Bring her around!"

The men complied without hesitation, and the *Aphrodite* pivoted, coming abreast of the other ship. Sophia stood transfixed as the flames crawled across the royal yard. The furled sail took fire like a scroll of paper.

"Volunteers!" Gray lifted a coil of rope from its pin. "Who'll board her with me? No men with wives or children."

Levi appeared at his side out of nowhere, strong and silent as ever. He and Gray exchanged nods of agreement.

"I'm in." O'Shea swung down from the yardarm and dropped to the deck with catlike grace. "Just like old times, eh, Gray?"

Gray shot an amused glance at his brother. "See?"

As the distance between the ships narrowed, the three men tested their ropes.

"I'll go, too." Davy pushed to the rail.

"No!" Sophia cried. "Gray, you can't let him."

"The ship could suffer my loss easier than most." The boy stood tall, rolling the sleeves of his tunic up over his elbows. "And I've no wife or children, sir."

"So you haven't," Gray said. "All right, then."

The four men grabbed hold of their ropes and climbed onto the rail, preparing to swing across the gap of churning sea to board the burning ship. No anxiety showed on Gray's face, only sharpened focus and grim determination. By contrast, Sophia was consumed with fear. She glanced up. The flames had reached the topgallant now. Dread numbed her entire body, and the bitter gale seemed to howl straight through her, whistling through her ribs and chilling her heart. She remembered the captain's words. *There could be fires throughout the ship . . . A keg of powder, one cask of rum, and . . .*

And he would be gone.

"Gray!" A gust of wind took her choked sob and flung it out to sea.

The captain strode forward, reaching for a coil of rope. "If you're determined to do this fool thing, I'm going with you."

"No." Gray's face was hard. "No men with wives or children." His gaze darted toward Sophia, then quickly away. If he read the desperate plea in her eyes, he did not acknowledge it. She winced, feeling the meaning of that dismissive glance. Whatever she was to him, she was something less than a wife. And he would never allow her to be more. She wasn't reason enough for him to live.

I don't want you.

Something inside her splintered and cracked. Sophia wrapped her arms tightly across her chest, as if she could hold the pieces together.

Gray turned back to his brother. "Fall back as soon as we're aboard, you hear? We'll signal when all's clear."

He hoisted his body's weight on the rope, the powerful brawn of his arms and back straining against the seams of his wet shirt. "The *Aphrodite*'s yours, Joss. Take care of her for me."

"Aye, I will." A knowing look passed between them. "I'll look after the ship, too."

CHAPTER
EIGHTEEN

Gray's boots hit the *Kestrel*'s deck with a hollow thud. Once the other three dropped over the rail, he began giving orders. The howling wind forced him to shout.

"O'Shea, take the wheel. Keep her steady, pointed into the gale. Otherwise, she'll be on her beam ends before we even get a whiff of smoke." The Irishman nodded and raced to the helm.

Gray looked to Levi. "Find some axes and start chopping down the mainmast. I'll join you."

His men dispatched, Gray peered up, squinting at the darkened sky rent by a line of bright flame. The fire was halfway down the mast now. With this unholy wind fanning the flames, they had only a matter of minutes before the fire reached the deck. No time to waste.

"I'll chop with Levi." Davy stood at his elbow. "I'm strong."

"No." Gray looked around. Where were the damn axes, anyhow? "I need you to search the ship. See if there are blazes in the hold. Look for injured, or anyone trapped. If you come across anything flammable—spirits, powder, medicines—you're to heave it overboard immediately, do you understand?"

The boy nodded, his face pale but determined. "Aye, captain." Davy's voice cracked, and Gray felt a twinge of guilt. He should have insisted the boy stay aboard the *Aphrodite*.

"I'm not your captain," Gray called after him.

"On this ship, you are." With a shrug, Davy hurried toward the hatch.

Gray strode toward the mainmast, looking for Levi. His boots crunched over something metallic. He stared down at the deck. Nails. Bent, fused together, some gnarled as tree roots. Good Lord, he'd heard of lightning strikes like this—jolts strong enough to rip nails right out of the mast and send them clattering to the deck—but he'd never seen such a thing, in all his years at sea. He hoped he'd never see it again.

A misshapen hunk of metal rolled to a stop at his feet, still smoking. Gray kicked the roundish lump. "What the devil is that?"

"I think it used to be the bell."

Gray's head snapped up, and he found two bedraggled sailors standing before him.

"What can we do?" the shorter of the two asked, rubbing his shoulder as though it ached.

"Are you unharmed?" Gray eyed the men from head to toe. Tattered clothing hung from their gaunt frames, and their hands were black with tar and soot. The acrid odor of singed hair assaulted his nostrils.

The sailors nodded. "Just rattled, is all," the taller one said. "Others weren't so lucky." He tilted his head toward a lifeless heap of rags on the opposite side of the deck. Mercifully, the dead sailor's face was hidden from view, but a charred hand still clutched the rigging.

Gray swallowed hard, tasting bile. "Where's your captain?" He brushed past the sailors. "And where the devil are your axes?"

"Don't know where the captain's at," one sailor answered. "Probably rummin' in his cabin. I'd like to think the bastard's dead, but we wouldn't be that lucky."

"As for the axes . . ." The taller seaman nodded

toward the rail, and Gray followed his gaze. A row of wooden hatchet handles stood at attention. Their hatchet blades, however, lay on the deck. Jolted from their handles, still smoking, half-melted . . . and completely, utterly useless.

Gray swore. Levi came bounding out from the galley, some sort of meat cleaver in one hand and a carving knife in the other. It was all Gray could do not to laugh till he cried. They were going to take down the mast with a meat cleaver?

Without a word, Levi handed him the knife and began attacking the mainmast with the cleaver. Well, apparently they were going to try.

Gray ran to the standing rigging, using the knife to saw through the ropes that connected mast and ship. If by some miracle Levi managed to cut through the mainmast, it couldn't fall clear with the rigging intact. The two sailors drew knives from their belts and began to assist. Despite the spray and wind, Gray's body quickly heated with the exertion. Sweat trickled down his brow, and he dabbed at it with his sleeve between blows. Eventually, he gave up the sawing motion in favor of full-armed swipes of the knife.

"How many crewmen?" he yelled at the sailors, hacking away at another rope. "Dead." *Thwack.* "Alive."

"There's eleven of us. Five were in the forecastle. Don't know how they fared. Two dead here on deck. A few others got blasted, but they're still alive. So far."

"What's in the hold?" His blow landed awkwardly, glancing the rail. Pain erupted in his elbow.

"Rum!" Davy scrambled toward them, juggling a small powder keg. Gray stopped mid-swing and stared at the boy. Terror was etched on his young face. "It's rum, Gray. The hold's full to bursting with it, and the—"

Davy tripped on a coil of rope, dropping the keg. Gray watched it roll back down the quarterdeck, trailing a thin line of powder as it went. *Perfect.* Just bloody wonderful.

Gray swung the knife again, fear cramping his side. "Is there fire below?"

"Not that I saw. But there are wounded men down there. One of them . . ." Davy's chest convulsed with a sudden heave, as if he would vomit. "One of them's burnt bad."

"Boats?" Gray looked to the sailors.

"Just one."

A wave of heat swamped them as the topsail caught fire, going up in flames like a dry leaf. Gray examined the shallow groove in the mainmast. Despite Levi's strength, he'd barely managed to score the trunk of pine. It would take far too long to fell it. By that time, the flames would be too low. The fire would reach the deck, ignite the powder, spread to the hold full of rum, and the entire ship would explode like a Bonapartist's grenade.

Bloody hell.

Levi kept swinging the tiny cleaver, while the rest of the men merely stared at Gray. Davy swallowed and shifted his weight, clearly awaiting direction. "Captain?"

The instant that word fell from Davy's lips, Gray knew several things. He knew he was now the de facto captain of this godforsaken ship. He'd boarded it and taken command, and now he had to stay with it until the end. He knew he could save some of the men, but not all. At this rate, they'd be lucky to get the boat lowered before the rum exploded, let alone bring the injured up from the hold. And he knew he couldn't leave the wounded behind and live with himself afterward. Which meant he wouldn't live. He'd never get back to the *Aphrodite*. Not to his business, not to his family.

Not to her.

He was going to die. Today.

Christ.

He ran both hands through his hair, pushing it off his brow, then took the cleaver from Levi. "Put in the boat. Raise the call to abandon ship." A hunk of charred yardarm dropped to the deck at his feet, forcing him to step back. "And be quick about it."

The men hurried to lower the jolly boat from the ship's stern, leaving Gray to stare up at the burning mainmast. The mast danced with flame like a giant candlewick. He made a fist and punched the stubborn column of wood, earning nothing but scraped knuckles and searing pain for his trouble.

"Fall, damn you." He leaned his shoulder against the mast and pushed, though he knew it a futile effort. Teeth gritted and heels dug into the grooves of the deck, he shoved again. *"Fall."*

Nothing.

An unfamiliar seaman's voice rasped through the gale. "Abandon ship! All hands, abandon ship! To the boat!"

A handful of sailors struggled up through the forecastle hatch, lurching their way toward the stern. If the men noticed a bearded madman attempting to topple the mainmast with his bare hands, they did not pause to spare him a second glance.

"Stop that bloody shouting!"

The surly, languid curse drew Gray's attention toward the stern. He watched as a lanky man in a black, brass-buttoned coat staggered out from the captain's cabin, rubbing his bleary face. Slack-jawed and blinking, he wore an expression that was one part bewilderment, two parts liquor.

The captain looked up at the encroaching flames and scowled. "What the devil—?"

Gray shook his head. Had the man slept through the whole damned ordeal? He'd lost at least two crewmen and his ship was poised to become an inferno, and this excuse for a commander had the idiocy to curse the alarm that roused him from his stupor?

The deck lurched, and the drunken captain grabbed a pin for support. With the next roll of the ship, he vomited wildly on his own boots.

Gray took two strides toward the helm and cupped his hands around his mouth. "O'Shea!"

The Irishman caught his gaze across the ship's wheel.

Gray indicated the retching officer. "Get him to the boat. And stay there yourself. Tell Levi to start pulling away. Now."

"What about you, Gray?"

"I'll swim out to you. Now go!"

"Aye, aye." O'Shea yanked on the captain's coat sleeve, practically carrying him toward the boat. They both disappeared over the ship's rail, and Gray watched the ropes securing the jolly boat reel out and then go slack.

They were away.

Gray sagged against the mainmast, feeling the flames above him singe his hair. He was going to die here, alone, leaving nothing to mark his time on this earth but a string of dashed expectations and broken promises. His legacy would fade faster than the wake of a porpoise.

Something popped overhead, and sparks showered down around him. Ducking, Gray buried his face against his arm. Perhaps, he thought, he *could* swim for it. There were injured men in the hold—how many? Four? Five? No way to save them now. But he could save himself. He could swim back to her. He'd swim miles to her, if that's what it took.

But could he live with himself afterward, knowing he'd abandoned five men to an agonizing death while he swam to safety?

An image of her loveliness bloomed behind his eyelids. Gray decided maybe he could.

Sliding his back down the mast, he sank to the deck and wrestled to remove his boots.

The flames had reached the standing rigging now. Above him, the tar sizzled and popped on the surfaces of the ropes, dripping to the deck like a black, sulfurous rain. His first taste of hell? The heat of the flames washed over him.

And then a familiar voice froze the very blood in his veins.

"What now, Captain?"

It couldn't be. Gray's head snapped up, and a curse tainted his rough exhalation. It was. *Davy.* "What the hell are you still doing here? You were supposed to leave with the boat!"

The boy shrugged. "I didn't. Thought you needed me."

Gray squeezed his eyes shut and let his booted foot fall to the deck. "Davy, I don't suppose you can swim?"

"No, Captain."

Gray swore again. He kicked the mast. Punched it. Stepped back, lowered his shoulder and rammed it with all his strength, all the while releasing a vicious stream of profanity.

Davy tilted his head and scratched his neck. "Don't think that's working."

"You're bloody right, it's not working," Gray shouted at him. "We're going to die, do you realize that?"

"Is there no other way to take a mast down?"

"I've taken dozens of masts down. But from my own damn ship, with the . . ." As Gray's voice trailed off, hope sparked in his chest. The idea was pure madness.

But better mad than dead. He wheeled to face the bow, a prayer caught in his throat as his eyes swept the deck. Finally, his gaze locked on the object he sought.

A six-pounder cannon, hunched low by the rail.

He strode toward it, the boy hurrying to follow. "Davy, do you know how to fire a cannon?"

"No, Captain."

After cutting the ropes with his knife, Gray swung the cannon one hundred and eighty degrees and shoved it to the center of the quarterdeck. "You're going to learn. Put your thumb here"—he indicated the vent hole at the top, and waited until Davy complied—"and don't remove it until I tell you to."

Gray retrieved the keg Davy had dropped earlier and broke it open with his knife, pouring a good third of its contents into the cannon. No time to measure out the charge. Better to err on the side of excess.

Now for the cannonballs. "We'll use a double shot," he explained to Davy. "We'll only get one try at this." Gray reached for the row of shot stored in the bulwark, only to snatch his hand back. The bloody things were still scorching to the touch. And worse. His heart sank as he gave the row an experimental kick.

The damned things were fused together. A caterpillar of iron.

Every profane word Gray had ever heard, read, uttered, or invented spewed forth from his mouth. *Don't panic,* he told himself, when Davy blanched. *Anything can go in a cannon. Anything metal, and preferably round.*

The gale howled through the sails, now lacy with flame. The ship gave a sudden lurch; the deck tipped. And the smoking remnants of the ship's bell rolled to rest at Gray's feet, like the answer to a prayer.

Using the cuffs of his shirt to buffer the heat, he threw the lump of metal into the cannon's mouth.

Gray gestured for Davy to remove his thumb. "Now, we need a fuse . . . and a spark."

"No shortage of those." Davy's straight-faced quip gave Gray a sudden surge of determination. He was not going to let this boy die. Crewmen with his good humor and courage were beastly hard to find. Crouching behind the cannon, he aligned the sights with the base of the mainmast, just below the spreading flames.

If he missed—or even if he hit his mark—this single shot could have the entire ship exploding into flame and ash. It was a desperate risk, for a desperate situation.

"Stand clear, to the side," he ordered Davy. "And cover your ears." Gray scrambled to pluck a glowing sliver of wood from the deck. He touched it to the fuse, clapped his hands over his ears, and ducked.

Boom.

The shot ripped from the cannon's barrel. A cloud of smoke and powder instantly engulfed them. Splinters of wood showered them, some piercing straight through Gray's shirt and lodging in his flesh. Blinded, deafened, choked, and gagged—Gray simply waited for one of his senses to return and let him know whether or not he'd survived.

The powder slowly cleared, and through the dissipating cloud, Gray saw the mainmast. Blasted on one side, but still standing. Still afire. Burning brighter still.

Gray jumped to his feet. "Fall, damn you."

The wind accelerated, and an eerie creaking sound pierced the air. Slowly, drunkenly, the mainmast splintered at its base and made an ungainly dive into the sea, severed rigging slithering behind it like eels.

"Jesus Christ." Gray slumped back to his knees.

And then—as if God Himself had heard him and decided to drown his blasphemous soul and be done with it—the skies opened up and vomited rain.

Stinging sheets of water scoured the deck, pelting them as they huddled by the cannon. For long moments the two of them crouched there, soaking up water like sponges. Gray's limbs were heavy with shock.

At last, Davy sputtered and shook himself like a wet dog, adding a horizontal spray of water to the vertical deluge. "Thank God." His boyish grin broke the ice encasing Gray's own reaction.

He laughed. What else could he do? He ought to have died. He was going to live. It was either laugh or weep, and he was already soaked with enough water to float a barrel.

"Don't relax yet. We're not done." He put a hand under Davy's arm and hauled the boy to his feet. "Find any able-bodied men still aboard and form a work chain. The ship's not out of danger yet. A slow fire might have sparked anywhere in her frame. We have to bring up that rum from the hold and dump it overboard. Then we'll see to the injured."

Davy paused as they moved toward the hatch. "If we're throwing the rum overboard . . . Can we at least drink some first? I could do with a swallow."

Gray laughed. "So could I."

Some time later, Gray swung his shaky legs over the rail of the *Aphrodite*.

Joss hurried to his side. "Any dead?"

"Two. And three more gravely wounded." Gray raked his wet hair away from his face. "Best to send the longboat for them. There doesn't seem to be any fire in the hold, but you know as well as I do it's too soon to tell. These things are known to flare up hours later. We've emptied it of anything incendiary, just to be safe."

Joss looked up at the sky. "Well, with this downpour, it seems less likely."

"Aye." Exhausted, Gray leaned against the rigging and wiped his brow with his forearm. "Everyone all right here?" He tried to keep his voice steady.

Joss nodded. "She's in my cabin, Gray. I think you'd better go to her."

"I don't think she'd want that." After the way he'd deserted her earlier, he assumed she'd be just as happy never to see him again.

"She's been sick with worry, Gray. I had to order her to go below. Even then, she'd only heed my cautions long after the rain doused the blaze. She'll be relieved to see you're well."

"She's just anxious for young Davy." Still, he couldn't douse the spark of hope that kindled in his chest. And he couldn't stay away. Giving Joss an affectionate punch on the arm, he climbed the stairs to the helm and opened the hatch.

Slowly, he descended into the murky cabin. Although it was still daytime, the storm clouds banked most of the sun's rays. Gray blinked, scanning the shadows. Then he saw her, silhouetted against the windows at the stern.

"Gray?"

He nodded. Then, realizing she probably couldn't discern the gesture in the dark, he cleared his throat and forced out, "It's me."

"Are you . . . are you well?"

"Yes." His eyes began to adjust to the dimness, and he could just make out the soft slope of her shoulder, her arms crossed over her belly. Her hair was loose, falling to her waist in heavy waves.

"Levi and O'Shea?" she asked, her voice tremulous. "Davy?"

"They're safe, too. The fire's out. It's all over."

She said nothing. Gray stood quietly for a moment, shifting his weight. *Go to her,* a voice inside him urged.

Take her in your arms. Beg her forgiveness. Say something; promise her anything.

God, what a coward he was. In truth, he'd been only too eager to board a burning ship and risk his life that afternoon. Because it was easier to walk through fire than to face this little governess, and the tempest of emotion she stirred in his heart.

The silence mocked him. He was on the verge of taking his leave when suddenly she ran to him, flinging her arms around his neck.

"Oh, Gray. I was so frightened. But I just knew you'd come back to me. You had to come back to me."

"Of course I did." Gray stood shocked and immobile as she clutched his neck, sobbing noisily against his shoulder. His hands dangled uselessly at his sides.

"Gray," she cried again and again. "Thank God you're safe."

Her affection overwhelmed him, as did her softness, her tears. Even after all he'd said to her, after all he'd done—she still gave a damn whether he lived or died. It was humbling. Incomprehensible. Wonderful. If he'd known this would be his reward, he would have fallen overboard weeks ago.

Finally, he drew a deep breath and wrapped his arms about her, clutching her tightly to his chest. "Shhh, sweet." With a trembling hand, he stroked her hair. The damp locks slid through his fingers like ribbons. "Don't cry. Everything's fine. It's all over now."

She sniffed and raised her face to his. He was still murmuring assurances and stroking her hair, and the sight of that perfect face tilted inches from his—it caught him completely unprepared. Her beauty hit him like a lightning bolt.

Her hands skimmed up his neck, tugging his face down to hers. Gray closed his eyes as she brushed a warm, feather-light kiss against his jaw. Another landed on his neck. Then the corner of his mouth. She pressed her cheek to his, and he felt her hot tears mingle with the cold rivulets of rain.

His heart squeezed. After the callous way he'd treated her, for her to hold him like this and kiss him so tenderly—it was the truest act of bravery Gray had ever seen. She was offering up her heart, fully expecting him to break it. And selfish bastard that he was, Gray had lost any will to push her away.

Maybe . . . just maybe, he didn't need to. He'd just boarded a ship, sprung its mast, destroyed its cargo—the same actions he'd performed time and again in the past, out of greed. But this time, he'd done them for different reasons entirely. Not to take, but to protect.

Just as he'd taken many—*too* many—women in his arms before, with only the most dishonorable of intentions. But this was different. So different. If he could seize a ship with honor . . . perhaps he could do this with honor, too. Not to take, but to protect. To cherish. To love.

She sobbed against his cheek again, and he pulled back. "Hush, love," he whispered, smoothing her hair behind her ear. He cupped her face in his hands and lowered his lips to hers in a gentle kiss. "It's all over now."

And it was. It was all over now. The fire was out, and the men were alive. And she was here in his arms, where she fit like she was fashioned for his embrace. Weeks of frustrated longing were finally at an end. Years of emptiness, too. It was all over now.

And Gray . . . Gray was finished. Done for. Completely and hopelessly lost in the softest, most tender embrace he'd ever known. He held her face in his hands, brushing light kisses over her lips. Kissing her slowly, carefully, as though he were only just learning about kissing—because he was. Not learning *how* to kiss, but learning *why* to kiss. Not in persuasion, not as a prelude to further liberties. Simply to discover the taste of her, delicate and fresh and exquisitely sweet. To tell her things he didn't dare express in words. To tell her things he had no words to express. He kissed her for no greater pleasure than to kiss, because at that moment, kissing her felt like the greatest pleasure imaginable.

He pressed his lips to her cheeks, her brow, her eyelids, her hair, interspersing his kisses with little endearments in every language he knew. Then, eyes closed, he rested his forehead against hers and waited. Leaving the choice to her.

With a little sigh, she melted in his arms, pressing the length of her body to his. Her breasts rubbed against his chest, deliciously warm and soft. Desire blazed through him. And suddenly, Gray was right back in the middle of an inferno.

She popped up on her toes, pressing her lips to his with a fierce urgency. An urgency he shared. The desperate energy that had fueled his race against the flames still ricocheted through his body. Gray felt it humming in his bones and pounding in his blood. And now he poured it all into kissing this woman, lashing his arms around her and lifting her body against his. Crushing her soft belly against his growing arousal.

Her lips parted beneath his, and he eagerly accepted the invitation. Their tongues tangled, tasted, teased, each of them giving and taking in return. Finally Gray broke away, sliding one hand down to cup her bottom as her fingers twined tightly into his hair.

"I'm so sorry," he said between kisses. "For what I said that night. For leaving you earlier. I never meant—"

"I know," she whispered, wrapping a leg over his hip

and shinnying up his body. Her lips grazed his ear. "I know. Just don't leave me again."

"Never." The word burst out like an oath or a prayer, and God help him, he meant it. "Never," he repeated, looking straight in her glimmering eyes. Then he sealed the vow with a kiss, deep and desperate and true. "Oh, God," he groaned when their lips finally parted.

She kissed him again, working her warm, slender fingers under the collar of his shirt to stroke the chilled flesh of his shoulders and back. He buried his face in her neck, inhaling the beautiful scent of her. He'd forgotten how roses smell sweetest after a rain. Trailing light kisses down to her collarbone, he began carrying her toward the bed.

"Make love to me, Gray."

She didn't need to ask it. They both knew what was going to happen. But Gray felt the significance of her words. He might have bedded ladies and whores the world over, but for the first time in his life, he was going to make love to a woman. And not just *a* woman. *His* woman.

And this idea that should have been so unthinkable, so frightening—to his surprise, Gray found it wildly arousing. They tumbled together onto the narrow bed, and she began pulling his shirt free of his trousers. He rose up on his knees and impatiently yanked it over his head.

He peered at her frock in the darkness.

Bloody hell. Stripes.

Gray started to roll her over, looking for laces or hooks or some other ridiculous device contrived by the devil to thwart men.

She shook her head. "Next time." She wriggled beneath him, drawing her skirts up to her waist. The erotic dance of her hips had him trembling with need. "Next time, we'll go slowly. We'll do everything you told me this morning, and more." She gasped as he palmed her breast through the wet muslin. Her fingers hooked under the waistband of his trousers, and she looked up at him with a bold, smoldering gaze. "But I need you now, Gray."

With a low groan, he leaned over to suck one pert nipple straight through the layers of shift and frock. She moaned and arched against him, working his buttons loose with one hand, until her fingers slid down into his smallclothes to caress the swollen head of his erection.

Oh, God. He needed her now, too. He needed her now, and again later, and perhaps a third time that night. And tomorrow and the next day and every day after that. He was pulsing with need, straining into her touch, and as her fingers curled around him, they both gasped.

She stroked him gently, so sweetly he wanted to weep for the joy of it. He slid one hand up her thigh to find her hot and wet and grinding against his palm. *Next time,* he promised himself. Next time, he would take the time to touch her and taste her and learn her responses and watch her beauty unfurl at the peak of passion.

But she needed him now, and he needed her now, and now wasn't a minute or even a second later. Now was *now.* Gray brushed her hand away, positioned himself at her hot, wet entrance, and thrust.

She cried out, digging her fingers into his arms so hard he nearly cried out, too.

Oh, God. She was so tight. Too tight. Fresh tears streamed down her cheeks even as she tried to look brave. And Gray finally understood that elusive, unnameable sweetness that always lingered about her, beneath the powder and rose water.

It was innocence.

His little siren was a virgin.

"Why—" His breath hitched in his chest as he struggled for control. "Oh, sweet, you should have told me the truth."

"I'm telling you now." She swallowed hard, sliding one hand up to cradle his face. "Only you, Gray. Now and always. Only you."

"But what about—"

She silenced him with a finger to his lips, then trailed the touch slowly down his chin, down the center of his chest. "There's never been anyone else. Only you."

Gray shook his head, uncertain what to believe. Her words were some sort of miracle, and so were her thighs cradling his hips, and her hair fanned out like a shining halo around her head. A fierce, primal joy flooded his chest, to know that she was his, and his alone.

His to possess; his to pleasure.

He shifted his weight on his hands, and as he did, he sank another inch into her. They both winced.

His to hurt.

"Sweetheart, I can't bear to hurt you."

"It's all right," she said through quivering lips. "Honestly, it feels better already."

He knew she was lying. He rocked his hips backward with every intention of withdrawing, but she hooked her legs over his.

"No," she gasped, her body tightening around his in every way imaginable. "You can't leave me. You promised."

He groaned as the exquisite friction pulled him back in. Gritting his teeth to restrain himself, he sank into her slowly. Her eyes grew wide, but she gave him a brave nod of encouragement.

"Yes," she breathed as he finally buried himself to the hilt and they were completely, perfectly joined. The feel of her surrounding him, holding him—it was like nothing he'd ever dreamed. He squeezed his eyes shut and rocked again slowly. Back and forth, he gently pistoned his hips, grinding against her. Until she said it again, this time releasing the word in an erotic sigh. "Oh, *yes.*"

It took every ounce of willpower Gray possessed not to lose control that instant and simply drive into her again and again. But she'd trusted him to make love to her, not rut with her. She'd trusted him to be her only one. Now and always. So he kept up the slow, steady rocking of his hips. Feeling her body caress his with each small, measured thrust.

She shut her eyes, and her head rolled back against the pillow. "Oh, Gray," she moaned, arching into his subtle thrusts now with tiny tilts of her hips. He bent to suckle her breast again, licking the soft peak through the rough, wet fabric.

She clutched his shoulders. He froze, panting above her. His hands fisted in the bed linens as he grappled for control.

"Are you all right?" he asked.

"I'm all right."

"Are you sure?"

"Yes, I'm sure," she said, a teasing note in her voice. She caressed his shoulders. Her fingers trailed down his chest, and she pressed her thumbs against his nipples.

Gray let out a hoarse groan. "I can't . . ." His voice trailed off as she craned her neck and kissed his chest. The sweep of her tongue against his neck pushed his restraint to its limit. "Sweet, stop. I want to make this good for you."

"It is good." Her teeth grazed his collarbone. "*You* are good for me." Her head fell back against the pillow, and she met his eyes. "There's no pain anymore."

This time, he believed her. He had to believe her, because his control was in shreds, and nothing but faith remained.

He drove into her now, thrust after blissful, unrestrained thrust. And when she cried out and clung to his neck, he knew it was with pleasure, not pain. Her core convulsed around him, pulling him toward release in waves of raw, mindless need. Then she cupped his face in her hands and blessed him with a single, sweet kiss.

And in the end, it was that kiss that proved his undoing. With a hoarse cry against her lips, he shuddered and collapsed, pumping his release into her. The last tremors of pleasure were still rippling through him, and already he wanted her again. Again, now, always, only.

He settled the length of his body over hers, guarding her between his arms. His rough, gasping breath precluded speech, but they needed no words. There *were* no words for the transcendent, floating happiness suffusing his limbs and filling his heart. Only kisses. Kiss after deep, heartfelt, unhurried kiss.

It was some time before Gray's awareness shifted from the wondrous taste of her soft, generous mouth to the strange, angular object pressing into his belly.

He propped himself up on one elbow and slid a hand up her hip, past the glorious Tropic where they remained joined even now, up over her belly to the notch between her ribs. His hand closed around a small, cloth-covered bundle strapped to her torso with bands of cloth. He frowned, feeling the solid object with his fingers, trying to learn its shape.

Money, he realized. It had to be money. He spanned his fingers over it, testing its size. Bloody hell. It was a great deal of money.

"Gray, I can explain."

CHAPTER
NINETEEN

"I'm waiting."

Sophia tensed at the sudden edge in his voice. Surely he couldn't be angry. Not after the pleasure they'd found, the connection they still shared.

"Gray," she murmured, stretching her neck to kiss him wherever she could reach. His hard chest, his powerful shoulders bracketing hers. She wanted to thank him, to bless him for the gift he'd given her. Such tenderness, and such pleasure.

Her mother, her sister, her married friends—in the weeks leading up to her wedding, there had been no shortage of women warning Sophia that her first experience in the marital bed would be painful, awkward, and blessedly quick. The ladies had varying opinions on whether the activity would improve with time, but predictions of an unpleasant wedding night were universal.

None of them, she thought with a secret smile, had met Gray. The power in his strong body, the passion he aroused in her, all tempered by such patience, the innate tenderness he hid so carefully from the world. There had been pain, yes. But the pain had been chased away by indescribable pleasure, intense and overwhelming, beyond anything she'd ever imagined.

And Sophia's imagination was vast.

Embers of desire still smoldered under her skin, on her

lips, between her legs. She tightened around him, wanting to preserve this moment forever. Lacing her fingers behind his neck, she attempted to pull him down for a kiss.

He wouldn't budge. "I'm waiting," he repeated tersely. "Explain."

She stroked the hair back from his face. "I promise I'll tell you everything. But for now . . . please, just hold me."

He swore, his coarse tone scraping against her nakedness. "I don't even know who I'm holding."

He released her abruptly, and Sophia gasped as he withdrew from her body. Somehow it hurt more than when he'd entered her. He rolled away, leaving her uncovered. Damp with rainwater, sweat, and tears. Cold.

"Of course you know me," she whispered. No one had ever made her feel so accepted as this man did. She feared no one else ever would.

He sat up, turning away and dropping his head in his hands. Sophia rolled onto her side and reached out cautiously to stroke his back. When her fingertip snagged on a sharp obstacle, she winced. "You have splinters in your back."

"Do I? Well, you have a small fortune between your breasts."

Sophia struggled to sit up, move closer. "Really, Gray. These must be painful. Let me—"

"Leave it be." He jerked away. Sophia curled her hand and let it fall to the bed. His voice measured, he continued, "Your name isn't even Jane Turner, is it?"

"The name Turner is . . . borrowed. Jane is mine." And it *was* truly hers, if only her middle name. That part could not count as a lie. Minimizing the number of her falsehoods seemed of sudden importance.

"You weren't ruined."

"But I was." Perhaps she had been a virgin until today, but her reputation was surely in tatters.

"Don't lie to me." He shot her a hard look, his eyes awash with anger. "You were a virgin."

Sophia didn't understand his ire. Yes, she'd deceived him, but shouldn't he be happy, that he'd been her first lover? Her *only* lover, if she had her wish? "Yes, but—"

"Then you weren't ruined. Though you are *now*, thanks to me." He swore again. "You lied to me. You knew I didn't want to take your innocence, so you tricked me into it. God, what a conniving little thing you are."

His words chilled her to the core. Sophia smoothed the fabric of her dress back down, covering her shivering legs. "Gray, it was not like that. You have to give me a chance to expl—"

"You're not even a governess, are you?"

She chewed her lip. "No."

"Of course not. No woman with those assets"—he gestured brusquely toward her breasts and the money strapped beneath them—"need seek employment. How much is there? Two hundred pounds? Three?"

"Nearly six."

"Bloody hell." He ran his hands through his hair, then curled them around the edge of the bed. "No one comes by that kind of coin honestly. Who are you then? A thief? A fugitive? Some sort of swindler?"

All of the above. Sophia clutched the blankets around her, as if they could protect her from his angry words. She knew this was a tangle of her own making, but she'd never dreamed it would be so difficult to make straight. Once he embraced her, she'd imagined, he would happily embrace the truth as well. She'd even expected he'd be amused, to hear the full story at last. But now . . . his obvious displeasure suggested otherwise. Fear built within her, swift and treacherous.

"Does it really matter?" she asked, her voice weaker

than she'd like. "After all that we've shared?" She slid one leg toward him, until her thigh grazed his fingertips.

"What we've *shared*?" He pulled his hand away. "What have you shared with me, but lies?"

How could he say such a thing? She'd shared everything with him. Her artistry, her most secret fantasies. Heavens, she'd *touched* herself in front of him. Now she'd given him her virtue, in a moment of passion and tenderness surpassing anything she'd ever known. And he was rejecting that gift, as though it were nothing. Rejecting *her*.

"Christ." Hiking his trousers to his waist, he stood and turned to face her. The look in his eyes was not quite revulsion, but rather an expression of utter disbelief. "I *told* you things. About myself, about my family. I told you things I've never told another soul. Now I learn you're no more than a stranger to me." He swore again.

"Must you persist in swearing?"

"Yes, I think I must. Damn it, I thought I was done bedding nameless women."

Now Sophia was growing angry, too. "I see. And now I suppose you intend to continue?"

He froze, arm extended to retrieve his shirt. For a long moment, Sophia stared at him. He wouldn't meet her eyes. Finally, he pulled the shirt over his arms and head, tucking it into his trousers with motions that bespoke controlled fury. "You're right," he said coolly, buttoning his falls. "After what we just did . . . it doesn't matter."

"What doesn't matter?" Sophia swallowed around the lump in her throat. "The truth? Or me?"

He pierced her with an icy look, one boot poised on the ladder leading up to the hatch. "How can you even ask me that?"

How can you be so cruel? A sob smothered the question. She hugged her arms across her chest, blinking away tears.

"Sweet." The slight rasp in his voice tugged her eyes back up. His gaze deepened, made room to hold hers. "Right now, there are dead and dying men up there, and a disabled ship in need of repair. At the moment, they are what matters. Stay here. I will come back." He mounted the ladder. "We'll deal with this later."

Then he was gone.

Sophia fell back onto the bed, curling into herself like the head of a fern. *We'll deal with this later?* How hateful that sounded. How final. She didn't want to be dealt with. She wanted to be comforted. She wanted to be held. She wanted something she hadn't felt in so long, she scarcely remembered how to name it—but she dared to imagine she deserved it, just the same.

She wanted to be loved.

He didn't come back that night. Her only visitors were Gabriel, who politely ignored her bedraggled, tear-stained appearance when he brought her evening tea and biscuit, and Stubb, who delivered her trunks to the captain's cabin. Evidently, the ladies' berths had been appropriated as a makeshift hospital for the *Kestrel*'s wounded.

Unfamiliar voices and late-night activity obscured the *Aphrodite*'s usual nocturnal symphony—bells and creaking wood and the reedy whistle of the breeze. Huddled in the center of the bed, Sophia drifted in and out of shallow sleep, straining her ears to catch any echo of his rich baritone, or the squeaking hinges of the hatch. If Gray did come to her, she wanted to be awake. But she kept watch in vain, and exhaustion finally claimed her with the first rays of dawn.

When she woke, it was to full daylight. Sophia bolted straight up in bed, her heart pounding. An argument was brewing directly above her, near the ship's helm.

Even with the hatch closed, she could make out not only Gray's voice, but the captain's, as well as O'Shea's thick brogue. And a few unfamiliar voices as well. Although he was not addressing her, the timbre of Gray's voice was as hollow and unforgiving as a bell struck on a winter morning—just the way she'd heard it last.

She rose from bed and went to the tiny round looking glass attached to the cabin wall, realizing with wonder that she hadn't looked in a mirror since leaving England. The image reflected there was greatly altered. Her skin was a shade or two darker—resembling bone more than porcelain—and lightly freckled from the sun. Some of the curves had sharpened to angles; her features caught more shadows now. When she squinted, faint lines pleated at the corners of her eyes, and even when she relaxed her expression, the lines had the audacity to linger. She was still beautiful, Sophia told herself, with no false or undue modesty. But it was no longer a pampered debutante's face that stared back at her.

She was a woman now. A fallen woman in truth, alone in the world, responsible for her own choices. She had to pull herself together, be strong. No more tears, she admonished herself, pressing the heels of her hands against her eyes. Gray could not ignore her forever. He would come to her eventually, most likely to hurl further angry accusations. When the time came, she would not weep or make excuses. She most certainly would not beg.

But by God, she would look pretty.

She washed her face and dabbed cold tea under her eyes to relieve the puffiness. Rifling through her trunks, she located her hairbrush and dusting powder. At least her hair, which had grown stiff with salt over the past three weeks, had been rinsed clean by yesterday's storm. Now dry, it tumbled about her shoulders in golden waves.

She'd washed out her sprigged muslin a few days ago, and it was as clean as it could get. When she reached into the trunk to retrieve the frock, however, her fingers lingered over a bundle at the bottom. Crisp tissue crackled under her touch, sliding over the silk beneath. She was tempted to unwrap the dress, to draw the fine fabric over her limbs and bathe her whole body in elegance as she hadn't done in weeks.

She resisted the temptation, reaching for the sprigged muslin instead. That tissue-wrapped dress was her best, and she was not yet sure Gray deserved her best. She was not convinced he even wanted it.

Powdered and dressed, her hair neatly coiled and pinned atop her head, Sophia peered into the mirror once again and pinched her cheeks to a high blush before mounting the ladder. The sounds of men arguing had grown louder.

She pushed open the hatch just a crack. Enough that she could distinguish the violent words being slung about like daggers and peer out at deck level. She recognized Gray's fine boots immediately, sooty as they were from the fire. He stood close to the rail, at the ship's stern. The sun was bright this morning; the men cast long shadows across the deck.

A gravelly, unfamiliar voice assailed her from somewhere near the ship's wheel. "I'm telling you, you bastard, you're going to pay for that rum. In gold or goods, I don't care which."

"Captain Mallory." Gray's baritone was forbidding. "And I apply that title loosely, as you are no manner of captain in my estimation . . . I have no intention of compensating you for the loss of your cargo. I will, however, accept your thanks."

"My *thanks*? For what?"

"For what?" Now O'Shea entered the mix. "For saving that heap of a ship and your worthless, rum-soaked arse, that's what."

"I'll thank you to go to hell," the gravelly voice answered. Mallory, she presumed. "You can't just board a man's craft and pitch a hold full of spirits into the sea. Right knaves, you lot."

"Oh, now we're knaves, are we?" Gray asked. "I should have let that ship explode around your ears, you despicable sot. Knaves, indeed."

"Well, if you're such virtuous, charitable gents, then how come I'm trussed like a pig?" Sophia craned her neck and pushed the hatch open a bit further. Across the deck, she saw a pair of split-toed boots tied together with rope.

Gray answered, "We had to bind you last night because you were drunk out of your skull. And we're keeping you bound now because you're sober and still out of your skull."

The lashed boots shuffled across the deck, toward Gray. "Let me loose of these ropes, you blackguard, and I'll pound you straight out of your skull into oblivion."

O'Shea responded with a stream of colorful profanity, which Captain Grayson cut short.

"Captain Mallory," he said, his own highly polished boots pacing slowly, deliberately to halt between Mallory's and Gray's. "I understand your concern over losing your cargo. But surely you or your investor can recoup the loss with an insurance claim. You could not have sailed without a policy against fire."

Gray gave an ironic laugh. "Joss, I'll wager you anything, that rum wasn't on any bill of lading or insurance policy. Can't you see the man's nothing but a smuggler? Probably wasn't bound for any port at all. What *was* your destination, Mallory? A hidden cove off the coast of Cornwall, perhaps?" He clucked his tongue. "That ship was overloaded and undermanned, and it would have been a miracle if you'd made it as far as Portugal. As for the rum, take up your complaint with the Vice Admiralty court after you follow us to Tortola. I'd welcome it."

"I'm not following you anywhere." Sophia could hear the scowl in Mallory's voice.

"Then what do you intend to do?" Captain Grayson asked. "Your ship is barely seaworthy. You have wounded men in dire need of a physician, and Tortola is the closest port. We could sink the *Kestrel,* if you prefer, and bring everyone aboard the *Aphrodite.* But that would mean forfeiting what cargo remains."

Someone spat, loudly and wetly.

"I'm not following you anywhere," Mallory repeated. "I'm not heading in for port, and I'll be damned if I let you brigands sink my ship. I'm going to repair my vessel and continue on. After I get my compensation, of course."

"Are ye mad?" O'Shea's voice rose a half-octave. "You'd not make the Tropic. You're one mast and at least four men down. Daft drunkard," he grumbled.

Gray's voice again. "I'll tell you why the daft drunkard doesn't want to harbor in Tortola. He knows I'd be entitled to salvage for saving his miserable craft. If he dared bring me into court, I'd walk away with everything. His rum would still be gone, and what's left of the *Kestrel* would belong to me. Isn't that right, Mallory?"

No answer. Just the light scuffling of bound boots. Sophia advanced one step up the ladder and pushed open the hatch a few inches more.

"Yes, he knows that ship is as good as mine." Gray's heavy footfalls underscored each phrase. Nearing Mallory, he continued, "And I'm of a mind to take her."

"You wouldn't dare." Mallory punctuated his reply with a spit and a curse, both indescribably crude to Sophia's ears.

"Gray," Joss began, "I'm not certain you can simply—"

"Oh, I assure you, it would be simple. As simple as the sixty-odd other times I've commandeered a vessel. What would you have me do, Joss? I didn't save that worthless bucket of timber just to watch it sink or sail off to its doom. The wounded need a doctor, the *Kestrel* needs a proper mast. I'm going to take her in to Tortola."

He was leaving this ship? Sophia pushed the hatch higher, needing to see more of him. His trousers and shirt hung limp and tattered from his frame. His loose posture was one of exhaustion. But even from her furtive vantage point, she could tell his expression was all seriousness. Her lungs seized. He couldn't be thinking to leave her again. He hadn't even dealt with her yet.

Mallory sneered. "You miserable, sniveling whoreson." He spat again, this time in Gray's face.

Gray slowly wiped his face on his shredded cuff. The two men glared at each other, the tension between them building, swarming, growing fists. Through the charged silence, Sophia heard the sound of knuckles cracking.

Then suddenly, Gray stood down. As he always did, he stole the advantage with a shrug and a lazy smile. *If I don't care about you,* that look said, *you can't possibly hurt me*.

Sophia was growing to hate that look.

"Mallory," he began on a tone of false conciliation, "by all means, let's do things the easy way. It would be a shame for this to turn violent." His voice darkened a shade. "I don't like violence."

He swung around to face Joss. "Send a party of able men to the *Kestrel,* to start rigging a jury-mast and fitting it with sails. You take the wounded on into port, and we'll limp behind as best we can. We'll meet up in Road Town."

"No!" Sophia threw open the hatch and stumbled out onto the deck, drowning Mallory's protest with her own. "Gray, you are *not* leaving me again. I won't let you."

His face was hard, unreadable as he quickly scanned her appearance. "What the devil are you doing on deck?"

"What am *I* doing? What are . . ." Her voice trailed off as she noticed the lascivious leer Mallory was dragging up and down her body. Sophia crossed her arms over her chest, disgusted. He was younger than she'd imagined from his voice, and thinner. But no less repulsive.

"Well, well," he clucked, narrow-set eyes peering at her around a hooked nose. "If she stays with this ship, I might stop protesting. Can't say I'd turn down a taste of that tart."

Her cheeks burning, Sophia turned to Gray. To her horror, she watched as his mouth tipped in a smirk. Almost a smile. Curse him, he even chuckled as he strolled back across the deck to face Mallory.

Was that how he saw her now, too? As a tart? Just another of his countless paramours? They might as well have been right back in that seedy tavern on the Gravesend quay, when she'd mistaken him for a gentleman—and he'd looked at her and seen only a bit of skirt.

"Mr. Mallory," he said, striking his habitual pose of arrogant swagger, "I'd like to thank you."

"For what?"

"For giving me an excuse to do this."

Gray swung his fist, putting the full force of his body behind the blow. The punch connected with Mallory's jaw, sending him reeling against the ship's rail. Before Sophia could even draw breath, Gray hit him again, this time delivering a solid blow to the stomach. With a choked groan, Mallory doubled over his boots and crumpled to the deck.

"I told you, I don't like violence," Gray forced out, shaking his hand as he stood over Mallory's writhing form. "But I'm not above using it."

Sophia's knees melted. She clung to the edge of the raised hatch for support. Tears stung her eyes, although she wasn't at all certain who or what she cried for.

"Put him in the brig," Gray said, without diverting his attention from Mallory.

"Can't," O'Shea said. "Brackett's in the brig. It's not big enough for two."

"Well, I can't have this cur aboard the *Kestrel*. He knows the vessel too well, might find some way to influence the crew." Gray looked to his brother. "I'll take Brackett with me."

Joss nodded. "You'll need a few able seamen as well." He turned to O'Shea.

The burly Irishman smiled. "I'm in."

"You're first mate, then," Gray said. He rubbed the back of his neck as he circled the whimpering figure on the deck. "I'll need Bailey, for sails and carpentry. And Davy, if you can spare him. Their cook was killed in the blast, so I'll need someone to manage the stores and pass around biscuit now and then."

"Then you'd best take a few of the goats, too," Joss said. "Stubb can't do the milking himself, not with wounded men to tend."

Gray nodded.

Sophia choked on a sob. Here he stood readying to leave the ship, making plans to take along sailors and Davy and goats and even that horrid Mr. Brackett . . . and ignoring her completely. He hadn't even cast a glance in her direction since Mallory's insult.

She sniffed loudly, wiping away tears with the back of one hand. *Fool girl*, she chided herself. Hadn't she vowed just minutes ago that she would not cry?

"Get below." The words could only be meant for her, though Gray did not turn his gaze. "Pack your things."

The captain shot Sophia a worried glance, then addressed his brother in solemn tones. "Gray, I don't think that's a good idea. She'd be much safer aboard the *Aphrodite*."

"I know," Gray said. "But I can't leave her." It was hardly a pledge of tenderness or emotion. Resentment hung from his words, making them heavy. Crushing.

"Are you certain?" Joss asked.

"I can't leave her," Gray repeated. Irony crept over his face, like the shadow of a passing cloud. "I gave my word."

Sophia stepped toward him. "Gray—"

"*Get. Below.*" Cold, demanding eyes finally met hers. "And stay there."

There was no disobeying that look, nor the blunted steel in his voice. Hands trembling and mind awhirl, Sophia went below.

And stayed there.

CHAPTER
TWENTY

It was midway through the dogwatch when the cabin door swung open with a rude creak, startling Sophia from her chair. Her stiffened joints protested the abrupt movement, and pain tingled through her limbs. She'd been sitting in that chair for hours.

"Are your things ready?" Gray asked, by way of greeting. Leaning one shoulder against the doorframe, he looked at the two trunks, packed and fastened shut. Sophia could sense him mentally weighing the baggage. He slumped further, his chest deflating with a slow exhalation. "Perhaps I'll have Levi fetch them."

Soot and dried blood streaked his face; shadows pooled under his eyes. He still wore the same bedraggled shirt and trousers, with the addition of an incongruently clean and tailored coat. Had it really been only yesterday morning, that he'd asked her permission to remove it? Indeed it had. *Will I shock you,* he'd asked, *if I remove my coat?* The absurdity of such a question now, after all that had passed between them. Drunken laughter bubbled up inside her, but she kept it corked.

Since that morning, she'd thought up a hundred things to say to him when this moment arrived. She'd narrowed them to a handful of possibilities, depending on his demeanor when he appeared. The cutting retort, the gentle plea, the abject apology and indignant defense . . . they all melted like snowflakes on her tongue.

"Oh, Gray," she said. "You must be so tired."

"Aye." The word was a ragged sigh, directed at his right boot. "I am."

His gaze lifted to hers then, his eyes shining with all the vulnerability he was simply too fatigued to mask. She ached to hold him. And from the yearning plainly writ on his face, she could tell he ached to be held. Only pride—and two packed trunks—stood between them.

He straightened and reached for the smaller of the trunks. "Let's go, then. It'll be dark before long."

The *Kestrel*'s jolly boat had been hoisted to the *Aphrodite*'s rail. It was a small craft, with two plank benches and a single pair of oars, not unlike the tiny rowboat that had conveyed her to the *Aphrodite*. Once Sophia and her trunks were deposited in the boat, Captain Grayson came by to offer words of farewell. She offered her hand, and he kissed it, making a smooth bow. The gesture surprised her. Sophia thought of him as so reserved and staid, in contrast to Gray. Apparently, the brothers shared a measure of charm, as well as their father's ears.

"You've been very kind to me," she said. "Thank you."

"You're not obliged to go. If you would prefer to remain aboard the *Aphrodite,* you've only to say the word."

Gray appeared behind his brother. His look to Sophia sparked with unspoken challenge.

"Thank you, Captain," she said. "I appreciate your concern, but Gray will look after me."

The captain smiled. "I'm certain he will. Until Tortola, then."

He bowed again and stepped aside so Gray could swing into the boat. The two men brushed shoulders in passing, in what Sophia assumed qualified as an acceptably masculine substitute for an embrace. How grateful she was to be female.

"What about the others?" Sophia asked, as the boat was lowered down to the sea. They sat facing each other on the two planks.

"Already aboard the *Kestrel*."

"Even the goats?"

"Yes," he replied, his voice humorless.

The boat hit the water's surface with a splash. A few shouts volleyed between Gray and the men above, and then the boat was loose, drifting quietly with the waves.

Gray reached for the oars. "We need to talk. Alone. And we may not have the chance once we're aboard the *Kestrel*. I'll be busy."

"Then I'll thank you now."

"For what?"

"For Captain Mallory."

"For hitting him, you mean?" He shook his head, looking off toward the horizon. "Save your thanks. I felt like hitting someone. He was convenient."

"Oh." Sophia searched the opposite horizon. Tears welled in her eyes again, much to her frustration.

"Jesus." He pulled hard on the oars. "I *never* hit people. Look what you've done to me. This was supposed to be the voyage I go respectable. Instead, I'm throwing fists, seizing ships, defiling virgins . . ."

Wincing at his harsh tone, Sophia sniffed and shifted sideways on the plank. Abruptly, he dropped the oars and began to wrestle with his coat.

"Why are you doing this?" Despite her bruised feelings, she caught the edge of one coat sleeve and held it as his arm slid loose.

"Easier to row with no coat." He wriggled free of the other sleeve.

"*Gray.*" She waited for him to meet her eyes. "You know that's not what I mean."

He folded the coat and handed it to her. "Here."

She stared at the bundle of wool. "What am I to do with it?"

"Sit on it," he said, thrusting it toward her. "You must be . . . tender." His gaze dropped briefly to her lap.

Sophia's face burned. She was indeed tender, and the wooden plank was torture beneath her thin skirts, but the presumptive manner of his gesture piqued her pride. She crossed her arms and glared at the proffered coat. "I might have been a virgin, Gray, but I've never been a fool. I knew it would hurt, but I wanted it anyway." She lifted her chin. "I knew you would hurt me."

His face hardened to stone. "Did you now?" He dropped the coat and reached for the oars. "Tell me," he asked on a vigorous pull, "did you pause to consider those you would hurt?"

Sophia fell silent. All was silent, save for the oars slicing briskly through the waves. The sun was an orange ember sliding toward the horizon, fizzling through layers of ashy, striated clouds. She inhaled deeply, letting the fresh, salty scent of the ocean fill her lungs—a relief from the brackish odor of bilge.

She gazed at the man across from her. *Her lover.* His powerful shoulders worked beneath his shirt as he pulled on the oars. The display of strength and agility, set to a steady rhythm . . . memories of their lovemaking assailed her with quiet force.

In some other place, under some other circumstance, they might have been a courting couple. Rowing across a placid lake, caressed by a glowing sunset. From a distance, this could have been the picture of romance.

But the reality was confusion, and resentment, and pain. Did she feel sorry for misleading him? Sophia considered. She was not sure she could. By his own admission, he would not have made love to her had she not. And she could not regret that exquisite pleasure; nor could she regret sharing it with *him*. She looked at the handsome, strong, charismatic, passionate, exhausted man across from her. Selfish and wicked though she might be, she could not feel sorry that he was now bound to her—that for good or ill, he had not left her behind.

Sophia was, however, unequivocally sorry for one thing.

"Gray," she said, "I'm so sorry I've hurt you."

His eyes flashed, and there was a slight hitch in his stroke. "Spare me your apologies. It's not me I meant to discuss."

"Then who?"

"Davy, of course. We'll be on this ship for a week or more, and that boy's suffered enough on both our accounts. You're to let him be, do you understand? No flirting, no sketching. It won't be easy for him, knowing why you're aboard."

Her heart lurched. "Davy *knows*?"

"Of course he knows. Everyone knows. There are no secrets on a ship, remember?" He gave her a wary, sidelong glance. "Well, evidently there are *some*."

"I've told you, I'm sorry." She bit her lip. "What more would you have me say?"

He stared at her for a long moment. Sophia resisted the impulse to look away. Would he question her in earnest now? Could she find the courage to answer?

"Nothing," he said finally, shaking his head. "I told you, it doesn't matter. Whatever you've done, whoever you are . . . so long as there's a chance you're carrying my child, I'm not letting you out of my sight."

She swallowed hard. Of course, the possibility of conceiving had occurred to her—how could it not?—but hearing it spoken aloud was another thing altogether. "So that's the reason you're bringing me along? Because I could be with child?"

He nodded. "When did you last have your courses?"

She blushed. No man had ever spoken to her of such things. "Just before we left England."

"Then we ought to know soon enough." The circular motions of the oars slowed, and his gaze burned into hers. "If you are breeding, I warn you now—you will marry me. I'll not allow you to run off and raise my child God knows where."

Her mouth fell open. He could not have cut her more deeply had he skewered her with a bayonet. *If* she was breeding, he would force her to marry him? Because he assumed otherwise she'd "run off"? And if she did not conceive, what then? Did he plan to toss her overboard? Her jaw and hands worked as she tried to match words to her anger. If only she could have painted it instead, with slashes of purple and violent splatters of red-tinged black.

She finally managed, "I will not be forced into marrying you, or any man. I've escaped that fate once before, and I can do it again. I have the means to care for a child, if need be." She patted the purse strapped beneath her stays. "And what does it signify to you, with your prodigious history? You probably have *countless* bastards, spread across four continents."

"No, I don't. My father brought enough bastards into the world, and I've never aspired to his example. That's why I've always been careful."

"Ah, yes. Caution and sheepgut, was it?"

"Precisely. Until yesterday." He gave a vicious yank on one oar, turning the boat as they neared the *Kestrel*. "Yesterday was my first time making that mistake."

"Well," she said bitterly. "How special that makes me feel. I'm glad to have been your first in some regard, even if only your first mistake."

He gave an exasperated sigh. From the *Kestrel*'s stern, someone tossed down a rope. Gray caught it and began securing it to the boat. "Yesterday was a first for me in many ways. I was . . . carried away. I wasn't thinking."

"You weren't thinking." Her heart was sinking faster than an anchor. God, could he make this any worse?

His gaze caught hers and held it. She felt searched, turned inside out. As though he could read some answer in her eyes, if only he looked hard enough. "No. I wasn't thinking, I . . ." He cleared his throat. "I suppose I was hoping."

Something cinched in her chest, constricting her lungs. She reached out to catch his hand in hers. "What about now, Gray? Are you still hoping now?"

Another rope fell from stern to boat. He reached for it, breaking their contact. Shaking his head, he said, "I don't even know what to think of you now."

"I see." Sophia drew her knees up and hugged them to her chest, burying her face in her stacked arms.

He sighed noisily. "Sweet." A light touch fell on her arm. Sniffing back tears, she looked up at him. "Do the hoping for us both, if it makes you feel better. At the moment, I'm just too damned tired."

The boat lurched into its ascent, startling a little gasp from her throat. His fingers latched protectively over her wrist. The embrace lasted only a moment, and then he let her go.

When the boat reached deck level, Sophia helped herself over the rail of the *Kestrel*. The light thud of her slippers hitting deck announced her presence to the ship at large. O'Shea and the other men turned to her, some offering curt words of greeting or nods. She tilted her head to examine the new jury-mast—a thin pole lashed to the charred, jagged stump of the mainmast. It gave the ship the look of a pruned rosebush, with a slender, green shoot branching out from old growth.

Davy stood some paces away on the quarterdeck, studiously testing the new mast's rigging. He did not turn her way.

"Davy," Gray called from behind her.

"Aye, Captain." The youth did not raise his head.

"I understand you've slung your hammock in the steerage compartment."

Davy's glance flicked toward them, and he gave a puzzled, "Aye."

"You're to move it to the forecastle at your first opportunity." Gray rounded Sophia and walked toward the boy. "On this ship, you're a sailor. You'll be expected to do a sailor's work, and you'll sleep where the sailors sleep. Do you understand?"

"Aye, aye, Captain." Davy's pale cheeks colored. With a quick nod, he went belowdecks. But not before throwing Sophia a wounded glance that drove a spear of pain straight into her heart. This should have been a momentous occasion for him, his promotion to the forecastle; a day of celebration and pride. And because of her, it was ruined.

Davy's wasn't the first young man's heart she'd broken. Nor was Gray the first grown man she'd hurt. She'd always been a selfish girl; she had no illusions otherwise. But this was the first time she'd been forced to bear witness to the consequences. She couldn't run away from this ship as she'd run from her wedding. Neither could she distract herself with thoughts of new ribbons or exhibitions or the Duchess of Aldonbury's card party Wednesday next. She had a front-row seat for the little tragedy she'd set in motion, and there would be no intermission.

There was a justice to it, she had to allow.

"And you"—Gray laid a hand on the small of her back and steered her down into the captain's cabin— "will stay here."

Sophia surveyed the cabin. Bed tucked into one corner, cabinets lining the other. In the center, a table and captain's chair. A thin slice of window spanning the stern. Much the same as the *Aphrodite*'s, if a bit more cramped.

"It's been cleaned and aired for you," Gray continued, his tone detached. "The linens are fresh, brought over from the *Aphrodite*."

"Thank you." She paced to the center of the cabin and turned to face him. "That was thoughtful."

"I'll have your trunks brought down. You're to stay here, do you understand?"

She nodded.

"No traipsing about the ship. And you'll keep this door bolted."

"Should I fear for my safety?"

He shook his head. "Brackett's confined below; he won't bother you. The *Kestrel*'s crew seem pleased with our change of course. But I don't know these men. And I can't trust those I don't know." He gave her a meaningful look as he turned to leave.

"Wait," she called after him. He paused in the door. "Where are you sleeping?"

"*When* I sleep, which I imagine will be infrequently, I'll bed down in the first mate's berth, just there." He nodded toward a small door just outside the entrance to her cabin. "But whether I'm on deck or below it, I'll never be far."

"Shall I take that as a promise? Or a threat?"

She sauntered toward him, hands cocked on her hips in an attitude of provocation. His eyes swept her body, washing her with angry heat. She noted the subtle tensing of his shoulders, the frayed edge of his breath.

Even exhausted and hurt, he still wanted her. For a moment, Sophia felt hope flicker to life inside her. Enough for them both.

And then, with the work of an instant, he quashed it

all. Gray stepped back. He gave a loose shrug and a lazy half-smile. *If I don't care about you,* his look said, *you can't possibly hurt me.* "Take it however you wish."

"Oh no, you don't. Don't you try that move with me." With trembling fingers, she began unbuttoning her gown.

"What the devil are you doing? You think you can just hike up your shift and make—"

"Don't get excited." She stripped the bodice down her arms, then set to work unlacing her stays. "I'm merely settling a score. I can't stand to be in your debt a moment longer." Soon she was down to her chemise and plucking coins from the purse tucked between her breasts. One, two, three, four, five . . .

"There," she said, casting the sovereigns on the table. "Six pounds, and"—she fished out a crown—"ten shillings. You owe me the two."

He held up open palms. "Well, I'm afraid I have no coin on me. You'll have to trust me for it."

"I wouldn't trust you for anything. Not even two shillings."

He glared at her for a moment, then turned on his heel and exited the cabin, banging the door shut behind him. Sophia stared at it, wondering whether she dared stomp after him with her bodice hanging loose around her hips. Before she could act on the obvious affirmative, he stormed back in.

"Here." A pair of coins clattered to the table. "Two shillings. And"—he drew his other hand from behind his back—"your two leaves of paper. I don't want to be in your debt, either." The ivory sheets fluttered as he released them. One drifted to the floor.

Sophia tugged a banknote from her bosom and threw it on the growing pile. To her annoyance, it made no noise and had correspondingly little dramatic value. In compensation, she raised her voice. "Buy yourself some new boots. Damn you."

"While we're settling scores, you owe me twenty-odd nights of undisturbed sleep."

"Oh, no," she said, shaking her head. "We're even on that regard." She paused, glaring a hole in his forehead, debating just how hateful she would make this.

Very.

"You took my innocence," she said coldly—and completely unfairly, because they both knew she'd given it freely enough.

"Yes, and I'd like my jaded sensibilities restored, but there's no use wishing after rainbows, now is there?"

He had a point there. "I suppose we're squared away then."

"I suppose we are."

"There's nothing else I owe you?"

His eyes were ice. "Not a thing."

But there is, she wanted to shout. *I still owe you the truth, if only you'd care enough to ask for it. If only you cared enough for me, to want to know.*

But he didn't. He reached for the door.

"Wait," he said. "There is one last thing."

Sophia's heart pounded as he reached into his breast pocket and withdrew a scrap of white fabric.

"There," he said, unceremoniously casting it atop the pile of coins and notes and paper. "I'm bloody tired of carrying that around."

And then he was gone, leaving Sophia to wrap her arms over her half-naked chest and stare numbly at what he'd discarded.

A lace-trimmed handkerchief, embroidered with a neat S.H.

CHAPTER
TWENTY-ONE

Gray left the cabin and went to work. He worked for days. He worked until he couldn't think, couldn't feel. His life became flips of the hourglass, clangs of the bell—increments of time too brief to allow anxiety for the future or regrets about the past. It was simply, always *now*. He concentrated on the task of each moment: the sail that wanted reefing, the brace gone slack. Getting the *Kestrel* from the crest of one wave to the next.

All the while, a deep, insidious current pulled on his heart. Resentment, confusion, fear. Uncertainty, in all its most sinister forms. By sheer force of will, he kept it at bay. A mere hint of uncertainty was all it required to taint authority in irrevocable fashion.

But for all his intensity of purpose, a mere moment in her presence was all it required to scatter his wits completely—he feared, in irrevocable fashion. In the clang of a bell, Gray was undone.

"What are you doing?"

The words fired from his mouth, like a salvo of rifle shots. She flinched with each one. But great God, he felt under attack.

What the devil was she doing in the galley? The galley was not where she ought to be. She ought to be in the captain's cabin, where she'd remained squirreled away for the past three days. Where he didn't have to look at this exquisite face, breathe this intoxicating fragrance, suffer these small earthquakes in his chest that left him reeling in his boots whenever she drew near.

"I'm serving dinner." She held out a deep wooden plate ladled with steaming chowder. "Are you always this late to mess?"

Gray stared at the plate. Then he stared at her. Which was a mistake.

Because he was starving, and she looked . . . delicious.

The galley was steamy and hot, as galleys tend to be. A high flush painted her cheeks and throat. Loose wisps of hair frizzled to tight curls at her hairline. Tiny beads of perspiration glittered on her décolletage, where her breasts pressed up like twin mounds of risen dough. Her skin glowed, and her eyes . . . God, her eyes positively sparkled. Plump lips curved in a self-satisfied, feline smile.

She had the look, the air—even the scent—of a recently-bedded, thoroughly-pleasured woman. And Gray's senses were under siege. All the desire that he'd been forcing down for the past three days tore free. It raced hot through his veins, swelled in his groin.

He resented it, resented this power she had over him. This was why she needed to stay where he'd put her, out of sight.

"What are you doing?" he growled again. "You shouldn't be here."

"I'm helping," she bit out, her smile fading to a tight line. Her eyes dulled in the space of a blink, and she slung the plate onto the table.

Gray slouched against the door and massaged his temples with one hand. Damn it, he was always the one to erase that smile from her face, douse that sparkle in her eyes. But he needed her to stay in that cabin. He could not look on her, be near her, think of her, and keep the

Kestrel afloat at the same time. No red-blooded man could.

"Go back to your cabin."

"No." She crossed her arms over her chest. "I'll go mad if I spend another day in that cabin, with no one to talk to and nothing to do."

"Well, I'm sorry we're not entertaining you sufficiently, but this isn't a pleasure cruise. Find some other way to amuse yourself. Can't you find something to occupy your mind?" He made an open-handed sweep through the steam. "Read a book."

"I've only got one book. I've already read it."

"Don't tell me it's the Bible."

The corner of her mouth twitched. "It isn't."

He averted his gaze to the ceiling, blowing out an impatient breath. "Only one book," he muttered. "What sort of lady makes an ocean crossing with only one book?"

"Not a governess." Her voice held a challenge.

Gray refused the bait, electing for silence. Silence was all he could manage, with this anger slicing through him. It hurt. He kept his eyes trained on a cracked board above her head, working to keep his expression blank.

What a fool he'd been, to believe her. To believe that something essential in him had changed, that he could find more than fleeting pleasure with a woman. That this perfect, delicate blossom of a lady, who knew all his deeds and misdeeds, would offer herself to him without hesitation. Deep inside, in some uncharted territory of his soul, he'd built a world on that moment when she came to him willingly, trustingly. Giving not just her body, but her heart.

Ha. She hadn't even given him her name.

"Are you ever planning to talk to me?" she asked. "Don't you have questions you want to ask?"

"Just one. Have you had your courses?"

"No. Not yet."

"Then we've nothing further to discuss."

"Not yet," she said meaningfully.

In truth, Gray wasn't certain how many answers he wanted, whether she carried his child or no. He knew he preferred silence to lies. It didn't matter one whit to him who she was, or what she'd done. Whether or not she'd taken lovers before, whether she had six shillings or six thousand pounds. It mattered that she'd lied. That even with her arms around him, her lips pressed to his mouth, her tight, virgin body yielding to his—she had always been holding something back.

In those dark, solitary watches over the past three nights, it had driven him quietly mad, wondering just how much of her he'd ever seen, ever held. He'd opened himself to her completely, and she'd been lying to him since the moment they'd met. In all those days aboard the *Aphrodite,* was a single one of her smiles ever truly for him? What fraction of her heart had she revealed to him, in all their conversations? When he'd held her, caressed her, *entered* her—had he finally reached some layer of her being where the lies ended and the real woman began?

Gray didn't even want to ask. Because he already knew the only answer that mattered. How much of her was *his*? Less than all.

And therefore, not enough.

"Sketching." He croaked the word. Clearing his throat, he continued, "Go to your cabin and draw, or paint. It kept you busy enough before."

"I've tried. I can't."

"What, no more paper?"

"No more inspiration. I . . . I've lost my heart for it, I think." With a shrug, she turned back to the stove and began stirring lazy figure eights in a bubbling pot. "Gray, be angry with me if you must. You've a right to be hurt. Call me vile names, think all the vengeful thoughts you wish. But you must allow me to do this. I want to help."

"I don't need your help."

"Yes, you do." She ceased stirring and leveled the ladle at him, wielding it like a sword. "You've eight men on this ship, performing the work of a dozen. I hear everything from that cabin. Do you think I don't know how hard you're working? That you're only resting every third watch, and sometimes not even that?"

Her voice lost its sharp edge, and she flung the ladle aside before wiping her brow with the back of her wrist. "If I run the galley, it frees Davy to stand a watch. If Davy's able to stand watch, you can get more rest."

Gray stared at her. He slowly shook his head. "Sweetheart—"

"*Don't.*" Her voice tweaked. "Don't call me that when you don't mean it."

"What am I to call you, then? Miss 'Turner'? Jane?"

"You're to call me Cook." With an impatient gust of breath, she blew a wisp of hair from her face. "If I knew how to reef a sail or splice a line, you'd be chasing me down from the rigging right now. I can't do a sailor's work, but I can do this. I've spent every morning with Gabriel since the *Aphrodite* left England, and I know how to pound a piece of salt pork."

"I can't allow you to do this sort of menial labor."

"You can't expect me to sit idly by and read or sketch in that cabin while you're working yourself to bones." She grabbed a smaller spoon from a hook on the wall and thrust it at him, handle-first. "I made you food, and you're going to eat it."

He accepted the spoon. It was that, or accept a spoon to the skull.

She kicked a stool toward him. "Now sit down."

Gray gave in. He did need rest, and having Davy on deck would be a boon. And, his stomach reminded him loudly, he'd scarcely tasted more than a biscuit in days. He'd avoided her since they boarded this ship, but she'd sensed these things somehow—his fatigue, his hunger. She'd sensed something else as well. He'd been giving orders for three solid days, and he needed a bit of ordering around. Given a choice between eating and working, his duty as captain demanded that work take priority. She left him no choice, so he sat and ate.

Still, he couldn't let her get away with it so easily. "If you're the cook," he said between mouthfuls, "I'm your captain. You can't continue speaking to me that way."

"You aren't dressed like a captain."

Gray looked down at his homespun tunic and the loose-fitting trousers cinched with a knotted cord. The clothes of a common seaman, borrowed from a sailor now dead. He hadn't the luxury of fine attire on the *Kestrel*. With the ship so undermanned, he had to be everywhere—climbing the rigging, down in the hold.

"Don't look apologetic. They suit you." Her gaze glanced off his shoulders, then dropped to the floor. "But I see you've kept the detested boots."

He shrugged, spooning up another bite of chowder. "I've broken them in now."

"And here I hoped you were keeping them for sentimental reasons."

She set a tankard of grog before him, the moment before he became aware of his own thirst. Gray reached for it, shaking his head. A long swallow of watered-down rum added fuel to his resentment. He'd allowed himself to become so transparent to her, while she remained an enigma to him. Her talents fit no logical pattern—sketching, painting, deceit, seduction, thievery . . . now the ability to pound biscuit and salted meat into a fair-tasting chowder? It was enough to make him abandon all hope of ever comprehending her.

Perhaps he never would. But it was another thought that had him hurrying through his food, desperate to put some distance between them. He might never understand her, Gray realized, but he could get dangerously accustomed to this other feeling.

Being understood.

"Just hold her steady, that's it. Don't lean too close, she might kick. Now firmly grasp her . . . her . . ."

Sophia was beginning to doubt the brilliance of this enterprise she'd suggested. She cleared her throat and affected a brisk, business-like tone. "Her teat?"

"Er, yes."

Thankfully, there was a brown-and-white nanny goat blocking her view of Davy's face, but she could hear the fierce blush in his voice.

"Take her teat," he said haltingly. "Like so."

She tilted her head to view the goat's underside, where Davy's thumb and forefinger curled around one knobby teat. Cautiously, she reached out to follow suit on her side. At the first brush of her fingers against the milk-swelled udder, the animal gave an annoyed shiver. Sophia snatched her hand back.

"Don't let her frighten you, Miss Turner. You can't be timid with a goat."

A nervous giggle escaped her. "Oh, I assure you, I can. I haven't your bravery, Mr. Linnet."

Her remark fell into the silence like a lead weight. Davy made no answer. *Drat.* Sophia chastised herself with a sharp tug on her apron. That was badly done of her. It was awkward enough that she'd asked him for milking lessons; to engage him in flirtation was unspeakably insensitive. Still, she needed to learn how to do this. Every hour Davy spent at milking was an hour he couldn't be standing watch.

Emboldened by the desire to complete this lesson quickly, she reached out in a flash, capturing the goat's second teat with her thumb and forefinger. "Like so?"

"Yes, miss. And now you roll your fingers down, one by one . . ." He demonstrated, and a jet of milk hit the tin pail with a sharp trill.

Sophia imitated his movements. Nothing happened. She tried again, earning only an impatient shuffle of the goat's hind legs.

"Try again, a bit faster this time."

She tried again, pulling harder. Nothing. The goat bleated, in seeming irritation at her ineptitude.

"Don't wring it, now. You want to coax the milk out, one finger at a time, see?" He sent a few more squirts of milk pinging into the pail.

Taking a deep breath, Sophia began again, painstakingly imitating the rolling pull of Davy's hand. When a thin stream of white shot from the teat, she could not suppress a small cry of elation. In truth, if she hadn't feared it would startle the nanny dry, she would have done a little dance. She tried again, with greater confidence. Another spurt of milk came forth.

"Good," Davy said, after she'd removed enough yellowish milk from the goat to cover the bottom of the pail. "You've the way of it now." He continued milking the other teat, and they settled into a quiet, contrapuntal rhythm.

"Did you do this often at home, then?" She hoped conversation would feel less stifling than silence.

"Often enough. Every day, when I was a boy."

Sophia smiled to herself. No, she supposed he wasn't

a boy any longer. "Who tends them now that you're gone?"

"My sisters, I expect."

"Sisters? Are they older or younger?"

"I'm in the middle. The eldest, she got herself married already. By the time I see her again, she'll have a brat of her own, I reckon." His voice deepened in pitch, as though the prospect displeased him.

"Shouldn't you like to be an uncle? Just think of the exotic tales and trinkets you'll bring home. You'll be a returning hero. The children will swarm around you like bees." She imbued her voice with a coy lilt. "All the girls will be mad for you."

He fell quiet again. Frustrated with herself, Sophia gave a harsh yank on the goat's teat and narrowly missed a swift kick to the thigh. It would seem she'd lost the ability to converse rather than flirt, if she'd ever developed that talent at all. What was her reasoning, precisely? That a man couldn't possibly hold himself in high esteem without the benefit of her flattery? Or that he'd see no reason to esteem *her* without it?

Davy finally said, "So long as I come home with my wages, I don't expect they'll turn me away."

She let the soft splashes of milk fill the silence. At length, she asked cautiously, "Aren't you happy for her, your sister who married?"

"I don't know that it matters, how I feel about it."

"But she's your sister. She matters to you."

His hand stilled on the teat. "The man she married, he's too old for her. My father's the one that arranged it. I think . . ." He squeezed out another jet of milk. "I think my father was in the man's debt, more than he could pay."

"I see."

Her dismay must have been evident. Davy's voice

grew robust with defense. "She weren't forced into it, mind. She didn't marry him against her will."

"No. No, of course not. Just against her heart. I do understand. It's the way of things for women, sometimes." After all, it had nearly been the way of things for her. "You don't suspect he'll mistreat her?"

"He'll treat her fair enough, I reckon. My father wouldn't have let her go, otherwise."

"Then that's some comfort."

"Aye." He shook a few last drops from the goat's teat, then released it completely. "Just the same, I didn't like it. I don't like to see her married to a man she didn't choose."

Sophia continued milking on her side, settling into a hypnotic rhythm. "Of course you don't. She's your sister. If you care for her, you want to see her well cared for. If you love her, you want to see her loved." If only she'd been so fortunate, to have a brother to want the same for her.

"Aye." His voice cracked slightly on the word, and he paused. It must have been a full minute before he spoke again. "He's a good man, the captain."

Her hand stilled. "The captain?"

"Gray. He's a good man, Miss Turner. He'll do right by you."

Sweet Heavens, the boy was giving her his blessing. Sophia didn't know what to say. It would probably wound his pride, to call him the loving brother she'd never had. Certainly, she couldn't tell him the truth of how matters stood between her and Gray. She didn't want to deplete the boy's faith in his captain's honorable intentions. To the contrary, she dearly wished to borrow it.

Sniffing, she let go of the goat's teat and brushed her hand on her skirts. "I think she's empty."

"Are you certain?" He reached under the goat and

gave the udder a brisk rub. Then he took the teat closest to Sophia and gave it a twist. A fresh stream of milk shot forth, glancing off the rim of the bucket and splashing her slippers.

"Take care!" With a little shriek of laughter, she pushed away from the goat's side. Davy tilted his hand and squeezed the teat again, this time splattering Sophia from crown to chest. Sputtering and wiping milk from her face, she scrambled to her feet. "Davy Linnet," she scolded, towering over both youth and goat. "You're a rascal."

"Am I?" He flashed her a lopsided, innocent grin. Shrugging, he dropped his gaze and emptied the last drops of milk into the pail. "Well, you're blushing."

Sophia made a show of huffing and crossing her arms, but she could not keep the laughter out of her voice. "Never say you've learned nothing from me, Davy. You might have shown me how to milk, but I've taught you to flirt."

"A fair bargain, then." He stood and took the goat by its collar.

"Perhaps. Mind you don't confuse the two talents. Keep your goats straight from your girls."

"That's easily done." Mischief twinkled sharp in his eye. "The goats don't blush."

"Son of a bitch."

Gray scowled at the ink spattering his trousers and pooling atop the toe of his boot. This was why captains had cabins. It was nigh on impossible to keep a proper log in the first-mate's berth, with only the most meager of lighting and this paltry writing surface jutting out from the wall, too narrow to accommodate both logbook and inkwell. And, he concluded as he frowned at the now-emptied latter, it was definitely impossible to keep a log without the benefit of ink.

He threw open the door of his berth and entered the captain's cabin, knowing it to be unoccupied. At this hour, she would be preparing dinner in the galley. Flinging the logbook and quill down on the table, he moved to search the built-in drawers for a fresh bottle of ink. He found none.

"Blast."

His eye fell on her trunks, stacked neatly in the corner. Surely she had a supply of ink, and quality ink at that. Without sparing a moment to second-guess the decision, he strode to her trunks and worked open the latches of the smaller trunk. He flipped it open.

It felt intimate, revealing. As if he'd unlaced her stays. And what treasures awaited him. Sheaves of paper, neatly wrapped in oilcloth and tied with efficient knots—knots that would do a sailor proud. Small bundles of brushes, smelling faintly of turpentine. And rows upon rows of her little bottles of ink and cakes of pigment. Of course, for Gray, the array of colors did not particularly impress. Rather, it was the care and precision with which they were packed that caused a sharp pinch in his chest. In this trunk was everything of delicacy, beauty, and painstaking care. Everything he admired in *her*, laid open for his examination, with no veneer of lies to obscure his view.

He looked his fill. He touched each item in the trunk, skipping his fingers from one object to the next. He couldn't bring himself to lift one out.

Until a small, leather-bound book wedged along one side caught his attention. Hooking a fingertip under the spine, he eased the volume up, and a title greeted him: *The Memoirs of a Wanton Dairymaid*. His shout of laughter rattled the bottles in their straw-buffered rows. So this was the one book she'd selected for the journey? A ribald novel?

Gray tipped the book into his hand. The binding was strained and the pages swollen—as though the entire volume had been dipped in water and dried. The cover fell open to reveal an elaborate frontispiece, depicting a buxom dairymaid wearing a straw bonnet, voluminous petticoats, and a knowing smile. On riffling the pages, it immediately became clear that the book's expanded bulk could be credited to the addition of numerous pen-and-ink illustrations.

He recognized her deft hand and eye for detail immediately. He flipped through the pages, past vignettes of the dairymaid and her vague-featured gentleman engaged in a courtship of sorts: a kiss on the hand, a whisper in the ear. By the book's midpoint, the chit's voluminous petticoats were up around her ears, and the illustrations comprised a sequence of quite similar poses in varying locales. Not just the dairy, but a carriage, the larder, in a hayloft lit with candles and strewn with . . . were those rose petals?

I'll be damned.

Gray was fast divining the true source of the French painting master's mythic exploits. More unsettling by far, however, as he perused the book, he noted a subtle alteration in the gentleman lover's features. With each successive illustration, the hero appeared taller, broader in the shoulders, and his hair went from a cropped style to collar length in the space of two pages.

The more pages Gray turned, the more he recognized himself.

It was unmistakable. She'd used him as the model for these bawdy illustrations. She'd sketched him in secret; not once, but many times. And here he'd nearly gone mad with envy over each scrap of foolscap she'd inked for one crewman or another. His emotions underwent a dizzying progression—from surprised, to flattered, to (with the benefit of one especially inventive situation in an orchard) undeniably aroused.

But as he lingered over a nude study of this amalgam of the real him and some picaresque fantasy, he began to feel something else entirely. He felt used.

She'd rendered his form with astonishing accuracy, given that it must have been drawn before she'd any opportunity to actually see him unclothed. Not that she'd achieved an exact likeness. Her virgin's imagination was rather generous in certain aspects and somewhat stinting in others, he noted with a bitter sort of amusement. But she'd laid him bare in these pages, without his knowledge or consent. God, she'd even drawn his scars. All in service of some adolescent erotic fantasy.

And now he began to grow angry.

He had been handling the leaves of the book with his fingertips only, anxious he might smudge or rip the pages. Now he abandoned all caution and flipped roughly through the remainder of the volume. Until he came to the end, and his hand froze.

There they were, the two of them. He and she, fully clothed and unengaged in any physical intimacies—yet intimate, in a way he had never known. Never dreamed. Sitting beneath a willow tree, his head in her lap. One of her hands lay twined with his, atop his chest. The other rested on his brow. The sky soared vast and expansive above, gauzy clouds spinning into forever.

The hot fist of desire that had gripped his loins loosened, moved upward through his torso, churning the contents of his gut along the way. Then it clutched at his heart and squeezed until it hurt. Somehow, this illustration was the most dismaying of all. So naïve, so ridiculous. At least the bawdy situations were plausible, if sometimes physically improbable. This was utterly impossible. To her, he'd never been more than a fantasy.

It occurred to Gray that more secrets might be packed within these trunks. If he sorted through her belongings, he might find the answers to all his questions. Perhaps answers to questions he'd never thought to ask. In spite of this, he let the lid of the trunk clap shut and fastened the strap with shaking fingers. He'd suffered as many of her fantasies as he could bear for one day.

It was time to acquaint her with reality.

CHAPTER
TWENTY-TWO

Reality was hitting Sophia hard. Or rather, kicking her hard, and leaving bruises the size and shape of a goat's cloven hoof. Reality was making her ache all over, in muscles she hadn't known she possessed.

Her first day as ship's cook had been novel, amusing. She'd experienced the thrill of competency and earning her own keep. Each fire built, each potato peeled, each squirt of milk into the pail was a small triumph. Just a few days later, she was fully prepared to admit defeat. Manual labor was not romantic in the least, and only dimly satisfying, in the way chewing rock-hard ship's biscuit satisfied one's hunger—begrudgingly, and at considerable expense of effort.

Once she assumed control of her inheritance, she intended to never boil water or tend a goat again. With a bit of prudence, her trust ought to keep her in servants for the remainder of her days. For the remainder of this voyage, however, she would toil or go hungry. And if there was one thing Sophia suspected would suit her less than a life of menial servitude, it was hunger.

The work suited Gray, though. He'd slipped into the role of *Kestrel*'s captain faster than he'd filled out a borrowed tunic and trousers. Authority was simply comfortable to him, like a second skin.

Despite all that had passed between them, despite his anger and hurt—at some deeper stratum of his being, he was more content than she'd ever seen him. He was pleased to be in command, to be on deck working rather than sitting idly below, and Sophia was pleased to see him where he belonged, living as he was meant to live.

Because she loved him, so much it hurt. She wanted him to be happy, whether or not that meant being with her. And if she never laid eyes on him again after they dropped anchor, she would carry this picture of him forever: Gray prowling the deck of the *Kestrel,* all confidence and energy and charisma, coordinating the movement of the sails and rigging as instinctively as he manipulated the fingers on his hand.

As for herself, the current picture was one she would endeavor to forget.

Toting a pail of hard-earned milk, she shouldered open the door to the storeroom to gather biscuit and salt-beef for the evening meal. Weak light spilled into the barrel-crammed space. She stomped hard on the floorboards: once, twice, three times. Then she counted ten and tried to ignore the sounds of rats scattering into the shadows. Heavens, if her mother could see her now. There weren't enough restoratives in Bath and Brighton combined to counteract the attack of nerves this scene would doubtless inspire.

When the sounds of scratching faded, she entered the storeroom and turned to rest the milk pail on a waist-high crate.

A hand clapped on her shoulder.

Milk sloshed over the side of the pail, dousing her hand and splattering her skirts. A startled cry whooshed out of her as an arm whipped around her waist. Her back collided with a wall of heat and muscle.

"Is this what you wanted?" The rough whisper warmed her ear.

"*Gray.*" She nearly fainted with relief. He held her tight

against him with one arm, his other hand skimming over the curve of her hip. "Gray, what on earth are you doing? You made me spill the milk, drat you."

"It won't go to waste." Resting his chin on her shoulder, he untangled her fingers from the pail's handle. Bending her arm at the elbow, he lifted her fingers to his mouth, sucking them clean one by one. His tongue traced each finger and the delicate webs between them, sending gooseflesh rippling down the backs of her legs.

"Isn't this what you wanted?" His fingers interlaced with hers, squeezing them until they hurt. "Your dream lover, lurking in the shadows of the stables, the larder . . . the storeroom? Lying in wait for his wanton dairymaid?"

Sophia froze. Dear God, he'd seen *The Book*. He nipped at the curve of her neck, and she gasped. "You—" She swallowed hard. "You had no right to look through that."

"You had no right to put me in it." She could hear the raw edge of anger in his voice. His fingers still gripping hers, he pressed her own hand to her breast. "But let's not dwell on rights, sweet. Not when wrongs are so much more interesting."

His hand flexed, digging her own fingers into the flesh of her breast. She felt the soft globe heating in her palm, the nipple firming to a tight knot.

"Gray." She tried for a reproving tone, squirming in his vise-like grip. His arm tightened about her waist, pulling her backside flush with his hips. The hard ridge of his arousal pulsed against the small of her back, hot and demanding. Her feeble attempts at resistance melted. Hadn't she been waiting days for just this? Longing for him to reach for her, take her in his arms? Yearning for the feeling of his strength surrounding her once more? Gentle or bruising—the precise manner of the gesture mattered little. What mattered was him. His warmth . . . his touch . . . his mouth . . .

"Did you think of me, as you lay in your bunk at night?" His hand kept kneading her fingers around her breast, chafing her palm against the aching peak. "Did you imagine these coarse hands pawing your body?" He dragged her hand to her other breast, groping impatiently. His lips traced the ridge of her ear, drew on the sensitive lobe with hot, wet suction. The nape of her neck prickled with excitement. Arousal washed through her, sweeping over the surface of her body and rushing together at the apex of her thighs. She closed her eyes and saw red waves of sensation pulse through her with each flick of his tongue against her ear.

Then his teeth closed down hard in a sharp burst of yellow. She gave a little cry, half pleasure and half pain.

"Did you ache for me here?" He pulled her hand down, thrusting it between her legs. Through the layers of shift and skirt, he ground her palm against her mound. She rocked against it, moaning a little. "You did, didn't you?" His index finger pressed hers into the soft folds of her sex. "Didn't you?" Another nip at her ear punctuated the question.

"Yes." Her breath dragged in and out of her, the air tasting dark and musky.

"Did you imagine me coming to you, in that berth at night? As you went about your day? Bending you over some obliging surface and hiking your skirts to your waist?" He untangled her hand from her skirts and pinned it to the crate before her, holding it immobile with the weight of his own. The splintery wood bit into her palm. He released her waist, and with his other hand he grasped a fold of her skirts, expertly drawing them up and up. She hadn't worn stockings or drawers since they entered the tropics, and the brush of fabric against the bare hollows of her knees sent pleasure shivering through her.

Leaning forward, he bent her at the waist and parted her legs with his thigh. Cool air licked over her inner thighs as he worked his trousers loose, and then his hard length sprang up to wedge snugly in her cleft. He rocked forward, rubbing slowly along the moist, swollen folds of her sex, drawing out the contact in one sweet, torturous, endless caress. She cried out with relief when the tip of him finally grazed that most sensitive bit of her flesh.

With his free hand, he swept her skirts up and away from her legs. "Look," he demanded, nudging her forward so her chin bent to her chest. "Look."

She obeyed, looking down to where the ruddy, swollen head of his arousal peeked out from her thatch of tight curls. The sight of their bodies locked together excited her beyond reason.

"It's what you wanted, isn't it? To look at it, touch it, feel it grinding against you. To satisfy all those schoolgirl curiosities about a man's body and how it fits with yours. To live out all the depraved little fantasies in that book of yours. This is what you've wanted all along, isn't it?" He pulled back, dragging his hard shaft through her softness until Sophia shuddered with pleasure. He thrust forward again. "Isn't it?"

"Yes," she gasped softly. Then louder, "Yes."

Something like a groan escaped him. "Well," he breathed against her ear, "I happen to have a few depraved fantasies of my own."

The words hummed in her ear, sending electric jolts of arousal straight to her core. She whispered, "Tell me."

Gray's heart thumped wildly in his chest, each beat matched by a pulse in his groin. Damn, but she was so hot, so wet. He dragged against her again, the friction of their bodies producing a liquid sound that was unspeakably erotic.

He'd meant to stop this here. Or, truthfully, a little ways back. He intended to make her admit that all she'd wanted from him was pleasure, a chance to explore her wanton fantasies. And then he'd planned to walk away, to tell her to find some other man to deceive and discard.

But he'd forgotten how she felt so good. How she felt so right.

"Tell me," she repeated, her voice husky. When he still hesitated, she added, "Show me."

And he found refusal was no longer within his power. This *was* what she wanted, he told himself. She wanted to explore passion and pleasure. Why should he deny her, deny himself?

He released her hand where it lay splayed on the crate. She remained in place, leaning forward at the waist. He settled both hands on her hips, lifting her up and firmly against him, and then he slid his hands up her ribcage, counting one slender rib for every narrow stripe of that damned button-less, hook-less, lacing-free, impenetrable muslin frock.

"My fantasies," he said hoarsely, hooking his index fingers under the neckline at the midpoint of her back, "start here."

He gripped the fabric and rent it to her waist in one swift motion. The striped muslin fell away, revealing her stays and a gauzy chemise beneath. He had her laces undone in the space of a breath. Ripping the chemise was the work of an instant, and then her back was exposed to him, elegant planes and graceful ridges and smooth, creamy skin. He ran his fingers over that silky expanse, watching her flesh quiver beneath his touch.

"And they continue here," he said, sliding his hands beneath the torn edges of the frock and around her ribcage. Easing her loosened stays aside, he took her bared breasts into his hands. Her breath was a sharp hiss as the soft, warm mounds filled his palms. He groped hungrily, thumbing her hard nipples as he nuzzled the curve of her neck.

She worked back and forth against him, stroking her moist, inviting heat over his aching erection. "And then?"

He pinched her nipples, rolling them between his thumbs and forefingers. She shivered as he swept his tongue over her neck and down between her shoulder blades. Oh, she tasted so good, both salty and sweet. "Then you moan my name."

"*Gray.*" The word was a throaty plea. His loins answered with a throb.

"You tell me you want me."

"I want you."

"Me, and no other."

"Only you, Gray, only you."

He slid his hands from her breasts to her hips and lifted, positioning himself at her entrance. "You tell me—"

He stopped himself, struck by the idiocy of what he'd nearly said: *You tell me you love me.* What a damn fool thought to entertain. This wasn't love to her, it was just fantasy and lewd imaginings. A chance to satisfy her youthful lust and curiosity. He'd been twenty once. He remembered what it was to chase pleasure, and he certainly hadn't confused it with love. He'd never contemplated love at all.

Until now.

She rocked backward, taking him into her. Beautiful, searing bliss enveloped him. She was all sweetness and heat and molten sighs, gripping him so tightly he could almost believe, for this moment, that she would never let him go.

He clutched at her hips, pulling her closer until they were fully joined. God, he was losing himself inside her, and it was too late to pull away. There was nothing he could do. Nothing but take the pleasure she offered and give it in return, and make this so damn good that so long as she lived, no matter how far she went from him, she would never, ever forget.

He took her in smooth, powerful strokes that had no end and no beginning, but built on one another—surely, steadily, relentlessly. He reached one hand around to cup her sex, part her gently, and strum the sensitive bud hidden there.

She moaned. She keened. She arched into his thrusts and took him deeper. And finally he felt the little flutters in her thighs and intimate muscles that told him her peak was near. He raced toward it with her, his cries joining hers as the pleasure consumed them both.

And then he simply held her, for as long as he dared.

"Well," he finally said, withdrawing from her body. "You got what you wanted, then." A bitter edge tainted the lingering tremors of pleasure singing through him. "We both did."

"Did we?" She pivoted to face him, and he choked on his breath. How dangerous her beauty was. He thought it might be the death of him. She smoothed the hair off his brow, and he winced at the tenderness in her touch.

"Gray, if you found my book, surely you must know that this kind of . . . encounter . . . is not all I want. I want so much more. And I want it with you."

He closed his eyes, and that picture of the two of them lounging under a willow tree appeared behind his eyelids. He shook his head to dispel it. "You want some fantasy, spun from a girl's imagination. You want a dream that can never come true."

The flush of her cheeks faded as she searched his face. "I suppose you're right. That dream can never come true, if you don't share it."

"It's not—"

"Enough about my dreams." She put a finger to his lips, then trailed the touch down his jaw. "What is it that *you* really want, Gray?"

He seized her shoulders. "I want no more lies. No more wild tales and secret fantasies. I want you to tell me everything. Who you are, where you came from, where you're going. Everything."

Something softened in those clear, lovely eyes. "I'm so sorry for deceiving you, for hurting you. But I was desperate, don't you understand? You were pushing me away, and I cared for you so much. And that was nothing, compared to what I feel for you now." She pressed her hand to his face. "Gray, I—"

"I don't want to hear this. I want the truth, not excuses."

She stiffened, withdrawing her touch. "Now *there* is a falsehood. No one ever wants the truth from me. They just want the pretty package it comes in. If you really wanted to hear the truth, you'd listen. My feelings for you, they're as true a part of me as my name, or my place of birth. But you never want to hear them. You just keep running away."

He swallowed, uncertain what to say.

"And of all the people to accuse me of dishonesty— the man who told me I was worth nothing to him but six pounds, eight shillings? The man who ordered me to go to my berth and thank Almighty God he didn't want me? You have no idea how your lies hurt me."

Oh, God. "Sweet, if I could only take back those words—"

"But you can't. You have to live with them now, just

as I do." Arms twisted behind her back, she adjusted and relaced her stays.

"Do you know what I think?" she asked, cocking her head and narrowing her eyes. "Never mind the lies— you were happy to be my first. I think you were damn near overjoyed to discover I was a virgin. I doubt you ever truly believed otherwise. It was only when you found the money that everything soured." She jabbed a finger in his chest. "I know precisely what you were hoping that day. You were hoping your pure, innocent virgin had come along, to spread her legs and redeem your sins with her mystical virtue. Well, surprise, Gray. I'm not perfect. I've sins enough of my own to deal with, and I'm not here to save you from yourself."

Once again, she left him with no words. She was getting far too good at that. Tightening the cord on his trousers, he released his breath in a bewildered sigh. It was so damned hard to argue with the truth. "Sweetheart—"

Holding her dress together with one hand, she threaded the milk pail over her other wrist. "I do have dreams, Gray. Beautiful dreams. And yes, depraved fantasies. I also have a heart. You're tangled up in all of them, and you can ignore me or run from me, but you can't ask me to deny my feelings any longer."

She stopped and studied him. Then she rose up on tiptoe and planted a kiss on his cheek. It struck Gray as a pitying sort of gesture, but he could not bring himself to spurn it.

"I know what you want, Gray. I know what it is you really need to hear. When you're ready to listen, come let me know."

Her kiss lingered, long after she'd gone.

"Something's amiss," Gray said, jerking his chin upward. "Fore topgallant lift."

The *Kestrel* crewman hoisted a lantern and peered up into the darkness. "Where, again? Can't say as I see it." Then he turned and peered at Gray. "It all looks right as roses to me."

"A line's gone slack." With an exasperated sigh, Gray extended a hand. "Lend me your marlinespike; I'll see to it myself."

The sailor did not argue, but handed over the marlinespike with a shrug. "You're the captain."

Gray scaled the foremast rigging, climbing hand over hand past the foresail and fore topsail yards. When he reached the topgallant, he made a perch for himself and rested. There was nothing wrong with the line, or the sail. He'd known that before he began climbing. But there was something amiss with him, and he needed the space and distance to examine it.

Cool night air buffeted him, rushing through the loose weave of his tunic and blasting the staleness from his skin. It felt almost as good as a proper bath.

Her question from that afternoon haunted him. What was it that he really wanted? For a self-centered libertine, it had been an oddly long time since he'd pondered that question. For the past two years, he'd poured, bled, and sweated himself into this shipping business. His goals were clear. He wanted Joss to become his partner; he wanted Bel to have her London debut; and he wanted to provide security and a measure of status for their family as a whole. But what did he want for himself? It had been years since he'd allowed himself to spin fantasies of a happy future—not since he was a youth of Davy's age. Happiness, he'd concluded, was meant for other men: men who lived honorably, kept their promises, built honest fortunes. Men who deserved it. Gray simply took pleasure where he found it, then left it behind. It was mad, and more than a bit dangerous, for a scoundrel like him to dream of lasting joy.

But now she was dreaming it for him. For them. Naïve, fanciful thing that she was, she genuinely believed they could live happily ever after. None of his angry words or dark confessions had persuaded her otherwise.

Remarkable. He'd finally met the one girl he couldn't disillusion.

And so, soaring through the darkness, rocked by waves and blanketed by stars, Gray decided to try an experiment. He shut his eyes and dared to dream.

He wanted someone to share his life. To share his burdens, his triumphs, his home and his bed. The longing assailed him, nearly flinging him from the mast with its intensity. It was as though a well of yearning existed inside him, deep and limitless, and he'd been keeping it tightly capped for years, lest he fall into it and drown. And now it flooded him, coursed in his veins like his lifeblood.

He wanted . . . he wanted so many things. Simple pleasures. To buy her a dozen muslin frocks to replace the one he'd destroyed today. To feed her succulent fruits and ripe cheeses and slices of roasted meat. To lay his head in her lap and feel her fingers in his hair, and listen to all her fanciful tales and dreams. To share thoughts without exchanging words. To lay with her, be in her, feel her body surround him as often as she'd allow. And a child . . . God, how he wanted a child. He'd been fighting that desire for more than a year, ever since he'd cradled his newborn nephew in his arms. It was irresistible in the most base, selfish way, this impulse to create a life. A child would be bound to love and admire him, no matter what he did. A child would be bound to accept his love. A child would bind him to her, forever.

Somehow it always circled back to her. He wanted her.

This was the voyage he'd meant to go respectable. He thought he'd lost that chance in the taking of her virtue, then the discovery of her lies and that bundle of gold beneath her stays. The futility of all his struggling had burned a black, smoking crater in his soul. But perhaps that was exactly what he'd needed: a blast to his petrified heart, and this resultant void that only she could fill. Perhaps, at long last, what he wanted and what was right were one and the same.

All that remained was to convince her. Well, there he had experience on his side. He knew a little something about conquest.

Gray spent an hour up there in the rigging, soaking up the darkness, gathering bravery from the wind. When the eight bells finally rang, they signified far more than a change of watch.

He was going to change his life.

CHAPTER
TWENTY-THREE

Sophia startled awake. By what dim, silvery light the cabin window afforded, she made out the silhouette of a man standing at the foot of the bed. He was tall—so tall his shadow spread up the wall and seeped into the ceiling cracks, like ink. It could only be Gray. She wondered how long he'd been standing there.

She rose up on her elbow. "What do you want, Gray?"

"I want you."

Heat swept her from crown to toes. She lay there waiting, suddenly uncertain how to speak or move or even breathe. The small sounds of waves lapping against the boat and canvas snapping in the breeze swelled to a deafening roar.

He leaned forward, placing one hand on either side of her legs. The bed creaked under his weight. Falling back on the pillow, Sophia let out a small squeak of her own.

He prowled up her body, moving forward on hands and knees, until he caged her completely. His scent, hot and male, engulfed her. The front of his shirt hung loose, and as he crawled over her, the fabric brushed against her belly, then her breasts. Her nipples peaked instantly.

His hand captured her chin, his thumb and fingers framing her jaw. Her pulse beat wildly against his palm. Though his face hovered mere inches above hers, she could barely make out his features. Moonlight glinted off the bridge of his nose and the neat, blunt edge of his teeth. He inhaled slowly, and Sophia could have sworn he sucked that breath straight out of her lungs.

He was everywhere around her—his strength, his heat, his rum-scented breath. She was powerless to do anything but stare up at him, eyes wide and straining in the dark. Her lips began to tremble.

He stilled them with his own. A brief, tender kiss that loosened every joint in her body. And now she trembled everywhere.

Still cupping her jaw, he broke the kiss. A breeze, ribbon-thin and cool as satin, rushed between their lips, only to be chased away by his hot, urgent whisper: *"I want you."*

This time, his mouth crushed down on hers, insistent and bruising. He lowered himself onto her, and Sophia thrilled to the way her body instinctively molded around his. Her lips parting to suckle his tongue, her breasts flattening under his chest, her thighs gripping his hips as he insinuated his legs between hers. And, oh God— when his hips forced her thighs wide and the hard ridge of his arousal pressed home through the layers of trousers and chemise—she was already softened and wet for him there.

Because she wanted him, too.

He ground his hips against hers, and she moaned around his tongue. There was nothing like the feel of this, his body hard and eager and crushed against hers. Knowing that she'd made him this way, driven him desperate with need until nothing—not pride or money or lies—could keep him away.

He pulled away suddenly, rising up to his knees. His shirt fluttered up over his head, a white sail caught in the moonlight and swept away into shadow. He reached between them, loosening the cord of his trousers. As he worked the knot, the back of his hand brushed against her mound, and Sophia gave a wanton sigh. When he finished, she bent her knees and hooked her toes under the loosened waistband. He leaned over her again, and she slowly dragged the trousers down over his hips, savoring the feel of hard muscle and downy hair under the arches of her feet. She felt his erection spring free and brush against her thigh. They moaned in unison.

And that was the final leisurely caress. They moved quickly now—to seize this time, this pleasure, this chance, before it could slip away into the night. He kicked off his trousers, and together they tussled with her chemise, bunching it up to her breasts and tugging it over her head.

"Gray," she whispered, reaching for him in the dark.

"I want you." He buried his face in her hair as they tumbled back onto the pillows. "God, how I want you. I want to kiss you." He pressed his lips to her ear, her neck, the small notch at the base of her throat. "Touch you." His hands, rough with fresh calluses, roamed over her breasts and hips, kneading greedy handfuls of flesh. "Lick you."

Sophia shivered at the mere words, and when his tongue made hot, wet contact with her skin, she gasped. A trail of gooseflesh rose up in the wake of his tongue as he traced the slope of her collarbone.

"I want to suckle you," he murmured against her skin, sliding down her body to draw her nipple into his mouth. She arched, gasping his name. He pulled gently at first, holding the tight bud firmly between his lips as his tongue flicked lightly over the peak. Sparks danced over her skin with each teasing caress. Then he sucked harder, catching her nipple between his teeth, and pleasure mingled with pain. Sophia twined her hands into his hair, digging her fingernails into his scalp—whether to wrench him away or hold him there forever, she didn't know.

Then he released her nipple, and his rough chin scraped against her breast. She opened her eyes to find him staring up at her, studying her intently in the darkness, as if counting her shallow breaths. Dark-blue eyes reflected tiny silver moons. All the while, his fingers toyed with her other nipple, pinching and rolling it until she bit back a moan.

"Sweet," he said, the smooth edge of his voice frayed. "I want to taste you. Let me taste you."

Hooking one arm under each of her knees, he sank between her thighs. Sophia gasped as he raised his shoulders, pushing her knees to her hips and spreading her legs wide. Her eyes squeezed shut. Never had she felt so naked, so exposed. She gave thanks for the robe of shadow night afforded her.

The darkness did not hinder Gray. His mouth went straight to her core. Sophia bucked when his tongue delved into the cleft of her sex.

"Shhh." The rush of his breath caressed her most intimate places. "Trust me."

Inhaling slowly, she willed herself to relax. "Yes."

He bent his head again, learning her body with his mouth, seeking the center of her pleasure. How could such tender, gentle exploration give rise to sensations so unbearably acute? His hands tightened over her hips, holding her down while his lips and tongue teased her most sensitive spot. And when his tongue dipped inside her, she cried out.

The climax burst through her, wave after wave of bliss rippling out from her center. And even as the tremors faded, he kept up his efforts, licking and gently suckling her swollen flesh.

"Gray," she panted, tugging on his hair. "Gray, *please*."

He unthreaded his arms from her legs and kissed his way up her belly before sitting back on his heels. "I want you." He pushed her knees wide. "I want to know that you will never spread these legs for another man." He wedged his hips snugly between her thighs and pushed into her, an inch. Sophia whimpered and reached for him.

He caught her hands in his, interlacing their fingers. Her arms bent at the elbows as he leaned forward, pinning her hands to the pillow.

"I want to know that no other man will ever have this." He pushed in a bit further.

It wasn't enough. Sophia strained toward him, wrapping her legs over his. "Gray. Oh, God. More."

He thrust into her roughly, his fingers tightening over hers. "I want you to know that you are mine." He withdrew and thrust again, this time sheathing himself to the hilt. "Mine." *Thrust.* "Mine."

Sophia's body sang under his tender assault, even as her heart ached. She longed to wrap her arms around him, draw him close. Whisper promises into his ear and hold him until he understood not just that she was his, but that he was *hers*. He was striving so hard to conquer her, but she knew all he wanted, in his heart, was to be claimed.

He held her hands in iron grips as he pushed into her, again and again. Sweat beaded on his brow, dripping onto her breasts and her neck. The bed protested his every stroke, and she moaned with it.

"I want you." Rasping breaths broke up his words; he punctuated each phrase with a thrust. "I want you . . . to be mine. Now. Always."

"Yes." She wrapped her thighs tightly over his hips, embracing him the only way she could. "Always."

"I want to fill you with my seed. I want you to bear my child." His pace quickened; his eyes squeezed shut.

"Gray," she gasped, feeling a rush of pleasure as he tilted his hips. Now his pelvis ground against hers, lifting her to a higher plane of ecstasy with each deep thrust. Her mouth fell open as pleasure mounted within her, spiraling up and up.

"I want you," he growled, his fingers tightening over hers. "I want the truth."

He froze. Time slowed, teetered on the edge of an abyss.

"I want the truth," he repeated, pushing into her again. Then he stopped, completely sheathed in her, the full length of him filling her, pressing hard against her womb. He released her hands and bent over her, burying his face in her neck.

"God, sweet, can't you understand? I want you. All of you. I want to know you, inside and out. I want you to know me. Nothing will change that, I swear to you. You can tell me anything. I'm ready to hear it."

With trembling hands, she cradled his head. "I love you."

"That's not . . ." He stiffened in her arms and began to withdraw. Sophia arched her body and clasped him to her, drawing him back in. "Oh, God," he groaned, sinking into her again. "You know that's not what I meant."

"Isn't it?" She wove her fingers into his hair and kissed his earlobe. "Gray, it's the truth. I love you."

The muscles of his neck went rigid under her fingertips. His hands slid down to cup her bottom, lifting her hips. Oh, and now he was so deep, so solid inside her. The tempo of his thrusts increased, driving her to a helpless crescendo.

Ragged breaths scorched her ear. "Tell me again. Tell me the truth."

"I love you."

Faster, now. Urgent. Desperate. She was soaring toward release.

"Tell me more," he demanded, his teeth scraping her shoulder.

"You love me, too."

His lips found hers, and then the truth was there—in this kiss, in their joining, in the exquisite pleasure that shuddered through them both and the hot bursts flooding her womb.

They collapsed together, damp with sweat and gasping for breath. He lay still only moments before starting again, seeding light kisses along her neck, palming her breast in his callused hand.

"You are so beautiful," he sighed into her hair.

She tried to check her girlish giggle, unsuccessfully. "Gray, it's dark as pitch. You can't even see me."

"Even in the dark," he murmured against her skin. "You are the most beautiful woman I've ever known, even in the dark."

Suddenly, it was tears Sophia fought to suppress. She lost that battle, too.

"I swear I'll never leave you," he whispered. "I said it before, and I mean it still. I don't care what you've done in the past, because your future is with me. If I never learn your name, it doesn't matter. I intend to give you mine."

He rose up on one elbow and smoothed the hair from her brow. His smile was a flash of white in the dark. "You can be 'Mrs. Grayson' to the world, but to me . . . to me, you'll always be 'sweet.' I don't think I could call you anything else."

Sophia swallowed hard. Did he mean what she thought he meant? "Are you certain? I may still get my courses."

"I'm certain. I've never been more certain."

"I thought you weren't the marrying sort."

"I wasn't. And it's a damn good thing, too, or I'd be

off with some inconvenient wife instead of here with you." His hand drifted down to her belly. "You could be carrying my child. I want our child. I want a life with you."

Hope fluttered in her chest. "Gray . . ."

"Shhh." He laid a finger against her lips. "Don't say anything, unless it's yes."

The silence was unbearable, the darkness palpable.

Gray kept his finger against her lips, suddenly afraid to move. If he released her and she didn't say yes . . .

Doubt seeped into his mind, inviting panic to follow. How had he come to care so deeply for this woman, in just a few short weeks? How had he come to care so deeply for anything? And how did he dare to believe he deserved her, deserved this happiness?

Her lips trembled under his touch; or perhaps his finger trembled against her lips. He felt as though a heavy weight balanced on the fulcrum of his heart. One sigh, one breath from her could topple it. Could crush him.

She swallowed, and beneath his fingertip, her lips thinned, separated. A slender crescent of white rent the dark. She was smiling.

Don't hope, he bade his hammering heart. *Women smile with regret as often as not.*

Slowly, he slid his finger downward, releasing her. The world stilled. He felt like a convict awaiting his sentence, absurdly hoping for life imprisonment.

"Yes," she whispered.

"Yes?" Hearing it once was not enough.

The crescent of white swelled, like a waxing moon. "Yes."

He clutched her shoulders. "Yes," he prompted again. Hearing it twice was not enough, either.

She hugged him close, her legs over his hips and her

arms linked around his neck. He was still inside her, and she tightened around him there, too. Arousal pulsed in his groin, and he began to thicken once again in her velvet embrace.

Craning her neck, she kissed him. "Yes," she murmured against his lips, over and over between hungry tastes. "Yes, Gray. Yes." Her head fell back against the pillow. "I love you."

Just like that, he was hard again. God, he would never get enough of this woman. *His* woman. And miracle of miracles, she hadn't had enough of him yet, either. Her pelvis rolled beneath his, sending currents of pleasure through him with each clever tilt. She stroked his back, her touch feather-light and cool against his skin.

"Sweet." He moved his hand between them, stroking her where their bodies joined. "I swear I'll take care of you. I'll make you happy." He prayed it was the truth.

"Mmmm," she moaned. "Oh, yes."

Once, twice, a dozen times. Gray could not hear that word enough. He loved her slowly, relentlessly, until she panted and sighed the words, "yes," "Gray," and "God" so many times they felt like sacred vows.

Then he watched her sleep curled up beside him, until dawn painted her nakedness in warm, glowing strokes of light. He'd made love to her four times now, he realized, but this was his first chance to truly look upon her body. She was every inch as lovely as he'd imagined, if not more. He felt a bit guilty, realizing he'd chastised her for sketching his likeness, when he'd been conjuring an image of her nude form nightly for weeks. The only difference was, he hadn't committed his fantasies to paper.

It would take a Renaissance master to capture this beauty.

Her hair spilled across the pillow and his outstretched arm, a million threads of the finest silk floss. When she woke, he vowed, he would brush it until it gleamed. He admired the smooth disc of her areola, relaxed in sleep. Then he blew surreptitiously across it, until it ruched to a tight rosette. His gaze wandered lower, to where her navel rose and fell with each breath, like a tiny cork afloat on her slightly rounded belly. An irregular birthmark stood out on the crest of her hip, like a splash of wine on snow.

He touched a finger to it, and she stirred.

"Don't look at that," she mumbled, rubbing sleep from her eyes. "I know it's horrid."

"Horrid?" Despite the pained expression on her face, he had to laugh. "Sweetheart, I can honestly say that there is nothing about you that's horrid in the least."

"My painting master would not agree."

The bitter taste of envy filled his mouth. "Do you know, that Frenchman of yours had better hope I never meet with him."

"Oh, no," she said quickly. "Not Gervais. Never Gervais. My painting master was an old, balding prig called Mr. Turklethwaite."

Gray's bafflement must have been obvious.

She went on, "There was never any Gervais. I mean, you know that I'd never taken a man to my bed, but you must understand . . . I've never allowed another man into my heart, either." She kissed his brow, then his lips. "I love you, only you."

God. How brave she was. Tossing those words about as though they were feathers. Could she possibly suspect how they landed in his chest like cannonballs, detonating deep in his heart?

Struggling for equanimity, he asked casually, "So when did this other painting master have occasion to see your birthmark?"

She laughed. "He didn't. But I painted something like

it once, on a portrait of Venus. I told him I thought it lent her an air of reality. Oh, how he scolded me. A lady who paints, he said—" She gave Gray a teasing look. "He would not apply the term 'artist' to a female, you see."

"I see."

"A lady who paints, he said, should approach the art as she would any other genteel accomplishment. Her purpose is to please; her goal is to create an example of refinement. A true lady would not paint an imperfection, he said, any more than she would strike a false note in a sonata. Beauty is not real, and reality is not beautiful."

Gray shook his head. "Remarkable. I believe I despise your real painting master even more than I hated the fictional one. I wouldn't have thought it possible."

She rose up on her elbows, her expression suddenly anxious. "Gray, how can you wish to marry me? There's so much you don't know. Some of it is ugly indeed."

"I know you are *mine*." Wanting to reassure her, he laced her fingers with his. "I meant every pledge I made to you aboard the *Aphrodite*. You are safe with me, and I will never leave you. I came to you with honorable intentions when we made love. I meant to marry you then, knowing no more of you than I do right now. I may not know your history, but I trust that I know your heart."

"Better than anyone." A little smile coaxed her lips apart, and he kissed them. First sipping gently at her upper lip, then savoring the plumpness of its counterpart below.

"And do you trust me? You can tell me everything. You do believe that?"

"Yes, certainly. And I will tell you everything." A hint of uncertainty flashed in her eyes, however, and she bit her lip. "In time."

Her reluctance wounded him, but Gray forced himself to feign patience. Pressing her further might yield answers, but not trust. He wanted to earn both. "Very well. In time."

She toyed with a lock of his hair. "There's so much to tell, is all. I'm uncertain where to begin."

"Well then. Let us begin with essentials. Are you free to marry me?" He exhaled slowly, in a pointed effort not to hold his breath.

"Of course. When I come of age, that is."

"Tell me your birthday."

She smiled. "The first of February."

"It will be our wedding day." He traced the shape of the birthmark on her hip. "Very convenient for me, for your birthday and our anniversary to coincide. I'll be more likely to remember both."

"I wish you would stop touching me there."

"Do you? Why?"

"Because it *is* ugly. I hate it."

He tilted his head, surprised. "I quite adore it. It reminds me that you are imperfectly perfect and entirely mine." He slid down her body and bent to kiss the mark to prove the point. "There's a little thrill in knowing no one else has seen it."

"No other man, you mean." He kissed her there again, this time tracing the shape with his tongue. She squirmed and laughed. "When I was a child, I would scrub at it in the bath. My nursemaid used to tell me, God gives children birthmarks so they won't get lost." Her mouth curled in a bittersweet smile. "Yet here I am, adrift on the ocean on the other side of the world. Don't they call that irony?"

"I believe they call it Providence." He tightened his hands over her waist. "You're here, and I've found you. And I take pains not to lose what's mine."

He kissed her hip again, then slid his mouth toward her center as he settled between her thighs.

"Gray," she protested through a sigh of pleasure. "It's late. We must rise."

"I assure you, I've risen."

"I've work to do." She writhed in his grip. "The men will be wanting their breakfast."

"They'll wait until the captain has finished his."

"Gray!" She gave a gasp of shock, then one of pleasure. "What a scoundrel you are."

He came to his knees and lifted her hips, sinking into her with a low groan. "Sweet," he breathed as she began to move with him, "you would not have me any other way."

CHAPTER
TWENTY-FOUR

Breakfast was late. Quite late, but served with a smile. And because the men were already at their duties, Sophia assumed the task of delivering Mr. Brackett's meal to the hold.

Bearing a tin plate of biscuits and a small pot of tea, she descended the long, narrow ladder, past the cabins and steerage, into the very belly of the ship.

"Mr. Brackett?" She paused at the bottom of the stair, uncertain in which direction he lay.

"Could that be Miss Turner?" His too-courteous voice scraped out from somewhere to the left. Sophia felt anxiety wing through her, but she did not allow it to build a nest. He was confined, she reminded herself. And he would be a fool to attempt any mischief with her.

"I've brought your breakfast." She walked in the direction of his voice, slowly, allowing her eyes time to adjust to the dim lighting in the hold. Eventually she found him, shackled and chained to a bilge pump. He looked healthy enough, if rather unwashed. The sharp features of his face appeared even more gaunt, and a growth of beard shadowed his jaw.

"Miss Turner," he said, clucking his tongue. "You came aboard this boat a respectable governess, and just look at you now. Grayson's made you his serving wench." He tilted his head. "And his whore."

Sophia's face burned. Her hands shook, and the hard biscuits rattled on the plate. "Don't you dare speak of him in that manner. You are not fit to scrape the tar from his boots. He is a better man than you could ever aspire to be, and what's more—he is a better person than I. He has sheltered you and fed you, when for what you did to Quinn and Davy, I would have gleefully thrown you to the sharks. As matters stand now, I shall settle for throwing your breakfast to the rats." She flung the plate, biscuits and all, into the furthest reaches of the hold. "Good day, Mr. Brackett."

Shaking, Sophia made her way up the stairs and stumbled wildly onto the deck.

"What is it?" Gray demanded, catching her in his arms. He searched her face and examined her limbs. "What's happened?"

She shook her head, dabbing at her eyes with her fingertips. "Mr. Brackett is a vile, hateful man."

"Did he hurt you? I'll kill him."

"No, don't. You'll make a liar of me." She smothered a burst of hysterical laughter with her palm.

Gray took her by the elbows and led her to sit down. "It's nothing," she insisted, soothed by his presence and strength. "He didn't hurt me. We just . . . had words, that's all."

"You're not to go down there again. Do you understand?"

"Believe me, I'd let him starve before I ventured down in that hold again."

"I'd be tempted to do just that—let him starve. But unfortunately, we won't be at sea long enough."

Sophia looked up, sniffing. "Are we so close to Tortola?" It wasn't the end, she reminded herself. Only the beginning. There would be other voyages, whole seas and continents to explore.

He nodded. "Just a day or two more." He pulled her to her feet and directed her toward the ship's rail. "Look."

A school of fish raced the *Kestrel,* a flurry of silver darts slicing through the foam. She glimpsed them easily through the unclouded waters. The tropical sea looked blue as sapphires from a distance, but clear as glass up close. To Sophia's astonishment, a few of the fish leapt from the water and sailed through the air on great wing-like fins, before disappearing once again beneath the waves.

"Flying fish. A sure sign we're close. And there's another." He pointed toward the tip of the foremast, where a large white gull perched serenely.

"A bird. I can't believe it's been a whole month since I've seen a bird." She turned to Gray. "And yet, I can't believe it's been only a month that I've known you. I can't decide whether it's been the longest month of my life, or the shortest."

His eyebrows gathered in an exaggerated frown. "I can't decide which pays me the fainter compliment."

"Neither," she teased, linking her arm in his. "To compliment you, I should tell you it has been the *best* month of my life. And it has." Truer words, she'd never spoken.

"Oh, nicely managed. My pride is rescued." Despite his air of nonchalance, his eyes held genuine emotion. They were fully blue today—a rich, azure blue, clear and inviting and endless. Just like the sea.

Sophia laughed to herself. How had she missed the obvious? All this time, she'd been puzzling out the color of his eyes. They were always shifting and changing, from green to blue to gray. And now she knew why. They always reflected the sea.

"Do you know," he said, "if you keep gazing at me

like that much longer, I shall be forced to pack you off belowdecks."

"Am I truly gazing?" She fluttered her lashes at him. "I am making a trip to the storeroom soon, you know. But mind—this is the last good frock I've got."

"Siren." He gave her a surreptitious pinch on the hip. "No, it's the cabin I have in mind for you, and you're going there alone. You need to rest." He walked her toward the hatch.

"You won't come rest with me?"

"If I come with you, neither of us will rest."

A current of pleasure shot straight to her center. Then a more practical thought intruded. "But what of the noon meal? It won't make itself."

At that instant, a flying fish as long as her arm sailed over the rail of the boat and flopped on the deck at their feet.

Gray looked at the thrashing fish, then raised his eyebrows at her. "Somehow I think we'll manage."

Hours later, Sophia woke alone in the dark. Her toes groped the floorboards for her slippers, and she wrapped a light blanket over her shift before heading abovedecks.

Stars greeted her, in divine multitudes. A million lights dancing, winking, shining merrily in the firmament. As though some mischievous seraph were crawling about the floor of Heaven, drilling little holes with an auger to let glory shine through.

She spied him at the helm, his back to her as he looked out over the *Kestrel*'s stern, elbows propped on the rail. The crewman at the ship's wheel politely ignored her as Sophia tiptoed past, through the swaying umbra of lamplight and into the shadows that cloaked Gray.

Noiselessly, she pressed her body to his, flattening her cheek against his back. He tensed at the initial contact, then relaxed an instant later. His fingers found hers as she crept one hand around his waist.

"You should be sleeping," he murmured. His amplified voice sounded delicious, traveling through the solid muscles of his back. She felt him, rather than heard him. Felt him everywhere.

"I was missing you." And, because she wanted to feel him speak again, she added in a suggestive voice, "Were you missing me?"

"Of course." He dragged her hand downward to present her with tangible proof of just how much he missed her. Sophia smiled against his back. He missed her greatly, she discovered, her fingers exploring. This was yearning on a grand scale, indeed.

He spoke again, sending pleasant tremors through her. "We'll make land tomorrow. In the morning, if the wind holds."

Now Sophia was the one to tense. He pivoted to face her, drawing her tight against his chest. "Nothing between us changes tomorrow." He lifted her hand to his lips and kissed it. "Except this," he said, rubbing her palm over his beard. "The first thing I'll do once we reach terra firma is shave. I'm going mad with itching."

She laughed, caressing his rough cheek with her thumb. "Then why haven't you shaved all along?"

"Feel this?" He dragged her fingertips over the narrow scar slanting across his chin. "This is what comes of shaving at sea."

"Truly?" She pulled back, blinking in the starlight to make out his features. "That's how you got that scar? You cut yourself shaving?" She could not help but laugh.

"I'm glad my vanity-occasioned injury amuses you so."

"I'm not laughing at you. I'm laughing at myself. That you cut yourself shaving . . . it isn't at all what I'd imagined."

"Oh, by all means, laugh. It was pure folly." He looked out over the waters. "Must have happened somewhere near this corner of the ocean, since we were only a day or so out from Tortola. I was coming home from England, after my father had died. I was so worried for my sister, Bel. She was just a child then. We hadn't seen each other in years, but from the moment she greeted me, I wanted her to feel reassured. I was so anxious to look responsible, capable . . ." She heard the wry smile in his voice. "Failing that, at least well-groomed. I was shaving when the storm hit. Lost my balance and fell—sliced open my chin, and blackened an eye, too. Instead of well-groomed and responsible, I showed up looking as though I'd been besieged by pirates."

"She was no less overjoyed to see you, I'm sure." Sophia rested her chin on his arm. "I look forward to meeting your sister. Will she like me, do you think?"

"She will love you." The soft murmur warmed her heart. Then he continued in a teasing tone, "Charity is her life's work. It's what Bel does best, devoting herself to the most wayward of souls."

"Well then, she will most certainly attach herself to me."

"I'm counting on it." He gathered her closer, then froze. "I've just realized something."

She looked up.

"Your little bundle's gone," he whispered, walking his fingers down the valley between her breasts. "You didn't pitch it overboard?"

She smiled. "It's beneath the mattress. I didn't want to feel it between us anymore. But supposing I *had* pitched it overboard, what then? I do hope you're not marrying me for my money."

"No." He laughed softly. "Six hundred pounds is no paltry sum . . . but no. It's not enough to persuade a man of my means. If it were six thousand, then you might have cause for concern."

And what if it were twenty thousand? Should I be concerned then?

Sophia rested her head on his shoulder. She knew he was only joking, that her money had no sway over his affections. He might have married for money years ago, if he'd wished. But still, she hesitated to divulge the remainder of her fortune, considering his angry reaction the first time.

Neither was she eager to tell him about Toby. How could she tell him that she'd just been betrothed to another solicitous, patient man whom she'd callously jilted and deceived? Gray would doubt her anew, she feared, and Sophia did not know how she would bear it. Better to wait until they were married. He could not doubt her love then.

She closed her eyes and let everything fall away. Everything but Gray. His thumb drew small, intimate circles on her back, and desire spiraled through her body. "Did you want to go below?" she asked.

An eager part of him jumped at the invitation, but the rest of him remained still. "In a bit." He put a finger under her chin and tilted her face to his. "Right now, I want to kiss my sweetheart under the stars."

She kept her eyes open as he bent his head to hers, taking in the silver-blue glow of his skin and the restless shadows the wind dragged from his hair. So handsome, even in the dark.

His breath caressed her lips first, gentle and warm. Then his lips whispered over hers, just a shade more insistent than breath. He licked lightly at the corner of her mouth, oiling the vulnerable hinge of her lips.

"Sweet," he murmured. She swallowed the word, felt it

slide from her throat to her belly, and lower . . . making her hungry for the warm press of his tongue against hers.

Oh, but he was a tease. All patient arrogance and devastating care.

Instead of taking her mouth, he slid a hand to the back of her neck, cradling her head and tipping it back to elongate the column of her throat. He scattered kisses there, hot sparks that danced along her exposed skin. She curled her fingers into his shirt and the rippling muscles beneath. Above them, strange constellations whirled through the night.

His mouth settled possessively over her ear, his breath heating the sensitive shell as his tongue traced its contours.

"You are mine," he whispered into her. "And the world is ours. There is nowhere beneath this sky that we do not belong together."

His tongue flashed into her ear, and her knees dissolved, leaving her no choice but to fall against him. To depend on him for her strength, her balance, and indeed her next breath, as now—at last—his lips covered hers.

Sophia's eyes fluttered shut, and now the stars were inside her. Bright constellations of desire—sparking, burning, whirling through the darkest parts of her being. Glorious. His tongue struck a subtle, coaxing rhythm, mating skillfully with hers. Breasts needy and aching, she pressed her body against his. She wriggled into his embrace until that iron-hard ridge of him nestled just where she needed it. Where they belonged together.

He growled, deep in his throat. She relished the feral sound, the lapse in his suave, sensual mastery of her. But she paused only a moment to savor that taste of power before yielding again, eagerly surrendering to the dangerous, unpredictable need she'd unleashed.

He roamed her body, stroking and tweaking her

everywhere she yearned for him. Soft caresses, rough pinches, sharp bites and gentle licks. He knew just where to place them, and in the precise sequence that rendered her panting and molten.

"Now," he grunted, clutching at her hips. "Now, we go below."

Gray delighted in going below. The little jolt of surprise she gave when he first kissed her there, that instinctive buck of her hips that thrust her heat against his mouth. That naughty little book of hers excluded some rather vital lessons in the art of passion, and he took great pleasure in completing her education.

And then he took his own pleasure in her.

Afterward, sweaty and sated, they lay naked atop the linens. Spread out on their backs as if floating, allowing the night air to cool their skin. Blissful exhaustion buoyed him into sleep.

He roused some time later, when she lit a candle.

"I know I've seen one here somewhere . . ."

Gray could barely muster the energy to lift his head. He caught sight of her, dressed in her shift and rummaging through drawers. "What are you looking for?"

"Aha!" She straightened triumphantly, holding a sharply gleaming object in her hand. A razor, he discerned. "There's a strop and a cake of shaving soap, too. I'll just fetch some water from the galley."

Before he could protest, she was out the cabin door, and Gray let his head fall back on the pillow. He must have dozed, because he opened his eyes to find her over him, tugging his head toward the edge of the bed and smoothing her palms over his face.

"Just lie still," she whispered, guiding him to pivot his body until the crown of his head rested against her chest. "Trust me, I've a very steady hand."

"I don't doubt it." She worked sharp-scented lather through the whiskers, and the aroma sliced through the fog of his brain, waking him a bit more.

"This time, you shall greet your sister looking resplendent. The picture of respectability; or at least, of good grooming."

He sighed as she smoothed the lather down his throat, her touch gliding over his skin. "Good. I shall need all the resplendence I can manage, in order to convince her. Although, I expect your presence will accomplish more in that respect."

"Convince her of what?"

"To come with us, of course." He paused as she laid the blade to his jaw and dragged it slowly up to his cheek. "Now that her mother's gone, and Mara, too . . . I can't allow her to continue living there alone."

"Mara?" She made another slow swipe with the razor.

"Joss's wife. Died in childbirth last year."

She paused. "How dreadful. Did the babe survive?"

"Yes. A boy, Jacob. Bel's looking after him now."

After rinsing the blade, she laid a hand to his cheek, rolling his head to the other side. Again, she began at his ear and worked inward.

"I wish you could have known my brother before," Gray continued. "Before Mara died, he was different. Things were different between us. More . . . brotherly."

"Grief changes people."

"So I've learned."

She tipped his head back to reach his throat. He steadied his breathing, fighting the urge to swallow as she scraped over his pulse. *Grief changes people.* How could it not? He realized now how unfair he'd been to Joss, denying him the time to grieve, the space to change. It was only now that he *could* understand it, when the very idea of losing this woman forced beads of cold sweat to his brow.

Closing his eyes, he reached up to squeeze her free hand. "Let us speak of happier things."

"Very well." He heard the smile in her voice. "Where shall we honeymoon? Will you take me to Italy, to see the Botticellis?"

"I will take you anywhere you wish. Anywhere under the sky."

A tender kiss landed on his eyelid. Then she fell silent, working toward the center of his chin, dipping the blade in a basin at his side between short, sure strokes. She was concentrating, he realized, working carefully around his scar. At last she set aside the razor, letting it sink into the basin with a soft splash, then dried his face with a cloth.

"Stay still." Her fingers ran lightly over his face, as if testing for any rough spots she'd missed. She traced the thin scar from his chin to his mouth. "So if this scar was self-inflicted, occasioned by vanity"—her hand slid down to the scar on his chest—"what of this? Not vanity, I think."

He shook his head, laying one hand over hers. "Pure stupidity, that one. But self-inflicted, just the same."

"It looks like a burn."

"It is."

Silence. His heart thumped against her palm.

"You don't have to tell me," she finally whispered.

"I want to," he replied, surprised to find it was the truth. How could he expect her to share her own secrets, if he withheld his? "But it's a long story."

"We have all night." He cocked his head and frowned up at her. "When I went to the galley, I told O'Shea you were ill," she admitted through a grin. "He'll not disturb us until they sight land."

He rolled onto his side and propped himself on one elbow, uncertain whether to scold or kiss her. She solved the dilemma by kissing him first, then nestling into the bed beside him.

"You need rest," she whispered, drawing his head to her shoulder. "Between keeping watch and keeping a mistress, you've scarcely slept in a week."

"You're not my mistress, you're my future wife."

"We're not married yet. And don't spoil my fun. It's my last chance to be anyone's mistress."

A savage joy swelled his heart. He wrapped an arm about her waist. "Yes, it is."

Gray held her in silence, considering the story he meant to tell. It was a story he scarcely understood himself, and he realized he would be relating it for his own benefit more than for hers. "You will have gathered that Joss's mother was my father's mistress. One of his mistresses, at any rate. She was a slave."

"I see." She stroked his hair.

"From the beginning, my father acknowledged Joss openly as his son. This was after my own mother's death, and before his bastards numbered so many as to make acknowledging them impractical. We were raised as brothers, during the day. Played together, dined together, took our lessons together. By night I stayed in the house, and Joss went to his mother in her quarters."

He frowned. "It's so odd now, to remember how I envied him. He had all the same privileges I enjoyed, with none of the expectations. To me, Joss seemed at home everywhere. It was only much later that I realized the opposite was true."

Pausing, he scrubbed a hand over his freshly shaven face. "It should not have been surprising, I suppose, that he grew to resent me. But it was. When my father talked of sending me back to England, to university—all I wished was to trade places with Joss and stay at home. All he wished was to have the chance to go. We argued all the time, and came to blows more than once."

"But such is the way between siblings," she interjected. "My sister and I quarreled constantly at that age."

"I suppose you're right. In the end, it was another fight that drew the line between us. On his way home from town one night, Joss found himself on the wrong side of some drunken louts. They decided it was time to put my brother in his place, so they beat and branded him."

Her hand froze in his hair. "Branded him?"

"It was done to slaves at one time, burning the owner's mark into their shoulder. A repulsive practice—not that slavery itself is not a repulsive practice in its own right. Branding has been out of favor on Tortola for generations, but Joss's attackers decided to resurrect the tradition." A wave of nausea rolled through him at the memory of his brother lying prostrate in his recovery bed for days on end. The odor of charred flesh giving way to the sickly smell of infection, then the sweet stench of laudanum overpowering all. These parts of the story, he would not share.

"Dear God." She resumed stroking his hair.

"I was due to leave for England before he'd fully recovered. I sat by his sickbed and promised him, when I had my own money I would come back for him and Bel, and we would all have the same luxuries, the same opportunities. We would share everything."

"Did that make him feel better?"

Gray smirked. "He told me to go to the devil. Mind, he was drugged and in pain, but it still killed me. I got roaring drunk, wildly sick, and then roaring drunk again. I didn't know how to convince him and remind myself that despite everything, we were brothers."

She gave a little gasp. Her hand left his hair and went to cover the scar. "Oh, Gray. You did this to yourself?"

He blew out a sigh. "Never underestimate the power of liquor and maudlin sentiment on an adolescent boy. I was so stupid. Botched the whole business. It had to be my chest, since I couldn't very well reach my own shoulder. Didn't heat the iron long enough, and of course my hand shook like a palm frond in a hurricane." He pushed her hand aside and traced the blurred, irregular pattern with his own fingertips. "God, did it hurt. Hurt all the way to England. It reminded me, all right. Reminded me that I should never have left. I felt so damned guilty for leaving him behind, I couldn't even bring myself to go to Oxford when we arrived. Stayed on that ship for more than a year.

"When I did finally go to England, it only made matters worse. I saw the life my father's family should have had. Society, wealth, rank, privilege. Not some nigh-on-biblical exile in a land of slavery and pestilence. I wanted— *needed*—to rebuild the fortune our father squandered. I hadn't a clue how to atone for his moral failings, much less correct my own. But I knew how to make a profit, and that's what I did. I wanted to give my brother and sister all the comforts and security they'd been denied."

His hand curled into a fist over his heart. "And how did I go about it? By breaking every promise I'd ever made. By denying my brother, taking his inheritance, selling his family's home out from under them, and dragging Joss out on the sea with me."

"To become privateers."

"We did have an unholy good time." Gray's lips curved in a cold smile. "We were like boys again, only armed with men's weapons: cannons, cynicism, anger at the world. France and England and America could blow one another to bits. We were there to collect the spoils. Toward the end of the war, we started planning Grayson Brothers Shipping. We'd set up offices in England, build more ships—bring Bel to London for her schooling and debut. We were supposed to be equal partners."

"So what happened?"

"Love, inconvenient thing that it is. Joss married Mara, got her with child. They didn't want to travel, so I went ahead to England and started building the business, gathering investors. Came back just in time to witness Jacob's birth, then Mara's death. Suddenly, Joss wanted nothing to do with the shipping business. Demanded his share of the prize to buy land on Tortola, of all places, and then just give it away."

Sophia frowned. "Give it away?"

"It was Bel's idea, a sugar cooperative. This is what happens when a girl's only friends are missionaries. The Quakers and Methodists have been buying up plantations and dividing them into smaller farms, for freedmen to make their own livelihood. The cooperative bit was Joss's notion—by sharing the cost and labor of refining the sugar, they might be able to eke out a profit."

"Well, that doesn't sound like a bad idea."

"No, it doesn't. It *sounds* like a bloody saintly idea. But in practice . . . it's a tremendous risk. And the farming life—it's hard, it's poor. It's less than they deserve." Gray swore into the night. "After all that time, all that work and sacrifice—to end right back where we'd started? I couldn't let Joss do it. I left."

"And took the money with you."

"He'll thank me eventually. Mara's death made my brother too cautious, that's all. Once he's been out on the sea long enough, he'll come around." He sat up in bed. "And I don't care if my sister claims she's happy dressing in rags and playing ministering Quaker. She is going to London for the most extravagant debut the *ton* has ever seen, and she will wear silk in every damned color of the rainbow. I didn't spend the past ten years lying, cheating, and stealing just so my brother and sister could continue on in the same miserable exile our father gave us. Damn it, I sold my soul for this."

"Shhh." She sat up behind him, draping her arms around his shoulders. "It's all right."

"It's not. Nothing's right. I've never done a right thing in my life, it seems."

"That makes a pair of us then." Her lips pressed against the spot under his ear. "But I believe we are right together, don't you? People like us . . . we have no talent for following rules. We can only follow our hearts. I've wronged people as well, but is it horribly wicked that I can't bring myself to regret it? It brought me to you."

He took one of her hands and kissed it. "You're so young, you can't know the meaning of true regret. It's never what you've done, love, it's what you've left undone."

He leaned against her, sighing into the comforting heat of her breasts. "I'll take you to Italy, sweetheart, I promise it. To Egypt and India, too, if you like. But it will have to wait until after Bel's season. I've put aside a dowry for her, enough to offset our provenance. We do come from gentry, and her mother was my father's second wife, so Bel isn't illegitimate. My aunt's agreed to help bring her out. And if being the well-dowered niece of a duchess isn't enough to turn heads, there is the fact that she's the second-most beautiful lady in the world."

Sliding from her embrace, Gray turned to face her. His compliment seemed to have bounced off her puzzled expression.

"Your aunt is a duchess?" she asked, her brow creasing. "Which one?"

"Oh, not a royal one. Camille Marie Augusta Glaston D'Hiver, Her Grace, the Duchess of Aldonbury. You're forgiven for never having heard of her." He leaned forward to kiss her neck. "Talent or no, it's time for me to follow the rules. I'll go to London and play their little game, attend their balls and parties, host a few of my own. Dress head to toe in the latest fashions, whether they suit me or not."

"What about me?"

"Oh, I'll be unfashionably faithful to you." He brushed her elegantly sloped nose with one fingertip. "Don't vex yourself, sweet. We'll tell everyone you're the daughter of a West Indian planter. I don't suppose you'll have much difficulty adopting the role."

She did not return his smile. "But Gray . . . what if I told you I don't want to go to London, don't want to play their little game?"

"Then I'd convince you otherwise." Giving her his best devilish grin, he leaned in to kiss her.

She put a hand to his chest, stopping him. "What if I told you I *can't*?"

"Of course you can." He pressed a firm kiss to her lips, shushing her objections. "And you will, for me. I must ask it of you. After Bel's settled and Joss assumes the partnership, then the world is ours to explore. But I have to see this through first, or . . ." He stroked her cheek. "Or I've done it all for nothing."

She stared at him for a long moment. "Not for nothing, Gray. You did it for them. And no matter what occurs, I'm certain they know it."

"I wish I had that certainty."

"You may borrow mine." She laid a hand on his cheek,

her eyes dewy. "I'm certain they know how much you love them."

For a moment, he feared she would cry. For a moment, he was mortally terrified that if she did, he would join her.

Then she cocked her head, and a knowing smile balanced out her poignant gaze. With a cheerful sniff, she straddled his lap and pushed back on his shoulders.

"Now." The word was a promising murmur as she pushed him back against the bed. "Let me show you how much I love you."

CHAPTER
TWENTY-FIVE

The dawn was cruel.

Sophia watched daylight creep across her beloved, stealing him from her with rosy fingers, one inch at a time. Sitting in the captain's chair, legs folded under her shift, she regarded Gray as he slept. He lay prostrate on the bed, the linens twisted about his body, one forearm draped over his eyes. It was the same position he'd lain in all night, since their lovemaking sent him into sleep.

When his seed had filled her, she'd sent up a silent prayer that it would take root. If she conceived, all choice would be taken from her. She couldn't leave him if she carried his child; she knew he wouldn't leave her. He would be forced to reconsider his plans in London, but the joy of a child might mitigate his disappointment. Life would write a different ending for them than either had imagined, but it might have been a happy one.

If only she'd conceived.

She'd held him inside her until she felt his gentle snores lifting his chest under hers. Then, leaving him to his well-earned rest, she rose quietly to perform her ablutions. And that was when she'd begun to bleed.

An hour's worth of silent, racking sobs later, Sophia curled into the chair and attempted to think.

Whatever was she going to do? How could she begin to tell Gray the truth? Perhaps she might start with that amusing tale of the red-faced bank clerk, how she'd charmed him into releasing five hundred pounds from her trust. She still suspected he'd have a good laugh at that.

But then she would have to tell him the source of her remaining one hundred. That it had been won at cards, and a fair bit of it at the Duchess of Aldonbury's own table. Should she tell Gray she'd been at school with his cousins? Stayed as a guest more than once in their family home? By now, Her Grace would have heard the sordid, albeit false, story of her elopement. She, like every other lady of the *ton,* would cut Sophia from her acquaintance as a matter of social necessity.

For Sophia, there could be no pretending, no adopting the role of a West Indian planter's daughter. Even if she could stomach the thought of further deceit—and she was not certain she could, even for Gray—if ever she returned to London, she would be a pariah. Her ruin would be a contagion to anyone connected with her.

She knew she ought to tell Gray the truth. But once she did, all the choices would be his. He might insist on marrying her anyway, thereby destroying his sister's prospects and his family's tenuous respectability—everything he'd worked so hard, sacrificed so much to attain.

Or . . . he might let her go.

Sophia buried her face in her hands. How could she tell him? How could she tell him what an inconstant, dishonest, scheming thing she had been, yet still make a claim on his honor? How could she force him to make this choice, between his love for his family and his promises to her?

How would she bear it if he chose them?

The irony of it all. If only she'd have been brave enough to stand up to her parents, to ask Toby to release her from their engagement instead of running away.

There would have been scandal, to be sure, but she still would have received the occasional invitation from old friends. And perhaps next Season, she would have attended a ball, a mad crush of a debut, and locked gazes with a tall, broad-shouldered gentleman sporting a roguish smile and an intriguing scar on his chin.

Perhaps he would have asked her to dance.

The sunlight gilded that scar now, as well as the larger one on his chest. How she envied those scars, the indelible marks he bore for love. One for his brother, one for his sister. In some primitive way, Sophia wanted to mark him, too. He might never see it, never know it—but in her heart, he would always be hers.

Rifling quietly through her trunk, she located an inkwell and a small paintbrush. As she settled beside him on the bed, he stirred . . . but did not wake. Instead, he rolled onto his side, away from her. Perfect.

Fortunately, Sophia had a deft touch and a steady hand. And Gray was exhausted and sleeping like the dead. She worked quickly, stealthily to create her mark. Just as she sat back to admire her sadly impermanent handiwork, footsteps pounded above and the cry rang out:

"Land ho!"

"There's the *Aphrodite*," Gray said, squeezed next to her in the jolly boat as a crewman rowed them toward Road Town. Of course, Gray had insisted she and her trunks be the first items taken ashore. He would not have left her behind.

He nodded toward his ship, moored on the other side of the harbor. "Probably arrived a few days ago now, so they'll be looking for our arrival. I wouldn't be surprised to see Bel waiting on the dock."

"I hope she is not there." The words popped out. She

ventured a glance at him, meeting with the expected frown.

"Why?" he asked. "I thought you looked forward to meeting her."

"I do," Sophia lied. "It's just, I don't feel ready, dressed like this. I should like to make a better first impression."

Gray looked resplendent indeed this morning, fitted out in a crisp lawn shirt, dove-gray trousers, and a royal blue coat that barely contained his massive shoulders. He must have been saving the outfit for just this occasion, his triumphant homecoming. Sophia felt drab and common at his side, dressed in her beleaguered sprigged frock. She, too, had an item of truly splendid attire she might have worn. But the silk gown remained wrapped in tissue at the bottom of her trunk. If she was truly going to do this—tell Gray the whole truth and give him a chance to let her go—well, to look that beautiful hardly seemed fair.

"Shall I introduce you as Jane, then?" He gave her a bemused look. "I can't even think of you as Jane. It's the wrong name for you entirely."

Sophia's hands curled into fists. He was giving her the perfect opportunity. She might as well do it now. "That's because it's not my name."

His jaw tightened, and his thumb ceased stroking her palm. In an instant, a wall of ice had formed between them.

Sophia forced herself to speak. "It's my middle name. You see, I . . . I . . ." Her courage failed. "My family always used my middle name."

His hard expression melted to a grin. "Another thing we have in common." He slid an arm about her waist, drawing her close.

Cursing her cowardice, Sophia leaned against him.

Just the thought of it . . . telling him everything, watching him struggle to choose between her and his dreams . . . She felt her bonnet ribbons constricting about her throat, cutting off her air. Desperation tugged at her, urging her to flee.

But this was not London. Tortola was so small, so uncrowded, so unfamiliar to her and known to Gray. From the boat she could see the settlement of Road Town rising up from the harbor like an amphitheater, all the largest buildings crowded near the water. People milled about the docks, nearly all of them shades of brown or ebony. How could a female, fair-skinned interloper like her possibly hope to disappear? Where would she turn, if he let her go?

The Walthams. She had this one connection. Perhaps they were still here. She could claim her acquaintance with Lucy. Better yet, she could claim to *be* Lucy. She still had the original letter, after all.

His confident baritone caressed her ear. "Don't be nervous. You're beautiful. I'm so proud of you, I think my coat will burst from it."

"It's lovely here," she said, wanting to change the subject.

"I suppose it is, to a newcomer. Though it's only home for me."

Sophia didn't think she could ever greet such a sight with indifference, even after decades. The lush, verdant island rimmed with white sand, set against a backdrop of azure sky . . . it would take her dozens of attempts to render these brilliant colors faithfully.

"Yes, there she is," Gray said as they neared the dock. "I think she's grown two inches since I saw her last." Releasing Sophia's waist, he cupped his hands around his mouth and called, "Bel!"

A young woman stood on the dock. She wore no bonnet, but shielded her eyes with both hands. At Gray's salute, she dropped one to her throat and raised the other in a wave.

From this distance, Sophia couldn't judge whether Miss Grayson had her father's ears, but her coloring was vastly different from either of her brothers'. She had olive skin and jet-black hair, so black it reflected a bluish gloss from the sky.

Heavens, Sophia thought as they docked. Miss Grayson was a *true* beauty. Hers was an exotic, medieval, operatic beauty—a beauty that radiated from within. The kind of beauty that inspired men to compose odes and wage wars, and inspired ladies to make unkind comments in retiring rooms. No wonder Gray would do anything for her.

How could Sophia ever withstand comparison to this creature? Drat. She should have worn the silk after all.

The young lady ran to meet their boat at the end of the dock. Her breathless greeting preempted any introductions. "Oh, thank God." She gulped for air. "Thank God you've arrived. They're coming for you, you know. They've already taken Joss." Her hand fluttered like a bird's wing. "Dolly, there's talk of hanging."

Dear Lord, had she just said—

"Hanging?" Gray helped Sophia out of the boat, then bounded onto the dock. He took his sister by the shoulders. "Bel, calm down. Tell me what's happened."

Miss Grayson swallowed hard. "When Joss brought the *Aphrodite* in, that horrid man . . . the other captain—"

"Mallory," Gray supplied impatiently.

"Yes, him. He went to the Vice Admiralty court and accused you of attacking him, taking his ship by force. They've put Joss in jail, and they're coming for you." She glanced over her shoulder. A trio of disconcertingly large men strode toward them. "They're charging you both with piracy."

At the word, Sophia went queasy. The dock lurched under her. She was on solid land now—or solid wood, at any rate—why did it still feel as though she were at sea?

Gray did not seem perturbed in the least. "I was expecting this. Mallory's nothing but a lying bilge rat, Bel. I'll have it straightened out in a minute, you'll see." He smiled at Sophia. "And then I've someone you'll be glad to meet."

Sophia and Miss Grayson barely had time to exchange befuddled looks before the men were upon them.

"Jenkins." Gray greeted the man in front with a nod. Sophia recognized his posture of effortless authority. "Always a pleasure."

"Welcome back, Gray. Good to see you, too." The man's gaze shifted to his companions, then back to Gray.

"What can I do for you, man? My sister tells me there's been a misunderstanding about the *Kestrel*."

"Seems so," Jenkins said. "Gray, I'm afraid you'll have to come with us straightaway. We've orders to hold you until the judge has a chance to question you and decide on charges."

"There won't be any charges," Gray said, chuckling. "But I'll be glad to come, just as soon as I've seen to my passengers and crew."

The man looked uneasy. "It'll have to be now, Gray." He made a motion to the two men in back, and they stepped forward, holding a pair of shackles between them.

Gray took a step back. "Surely there's no need for chains." He looked from one soldier to another. "I'm a patriot. I brought more than sixty prizes into this harbor and surrendered them all to the Crown. Burton knows that."

"Burton's been gone eight months. The new judge— he's called Fitzhugh—well, he wants you brought in wearing chains, public-like. Fond of display, this one." Jenkins shuffled his feet. "We'll leave the shackles loose. Just come willingly, Gray. Let's not make it an ugly display."

Gray swore with exasperation, but he didn't resist. Stepping a few yards back, he held out his hands. Jenkins directed the two younger soldiers as they fitted metal bands around his wrists.

Sophia touched Miss Grayson's shoulder. "He'll be fine," she whispered, as much to herself as to her companion. "He's done nothing wrong."

"I know." The young lady sniffed. "Dolly always finds a way out of these things."

"Who's Dolly?"

"Why, my brother."

Sophia blinked. Was there a third Grayson brother with square-tipped ears?

"You probably call him Gray," the young lady continued, giving her a cautious smile. "Most people do."

Dolly was Gray? Oh dear. No wonder his sister was the sole lady on earth permitted to address him by his Christian name.

The soldiers began shackling his legs now, working awkwardly to fit the bands around Gray's ankles.

"I thought his name was Benedict," Sophia murmured.

"Oh it is, but that was our father's name. He's always gone by his middle name, Adolphus. Dolly." Miss Grayson turned to her. "You know my brother quite well, then. Forgive me the lapse in etiquette, we haven't even been introduced." She dropped a little curtsy. "I'm Isabel Grayson. Were you a passenger on the *Kestrel*?"

"No, I left England on the *Aphrodite*. Didn't Joss mention me?"

Miss Grayson shook her head. "We didn't have much time to speak. But if Dolly says I'll be glad to meet you, I have a fair guess . . ." Suddenly she grasped Sophia's hand. "You must be one of Mr. Wilson's friends, with the West Indian Missions League. I'm so glad you've come. We've so many plans for the sugar cooperative. And we can take you to the judge. Even if he won't believe Dolly, surely he cannot discount the testimony of a missionary."

A missionary? Sophia's mind whirled. Of all the preposterous assumptions . . . oh, but if only it were true. Then she might have been some help to Gray. But she, a fallen woman, a liar and a thief, walking into a courtroom to speak on his behalf? She could do his cause nothing but harm.

Oh God. He was better off without her.

Finally, the soldiers finished their task. At the sight of her brother in chains, Miss Grayson began to weep.

"All right, Jenkins," Gray muttered, his voice seething. "I'm wearing your shackles. I'll come willingly. Surely you can spare me a minute first." At the command in his eyes, the men fell back a few paces.

Gray turned to his sister. "Bel," he said quietly, "there's a handkerchief in my breast pocket. Take it." She obeyed, and wiped her eyes. He smiled down at her. "Now is this any way to greet your prodigal brother? I'd planned to come home a respectable tradesman." He glanced toward Sophia. "Not just that, but a family man. Instead, I stand before you as a pirate in chains."

He laughed, but Sophia wanted to cry. Once again, his best efforts at brotherhood had been twisted and distorted by fate. She could see in his expression how it wounded him. The thought of tainting Miss Grayson's prospects, being the cause of that pain . . .

"Just the same," he teased his sister, "I'd rather hoped for a kiss."

Miss Grayson gave him a tremulous smile and went up on tiptoe to plant a kiss on his cheek.

"That's better. Now don't worry. I'll have this straightened out directly." His eyes went back and forth between Sophia and his sister. "In the meantime, the two of you can become acquainted." He rattled his chains, adding a self-deprecating roll of his eyes. Then he walked a few paces back, toward the men.

Sophia's dizziness increased, and the dock seemed to roll beneath her again. She felt as though she would become ill, or fall. And with Gray chained like a criminal, who would catch her?

She closed her eyes. If she ran now . . . he couldn't catch her.

She had to go. If she were a better person, a *good* person, she might have gathered the courage to tell the truth and accept her fate. She might have even been able to help him. But if she were a good person, she would not have been here in the first place. She didn't know how to change her colors, any more than a dolphin-fish knew how to change its iridescent scales.

She knew how to lie. She knew how to run.

There was only one way she could set Gray free.

She rushed after him as he ambled down the dock, joking with his captors.

"Gray," she whispered, clutching his bound wrist.

"Don't be anxious, sweet," he murmured, low enough that only she could hear. "I know these men. I've lined their pockets for years. They're not going to hang me. I'll have it all sorted out soon enough."

"I'm certain you will." She swallowed back a wave of nausea. "But . . . I won't be here when you do." He deserved this much, to hear it from her. Just as Toby had deserved the same. Gray was right. She didn't regret the things she'd done, but what she'd left undone.

He tensed. "What do you mean?"

"I have to leave."

He stared at her, his eyes wide with disbelief.

"My courses came," she whispered. "There'll be no child."

"You know that's not the reason—"

"No, it's not the reason. It's not why I'm leaving."

His expression hardened to anger. "What the devil are you saying?"

Be strong, she told herself. *Cut the line cleanly; don't dangle false hope.* "I just have to leave. Gray, please don't make this harder than it is. You don't understand."

His hand encircled her wrist, like a cuff. "You're damned right I don't understand. And I'll be damned if I'll make it easy. Were you lying to me when you agreed to marry me? When you told me you . . ." He lowered his voice. "When you told me you loved me?"

"It doesn't matter if I love you."

He swore violently. "It matters to me."

Surreptitiously, she wrestled against his grip. She kept her voice low. "Gray, we can't be together. We just can't." She finally wrenched her arm from his grasp and turned away, her gaze dropping to her feet. He made a motion toward her, but the chains cut it short.

"Look at me, damn it," he growled.

She did. "Gray, I—"

"If you leave me, I will follow you. And I will find you. I've the fastest ship on the sea, and boundless determination. I don't lose what's mine." His eyes burned into hers. "I will find you."

She shook her head. "Please," she whispered. "Don't try. You won't find me. You don't even know my name."

He flinched. Good. She'd struck a blow.

Soldiers took him by either arm. Gray tried to shake them off. "I'm not done here, damn it."

"Sorry, Gray," Jenkins said. "It's time we took you in. Your sister can visit you at the jail." He gave Sophia a cautious look. "Don't know about your sweetheart."

"I won't be visiting," Sophia said. "And I'm not his sweetheart."

He winced this time, as if she'd dashed saltwater in an open wound.

Tears stung her eyes. She whispered, "Go with them. Don't let them drag you by the chains. You wouldn't want Bel to see you that way."

"Listen to the lady, Gray."

The men pulled him back a step, and Gray's feet moved under him. He hesitated, still staring cold fury into her eyes. "We're not finished. I will find you." Then he turned and let them lead him away.

Oh, Gray. We were finished before we began.

Miss Grayson came to her side, crying into her brother's handkerchief. Together they watched him disappear down the dock. The crowd parted around him as the soldiers marched him into a narrow street and out of view.

There, it was done. She'd never hold him again. The pain of it threatened to split her in two.

"Will you be coming with me, Miss . . . ?" Miss Grayson asked. "I'm so sorry, I never did learn your name."

Sophia turned to the young woman. The irony twisted in her heart. Hathaway, Turner, Waltham . . . She might assume any identity she wished, claim any name for her own.

Any name, that is, save the one she truly wanted.

Mrs. Sophia Grayson.

CHAPTER
TWENTY-SIX

"Joss. What the devil is going on?" Gray shuffled into the dank cell. The guard released him from his shackles and left, clanging the door shut and securing the formidable lock.

His brother rose to greet him. "Evidently, we're pirates."

"Says Mallory, I gather."

"Yes." Joss sank back to a crouch and leaned against the wall. "Swine went for the officers the instant we made port. I should have kept him in the brig until you arrived."

"Why didn't you?"

Joss shrugged. "He kept shouting and spitting. It was damn annoying." He swiped his cuff across his face. "Besides, I didn't think they'd pay him any mind. Your reputation is worth gold here, quite literally."

"It *was*. Not any longer, I gather."

"Once the judge hears your side of things, he'll set us free."

"Damn right, he will." *And he'd better do it soon.* She thought to leave him, did she? There wasn't anywhere she could go, on this island or from this island, that he couldn't follow her. A few hours' delay, even a few days—he'd track her down. And when he did, this time he would demand some answers.

Gray looped an arm through the bars of the door. "What's Mallory told him? Do you know?"

"That we attacked the *Kestrel* without provocation, destroyed her cargo." Joss lifted an eyebrow. "Shot down her mast with our cannon."

"The blackguard." Gray made a fist around the bar. "Why didn't I let him go down with his miserable ship?"

"Ah, I expect you were enjoying playing the hero too much. Bent on impressing the ladies, you know. How is the lovely Miss Turner, by the way?"

Gray's chest deflated. "I don't want to talk about it."

"Good God, man, what did you do?"

"I asked her to marry me."

Joss gave a low whistle. "And?"

"And—" Gray grabbed the bars with both hands and pushed back. "I don't want to talk about it."

He didn't want to think about it, either, but he could hardly keep from doing so. What had frightened her? For all her brave talk, Gray was certain he'd seen fear in her eyes. Was it watching him put in chains that had spurred her to flee? Perhaps she had her own reasons to avoid arrest.

"Her name isn't even Jane Turner," he said bitterly. "She's not even a governess. She's some sort of conniving little thief with six hundred pounds beneath her stays."

"I thought you didn't want to talk about it."

Gray shot his brother a look. It was then that he noticed the haggard shadows on Joss's face, and the bruise purpling beneath his left eye. "No, let's talk of other things. How long have you been here?"

"Two days."

"The guards give you that?" Gray gestured toward his own eye.

Joss shrugged.

Gray released a string of oaths. "Which one was it? He'll pay for it with his life, I swear to you."

"Settle down, Gray. And for God's sake, don't go punching yourself in the eye just to even the score."

Gray shot him a look. "Not amusing, Joss."

"Oh yes, it is. Give me credit for a joke when I make one. It's nothing, Gray. I've had worse. *You've* given me worse. And it's no more than a man can expect, I suppose, when he's an alleged pirate."

"Piracy charges." Gray cracked his neck. "What a joke." This was the voyage he'd finally gone respectable, and what had it gotten him? Jilted and jailed. No good deed went unpunished.

A few hours later, the guard sauntered back down the corridor. "You've a visitor, gentlemen. A lovely miss."

An irrational surge of hope rose up in Gray's breast. *She came back,* some fool voice whispered. *She wouldn't leave you.*

Light footfalls sounded on the stone floor, and a figure emerged from the darkness. Of course. It was Bel.

"Joss. Dolly."

She clung to the bars, and the two of them joined her from the other side.

"How's Jacob?" Joss's voice was tight. "How's my son?"

"He's fine, Joss. A bit taller than he was when you saw him last, and twice as mischievous. A Grayson man, through and through. He's been asking for his papa." She sniffed back tears.

"I've spoken with my friend, Mr. Wilson," Bel continued. "You'll remember him, Joss. He's the one who used to be a solicitor in London, before he devoted his life to charity." Her gaze flitted toward the guard and she lowered her voice. "He's made some inquiries. He says . . . He says your situation doesn't look good."

"What does that mean?" Joss asked. "Surely once the judge has the story from Gray, he'll not press any charges."

"That's just the problem," Bel said. "It's Mallory's word against Gray's."

"And mine," Joss said. "And every crewman's aboard the *Aphrodite* and the *Kestrel*."

"Not every crewman. There's someone . . . an officer who just arrived today, who's taking Mallory's side."

"Brackett." Gray released a groan. "The bastard."

"And the other crewmen, Mr. Wilson says their testimony could be too easily disregarded, since they might face charges themselves."

"What sort of charges could they face?" Joss asked.

"Piracy, for the crew of the *Aphrodite*. Mutiny, for the *Kestrel*'s men."

Gray swore under his breath. No, their situation did not look good. "So we bribe the judge. Every man has his price."

"We can't." Bel shook her head.

"Bel, this is no time for scruples. This is hanging we're discussing."

"I mean it won't work," she continued. "Mr. Wilson knows something of this Mr. Fitzhugh. He's ambitious, Mr. Wilson says, eager to make a name for himself and obtain a better post. That's why he'll press charges on such slender evidence. He means to make an example of Gray."

Joss turned to Gray. "Why would he make an example of you?"

Gray clenched his jaw. He knew precisely why. "Not all privateers stopped seizing ships with the end of the war. Some of them kept right on plundering, even without letters of marque. They're pirates now, with no allegiance to the Crown. It's a problem for honest merchants. Like me," he added ironically.

Understanding lit his brother's eyes. "And the best way to discourage privateers from turning pirate . . ."

"Is to capture the most successful privateer of them all. And hang him." Gray turned and paced away from the door. "This Fitzhugh plans to make his career on my neck. Goddamn it."

"Dolly, please don't curse." Bel's voice cracked as she spoke. "We need God on our side now."

"Seems no one else is," Joss added.

"There's to be a sort of hearing tomorrow," Bel said. "The judge will hear testimony and decide whether he has sufficient evidence to convene a court of piracy."

"A court of piracy?" Joss repeated.

"Yes," Gray said, "in order to charge us, he has to summon representatives of the governor, all the way from Antigua. It's no small undertaking. He won't go to the trouble if he's not certain we'll hang."

"I see," Joss said. "It would seem much hinges on to-morrow."

"Everything hinges on tomorrow." If he didn't walk free tomorrow, she'd be too far away. He might truly lose her. Damn.

Bel reached for his hand through the bars. Gray accepted the comfort of her small, chilled fingers wrapped around his own.

"Mr. Wilson will try to intercede for you," she said. "The rest of us will pray."

Gray squeezed her fingers. "You do that." If Bel prayed, God might actually listen. "What of Miss Turner?" The question was out before Gray could stop it.

"Who?" A strange look crossed Bel's face. "I don't know any Miss Turner."

"The lady from the dock, Bel. What happened to her?"

Bel frowned. "I don't know," she whispered, eyes downcast. "She said someone would be meeting her, and then Mr. Wilson found me, and . . ."

"And she left." Gray pressed his forehead to the bars. *Christ*. She'd truly left. She'd truly left *him*. Until that moment, he hadn't believed she could do it.

He must have done something wrong. Perhaps he ought to have demanded her secrets. Perhaps he should have held back some of his. Or maybe . . . God, maybe she'd been playing him for a fool all along.

"I'm sorry," Bel said. "I suppose she just slipped away."

"I can't believe I lied to him," Miss Grayson said, opening the green plantation shutters to admit a sultry breeze. "I've never lied to my brother in my life."

Cringing, Sophia sat on the edge of the bed. As if all her own lies to him weren't bad enough, now she'd gone and corrupted Gray's sister. "I'm sorry to ask it of you," she said. "But it was for his benefit. If my name reached the judge's ears today, he might not believe my story to-morrow."

"But how could the judge not believe the truth?"

How, indeed. Sophia's lies were growing so numerous, even she couldn't keep them straight. But when she'd assumed Sophia to be a missionary, Miss Grayson had handed her the perfect way to help Gray, as well as the perfect escape. One more day of deceit—in this, her most challenging role yet—and she would be done.

Miss Grayson sat down beside her. "I suppose it was in service of the greater good. But the look on Gray's face when I told him you'd gone . . . He was—"

"Furious, I'd imagine."

"No," Miss Grayson said, surprised. "Not angry at all, just . . . disappointed, I think. His face went very grim.

For all his initial resistance to the sugar cooperative, he must be attached to the idea now." She beamed at Sophia. "That must be your good influence, Miss Turner."

Sophia thought it best to change the subject. "This isn't your bedchamber, is it? I couldn't put you out, you've been so kind."

Gray had not been exaggerating when he described his sister's kind nature. Indeed, Bel seemed to Sophia some kind of saint. While Bel had visited her brothers in jail, Sophia had been offered a series of small miracles: a bath in fresh, fragrant, heated water; a feast of tropical fruits and risen bread and unsalted meat; a freshly laundered dress; a soft, clean bed in this bright, airy chamber. If Gray had only been with her, Sophia would have felt welcomed into Heaven.

"No, this isn't my bedchamber," Bel answered. "It was once my mother's, but no one has used it in years."

"Has your mother been gone so long, then?" From what Gray had told her, she'd thought Bel's mother had died more recently.

"She died a little over a year ago. But we had to move her from this room several years earlier, when she first took ill." Bel opened a door between the windows, and beckoned Sophia. "Come have a look."

Sophia stepped through the door and emerged onto a stone-tiled portico framed by a Grecian colonnade. Beyond the railing, a lush, green valley fell away from the house, the hillsides blanketed with fields. In the distance, two craggy mountains framed a wedge of ocean blue. "How beautiful," she breathed. "I can see all the way to the harbor."

"Yes. It's a lovely vista. Transporting household goods to the top of a mountain isn't especially convenient, but one can't complain in the face of such grandeur."

"Why did you move your mother to a different chamber?" she asked. "I should think this vista would cure all manner of ills."

"Perhaps, for some. Though in my mother's case, the risk was too great." She gave Sophia a melancholy smile. "She suffered an attack of brain fever, you see, when I was just a girl. She survived, in body—but her mind was never quite the same. For the rest of her life, she was prone to fits of . . . unpredictability. For her safety, we moved her to a room facing the mountainside, below-stairs."

Sophia bent and peered down over the rail at the mossy limestone boulders below. It was a long way down. To think, Bel had grown up concerned that her mother would fling herself off this portico? If her own mother stood in the same place, she would think only of hanging draperies. Sophia felt a sudden swell of gratitude for her boring, sheltered childhood.

"The land you see below used to be my father's plantation. Now the family owns only the house."

"Were you angry, when Gray sold it?"

Bel turned to her. "But how would you know about—" Her eyes widened with understanding. "Ah, I can guess. My brothers are still fighting?" She shook her head. "He did the right thing, selling the plantation. Joss would have done the same. As would I have done, if these matters were ever placed in ladies' hands."

Below them, dusk painted the valley purple with shadow. Sophia gathered the borrowed shawl about her shoulders. "But I don't understand. If Gray and Joss were in agreement then, why do they keep arguing now, over the sugar cooperative?"

"Why do men argue over anything?" Shrugging, Bel continued, "I wish I'd never suggested using the priva-teering money. My brothers have drawn such lines over the notion, and now neither will back down. It's nothing but a source of acrimony. Now the cooperative's coming to pass anyway, thanks to mission-minded Christians like you, and Mr. Wilson."

Sophia chewed her lip. And when it was revealed that she was not a mission-minded Christian and the cooperative did not come to pass—would Gray and Joss keep arguing then? But she couldn't worry about that now.

Bel asked, "Are you sure we should not tell Mr. Wilson you've arrived?"

"No," Sophia blurted out. "Not if he's advising your brothers. I must seem perfectly impartial, you see." That was all she needed, for this poor Mr. Wilson to contradict her story—or worse, become entangled in her deceit.

Bel stared at her hands, loosely linked on the railing. "He wants to marry me. Mr. Wilson, I mean."

Sophia felt a pang of disappointment on Gray's behalf. "Of course he does," she said, forcing a playful tone, wondering how this young woman could be unaware of her beauty and its power over men. Didn't she know she might marry whomever she pleased? "What man would not wish to marry you?"

"Perhaps men desire me, but desire is not a foundation for marriage." Bel crossed her arms over her breasts in a self-conscious gesture.

Ah. She was not so unaware after all.

Sophia asked, "Do you wish to marry Mr. Wilson?"

"I don't know. He is a kind, decent man, and we share a dedication to charity. We would make a good life together. I don't love him, if that's what you're asking. But then, I don't wish to marry for love."

Sophia laid a hand on Bel's wrist. "You deserve to be loved. And that is all Gray wishes to give you. You needn't marry the first man to offer you companionship and a home. Your brother would gladly provide for all your needs. He wants so desperately to make you happy."

Bel sighed. "He wants to take me to London, dress me up in silks and jewels, and parade me before the aristocracy—the very people who profit from every instance of human misery on this island. How could that make me happy?"

Sophia fell silent for a moment, watching the clouds turn vibrant shades of pink and orange in the glow of the setting sun. "I do sympathize with you. More than you know."

Of course, she had fled England for much the same reason that Bel resisted leaving her home. Neither of them wanted to be put on display, forced into marriage at their guardians' behest. But now Sophia understood that Gray's plans had nothing to do with currying society's favor and everything to do with his deep love for his sister, and his desire to give her the best life he could. It was impossible not to wonder—had her parents wanted the same for her? Had their misguided, social-climbing machinations truly been born of love?

Perhaps. But now she would never know.

"Miss Grayson, please promise me one thing. After tomorrow, promise me you will sit down with Gray and tell him . . ." Sophia stopped. She had meant to say, *tell him honestly what you've told me, tell him all your hopes and dreams. And then listen to him, allow him to explain his dreams for you, for the family.*

But really, there was only one thing Gray needed to hear—and then the rest would fall into place. The same words that could have changed everything for her.

"Tell him you love him," she said. "He needs to hear it."

"Of course I will."

"You must promise me."

Bel smiled. "I promise you."

"Good." Sophia squeezed Bel's arm before releasing it. *Good.* A sense of relief descended on her as evening turned to night. With that promise, she felt a certainty that tomorrow everything would be set right. So long as Gray knew he had his sister's unconditional love.

Now, Sophia just needed to do her part: making sure he lived to hear it.

By the break of dawn, Gray knew he was a dead man. One way or another.

He'd paced the cell's perimeter all night, his thoughts circling like his feet. She was gone, he knew it. He felt it. It was still within his power to trace her, with ships and men and gold at his disposal. But dead men typically didn't have those resources.

What was he going to do? He could argue his case, make a defense. Morally and legally, Gray knew he was in the right. But if Fitzhugh was truly determined to make him an example, the facts mattered little. His fate would already be sealed. And Gray's fate was not just his, but Bel's, and Jacob's, and Joss's. Could he gamble his entire family's future on an attempt at freedom, on this slim hope of finding her?

Crouching to the floor, he nudged his brother awake. "Joss. *Joss.*"

Joss stirred and rubbed his eyes. "What do you want, Gray?"

"I want you to listen to me. I've been thinking about this all night. When we're in this hearing today, I want you to let me do the talking."

"Do I ever have a choice?" Joss stretched. "I don't expect either one of us will be offered much opportunity for speech-making. Don't count on charming your way out of this one."

"I'm not planning to charm *my* way out of anything.

It's your skin I'm trying to save. I mean it Joss, not a word. There are papers already drawn up in England. The business, the ships—if I die, my will leaves it all to you. There are trusts for Bel and Jacob." Gray let his head fall back against the stone wall and rubbed his temples. "Had it drawn up the same time as the partnership papers. I was hoping you'd sign them this year."

"Now I'm awake." Joss's eyebrows lifted. "What are you on about? Don't turn martyr on me, Gray."

"I can't risk both of us dying, Joss. Don't you understand? Where would that leave Bel and Jacob?" Gray rose and began to pace the cell with agitation. "One of us needs to walk out of here alive, for them. I've decided to plead guilty in exchange for your freedom, and that of the crew. I'll say you objected, but I coerced you into engaging the ship. Beyond that . . . you never boarded the *Kestrel*, Joss. They've got no evidence against you. So just keep quiet and play along."

"You mean play dumb. You mean play the ignorant Negro incapable of thinking for himself." He drew his knees to his chest and stacked his arms atop them. "Is that what you mean, Gray?"

"No." Gray stopped pacing. He looked his brother in the eye. "Yes, Joss. That's exactly what I mean."

Joss stared at the floor for a moment. Then he shook his head slowly. "No."

"What do you mean, no? You can't possibly say no."

"I assure you, I can. And I believe I just did." Joss stood, brushing his trousers clean as he rose to his feet. "Here, let me demonstrate the possibility again. *No.*"

"You'd rather hang?" Gray crossed the small cell in two paces, coming toe-to-toe with his brother. "Joss, you have a child who needs you. A sister who needs you. Hell, I'm your brother—and I need you, too. I need you to take care of them for me."

"I won't do it, Gray."

"Damn it. I'd never have dreamed you could be this selfish, to sacrifice your own son's security for the sake of your pride."

"It's not just my pride you're asking me to sacrifice. It's my dignity. My humanity, for God's sake. I'd rather Jacob grow up a pirate's orphan than the son of a slave."

"You were never a slave."

"You know what I mean. I want my son to make his own way in the world, with his own wits and courage. What example do I give him if I swear before God and England that I can't be held responsible for my own actions?"

Gray turned on his heel and strode to the far corner of the cell. He braced one arm against the wall and covered his face with the other hand, trying to concentrate.

Damn it all to hell. Joss and his stubborn, foolish pride. Gray had to convince him—someway, somehow. They couldn't both die. He simply couldn't allow it to happen. The very idea of Bel and Jacob left alone in the world made his limbs go numb.

Joss cleared his throat. "You've been trying to manage my life for years now, Gray. If you're suddenly in the mood to make a grand sacrifice, do me this favor: For once, let me be my own man."

The anger in his brother's voice stiffened Gray's spine. "What is that supposed to mean?"

"You've given me no choice in any of this. You sold my home out from under me and forced me out on the sea the first time. You knew I wanted to settle here after . . . after Jacob was born, but you dragged me back out again. If I'm going to die, at least let me go to my grave with a shred of autonomy."

Now Gray was angry, too. "You love the sea, Joss. I know you do. At least you did, before Mara died and took the best half of you with her." He saw his brother wince at the mention of his wife. Good. It was long past time they stopped mincing around it. "We had plans. We were supposed to be partners. You're the one who went back on his word, decided he'd rather dig in the dirt and indulge this ridiculous scheme of Bel's."

"It isn't a ridiculous scheme."

"Come now, a sugar cooperative?" Gray scoffed. "One season, and you'd be bankrupt. And then how is your son supposed to respect his father, the sharecropper? How is anyone going to respect you?"

"Here's a better question. Why doesn't my own brother respect me? You've never once trusted me to make my own decisions."

"That's because you make stupid decisions!"

Joss glared at him. He took a slow breath before continuing. "No, it's not. It's because you're forcing me into a life I don't want, just to assuage your own guilt. It's because you're legitimate, and I'm a bastard. It's because you're white, and I'm black."

"Damn you, Joss. It's because we're brothers. Stop trying to make every argument about our disparities. You're my little brother, and I've a God-given right to care about you." Gray ran both hands through his hair. "We had fun all those years, chasing down packet ships. Things were good between us, until Mara died. We had plans. You reneged on them and made me the villain. Is it really so terrible, that I want something better for you, for our family?"

Joss blew out a breath. "No. It's not."

"Then why are you so damn angry with me? For leaving with all our proceeds?"

"For leaving at all." Joss stalked to the far corner of the cell. "When Mara died, it was hell for me. It wasn't easy for Bel either. They were close. So Bel and I didn't leap at the chance to go off to London and leave the only home we've ever known. Can you honestly blame us? We were grieving. We needed you, Gray. I needed you. All that huffing and storming you did, about what was best for the family . . . Well, your family needed a brother, and you just left."

Gray stared at him for a moment and swallowed hard. "I knew you were hurting. Don't you know it was killing me, to just stand by and watch grief eat you alive? There wasn't anything I could do, save securing our future, providing a home. Perhaps I went about it all in the wrong way, but it doesn't mean I don't care."

"I know." Joss put a hand to his face. "I know."

"Do you?" Gray waited until his brother looked up. "Joss—" His voice cracked, and he tried again. "No matter how old we get, you're still my little brother. While there's breath in my body, I can't allow you to hang. Don't ask it of me."

"But it's all right for you to ask it of me? You're not the only one capable of brotherly affection, you know." Joss crossed the cell and stood before Gray. "It's not your fault, whatever happens. You do understand that?" He put a hand on Gray's shoulder. "I know you've always tried to do your best by me, in your own insufferable, arrogant way. You've been a decent brother, Gray. And a damn good friend."

Gray swore. He looked to the side, then back at his brother. "Fair warning, Joss. If you don't take your hand off me . . . I will have to hug you."

Joss laughed. "After that speech, I'd be damn disappointed if you didn't."

Gray grabbed his brother in a rough embrace. Joss thumped him on the back as he hugged him close.

"What's all this talk about dying, anyway?" Joss asked, pulling away with moist eyes and a sly smile. "We've cheated death before. I reckon we've one more life in us yet. Maybe Wilson will come up with something. Or Bel will work a miracle."

"Maybe." Gray heaved a rough sigh and slid down the wall until he sat on the floor, legs outstretched.

Joss joined him. "I mean it, Gray. No more talk of hanging or noble sacrifice."

Very well, Gray thought. *I won't talk about it.*

"Allow yourself a moment of optimism. It's not just me and Bel and Jacob you've got to live for, you know. There's a beautiful miss out there somewhere who'd be heartbroken to see you hanged."

"There are beautiful women all over the world who'll be heartbroken to see me hanged," Gray said dryly. "But the only one I care about is gone."

"You don't know that."

"Oh, she's gone all right. Do you know, she claimed to love me. What a fool I was, to believe it."

"Is it so hard to believe?" Joss nudged Gray's arm. "It's not as though she's the only one."

"More fool you," Gray grumbled. He let his head fall back against the stone wall and stared up at the cell's single window. Slices of bright sky winked at him from behind the rusted iron bars. It hurt his eyes to look at, but the discomfort was preferable to darkness. "To fall in love now, of all times . . . after I've successfully avoided it all my life."

"Avoided it? To the contrary, I think you've conducted a rather thorough search of the globe for it."

Gray thought on this for a minute. Damn, he hated it when Joss was right.

It was just as well she'd left. He knew what he had to do today; it would only have been harder, had she stayed. Still, as always, he regretted what he'd left undone. Unsaid.

"I never told her I loved her. What an ass I am. No wonder she left. I mean, I *told* her in a dozen different ways, but I never said the words."

"Are they so hard to say?"

"Yes, but . . . I don't know. They shouldn't be." Gray shook his head. "Do you know, that fifteen-year-old boy had the courage to say in front of the whole crew what I couldn't bring myself to whisper in the dark? He'll make a fine officer someday, Davy Linnet. Got bigger stones than either of us, I'd wager."

Joss snorted. "Speak for yourself."

Laughter erupted in Gray's chest. God, he was going to miss Joss. He hoped his brother could forgive him one day, for betraying his trust this last time.

"Joss." Gray swallowed the lump rising in his throat. "I love you. Whatever happens, I want you to know that."

Joss propped an elbow on Gray's shoulder. "It's nice to hear it. But I knew that already—never had a doubt in my mind, actually. I'd imagine she knows you love her, too. You'll have a chance to say the words."

Gray rubbed his temples. What could he say? He had but a few days left in this world, and no hope of seeing her in the next. But he had to keep up the illusion of optimism, for Joss's sake. "Supposing I did find her? What if I tell her I love her, and she still walks away?"

"I don't know what to tell you there. There aren't any guarantees in love. I know as well as anyone how fleeting it can be."

Gray winced, knowing that Joss referred to Mara.

Joss fell silent for a moment, then continued in a low voice, "You may not be able to hold on to her forever. But I don't think you'll regret trying. I don't."

Gray felt tears burning at the corners of his eyes. He sniffed and looked away quickly, searching his mind for something witty and irreverent to say. He was saved the effort when Joss spoke again.

"That girl loves you, Gray. We're going to get out of this, and when we do—I'd bet a hundred sovereigns to one, Sophia will be there waiting for you."

"Sophia?" Gray blinked. "Her name is *Sophia*?"

Joss chuckled. "I was right. You didn't know."

"But—" Gray scratched the back of his neck. "But how did *you*? Since when have you known her name?"

Joss shrugged, his expression composed. "Since sometime yesterday." He laughed at Gray's befuddled silence. "When you dropped your trousers to take a piss. It's painted on your arse."

CHAPTER
TWENTY-SEVEN

"The *Aphrodite* hailed us, so we approached. Backed our sail, prepared to speak. Bastards had us right where they wanted us. Before my officer even called out our port of origin, he"—Mallory jabbed a finger at Gray across the courtroom—"was blowing our mainmast away. You've only got to look at my ship to find proof enough of that."

Judge Fitzhugh nodded gravely. "Continue."

Gray's teeth ground like millstones. At this rate, they wouldn't need a hanging. The effort required to hold his tongue in the face of these scurrilous falsehoods—it was likely to kill him.

But he had to remain composed. Argument served no purpose now. Whether he dangled at the end of a rope or imploded from sheer irritation, the result would be the same. It all ended here. Here in this stifling chamber with its weathered paneling and scent of decay. In this very room he'd been awarded scores of prizes, stolen his entire fortune from the unfortunate merchants who chanced to cross the *Aphrodite*'s course. He'd bartered his soul in this court. There was a strange justice to it, that his life should be traded here, too.

"Well, he boarded the *Kestrel*," Mallory continued, sneering at Gray. Beneath the table, Gray's hand balled into a fist. "Him and his men. He had me bound in ropes, took command of the ship, and raided my cargo."

Fitzhugh cocked an eyebrow. "And all this with no provocation."

"None whatsover."

Gray tightened his fist until his knuckles cracked. Behind him, the crewmen of the *Aphrodite* and *Kestrel* grumbled loudly in protest. With a sharp look over his shoulder, he quelled the dissent.

Next to him, Joss nudged Mr. Wilson. "Lying bastard. Ask him about the storm," he whispered. "The fire. The rum."

"Don't." Gray cleared his throat. "He'll only spin more lies. And this court isn't interested in the truth. No more than it was when we brought in ships we'd seized. Judges in this court care only for the prize."

"But there's no prize at stake here," Joss argued.

"Oh, there is. It's just not a ship."

The judge finished his questioning of Mallory, then turned to Gray. "Mr. Grayson, please stand."

"Joss," Gray murmured. "I shouldn't have forced you into taking the *Aphrodite*. It's my fault you're here, and I'm going to fix it. Take the money, do whatever makes you happy. Sell the ships, plant sugarcane—"

"What are you on about?" Joss whispered. "Don't do something stupid, Gray."

"Mr. Grayson," Fitzhugh called out, impatient. "You will stand."

Gray whispered to his brother, "I'm not doing anything stupid. For once, I'm doing something right." He pushed back his chair and stood, bringing himself to eye level with the judge seated at the elevated bench.

Fitzhugh couldn't have been much older than Joss. Sallow, thin, and sweating profusely from under his wig, he appeared ill-adjusted to the tropical climate. He had the look of a boy in a man's attire—a boy who'd been on the losing end of many a schoolboy brawl. Presumably in an attempt to appear older, or perhaps wiser, he affected an overly stern mien that belonged to a caricature. But it was the look in Fitzhugh's eyes that amused Gray. Anticipation, laced with awe. No doubt the judge had heard tales about him; Gray's privateering success had been a matter of local pride.

Gray didn't expect the measure of reverence in Fitzhugh's gaze would work to his advantage, however. Rather, he suspected it would make the judge all the more eager to see Gray brought low. He was the seafaring equivalent of the school bully, and this was Fitzhugh's chance to finally beat one down.

Just to provoke him further, Gray spoke first. "This is an informal hearing, I understand. This court has no power to convict on charges of piracy."

Fitzhugh's eyes narrowed within their round wire frames. "Not alone, Mr. Grayson. It does, in concert with the governor."

"Who would be most displeased to be summoned from Antigua without sufficient cause."

After a moment's hesitation, Fitzhugh replied, "That is the purpose of this hearing today, Mr. Grayson. To establish sufficient cause." The judge scowled at him, and Gray nearly laughed. For all his facial acrobatics, Fitzhugh had already ceded control of their conversation. The courtroom was Gray's to command.

He relaxed his posture and allowed himself a grin. "You look familiar to me, Mr. Fitzhugh. I believe we must have met at Oxford?"

The judge harrumphed. "I sincerely doubt it."

"Ah. Not an Oxford man, then. Cambridge?"

"Edinburgh."

"Oh. *Edinburgh*. I suppose now the war's over, the

Admiralty's relaxing its standards?" Gray studied him. "Still, your face is so familiar to me. Did we meet in Town? At White's, perhaps."

"No." Fitzhugh's mouth thinned to a line. "Not that it's of any relevance, but I am certain we have never been introduced, Mr. Grayson."

"Not a member of White's then? Pity. Well, I must be mistaking you for someone else." He watched a flush seep out from beneath Fitzhugh's wig. "At any rate, I've been friendly with every judge to pass through this post in recent years, and I see no reason you should be different. I trust we may speak as gentlemen, seeing as how this is an informal proceeding."

"Actually, this—"

"I do understand your predicament, Mr. Fitzhugh. A great deal of wealth changed hands in this courtroom once. Plenty of excitement, during the war. A judge could build a reputation on it, not to mention a fortune. But now . . . what sort of matters come before you? Insurance claims? Difficult to distinguish yourself with those cases. Your superiors are likely to forget about you completely. You may find yourself in this post for the remainder of your days." He chuckled at Fitzhugh's chagrined expression. "Oh, don't despair. With luck, a fever will take you before you die of boredom."

Laughter rippled through the courtroom. The judge rapped his gavel until the assembly hushed. "Mr. Grayson. You stand before this court accused of piracy, a hanging offense. You will refrain from making speeches and allow me to pose the questions."

"If I'm to be hanged, where's the benefit in decorum?" When the next wave of laughter faded, Gray lowered his voice and approached the bench. Contempt glimmered in the judge's eyes. Good. He'd be only too eager to see Gray dead. "I know what you want, Fitzhugh. I'll give it to you. I'm prepared to plead guilty to all your charges. You can build your career on my grave, claim your promotion, and return to England. I still doubt they'd allow you in White's. But the questions, and the charges, begin and end with me. Do we understand each other?"

"You'll plead guilty. To piracy."

Gray nodded. "I'll put on a show if you like, to make things interesting. In the end, you'll have your hanging. But only one. Once I've admitted fault, you'll call an end to this 'informal proceeding,' and everyone else in the room walks free."

Fitzhugh smiled. "Very well."

"I want your word. And if you cross me, by God I swear I'll hunt you down in hell."

"You have my word. Do I have yours?"

Gray gave him an easy grin. "My word as a gentleman." He stepped back from the bench and addressed the courtroom. "Everything Captain Mallory testified is the truth."

An outcry rose up among the men. Fitzhugh banged his gavel to no avail, until Gray motioned for silence.

It took great effort to ignore the look of betrayal in Joss's eyes. But ignore it he did.

"I hailed the *Kestrel* as a friendly vessel. I boarded the ship without permission. I took command of her crew. I shot her mast down with a cannon. And I destroyed a large part of her cargo." Gray ticked off the facts on his fingers. "All truths. If those actions make me a pirate, then I'm a pirate." Gray spoke over a chorus of objections. "And neither I, nor the honorable Mr. Fitzhugh"—he swept the room with a meaningful glare—"care to hear any argument to the contrary. Do you follow me?"

He looked his men in the eye—O'Shea, Quinn, Levi, Stubb, and all the others, right down to Davy—until they absorbed his meaning and the obedience he demanded. He kept his jaw firm, shoulders squared, gaze unwavering. Not even a blink. The bravado came to him easily enough, when the actual dying was weeks away. There would be time enough later for trembling. Then he would be alone.

He turned back to face the bench. "Now then, Mr. Fitzhugh, you have your pirate. Do you suppose we can conclude these proceedings?"

"Yes, well . . ." Fitzhugh coughed. "In light of your testimony, Mr. Grayson, which is supported not only by Captain Mallory's account but by that of your own first mate, Mr. Brackett, I find sufficient cause to hold you on a charge of piracy, a crime against the Crown. Arrangements will be made for your trial."

The room was silent, save for the cackling laughter of Mallory. "Grayson, I'm going to dance on the day that you swing."

"If he swings, I swing with him." Joss rose to his feet.

Gray drilled his brother with a glare. "Joss, no." *Sit down, damn you. Think of our sister. Think of your son.*

"I'm the captain of the *Aphrodite*." Joss's voice rang through the courtroom. "I'm responsible for the actions of her passengers and crew. If my brother is a pirate, then I'm a pirate, too."

Gray's heart sank. They would both die now, he and his idiot of a brother.

Joss walked to the center of the courtroom, the brass buttons of his captain's coat gleaming as he strode through a shaft of sunlight. "But I demand a full trial. I will be heard, and evidence will be examined. Logbooks, the condition of the ships, the statements of my crew. If you mean to hang my brother, you'll have to find cause to hang me."

Fitzhugh's eyebrows rose to his wig. "Gladly."

"And me."

Gray groaned at the sound of that voice. He didn't even have to look to know that Davy Linnet was on his feet. Brave, stupid fool of a boy.

"If Gray's a pirate, I'm a pirate, too," Davy said. "I helped him aim and fire that cannon, that's God's truth. If you hang him, you have to hang me."

Another chair scraped the floorboards as its occupant rose to his feet. "And me."

Oh God. O'Shea now?

"I boarded the *Kestrel*. I took control of her helm and helped bind that piece of shite." The Irishman jutted his chin at Mallory. "Suppose that makes me a pirate, too."

"Very good." Fitzhugh's eyes lit with glee. "Anyone else?"

Over by the window, Levi stood. His shadow blanketed most of the room. "Me," he said.

"*Now,* Levi?" Gray pulled at his hair. "Seven years in my employ, you don't say a single goddamned word, and you decide to speak up *now*?"

Bloody hell, now they were all on their feet. Pumping fists, cursing Mallory, defending Gray, arguing over which one of them deserved the distinction of most bloodthirsty pirate. It would have been a heartwarming display of loyalty, if they weren't all going to die.

"You see?" Gray recognized Brackett's voice. "They're nothing but lawless brigands, just as I said!"

Fitzhugh banged his gavel over and over, as though he were cobbling together a new bench up there. "Silence!" His voice cracked with the shout. "Silence, all of you! I will have order!"

Eventually, a lull in the mayhem occurred—not precisely a pause, but rather a collective drawing of breath, that the yelling might continue. The judge took advantage of the moment, leaping to his feet and indiscriminately throwing his gavel into the crowd. This proved a far more effective use of the implement. The screech of pain from Mallory ripped through the chaos, and all swiveled to face its source.

"Anyone"—Fitzhugh's breath heaved, and his wig was askew—"who participated in the unlawful seizure of the *Kestrel* will be condemned as a pirate and made to pay with his life. I'll hang the whole lot of you, you miserable, bloody louts!"

This, Sophia took as her cue.

With a parting squeeze of Miss Grayson's hand, she stepped into the courtroom. Lifting her voice, she called out, "Then you will have to hang me, too."

Ah, now it was silent. Only silk and crinoline had the temerity to whisper as she advanced to the center of the courtroom.

My, how she'd missed this. Making an entrance.

Sophia smoothed one gloved hand over her rose silk skirt, guiding it around the furniture. How glad she was now, that she had surrendered trunk space to vanity and brought this gown with her. Extravagant beauty did come in useful, in emergencies such as these.

She felt the men's stares on her as she glided through the crowd, chin lifted, carriage erect. It was tempting to meet their gazes, favor each of her friends with a warm smile. She resisted, however, saving her practiced debutante's blush for the only man who mattered.

The pale, gawping man in a wig.

"Your honor," she said sweetly, holding her skirt out with one hand as she made a smooth curtsy.

"Who . . . who are you?"

Sophia saw at once Mr. Fitzhugh would serve perfectly. Young and pale; rather unattractive and exceedingly awkward. A man with little confidence or experience where ladies were concerned. Gentlemen of his sort were easily led, easily deceived.

But then, deceit was not her purpose any longer. Today she would finally tell the truth.

"I am Miss Sophia Jane Hathaway, of Kent. And, from what I understand of these proceedings, it would seem that I am a pirate."

"You, miss. A pirate?"

Sophia toyed with the neckline of her bodice. "You did say that anyone who participated in the seizure of the *Kestrel* would be hanged as a pirate?"

The judge swallowed, then nodded.

She moved her hand up to stroke the delicate skin of her throat. "My Heavens. Then you shall have to hang me, too. Perhaps my execution will not advance your career as some others' would, but this is of little consequence in the pursuit of justice. Am I right, your honor?"

"Not at all," he replied, incongruently nodding in agreement. His gaze jerked up from her throat to her eyes. "Er . . . that is to say . . ."

Sophia cocked her head and frowned. "You will need to question me, I presume? Obtain my testimony?"

"Y-yes."

When the silence proved no questions were forthcoming, she offered, "Perhaps I should simply begin at the beginning?"

He sighed gratefully. "That would be best."

"Very well."

And now—only now—she allowed herself a glance at Gray. She'd done her best to resist looking in his direction, even though his presence had pulled at her like a magnetic force from the moment she'd entered the room. She felt precisely where he was, understood exactly how many degrees she must turn her neck to meet his gaze.

She hadn't counted on how difficult it would be to turn away. There were a hundred emotions churning in his eyes—questions and accusations, and pleas and promises, too—and now her own eyes welled with tears.

Stop this. You have a whole life ahead of you to cry.

With a bracing sniff, Sophia turned back to the judge. "Mr. Grayson has given you an accurate, yet incomplete account of events." She pulled out an embroidered handkerchief and hastily dabbed at her eyes before pressing it to her décolletage. "I hope your honor will permit me to acquaint you with more of the truth."

Just not quite all of it.

"As I told you, my name is Sophia Jane Hathaway, though the men in this room know me as Jane Turner. My father, Mr. Elias Hathaway, is a gentleman of considerable wealth and modest consequence. I traveled under an assumed name because I left England without his permission. Or knowledge." Guilt pricked at her heart. The anxiety her family must have endured. Perhaps by now they believed her dead.

Fitzhugh squinted at her through his spectacles. "You were running away?"

She nodded. "I was to be married, you see. To a man I did not love."

It was clear in the judge's expression that he did not see. "You were to be married against your wishes. So—logically—you absconded, unescorted, with the aid of these brigands, to the West Indies." He glared at Gray. "Perhaps I shall add kidnapping to the charges."

"Oh, no! You misunderstand." Sophia chewed her lip. Why was telling the truth so much more complicated than lying? She hardly knew how to explain the reasoning that had taken her from "I cannot marry Toby" to "I must board a ship bound for Tortola." At the time, it had made some sense to her, in her desperation. Now she saw what anyone in his right mind could see: that she should have simply broken her engagement.

But then, as now, the truth had been so much more difficult than a lie.

"I assure you, neither Captain nor Mr. Grayson knew my true identity. I led them to believe I was a governess, en route to a new post." Sophia took a step closer to the bench, placed one gloved hand upon the lip of wood and leaned toward him in confidence. Fitzhugh fidgeted with his wig, clearly both unnerved and flattered by her nearness. Very good.

She made her voice breathy and reverent. "Your honor, I sense that you are a man of principle, and ambition. I believe you can understand this, that I sought some greater purpose to my existence. I wanted to experience real life, find my true passion."

"And did you?" He swallowed. "Find your . . . er, passion?"

"Oh, yes." She smiled beatifically. "Mr. Grayson showed it to me."

A low murmur rippled through the courtroom. Sophia ventured a quick glance at Gray. Gone were the accusations and questions in his gaze; all that remained to him was blank confusion. Well, that and his roguish good looks. But to her, everything was finally clear. She'd wanted to experience real life—but how could she, until she ceased running away from it? This was her life, and no one else's. This was her story to tell, her picture to paint.

"Mr. Fitzhugh," she said, "may I tell you about the seizure of the *Kestrel*? I watched it all from the deck of the *Aphrodite* that day." At his nod, Sophia continued. "There was a terrible gale. The clouds were churning and green as the sea, and just as the two ships approached, the sky cracked with lightning. It struck the *Kestrel*'s mainmast, setting the tip afire. With no regard for their own safety, Mr. Grayson and a few of his bravest men boarded the ship to help. Their aim was to aid the *Kestrel*'s stunned crew in cutting away the mast before the flames reached the deck. But there was no time, and with a hold full of smuggled rum, the ship was certain to explode."

Mr. Fitzhugh hung on her words, though his eyes seemed fixed to her bosom. "And . . . ?"

"Mr. Grayson sent all able men away in the boat, save Mr. Linnet." She searched out Davy's smooth face in the crowd. "And together they shot down the mast with the *Kestrel*'s own cannon, dousing the fire in the sea."

"Remarkable," the judge whispered.

"Is it not?" Pride brought a smile to her face. "It was the truest act of valor I have ever witnessed. Mr. Grayson saved many lives that day. Including the life of Captain Mallory, who now has the malicious cowardice to accuse innocent men of piracy rather than lose his own ship as salvage."

Sophia leaned closer. "Do you know, Mr. Fitzhugh, that Captain Mallory would have denied his injured crewmen medical attention, when a port was only a few days' sail away? This is why Mr. Grayson seized the *Kestrel,* sending his own ship ahead with the wounded. If that be an act of piracy, then he is the most honorable pirate to ever live. And as I also joined the crew that seized the *Kestrel,* I am proud to declare myself a pirate, too."

"You joined the crew?"

"Yes, I became ship's cook. They were undermanned, you see." Sophia loosened one glove and removed it, revealing her calloused, knife-scored hand. "Your honor, I am a gentlewoman. I have never performed such labor in my life, but I was glad to do it to help these men. My life changed the day of that storm. I shall never be the same again." *In more ways than you would suspect,* she thought with some amusement. But the statement was the truth.

She turned to Gray, who wore a half-smile of his own. It was a comfort to know they still shared something, if only a private joke.

"Even now, this innocent man would sacrifice himself to save his brother and crewmen from the hangman's noose. Mr. Grayson's courage and fortitude are an example to me," she said, dabbing at her eyes with the handkerchief. "They should be an example to us all."

Oh come now, Gray's smirk chided her. *Don't take it too far.*

"An example . . ." Fitzhugh spoke in a slow tone of discovery. "Of honor?"

"She's a liar!" Mr. Brackett pushed to the front of the room, carving his way through the assembly with his blade-thin nose and sharp elbows. "She's a liar and a whore. They're lovers, she and Grayson. Her whole story is a falsehood, fabricated to save his miserable neck."

Sophia's heart seized. The crowd held its breath. *Please don't ask it,* she silently implored the judge. It felt so good to finally stand before Gray, these men, the world, and tell the truth. Could she bring herself to deny him now, even to save his life? *Please, just don't ask.*

"Miss Hathaway?" The judge adjusted his spectacles and peered at her. "What, precisely, is the nature of your relationship with Mr. Grayson?"

"My . . . relationship?" Turning away, Sophia closed her eyes briefly, then opened them again. *I'm sorry,* she mouthed to Gray. He gave her a barely perceptible nod, his expression hard. He was wiping all emotion from his face, expecting her denial.

She had to say it; she had no choice. "I love him."

Surprise melted the ice in his gaze. Soon his eyes were shining with approval. Approval, and love.

Her heart soared. For this one moment, they loved each other, and the rest of the world could go hang. "I love him," she repeated, simply because she could. Because it was the truth.

Now the truth was out, suspended in the humid silence—a sketch of it, at least. It still remained within Sophia's ability to shade it. Collecting herself, she took advantage of the stunned pause. "As is my Christian duty, your honor. To say I felt anything less for him would be not only a falsehood, but a sacrilege."

The judge scratched his wig.

"No," Brackett protested. "She's a liar, I tell you!"

"I assure you, I speak only the truth. What motive do I have to lie?" Sophia tugged on her glove, working her fingers into the slender tips. "Indeed, I have come to care deeply for many of the men in this courtroom. But anyone who would insinuate that I give this truthful testimony in hopes of resuming some relationship with Mr. Grayson, friendly or otherwise, would be mistaken. I esteem the man, your honor. I admire him greatly, and his example of honesty and courage has altered the course of my life. But beyond today, I do not expect to ever meet with him again."

Gray took a step forward. "You can't mean—"

Sophia froze him with a look. "Yes, Mr. Grayson, I mean that my mission here has already been completed."

He stared at her, clearly baffled. Adorably so.

"Since leaving England, I have resolved to never marry," she said, directing her statement at the judge, "but to devote my fortune to charity. I have twenty thousand pounds, you see—or I shall have in a matter of days, when I reach my majority. It was to have been my dowry, but this very morning I have pledged it toward the purchase of Eleanora plantation from Mr. George Waltham, to establish a sugar cooperative for freedmen."

"A sugar cooperative?" Gray and Fitzhugh spoke as one.

There. Now Gray and Joss had nothing further to argue over, no years-old dispute to drive them apart. They could start over, sit down and discuss their future with open minds and open hearts. It was likely too late for Sophia's own family, but she could not pass up this chance to heal theirs.

"Mr. Wilson and Miss Grayson can provide you with any evidence you may require on that matter." She folded her handkerchief. "As for me, I fear I must be going."

"Going?" Again, Gray and Fitzhugh spoke in unison, and each glared at the other, clearly annoyed.

"Now that my mission has been completed, I must return to England. I have given only earnest money, you see, some six hundred pounds. The rest of the transaction must be completed in London. And I . . . I must return to my family, though I do not know how they will receive me. After this adventure, I doubt I shall be received by even my closest friends. Most certainly not by the likes of Mr. Grayson's family." He had to understand this, the reason she must leave.

"Mr. Grayson's family?" the judge asked.

"Didn't you know? Your honor, he is the nephew of a duke. I played cards with his aunt, the Duchess of Aldonbury, every third Wednesday." She gave Gray a cautious look. "Her granddaughter, Lady Clementina Morton, was at school with me. I was even so fortunate as to be a guest in their home, your honor, but that is not a pleasure I shall ever have again. Her Grace is a lady of elevated rank and limited forgiveness. Were I the ambitious sort, Mr. Fitzhugh, I should not wish to cross her."

The judge blanched to the color of parchment.

Sophia busied herself with the cord of her reticule. "No, I shall be ruined in society's eyes, though my conscience is clear. I must go home and throw myself on the mercy of my family. If they spurn me . . ." She shrugged. "Perhaps I shall become a governess."

A sense of satisfaction filled her. Yesterday, she'd planned to lie—to walk into this courtroom and pretend to be the sort of honest, selfless woman who could have helped Gray's cause. Now she had given everything— her fortune, her reputation, her future—to make it the truth. Not just to save Gray's life, but to redeem hers.

What a fool she'd been, always blaming the world for not seeing the person beneath the vast fortune. The truth was, she'd spent her life afraid—hiding behind wild lies and fantasies—because she hadn't believed in herself, in her own value.

That all ended today. Here, in this courtroom, the truth was worth something. *She* was worth something. The world was welcome to shun her now. For the first time in a long while, Sophia liked herself.

She would have no regrets.

She turned a slow circle, letting her gaze linger on each of her friends one last time. "I sail for Antigua immediately, where I understand I may board an English frigate." Her gaze settled on Gray. "So this is good-bye."

Gray nodded. Of course, now that he understood everything—how her past would inevitably poison his family's future—he was letting her go.

"Farewell, then. Unless . . ." She addressed Fitzhugh with perfect innocence. "But you didn't *really* mean to charge us all with piracy?"

He blinked.

Sophia smiled. "I didn't think so."

CHAPTER
TWENTY-EIGHT

Whether one strolled the park or traveled the globe, the journey home invariably seemed shorter than the journey abroad. It felt only a matter of hours before the *Polaris* crossed the Tropic, although Sophia knew days had passed. Very little fanfare had accompanied the occasion: a bit of singing among the sailors, a collection of shillings in a tarred cap, to which she contributed from her dwindling purse.

Perhaps the subdued celebration could be credited to the scarcity of passengers aboard the frigate. She was accompanied only by the ship's supercargo, and the widow and two grown sons of an Antiguan planter. However, Sophia thought it more likely that the character of the captain, the perpetually dour Captain Herring, was to blame. As herrings went, he seemed to be of the kippered variety.

No, the *Polaris* was not the *Aphrodite*, nor even the *Kestrel*. And for this, perhaps Sophia ought to have been grateful. In an atmosphere of camaraderie and merriment, her melancholy might have drawn notice. But if anyone took note of her remote behavior or persistently moist eyes, it was only to suggest a remedy for cold.

If only there were a cure for heartache.

On fine afternoons like these, she spent long hours staring out over the sea. She had no more paper or canvas; even her little trunk of paint and brushes had been left behind. But it soothed her, blending pigments in her mind to capture the ever-shifting colors of the waves: today, a base of Prussian blue, tinted with cobalt green. The same shade would be reflected in his eyes, if Gray were there with her. She could almost imagine he was.

Almost.

Sophia shook her head, dismayed. It would seem she'd finally discovered the limits of her vivid imagination.

Still, whenever a sail appeared on the horizon, a ridiculous hope bloomed in her heart. She peered out over the waves, anxious to glimpse the profile of the ship, the style of its rigging. Any square-rigged ship spurred an irrational acceleration of her pulse. When a closer view—or the ship's disappearance over the curve of the earth—proved it was not the *Aphrodite,* she would chide herself for her foolish tears.

He knows the truth now, she told herself. *He understands everything. And he has let you go.*

When a sail appeared this afternoon, her ordeal was mercifully brief. The ship sighted at their stern quickly revealed itself to be a schooner, its large, triangular sails jutting up from the sea like a row of shark's teeth. As the ship drew closer, unease spread through the crew like a contagion.

"Don't like it," the first mate said. "The way she's bearing down on us, as if she were in pursuit. If they want to speak, why don't they fire a signal?"

"What colors is she flying?" the captain asked. "That's a Baltimore-built ship, to be sure. Could be privateers, though, sailing under a Venezuelan flag."

"Not flying any colors that I can see," the officer reported, squinting into his spyglass. "She's heavily armed, riding high on the waves. Can't be much cargo to speak of in that hold."

"Pirates." The captain let out a string of oaths. Not particularly imaginative ones, but uttered with conviction nonetheless. Sophia drifted toward the stern, drawn by the sight of the jagged sails slicing toward them.

"She has the advantage of the wind, Captain. Gaining fast. Still no colors, but I can almost make out the name of the craft. Hold there . . . she's tacking to the wind. Ah." He lowered the spyglass. "Named the *Sophia*."

Her heart gave a queer flip. *No. It couldn't be. Surely it was merely one of life's cruel coincidences.*

"Shall I send up the alarm, Captain? Ready the cannon?"

"No!" Sophia cried.

The captain and officer turned on their heels to face her.

"I . . . I believe I may know this ship, sir." She looked to the first mate. "Might I borrow your spyglass?"

She took it from his hand without waiting for permission, then fitted it to her eye and looked sharp toward the horizon. There it was, the schooner. Through the narrow lens, she stared down the ship's prow. Scanning the sails, the rigging, the deck. The jib blocked her view, drat it. There, they tacked the sails and the ship pivoted slightly. She could almost make out the figure of a man on the quarterdeck.

Beside her, the first mate shifted his weight. "Beg pardon, miss, but—"

"Levi!" A towering figure came into focus. It had to be Levi, so impossibly large. She directed the spyglass up to the rigging, searching . . . searching . . . *Quinn*. There was no doubt in her mind. The man had hams where his fists should be.

A shot boomed across the waters, and Sophia jumped. "No," she cried. "You mustn't fire! They're not pirates." She swiveled to face the first mate. "That is . . . they *may* be pirates, of a sort. But I promise you, they're no threat to this ship."

"That was only their signal shot, miss." The first mate called over to the captain. "Do we wish to speak with them, sir?"

The captain grumbled, "Whether we wish it or not, it appears they're determined to speak with us. Square the yards and come about, then."

The whole ship began a slow, creaking pirouette, and Sophia went dizzy with anticipation. Had he truly come for her? She supposed Levi and Quinn could have taken employment with another ship. Perhaps Gray wasn't even aboard. Despite her best efforts to remain calm, she could not help pinching a blush to her cheeks and smoothing back stray locks of hair. If only there were time to change her gown.

The officers strode toward the bow of the ship now, and Sophia hurried after them. The forecastle was crowded with curious sailors, obstructing her view of the clipper as it drew near.

"Ahoy!" a seaman called out. "The English frigate *Polaris,* ten days out from Antigua, bound for Portsmouth."

"Ahoy, yerself!" It was O'Shea's rough brogue. She'd never heard sweeter music. "This be the clipper *Sophia,* of no particular country at the moment. Seven days out from Tortola, bound for . . . well, bound for here. Captain requests permission to board."

Gray. It had to be Gray.

The officers of the *Polaris* exchanged wary looks.

"Oh, for Heaven's sake." Sophia pushed forward to the ship's rail and cupped her hands around her mouth, calling, "Permission to board granted!"

A cheer rose up from the other ship's deck. "It's her, all right!" a voice called. Stubb's, Sophia thought.

Oh, but she hardly cared who was on the other deck. She cared only for the strong figure swinging across the watery divide as the two ships came abreast. Turning back toward the center of the ship, she pushed her way through the sweaty throng of sailors, desperate to get to him. Her foot caught on a rope, and she tripped—

But it didn't matter. Gray was there to catch her.

And he was still wearing those sea-weathered, fire-scarred boots. No doubt for sentimental reasons.

"Steady there," he murmured, catching her by the elbows. She looked up to meet his beautiful blue-green eyes. "I have you."

"Oh, Gray." She launched herself into his arms, clinging to his neck as he laughed and spun her around. "You're here."

"I'm here."

And he was. Every strong, solid, handsome inch of him. Sophia buried her face in his throat, breathing in his scent. Lord, how she'd missed him.

She pulled away, bracing her hands on his shoulders to study his face. "I can't believe you came after me."

"I can't believe you actually left." He lowered her to the deck, and her hands slid to his arms. "I thought you were bluffing with that bit. I'd have never allowed you to go."

Sophia shook her head. "I didn't say a word in that courtroom that wasn't true. I didn't want to lie to you anymore, Gray. Even if we can't be together . . . I just couldn't leave without telling you the truth."

"Who says we can't be together?" His brow furrowed.

"Surely you must understand. I'm ruined, most thoroughly. You've worked so hard to regain your family's place, you have such hopes for your sister. If you marry me, all those plans will be ruined, too. I couldn't ask it of you." Her eyes fell to his lapel, and she lowered her voice. "Unless . . . I could stay on as your mistress, perhaps. If we kept the arrangement quiet, it would not reflect on Bel. It's what the *ton* will expect of me, now that I'm a fallen woman."

He cupped her chin and lifted her face. "Don't ever speak of yourself that way." His voice was fierce; his gaze, intent. "And don't ever refer to yourself as my mistress again. I will have you as my wife, or nothing."

She let her hands fall to her sides. "Then I suppose it will have to be nothing."

Gray swore. "Do you honestly believe I've chased you out to the middle of the ocean for nothing?"

"But what about your aunt, your connections? Your sister's prospects—"

He shook his head. "The only prospects Bel cares about are the prospects of ministering to flea-bitten orphans, of which I've assured her London has plenty. She'd only agree to come with me after I promised *not* to give her a debut. If she marries at all, she'll likely marry some Quaker, or maybe a pitiful war invalid."

"She's come with you?"

"See for yourself." Gray nodded toward the deck of his ship. Yes, there she was. The dark-haired young lady gave a friendly wave. Sophia suddenly became aware of how many people were watching them, on both ships.

She cleared her throat. "And what of your brother?"

"Joss? He'll be bringing the *Aphrodite* to England, once he takes care of her cargo. After that, he's thinking of studying law. I'll manage the shipping business, Bel will have her charities. The family will be together; that's the important thing." He smiled. "Mr. Wilson's agreed to manage your sugar cooperative, in case you're wondering."

Hope fluttered in her chest. "Are you sure you want to marry me? I'm quite destitute now, you realize."

Gray laughed. "Look at that ship. That clipper cost me a queen's ransom, even with the *Kestrel* thrown in the bargain. But it was the fastest ship to be had." He took her hands in his. "Forget money. Forget society. Forget expectations. We've no talent for following rules, remember? We have to follow our hearts. You taught me that."

He gathered her to him, drawing her hands to his chest. "God, sweet, don't you know? You've had my heart in your pocket since the day we met. Following my heart means following you. I'll follow you to the ends of the earth if I have to." He shot an amused glance at the captain. "Though I'd expect your good captain would prefer I didn't. In fact, I think he'd gladly marry us today, just to be rid of me."

"Today? But we couldn't."

His eyebrows lifted. "Oh, but we could." He pulled her to the other side of the ship, slightly away from the gaping crowd. Wrapping his arms around her, he leaned close to whisper in her ear, "Happy birthday, love."

Sophia melted in his embrace. It was her birthday, wasn't it? The day she'd been anticipating for months, and here she'd forgotten it completely. Until Gray had appeared on the horizon, she hadn't been looking forward to anything.

But now she did. She looked forward to marriage, and children, and love and grand adventure. Real life and true passion. All of it with this man. "Oh, Gray."

"Please say yes," he whispered. "*Sophia.*" The name was a caress against her ear. "I love you."

He kissed her cheek and pulled away. "I've been remiss in not telling you. You can't know how I've regretted it. But I love you, Sophia Jane Hathaway. I love you as no man ever loved a woman. I love you so much, I fear I'll burst with it. In fact, I think I *shall* burst if I go another minute without kissing you, so if you've any mind to say yes, I'd thank you to—"

Sophia flung her arms around his neck and kissed him. Hard at first, to quiet the fool man; then gently, to savor him. Oh, how she loved the taste of him, like freshly-baked bread and rum. Warm and wholesome and comforting, with just a hint of spice and danger. "Yes," she sighed against his lips. She pulled back and looked into his eyes. "Yes, I will marry you."

His arms tightened about her waist. "Today?"

"Today. But you must let me change my gown first." Smiling, she stroked his smooth cheek. "You even shaved."

"Every day since we left Tortola." He gave her a rueful smile. "I've a few new scars to show for it."

"Good." She kissed him. "I'm glad. And I don't care if society casts us out for the pirates we are, just as long as I'm with you."

"Oh, I don't know that we'll be cast out, exactly. We're definitely not pirates. After your stirring testimony"—he chucked her under the chin—"Fitzhugh decided to make the best of an untenable situation. Or an unhangable pirate, as it were. If he couldn't advance his career by convicting me, he figured he'd advance it by commending me. Awarded me the *Kestrel* as salvage and recommended me to the governor for a special citation of valor. There's talk of knighthood." He grinned. "Can you believe it? Me, a hero."

"Of course I believe it." She laced her fingers at the back of his neck. "I've always known it, although I should curse that judge and his 'citation of valor.' As if you needed a fresh supply of arrogance. Just remember, whatever they deem you—gentleman or scoundrel, hero or pirate—you are *mine*."

"So I am." He kissed her soundly, passionately. "And which would you prefer tonight?" At the seductive growl in his voice, shivers of arousal swept down to her toes. "Your gentleman? Your scoundrel? Your hero or your pirate?"

She laughed. "I imagine I'll enjoy all four on occasion. But tonight, I believe I shall find tremendous joy in simply calling you my husband."

He rested his forehead against hers. "My love."

"That, too."

EPILOGUE

London, five weeks later

Sophia did not expect anyone to come calling today. They'd made their quiet arrival at Gray's town house just a few days ago, and the only two letters she'd posted—one to her mother, the other to her sister—had thus far gone unanswered. It was too soon to hope for a reply.

Yet there Hurst stood in the doorway, a card on his salver. "A caller for you, ma'am. Lady Lucinda Trescott, the Countess of Kendall."

"It *is* you!" Lucy angled around the manservant, pushing her way into the salon. "I heard you were back, but I couldn't believe it until I saw for myself."

"Lady Kendall." Astonished, Sophia rose to her feet, as did Bel. "Allow me to introduce my sister-in-law, Miss Grayson. However did you know I was here?"

"Are we to be so formal then? Must I call you *Lady* Grayson?" With a polite nod to Bel, Lucy crossed the room and caught Sophia in an exuberant hug. "Jeremy heard word of your husband's commendation. That's how I knew you were here." She surveyed Sophia from head to toe. "Now tell me, wherever have you *been*?"

"To visit your cousins, actually." Sophia's attention shifted to the strange bump obstructing their embrace. "Lucy, you're with child!"

Smiling, Lucy pulled Sophia's hand against her rounded

belly, placing her own hand on Sophia's flat stomach. "And you're not. At least, not discernibly."

No, not discernibly. Sophia smiled, keeping her suspicions to herself.

"Well," Lucy said, "that will disappoint the gossips."

At the mention of gossip, Sophia cringed. "Lucy, you shouldn't even be here. A countess can't be associated with such scandal."

"Scandal? Your husband's to be knighted. They're making him out to be Lancelot, Robin Hood, and Lord Nelson all rolled into one. You'll be guests of honor at every table in London." Lucy craned her neck to peek into the corridor. "Where is this living legend, anyway?"

"Gray? He's at his shipping office." Sophia directed her friend to a chair. "But even if he is to receive a commendation, surely I will not be welcome at those dinner tables. I'm ruined, most thoroughly."

"Because you broke your engagement?"

"Because I eloped with a fictional Frenchman!"

"You mean Gervais?" Lucy laughed. "Oh, no one knows about that. Your parents told everyone you'd taken ill and been sent to the seaside to recover. There may have been a few rumors to the contrary, but the fact that you fell into mad, passionate love with a heroic sea captain corroborates the tale quite nicely. You did fall into mad, passionate love with him, didn't you?"

Sophia nodded, numb with disbelief. Could it be true? Her parents, her sister, her jilted betrothed, her friends . . . they had all kept her escape secret?

"Oh, I knew it!" Lucy clapped her hands. "You must tell me everything."

"Perhaps another day." Sophia cast a glance at Bel.

"I see," Lucy whispered, following her gaze. "The story is that good, is it? Well, I suppose it will keep for another visit." She gave Sophia an appraising look. "If you've been ruined, I must say it suits you. You look very well."

"And breeding suits you. You are radiant."

Lucy made a dismissive wave, but the assessment was true. While Sophia would never have called her friend a great beauty before, she merited the term now. The pregnancy rounded off Lucy's sharp angles, and her dark-brown hair positively gleamed.

The maid entered, bearing a tray laden with tea service and refreshments.

"Isabel, would you be so good as to pour?" Sophia asked.

"Certainly."

While the young lady busied herself with teacups, Sophia drew her chair closer to Lucy's. "How is Toby?" she whispered. "I can't believe he never said a word about Gervais, when he had every motive to humiliate me publicly and demand restitution. Was he horribly hurt when I left?"

"Which answer are you hoping to hear? That he has endured great agony for love of you, or that he has forgotten you already?" Lucy laid a hand over Sophia's. "He has suffered, but I believe his pride incurred a deeper wound than his heart. Regardless, he is too good to humiliate anyone or make demands. He and Felix searched all England for you. You had us quite anxious, you know."

Guilt pinched in Sophia's chest. "How you all must hate me."

Lucy squeezed her hand. "How grateful we all are to have you safely home. I'm certain your family will feel the same. How could they complain? They'll have a title in the family now, just as they always wanted."

Bel interrupted their conference, a teacup and saucer balanced in either hand.

"Miss Grayson," Lucy asked, accepting her teacup, "are you to have a debut this Season?"

"Oh, no." Bel handed the other cup to Sophia.

"Maybe you should reconsider." Sophia perked, thinking of the possibilities. "We had thought a formal presentation imprudent," she told Lucy, "given my situation. But if the scandal has truly been contained . . . Bel might look as high as she wishes. She could even marry a lord, should she so desire."

"But I don't want to marry a lord," Bel protested.

"No, you don't." Lucy reached for a teacake. "It's not nearly as amusing as it sounds. People have such wearying expectations. Ever since my husband took up his seat in Lords, it's been one thing after another. I'm always being asked to subscribe to Lady Thus-and-so's charitable society or purchase vouchers for some benefit musicale."

"Truly?" Bel sipped her tea, looking pensive.

"Jeremy gives me more money than I know what to do with, so naturally I support them all. But worse, people are continually asking my opinion on lofty topics . . . as if *I* understand tariffs or navies. I try to smile and change the subject, but they insist on assigning me a ridiculous amount of influence, simply because my husband's stared down a few fusty members of Parliament." Lucy took a bite of cake. "Whatever you do, don't marry a lord."

"What interesting advice." Bel put down her teacup.

Sophia touched Bel's wrist. "We're only teasing. You shall marry for love. Your brother would not have it any other way."

"If that is so, than I doubt I shall marry at all," Bel said. "My heart is already so full, with devotion to my family and passion for God's work. There cannot be room for romantic love, too."

"The heart is not the only organ involved." Lucy gave Sophia a wicked smile.

"Perhaps I could be persuaded to marry," Bel continued, "if I could find a man of consequence and principle, who possessed a keen sense of justice and shared my passion for charity . . ."

"I hope you do find such a man," Sophia said. "But, Bel . . . to have a happy marriage, two people must share a passion for something other than charity."

Bel looked up. "Truly? Like what?"

Lucy broke into laughter, and Sophia could not help but join her.

"No, really," Bel insisted, looking from one to the other. "Tell me what you mean."

"Miss Grayson, never fear," Lucy said. "We will expand your education." She looked to Sophia. "You do still have *The Book*?"

Sophia choked on her tea. Under no circumstances would she permit Gray's sister so much as a glance at that book—not after the way she'd illustrated it.

"Well," she hedged, avoiding Lucy's inquisitive look, "you see, it isn't—"

The housekeeper saved her, thank goodness.

"Beg pardon, my lady. There's an urgent matter requiring your attention." Mrs. Prewitt gave a cryptic nod and disappeared into the corridor.

With relief, Sophia muttered her excuses to Lucy and Bel as she rose to her feet. By the time she reached the hallway, however, the housekeeper had disappeared. Frowning, she wandered toward the rear of the house. Perhaps there was some problem in the kitchens, or with the coal delivery?

As she passed the door to Gray's study, a familiar, muscled arm shot out into the corridor, catching her by the waist.

Laughing, she stumbled into the room, quickly finding herself caught between cool walnut paneling at her back and the hot, solid wall of man before her. Ever since their wedding—or since the *Kestrel* storeroom, more likely—Gray seemed to find it an irresistible challenge, to catch her unawares in an unlikely location and pull her into a feverish embrace.

Sophia had no wish to discourage the habit, but this wasn't the ideal time for a tryst. "Gray," she chided between kisses, "what are you about? The housekeeper said there was an urgent matter requiring my attention."

"And so there is. I require your attention. Most urgently." His hands slid to her bottom, and he lifted her easily, pinning her to the wall with his hips. The beaded ridges of the wainscoting dug into her spine. "Don't think we've used this room yet," he murmured, nibbling at the curve of her neck.

"I'm entertaining," she protested.

"Yes, you are," he said, grinding against her. "Highly entertaining."

Sophia sighed with pleasurable frustration. "I mean, I have a guest. Lady Kendall's in the salon, with Bel." She levered her arm against his chest, carving out some space between them. "And I thought you were at your shipping office."

"Yes, well . . ." Mischief gleamed sharp in his eyes. "I decided to go riding instead."

"Riding? To where?"

Relaxing his grip on her bottom, he slid her downward until her toes met the floor. "Out to Kent."

Her breath caught. There wasn't any reason for him to go to Kent, not unless he meant to visit—

"Gray, you didn't."

"I did." His expression turned to seriousness. "Don't be angry, sweet. I know you wrote to them, but . . . I felt I owed your father that much, to pay a call and face matters straight on. It's the man's way, you understand."

She nodded, a lump of anxiety forming in her throat. She wouldn't have asked him to call on her father, but she understood why he had. It wasn't just the man's way, it was the honorable thing to do—and therefore, she knew Gray couldn't have done otherwise. He truly was the best of men.

With unsteady fingers, she smoothed the lapel of his coat. "Dare I ask how you were received?"

"Warily, at first. Then somewhat belligerently." His eyebrow quirked. "But my reception improved markedly, once I extended the invitation to a dinner party with my aunt."

A rueful smile curved Sophia's lips. Yes, that would be her parents' reaction. They'd dine with the Devil himself, if a duchess were in attendance. "They are dreadful, aren't they?"

He shrugged. "Isn't everyone's family? I doubt your father and I will ever be great friends, but we did discover one interest in common."

"What's that?"

"You." Strong fingers cupped her chin. "We both want to see you happy. We both love you."

For a moment, Sophia did not trust herself to speak. Relief and joy swelled within her, until there was room for nothing else.

His lips brushed hers in a gentle kiss. "Am I forgiven, for not telling you first?"

Yes, yes. Forgiven, cherished, treasured, adored. Loved, beyond reason.

"I suppose," she said coyly, tracing the line of his jaw with her fingertips. "So long as you will extend me the same forgiveness."

"Why?" His eyes narrowed. "Have you been keeping secrets again?"

"Just one." Smiling, she took his hand and pressed it meaningfully against her gently rounded abdomen. "A very, very tiny one."

ACKNOWLEDGMENTS

This book is the product of more than a year's work. Courtney Milan and Amy Baldwin were there from the roughest of rough beginnings. Lindsey helped point the way when I was hopelessly adrift. Lenore, Maggie, Elyssa, Manda, Darcy, Lacey, and Erica all came along for the ride, reading drafts and providing invaluable perspective. Thanks to Jennifer, for really, truly going sailing with me. And lastly, much gratitude to my editor, Kate Collins, for helping me shape the manuscript into an even stronger story.

A note to readers: In this story, "dolphin-fish" refers to the deep-sea fish we now commonly call mahi-mahi—not the friendly, intelligent mammals we know as dolphins today. Please be assured that no dolphins, fictional or otherwise, were harmed in the writing of this book!

Read on to catch an
exclusive sneak peek at

A Lady of Persuasion

the final installment of
Tessa Dare's historical romance trilogy!

Coming in September 2009 from Ballantine Books
Available wherever books are sold

Sir Tobias Aldridge was contemplating an act of cold-
blooded murder.

Failing that, an act of barbarous incivility.

By nature, Toby wasn't one to hold a grudge. As a
gentleman of rank, wealth, and unarguable good looks,
he'd never received a slight he couldn't simply laugh off.
He called every man friend, and no man enemy.

Until now.

"So that's him." Toby glared at the man twirling a fair-
haired beauty across the gleaming parquet—Benedict
"Gray" Grayson. The scoundrel who'd stolen Toby's
bride, his future, and his very respectability, then returned to a bloody hero's welcome.

"That's him. Here, have a brandy." His host, Jeremy
Trescott, the Earl of Kendall, extended a glass.

Toby accepted the drink and downed a quick, blistering swallow. "I could call him out," he murmured behind the glass. "I could call him out and shoot him dead
tonight, in your garden."

Jeremy shook his head. "You're not going to do that."

"Why not? You don't think I have it in me?" Toby

gave a bitter laugh. "Don't you read the papers, Jem? That affable Sir Toby is a phantom of the past, and good riddance to him. Where did honor and decency get me, I ask you? Jilted, and replaced by a thieving, unprincipled bastard."

"Gray's not a bastard. He's the legitimate nephew of a duchess."

Toby gave a humorless chuckle. "Oh, yes. And now a knight, as well. What isn't he? If you listen to the talk, *Sir* Benedict's a shipping financier, a West Indian planter, a feared privateer, a paragon of valor . . ." He shook his head. "I know the truth. He's the thieving bastard who seduced my intended bride. It's within my rights to call him out."

"Even if you *could* do it," his friend said tersely, "you're not going to do it. This is Lucy's first ball. She's been planning it for months. If you turn it into scandal-sheet fodder, I'll take you into the garden and gut you myself."

"Well, if you didn't want scandal, you shouldn't have invited me. So long as I have the devil's own reputation, I might as well live up to it."

"You ought to rise above it." Jeremy lowered his voice. "Listen, you're bound to meet with them at some point. Gray's bringing out his younger sister this year, and they'll be at every major social event. Best to make your public reconciliation now and quell the gossip. Why do you think Lucy and I planned a ball so early in the Season?"

"Because if you waited a few months she'd be too round?" Eager to change the subject, Toby clapped his friend on the shoulder. He had no intention of reconciling with Grayson, publicly or otherwise. Ever. "Congratulations, by the way."

"How did you know Lucy's with child?"

Toby made eye contact with his friend's wife across the ballroom, as she weaved through the crush of guests. For years, Lucy Waltham Trescott had dogged their annual hunting excursions at Henry Waltham's estate. She'd harbored a girlish infatuation for Toby, but had forgotten him quickly enough when Jeremy captured her heart last autumn.

He said, "I've three older sisters, and ten nieces and nephews to date. I can tell. A woman's face gets a bit rounder, her hair shines. And her bosom, it . . ." Jeremy shot him a glare. Toby took another sip of brandy. "Right, well. I can just tell."

Lucy reached them, and Toby fortified his smile. He'd be damned if he'd let this assembly catch him wearing any expression other than his usual rakish grin.

"Toby!" Lucy exclaimed, taking his hands. "I'm so glad to see you."

"Look at you, Luce." He gave her a sweeping gaze and an appreciative wink. The once-hoydenish twig of a girl had blossomed into the lovely, confident Countess of Kendall. "Stunning. Most beautiful lady in the room."

Lucy made a dismissive wave of her hand, but behind the gesture she blushed to the ears. Just as he'd known she would. Toby leaned in to kiss her cheek, ignoring Jeremy's forbidding glare.

"I know you say that to all the ladies," Lucy said. She gave him a cautious look. "Sophia looks well, doesn't she?"

"Oh, she's radiant." Toby forced his grin wider as the Graysons waltzed by, Sophia's flaxen hair and porcelain complexion an elegant ivory blur. "Incandescent, even. She has the look of a woman in love."

Sophia had never looked incandescent with him.

Lucy seemed to read his thoughts. She laid a hand on his sleeve. "Toby. You weren't in love with her, either."

Toby shrugged. Lucy spoke the truth, but the truth didn't help.

"What's done is done. You've got to move on." Jeremy nodded toward the crush of guests. "It's a new Season, man. There's a fresh crop of debutantes just waiting to experience the renowned Sir Toby charm. Surely one of them has caught your eye."

Toby considered. True, a fresh conquest might provide a welcome diversion from murderous rage. He'd always been a favorite with the debutantes. But lately, there was scarcely any challenge to it. His scandal-sheet notoriety as the "Rake Reborn" had the mamas on alert and the young ladies in a flutter. All he had to do was appear.

"Now that you mention it, there was one . . . just one." Toby scanned the ballroom for a glimpse of vibrant emerald silk. There was only one lady who'd caught his eye even briefly since he'd made his entrance. He knew he'd never seen her before—he certainly wouldn't have forgotten her if he had.

Ah, there she was. An intriguing dark-haired beauty unlike any other lady in the room. Unlike any lady he'd ever seen. Until now, he'd caught only glimpses of her through the churning sea of dancers—a flash of emerald, a cascade of raven hair, a swatch of honey-gold skin. Now she lined up with the ladies in preparation for a reel, and he had his first opportunity to study her in full view.

She was tall. Not nearly so tall as he, but taller than the ladies she stood among, and possessed of a lushly proportioned figure. The cut of her gown was modest, but she was the kind of woman who managed to look indecent, even fully clothed. Hers was a body plucked straight from some exotic harem fantasy—full breasts, flared hips, long legs.

Toby watched as she favored her dance partner with

the hint of a smile. That subtle curve of her lips was somehow more sensuous than any other curve of her body. Desire sparked through him, surprising him with its intensity. His whole body thrummed with that base, ineloquent instinct in which every seduction, no matter how suave, took its root:

I want that.

Who was she? She was in her first Season, most certainly. With her beauty, she could not last more than a few months on the marriage mart, even if her dowry were made up of cockleshells.

Toby shifted to view the row of gentlemen lined up opposite, to discern the identity of her partner. "Bloody hell."

It couldn't be. She was partnered with Grayson, the thieving bastard. It wasn't enough he'd already stolen the woman Toby had planned to marry—now he had to strut and impress the debutantes, too? Damn it, they were Toby's territory. Now what had begun as vague, lustful inclination firmed into a plan:

I want that.

And I'm going to take it.

"Fancy a reel, Luce?"

"Why, I had not—"

Without waiting for her answer, Toby took Lucy by the hand and tugged her onto the dance floor, wedging their way into the queued-up dancers just instants before the music began. He'd positioned himself at Grayson's shoulder, and though he bowed to Lucy as the first chords were struck, he kept his gaze slanted toward the beauty in green silk beside her.

The dance was one patterned in groups of three couples, requiring much interchange between adjacent partners—just as Toby had hoped. At regular intervals, he would have occasion to take his emerald-clad vision by the hand, exchange a few words, twirl her dizzy, and—if all that failed to render her breathless—flash his most winning smile.

But all in good time.

Winning over a lady was a matter of strategy, of patience. The first contact must not be skin-to-skin, nor even glove-to-glove, but solely eye-to-eye. Toby moved forward to bow to her, his gaze riveted to hers. Her eyes were remarkable. Wide-set, almond-shaped, and fringed with sable lashes. So large and serious, they seemed to swallow up the rest of her face. For a moment, Toby let himself sink into those dark, placid pools.

He had a devil of a struggle fishing himself back out.

A few bars later, he was still recovering when the pattern compelled him to take her hand. He seized her gloved fingers firmly. The soft fabric heated between them as they circled, becoming warm and pliant as skin. Her bare flesh would feel like this, he thought. Satin-smooth. Supple. Hot to the touch as his hands glided under that cool silk to explore her every enticing curve. It would have the texture of cream against his tongue.

Lord. Toby hauled on his mental reins before those thoughts carried him away. Never before had he felt such a thrill simply taking a lady's hand. But then, never before had he seduced a woman straight from the arms of his enemy.

"*Toby.*" Lucy beckoned him with a twitch of her fingers, and Toby realized they'd fallen behind in the pattern.

"Right. Beg pardon." He leapt forward to claim Lucy's hands and sweep her down the dance. "And I apologize in advance, for what is about to occur."

Her eyes flared. "Toby, no. You can't make a scene."

"Oh, but I could. I could denounce Grayson and Sophia in front of the entire ballroom. Everyone thinks they're the golden couple, the freshly knighted hero and his beautiful, innocent bride? I could expose the truth."

"And I could expose your innards." Lucy's fingernails dug into his arm, proving a fierce huntress still prowled that elegant exterior. "You wouldn't dare. I've been planning this evening for months, Toby."

The dance parted them before Toby could respond. Then the lady in green silk smiled, and something in his chest pulled tight. He couldn't have spoken if he'd tried. It was perfect, that smile, comprised of full, sensuous lips the color of fine Madeira. Lips designed for sin, framing an innocent row of pearly teeth. And about the corners of her mouth, the slightest hint of melancholy— just enough to intrigue the mind, stir the heart. Those lips defied mere admiration; they wanted a kiss.

There was only one thing wrong with that smile.

It wasn't directed at him. That bastard Grayson was its lucky recipient, and it was all Toby could do not to thrust out his boot and trip the man as he moved forward to take the beauty's hands.

Tempting, that idea, but inconceivable. Toby might scuff his boot.

No, he would exact his revenge more subtly, more justly. No messy duel, no public denouncement. Did not the Bible advise an eye for an eye, a tooth for a tooth . . . or, in this case, a lady for a lady?